SCIENCE FICTION is the literature of awareness, of perception—of our time, and of other times, of the human condition as it is and of what it might be.

TERRY CARR, the distinguished editor, makes his first appearance on the Ballantine list with a collection that represents the cream of science fiction's recent stories: lyrical or down-beat, mystical or hardcore, adventurous or contemplative—these stories are all turn-ons to the potentials of reality.

RECENT SCIENCE FICTION TITLES
FROM BALLANTINE BOOKS

Contents

INTRODUCTION

When you're editing an anthology of the best science fiction stories of the year, as I've been doing for eight years now, you often find yourself mentally charting the ebb and flow of trends in the work that's being published. In the past half-dozen years, for instance, we've seen an influx of fine new writers who brought with them the so-called "new wave" styles of writing: experimental prose, hard-edged realism, shiftings of reality, or sometimes straightforwardly angry "downbeat" stories. The readers, critics, fans and other writers in the field were either delighted or appalled by such writing, and authors like Thomas M. Disch and Norman Spinrad became centers of rather fierce controversy.

Reading the manifestos and denunciations produced during this internecine battle, and hearing the arguments that so often sprang up at gatherings of science fiction people, a person could easily have come away with the impression that the sf field was falling apart, losing coherence and direction. But through it all I remembered a delightful description that I read years ago of the audience reaction to the premiere performance of Stravinski's *Rite of Spring*: There were boos and catcalls; there were cheers and clapping; and there was, before long, a full-scale riot as the members of the audience fought over their differing reactions to the music. "That is what I call a strong aesthetic response," said the narrator.

And of course he was right. A field of art that can involve its fans so intensely is very far from extinction, and obviously the same is true of science fiction today. By now the "new wave" as such has come and gone; those stories that could stand on their own merits have done so, and those writers whose work stood up to the glare of controversy have become respected "regulars" within the field. And already another generation of writers is upon us, people who read the best experimental sf and the best of all other kinds, and who have gone on to create stories that range the entire spectrum of science fiction's possibilities. Ursula K. Le Guin is such a writer; so is Alexei Panshin; and so is at least one man who was writing science fiction for ten years before the "new wave" hit the field: Robert Silverberg.

These writers, and many others, realize a truth basic to all art, not just the art of science fiction writing. Innovations are positive to the extent that they open doors, and an avant garde which seeks to destroy rather than build will only destroy itself all the faster. And when a "wave" has passed, what it leaves behind will be its positive contributions, so it behooves us to become literary beachcombers.

Personally, I thought most of the work produced during the height of the "new wave" was just as bad as bad science fiction has always been; if there was an effective difference to me, it was only that I sometimes had to read a story more carefully to discover that I disliked it. But bad fiction is quickly unimportant; it's forgotten, while the good stories remain in our memories. And there were many, many fine stories produced in the late sixties, new themes explored or old ideas seen afresh. The entire field of science fiction is richer for these stories.

Flashy experimental writing is no longer "in" in science fiction, if it ever was. What we're concerned with now is what has always concerned us: exploration. The wonders of an infinite universe still lie before us, and the wonders of mankind's own potential are opening up at an ever accelerating rate. Science fiction is a literature of expansion, and it is now in its most exciting period. If we ever lacked the literary tools to cope with the riches of our imagination, that's certainly not true now; and so the stories we read this year, and shall read in the future, can realize more fully than ever before the sense of awe and majesty that the universe requires.

The specific technique isn't important. It may be beautiful romantic imagery, such as in Poul Anderson's "The Queen of Air and Darkness"; it may involve detailed descriptions of the exploration of alien worlds, as in Arthur Clarke's "A Meeting With Medusa"; it may be a vivid evocation of internal experience, such as Robert Silverberg's "In Entropy's Jaws," or satire, like George Alec Effinger's "All the Last Wars At Once," or any of an endless variety of approaches to fictional creation. What matters is the pleasure we experience in reading these stories, and when the whole range of literary technique is used to evoke the wonder, scope and beauty of the universe—yes, and its dangers too—then we have a genre that cannot fail to be exciting.

This year's collection of stories provides many examples of science fiction's growth and variety. There will be more to come tomorrow. (There is always more to come tomorrow.)

TERRY CARR

Berkeley, California
January 14, 1972

OCCAM'S SCALPEL

Theodore Sturgeon

With everyone talking about pollution and its implications for the future, it's not surprising that science fiction should have joined the chorus of speculation and foreboding—for the future, good or bad, is science fiction's domain. Here Theodore Sturgeon offers his own comment on our plight: an ingenious idea, told with the Sturgeon flair.

I

Joe Trilling had a funny way of making a living. It was a good living, but of course he didn't make anything like the bundle he could have in the city. On the other hand he lived in the mountains a half mile away from a picturesque village in clean air and piney-birchy woods along with lots of mountain laurel, and he was his own boss. There wasn't much competition for what he did; he had his wife and kids around all the time and more orders than he could fill. He was one of the night people and after the family had gone to bed he could work quietly and uninterruptedly. He was happy as a clam.

One night—very early morning, really—he was interrupted. *Bup-bup, bup, bup.* Knock at the window, two shorts, two longs. He froze, he whirled, for he knew that knock. He hadn't heard it for years but it had been a part of his life since he was born. He saw the face outside and

1

filled his lungs for a whoop that would have roused them at the fire station on the village green, but then he saw the finger on the lips and let the air out. The finger beckoned and Joe Trilling whirled again, turned down a flame, read a gauge, made a note, threw a switch and joyfully but silently dove for the outside door. He slid out, closed it carefully, peered into the dark.

"Karl?"

"Shh."

There he was, edge of the woods. Joe Trilling went there and, whispering because Karl had asked for it, they hit each other, cursed, called each other the filthiest possible names. It would not be easy to explain this to an extra-terrestrial; it isn't necessarily a human thing to do. It's a cultural thing. It means, I want to touch you, it means I love you; but they were men and brothers, so they hit each other's arms and shoulders and swore despicable oaths and insults, until at last even those words wouldn't do and they stood in the shadows, holding each others' biceps and grinning and drilling into each other with eyes. Then Karl Trilling moved his head sidewards toward the road and they walked away from the house.

"I don't want Hazel to hear us talking," Karl said. "I don't want her or anyone to know I was here. How is she?"

"Beautiful. Aren't you going to see her at all—or the kids?"

"Yes but not this trip. There's the car. We can talk there. I really am afraid of that bastard."

"Ah," said Joe. "How is the great man?"

"Po'ly," said Karl. "But we're talking about two different bastards. The great man is only the richest man in the world, but I'm not afraid of him, especially now. I'm talking about Cleveland Wheeler."

"Who's Cleveland Wheeler?"

They got into the car. "It's a rental," said Karl. "Matter of fact, it's the second rental. I got out of the executive jet and took a company car and rented another—and then this. Reasonably sure it's not bugged. That's one kind of answer to your question, who's Cleve Wheeler. Other answers would be the man behind the throne. Next in line. Multifaceted genius. Killer shark."

"Next in line," said Joe, responding to the only clause that made any sense. "The old man is sinking?"

"Officially—and an official secret—his hemoglobin reading is four. That mean anything to you, Doctor?"

"Sure does, Doctor. Malnutritive anemia, if other rumors I hear are true. Richest man in the world—dying of starvation."

"And old age—and stubbornness—and obsession. You want to hear about Wheeler?"

"Tell me."

"Mister Lucky. Born with everything. Greek coin profile. Michaelangelo muscles. Discovered early by a bright-eyed elementary school principal, sent to a private school, used to go straight to the teachers' lounge in the morning and say what he'd been reading or thinking about. Then they'd tell off a teacher to work with him or go out with him or whatever. High school at twelve, varsity track, basketball, football and high-diving—three letters for each—yes, he graduated in three years, *summa cum*. Read all the textbooks at the beginning of each term, never cracked them again. More than anything else he had the habit of success.

"College, the same thing: turned sixteen in his first semester, just ate everything up. Very popular. Graduated at the top again, of course."

Joe Trilling, who had slogged through college and medical school like a hodcarrier, grunted enviously. "I've seen one or two like that. Everybody marvels, nobody sees how easy it was for them."

Karl shook his head. "Wasn't quite like that with Cleve Wheeler. If anything was easy for him it was because of the nature of his equipment. He was like a four-hundred horsepower car moving in sixty-horsepower traffic. When his muscles were called on he used them, I mean really put it down to the floor. A very willing guy. Well—he had his choice of jobs—hell, choice of careers. He went into an architectural firm that could use his math, administrative ability, public presence, knowledge of materials, art. Gravitated right to the top, got a partnership. Picked up a doctorate on the side while he was doing it. Married extremely well."

"Mister Lucky," Joe said.

"Mister Lucky, yeah. Listen. Wheeler became a partner and he did his work and he knew his stuff—everything he could learn or understand. Learning and understanding are not enough to cope with some things like greed or unexpected stupidity or accident or sheer bad breaks. Two of the other partners got into a deal I won't bother you with —a high-rise apartment complex in the wrong place for the wrong residents and land acquired the wrong way. Wheeler saw it coming, called them in and talked it over. They said yes-yes and went right ahead and did what they wanted anyway—something that Wheeler never in the world expected. The one thing high capability and straight morals and a good education doesn't give you is the end of innocence. Cleve Wheeler was an innocent.

"Well, it happened, the disaster that Cleve had predicted, but it happened far worse. Things like that, when they surface, have a way of exposing a lot of other concealed rot. The firm collapsed. Cleve Wheeler had never failed at anything in his whole life. It was the one thing he had no practice in dealing with. Anyone with the most rudimentary intelligence would have seen that this was the time to walk away—lie down, even. Cut his losses. But I don't think these things even occurred to him."

Karl Trilling laughed suddenly. "In one of Philip Wylie's novels is a tremendous description of a forest fire and how the animals run away from it, the foxes and the rabbits running shoulder to shoulder, the owls flying in the daytime to get ahead of the flames. Then there's this beetle, lumbering along on the ground. The beetle comes to a burned patch, the edge of twenty acres of hell. It stops, it wiggles its feelers, it turns to the side and begins to walk around the fire—" He laughed again. "That's the special thing Cleveland Wheeler has, you see, under all that muscle and brain and brilliance. If he had to—and were a beetle—he wouldn't turn back and he wouldn't quit. If all he could do was walk around it, he'd start walking."

"What happened?" asked Joe.

"He hung on. He used everything he had. He used his brains and his personality and his reputation and all his worldly goods. He also borrowed and promised—and he worked. Oh, he worked. Well, he kept the firm. He cleaned out the rot and built it all up again from the inside, strong and straight this time. But it cost.

"It cost him time—all the hours of every day but the four or so he used for sleeping. And just about when he had it leveled off and starting up, it cost him his wife."

"You said he'd married well."

"He'd married what you marry when you're a young block-buster on top of everything and going higher. She was a nice enough girl, I suppose, and maybe you can't blame her, but she was no more used to failure than he was. Only he could walk around it. He could rent a room and ride the bus. She just didn't know how—and of course with women like that there's always the discarded swain somewhere in the wings."

"How did he take that?"

"Hard. He'd married the way he played ball or took examinations—with everything he had. It did something to him. All this did things to him, I suppose, but that was the biggest chunk of it.

"He didn't let it stop him. He didn't let anything stop him. He went on until all the bills were paid—every cent. All the interest. He kept at it until the net worth was exactly what it had been before his ex-partners had begun to eat out the core. Then he gave it away. Gave it away! Sold all right and title to his interest for a dollar."

"Finally cracked, hm?"

Karl Trilling looked at his brother scornfully. "Cracked. Matter of definition, isn't it? Cleve Wheeler's goal was zero —can you understand that? What is success anyhow? Isn't it making up your mind what you're going to do and then doing it, all the way?"

"In that case," said his brother quietly, "suicide is success."

Karl gave him a long penetrating look. "Right," he said, and thought about it a moment.

"Anyhow," Joe asked, "why zero?"

"I did a lot of research on Cleve Wheeler, but I couldn't get inside his head. I don't know. But I can guess. He meant to owe no man anything. I don't know how he felt about the company he saved, but I can imagine. The man he became—was becoming—wouldn't want to owe it one damned thing. I'd say he just wanted out—but on his own terms, which included leaving nothing behind to work on him."

"Okay," said Joe.

Karl Trilling thought, *The nice thing about old Joe is that he'll wait. All these years apart with hardly any communication beyond birthday cards—and not always that—and here he is, just as if we were still together every day. I wouldn't be here if it weren't important; I wouldn't be telling him all this unless he needed to know; he wouldn't need any of it unless he was going to help. All that unsaid—I don't have to ask him a damn thing. What am I interrupting in his life? What am I going to interrupt? I won't have to worry about that. He'll take care of it.*

He said, "I'm glad I came here, Joe."

Joe said, "That's all right," which meant all the things Karl had been thinking. Karl grinned and hit him on the shoulder and went on talking.

"Wheeler dropped out. It's not easy to map his trail for that period. It pops up all over. He lived in at least three communes—maybe more, but those three were a mess when he came and a model when he left. He started businesses—all things that had never happened before, like a supermarket with no shelves, no canned music, no games or stamps, just neat stacks of open cases, where the customer took what he wanted and marked it according to the card posted by the case, with a marker hanging on a string. Eggs and frozen meat and fish and the like, and local produce were priced a flat two percent over wholesale. People were honest because they could never be sure the checkout counter didn't know the prices of everything—besides, to cheat on the prices listed would have been just too embarrassing. With nothing but a big empty warehouse for overhead and no employees spending thousands of man hours marking individual items, the prices beat any discount house that ever lived. He sold that one, too, and moved on. He started a line of organic baby foods without preservatives, franchised it and moved on again. He developed a plastic container that would burn without polluting and patented it and sold the patent."

"I've heard of that one. Haven't seen it around, though."

"Maybe you will," Karl said in a guarded tone. "Maybe

you will. Anyway, he had a CPA in Pasadena handling details, and just did his thing all over. I never heard of a failure in anything he tried."

"Sounds like a junior edition of the great man himself, your honored boss."

"You're not the only one who realized that. The boss may be a ding-a-ling in many ways, but nobody ever faulted his business sense. He has always had his tentacles out for wandering pieces of very special manpower. For all I know he had drawn a bead on Cleveland Wheeler years back. I wouldn't doubt that he'd made offers from time to time, only during that period Cleve Wheeler wasn't about to go to work for anyone that big. His whole pattern is to run things his way, and you don't do that in an established empire."

"Heir apparent," said Joe, reminding him of something he had said earlier.

"Right," nodded Karl. "I knew you'd begin to get the idea before I was finished."

"But finish," said Joe.

"Right. Now what I'm going to tell you, I just want you to know. I don't expect you to understand it or what it means or what it has all done to Cleve Wheeler. I need your help, and you can't really help me unless you know the whole story."

"Shoot."

Karl Trilling shot: "Wheeler found a girl. Her name was Clara Prieta and her folks came from Sonora. She was bright as hell—in her way, I suppose, as bright as Cleve, though with a tenth of his schooling—and pretty as well, and it was Cleve she wanted, not what he might get for her. She fell for him when he had nothing—when he really wanted nothing. They were a daily, hourly joy to each other. I guess that was about the time he started building this business and that, making something again. He bought a little house and a car. He bought two cars, one for her. I don't think she wanted it, but he couldn't do enough—he was always looking for more things to do for her. They went out for an evening to some friends' house, she from shopping, he from whatever it was he was working on then, so they had both cars. He followed her on the way home and had to watch her lose control and spin out. She died in his arms."

"Oh, Jesus."

"Mister Lucky. Listen: a week later he turned a corner downtown and found himself looking at a bank robbery. He caught a stray bullet—grazed the back of his neck. He had seven months to lie still and think about things. When he got out he was told his business manager had embezzled everything and headed south with his secretary. Everything."

"What did he do?"

"Went to work and paid his hospital bill."

They sat in the car in the dark for a long time, until Joe said, "Was he paralyzed, there in the hospital?"

"For nearly five months."

"Wonder what he thought about."

Karl Trilling said, "I can imagine what he thought about. What I can't imagine is what he decided. What he concluded. What he determined to be. Damn it, there are no accurate words for it. We all do the best we can with what we've got, or try to. Or should. He *did*—and with the best possible material to start out with. He played it straight; he worked hard; he was honest and lawful and fair; he was fit; he was bright. He came out of the hospital with those last two qualities intact. God alone knows what's happened to the rest of it."

"So he went to work for the old man."

"He did—and somehow that frightens me. It was as if all his qualifications were not enough to suit both of them until these things happened to him—until they made him become what he is."

"And what is that?"

"There isn't a short answer to that, Joe. The old man has become a modern myth. Nobody ever sees him. Nobody can predict what he's going to do or why. Cleveland Wheeler stepped into his shadow and disappeared almost as completely as the boss. There are very few things you can say for certain. The boss has always been a recluse and in the ten years Cleve Wheeler has been with him he has become more so. It's been business as usual with him, of course—which means the constantly unusual—long periods of quiet, and then these spectacular unexpected wheelings and dealings. You assume that the old man dreams these things up and some high-powered genius on his staff gets them done. But it could be the genius that instigates the moves—who can know? Only the people closest to him —Wheeler, Epstein, me. And I don't know."

"But Epstein died."

Karl Trilling nodded in the dark. "Epstein died. Which leaves only Wheeler to watch the store. I'm the old man's personal physician, not Wheeler's, and there's no guarantee that I ever will be Wheeler's."

Joe Trilling recrossed his legs and leaned back, looking out into the whispering dark. "It begins to take shape," he murmured. "The old man's on the way out, you very well might be and there's nobody to take over but this Wheeler."

"Yes, and I don't know what he is or what he'll do. I do know he will command more power than any single human being on Earth. He'll have so much that he'll be above any kind of cupidity that you or I could imagine— you or I can't think in that order of magnitude. But you see, he's a man who, you might say, has had it proved to him that being good and smart and strong and honest doesn't particularly pay off. Where will he go with all this? And hypothesizing that he's been making more and more of the decisions lately, and extrapolating from that—where is he going? All you can be sure of is that he will succeed in anything he tries. That is his habit."

"What does he want? Isn't that what you're trying to figure out? What would a man like that want, if he knew he could get it?"

"I knew I'd come to the right place," said Karl almost happily. "That's it exactly. As for me, I have all I need now and there are plenty of other places I could go. I wish Epstein were still around, but he's dead and cremated."

"Cremated?"

"That's right—you wouldn't know about that. Old man's instructions. I handled it myself. You've heard of the hot and cold private swimming pools—but I bet you never heard of a man with his own private crematorium in the second sub-basement."

Joe threw up his hands. "I guess if you can reach into

your pocket and pull out two billion real dollars, you can have anything you want. By the way—was that legal?"

"Like you said—if you have two billion. Actually, the county medical examiner was present and signed the papers. And he'll be there when the old man pushes off too—it's all in the final instructions. Hey—wait, I don't want to cast any aspersions on the M.E. He wasn't bought. He did a very competent examination on Epstein."

"Okay—we know what to expect when the time comes. It's afterward you're worried about."

"Right. What has the old man—I'm speaking of the corporate old man now—what has he been doing all along? What has he been doing in the last ten years, since he got Wheeler—and is it any different from what he was doing before? How much of this difference, if any, is more Wheeler than boss? That's all we have to go on, Joe, and from it we have to extrapolate what Wheeler's going to do with the biggest private economic force this world has ever known."

"Let's talk about that," said Joe, beginning to smile.

Karl Trilling knew the signs, so he began to smile a little, too. They talked about it.

II

The crematorium in the second sub-basement was purely functional, as if all concessions to sentiment and ritual had been made elsewhere, or canceled. The latter most accurately described what had happened when at last, at long, long last, the old man died. Everything was done precisely according to his instructions immediately after he was certifiably dead and before any public announcements were made—right up to and including the moment when the square mouth of the furnace opened with a startling clang, a blare of heat, a flare of light—the hue the old-time blacksmiths called straw color. The simple coffin slid rapidly in, small flames exploding into being on its corners, and the door banged shut. It took a moment for the eyes to adjust to the bare room, the empty greased track, the closed door. It took the same moment for the conditioners to whisk away the sudden smell of scorched soft pine.

The medical examiner leaned over the small table and

signed his name twice. Karl Trilling and Cleveland Wheeler did the same. The M.E. tore off copies and folded them and put them away in his breast pocket. He looked at the closed square iron door, opened his mouth, closed it again and shrugged. He held out his hand.

"Good night, Doctor."

"Good night, Doctor. Rugosi's outside—he'll show you out."

The M.E. shook hands wordlessly with Cleveland Wheeler and left.

"I know just what he's feeling," Karl said. "Something ought to be said. Something memorable—end of an era. Like 'One small step for man—' "

Cleveland Wheeler smiled the bright smile of the college hero, fifteen years after—a little less wide, a little less even, a great deal less in the eyes. He said in the voice that commanded, whatever he said, "If you think you're quoting the first words from an astronaut on the moon, you're not. What he said was from the ladder, when he poked his boot down. He said, 'It's some kind of soft stuff. I can kick it around with my foot.' I've always liked that much better. It was real, it wasn't rehearsed or memorized or thought out and it had to do with that moment and the next. The M.E. said good night and you told him the chauffeur was waiting outside. I like that better than anything anyone could say. I think he would, too," Wheeler added, barely gesturing, with a very strong, slightly cleft chin, toward the hot black door.

"But he wasn't exactly human."

"So they say." Wheeler half smiled and, even as he turned away, Karl could sense himself tuned out, the room itself become of secondary importance—the next thing Wheeler was to do, and the next and the one after, becoming more real than the here and now.

Karl put a fast end to that.

He said levelly, "I meant what I just said, Wheeler."

It couldn't have been the words, which by themselves might have elicited another half-smile and a forgetting. It was the tone, and perhaps the "Wheeler." There is a ritual about these things. To those few on his own level, and those on the level below, he was Cleve. Below that he was mister to his face and Wheeler behind his back. No one of his peers would call him mister unless it was meant as the herald of an insult; no one of his peers or immediate underlings would call him Wheeler at all, ever. Whatever the component, it removed Cleveland Wheeler's hand from the knob and turned him. His face was completely alert and interested. "You'd best tell me what you mean, Doctor."

Karl said, "I'll do better than that. Come." Without gestures, suggestions or explanations he walked to the left rear of the room, leaving it up to Wheeler to decide whether or not to follow. Wheeler followed.

In the corner Karl rounded on him. "If you ever say anything about this to anyone—even me—when we leave here, I'll just deny it. If you ever get in here again, you won't find anything to back up your story." He took a complex four-inch blade of machined stainless steel from his belt and slid it between the big masonry blocks. Silently, massively, the course of blocks in the corner began to move upward. Looking up at them in the dim light from the narrow corridor they revealed, anyone could see that they were real blocks and that to get through them without that key and the precise knowledge of where to put it would be a long-term project.

Again Karl proceeded without looking around, leaving go, no-go as a matter for Wheeler to decide. Wheeler followed. Karl heard his footsteps behind him and noticed with pleasure and something like admiration that when the heavy blocks whooshed down and seated themselves solidly behind them, Wheeler may have looked over his shoulder but did not pause.

"You've noticed we're alongside the furnace," Karl said, like a guided-tour bus driver. "And now, behind it."

He stood aside to let Wheeler pass him and see the small room.

It was just large enough for the tracks which protruded from the back of the furnace and a little standing space on each side. On the far side was a small table with a black suitcase standing on it. On the track stood the coffin, its corners carboned, its top and sides wet and slightly steaming.

"Sorry to have to close that stone gate that way," Karl said matter-of-factly. "I don't expect anyone down here at all, but I wouldn't want to explain any of this to persons other than yourself."

Wheeler was staring at the coffin. He seemed perfectly composed, but it was a seeming. Karl was quite aware of what it was costing him.

Wheeler said, "I wish you'd explain it to *me*." And he laughed. It was the first time Karl had ever seen this man do anything badly.

"I will. I am." He clicked open the suitcase and laid it open and flat on the little table. There was a glisten of chrome and steel and small vials in little pockets. The first tool he removed was a screwdriver. "No need to use screws when you're cremating 'em," he said cheerfully and placed the tip under one corner of the lid. He struck the handle smartly with the heel of one hand and the lid popped loose. "Stand this up against the wall behind you, will you?"

Silently Cleveland Wheeler did as he was told. It gave him something to do with his muscles; it gave him the chance to turn his head away for a moment; it gave him a chance to think—and it gave Karl the opportunity for a quick glance at his steady countenance.

He's a mensch, Karl thought. *He really is . . .*

Wheeler set up the lid neatly and carefully and they stood, one on each side, looking down into the coffin.

"He—got a lot older," Wheeler said at last.

"You haven't seen him recently."

"Here and in there," said the executive, "I've spent more time in the same room with him during the past month than I have in the last eight, nine years. Still, it was a matter of minutes, each time."

Karl nodded understandingly. "I'd heard that. Phone calls, any time of the day or night, and then those long silences two days, three, not calling out, not having anyone in—"

"Are you going to tell me about the phony oven?"

"Oven? Furnace? It's not a phony at all. When we've finished here it'll do the job, all right."

"Then why the theatricals?"

"That was for the M.E. Those papers he signed are in sort of a never-never country just now. When we slide this back in and turn on the heat they'll become as legal as he thinks they are."

"Then why—"

"Because there are some things you have to know." Karl reached into the coffin and unfolded the gnarled hands. They came apart reluctantly and he pressed them down at the sides of the body. He unbuttoned the jacket, laid it back, unbuttoned the shirt, unzipped the trousers. When he had finished with this he looked up and found Wheeler's sharp gaze, not on the old man's corpse, but on him.

"I have the feeling," said Cleveland Wheeler, "that I have never seen you before."

Silently Karl Trilling responded: *But you do now.* And, *Thanks, Joey. You were dead right.* Joe had known the answer to that one plaguing question, *How should I act?*

Talk just the way he talks, Joe had said. *Be what he is, the whole time . . .*

Be what he is. A man without illusions (they don't work) and without hope (who needs it?) who has the unbreakable habit of succeeding. And who can say it's a nice day in such a way that everyone around snaps to attention and says: *Yes, SIR!*

"You've been busy," Karl responded shortly. He took off his jacket, folded it and put it on the table beside the kit. He put on surgeon's gloves and slipped the sterile sleeve off a new scalpel. "Some people scream and faint the first time they watch a dissection."

Wheeler smiled thinly. "I don't scream and faint." But it was not lost on Karl Trilling that only then, at the last possible moment, did Wheeler actually view the old man's body. When he did he neither screamed nor fainted; he uttered an astonished grunt.

"Thought that would surprise you," Karl said easily. "In case you were wondering, though, he really was a male. The species seems to be oviparous. Mammals too, but it has to be oviparous. I'd sure like a look at a female. That isn't a vagina. It's a cloaca."

"Until this moment," said Wheeler in a hypnotized voice, "I thought that 'not human' remark of yours was a figure of speech."

"No, you didn't," Karl responded shortly.

Leaving the words to hang in the air, as words will if a speaker has the wit to isolate them with wedges of silence, he deftly slit the corpse from the sternum to the pubic symphysis. For the first-time viewer this was always the difficult moment. It's hard not to realize viscerally that the cadaver does not feel anything and will not protest. Nerve-alive to Wheeler, Karl looked for a gasp or a shudder; Wheeler merely held his breath.

"We could spend hours—weeks, I imagine, going into the details," Karl said, deftly making a transverse incision in the ensiform area, almost around to the trapezoid on each side, "but this is the thing I wanted you to see." Grasping the flesh at the juncture of the cross he had cut, on the left side, he pulled upward and to the left. The cutaneous layers came away easily, with the fat under them. They were not pinkish, but an off-white lavender shade. Now the muscular striations over the ribs were in view. "If you'd palpated the old man's chest," he said, demonstrating on the right side, "you'd have felt what seemed to be normal human ribs. But look at this."

With a few deft strokes he separated the muscle fibers from the bone on a mid-costal area about four inches square, and scraped. A rib emerged and, as he widened the area and scraped between it and the next one, it became clear that the ribs were joined by a thin flexible layer of bone or chitin.

"It's like baleen—whalebone," said Karl. "See this?" He sectioned out a piece, flexed it.

"My God."

III

"Now look at this." Karl took surgical sheers from the kit, snipped through the sternum right up to the clavicle and then across the lower margin of the ribs. Slipping his fingers under them, he pulled upward. With a dull snap the entire ribcage opened like a door, exposing the lung.

The lung was not pink, nor the liverish-brownish-black of a smoker, but yellow—the clear bright yellow of pure sulfur.

"His metabolism," Karl said, straightening up at last and flexing the tension out of his shoulders, "is fantastic. Or was. He lived on oxygen, same as us, but he broke it out of carbon monoxide, sulfur dioxide and trioxide and carbon

dioxide mostly. I'm not saying he could—I mean he had
to. When he was forced to breathe what we call clean air,
he could take just so much of it and then had to duck out
and find a few breaths of his own atmosphere. When he
was younger he could take it for hours at a time, but as
the years went by he had to spend more and more time
in the kind of smog he could breathe. Those long disap-
pearances of his, and that reclusiveness—they weren't as
kinky as people supposed."

Wheeler made a gesture toward the corpse. "But—what
is he? Where—"

"I can't tell you. Except for a good deal of medical
and biochemical details, you now know as much as I do.
Somehow, somewhere, he arrived. He came, he saw, he began to make his moves. Look at this."

He opened the other side of the chest and then broke
the sternum up and away. He pointed. The lung tissue was
not in two discreet parts, but extended across the median
line. "One lung, all the way across, though it has these two
lobes. The kidneys and gonads show the same right-left
fusion."

"I'll take your word for it," said Wheeler a little hoarsely.
"Damn it, what *is* it?"

"A featherless biped, as Plato once described homo sap.
I don't know what it is. I just know *that* it is—and I thought
you ought to know. That's all."

"But you've seen one before. That's obvious."

"Sure. Epstein."

"Epstein?"

"Sure. The old man had to have a go-between—someone
who could, without suspicion, spend long hours with him
and hours away. The old man could do a lot over the phone,
but not everything. Epstein was, you might say, a right
arm that could hold its breath a little longer than he could.
It got to him in the end, though, and he died of it."

"Why didn't you say something long before this?"

"First of all, I value my own skin. I could say reputation,
but skin is the word. I signed a contract as his personal
physician because he needed a personal physician—another
bit of window-dressing. But I did precious little doctoring
—except over the phone—and nine-tenths of that was, I
realized quite recently, purely diversionary. Even a doctor, I

suppose, can be a trusting soul. One or the other would call and give a set of symptoms and I'd cautiously suggest and prescribe. Then I'd get another call that the patient was improving and that was that. Why, I even got specimens—blood, urine, stools—and did the pathology on them and never realized that they were from the same source as what the medical examiner checked out and signed for."

"What do you mean, same source?"

Karl shrugged. "He could get anything he wanted—anything."

"Then—what the M.E. examined wasn't—" he waved a hand at the casket.

"Of course not. That's why the crematorium has a back door. There's a little pocket sleight-of-hand trick you can buy for fifty cents that operates the same way. This body here was inside the furnace. The ringer—a look-alike that came from God knows where; I swear to you I don't—was lying out there waiting for the M.E. When the button was pushed the fires started up and that coffin slid in—pushing this one out and at the same time drenching it with water as it came through. While we've been in here, the human body is turning to ashes. My personal private secret instructions, both for Epstein and for the boss, were to wait until I was certain I was alone and then come in here after an hour and push the second button, which would slide this one back into the fire. I was to do no investigations, ask no questions, make no reports. It came through as logical but not reasonable, like so many of his orders." He laughed suddenly. "Do you know why the old man—and Epstein too, for that matter, in case you never noticed—wouldn't shake hands with anyone?"

"I presumed it was because he had an obsession with germs."

"It was because his normal body temperature was a hundred and seven."

Wheeler touched one of his own hands with the other and said nothing.

When Karl felt that the wedge of silence was thick enough he asked lightly, "Well, boss, where do we go from here?"

Cleveland Wheeler turned away from the corpse and to Karl slowly, as if diverting his mind with an effort.

"What did you call me?"

"Figure of speech," said Karl and smiled. "Actually, I'm working for the company—and that's you. I'm under orders, which have been finally and completely discharged when I push that button—I have no others. So it really is up to you."

Wheeler's eyes fell again to the corpse. "You mean about him? This? What we should do?"

"That, yes. Whether to burn it up and forget it—or call in top management and an echelon of scientists. Or scare the living hell out of everyone on Earth by phoning the papers. Sure, that has to be decided, but I was thinking on a much wider spectrum than that."

"Such as—"

Karl gestured toward the box with his head. "What was he doing here, anyway? What has he done? What was he trying to do?"

"You'd better go on," said Wheeler; and for the very first time said something in a way that suggested diffidence. "You've had a while to think about all this. I—" and almost helplessly, he spread his hands.

"I can understand that," Karl said gently. "Up to now I've been coming on like a hired lecturer and I know it. I'm not going to embarrass you with personalities except to say that you've absorbed all this with less buckling of the knees than anyone in the world I could think of."

"Right. Well, there's a simple technique you learn in elementary algebra. It has to do with the construction of graphs. You place a dot on the graph where known data put it. You get more data, you put down another dot and then a third. With just three dots—of course, the more the better, but it can be done with three—you can connect them and establish a curve. This curve has certain characteristics and it's fair to extend the curve a little farther with the assumption that later data will bear you out."

"Extrapolation."

"Extrapolation. X axis, the fortunes of our late boss. Y axis, time. The curve is his fortunes—that is to say, his influence."

"Pretty tall graph."

"Over thirty years."

"Still pretty tall."

"All right," said Karl. "Now, over the same thirty years, another curve: change in the environment." He held up a hand. "I'm not going to read you a treatise on ecology. Let's be more objective than that. Let's just say changes. Okay: a measurable rise in the mean temperature because of CO_2 and the greenhouse effect. Draw the curve. Incidence of heavy metals, mercury and lithium, in organic tissue. Draw a curve. Likewise chlorinated hydrocarbons, hypertrophy of algae due to phosphates, incidence of coronaries . . . All right, let's superimpose all these curves on the same graph."

"I see what you're getting at. But you have to be careful with that kind of statistics game. Like, the increase of traffic fatalities coincides with the increased use of aluminum cans and plastic-tipped baby pins."

"Right. I don't think I'm falling into that trap. I just want to find reasonable answers to a couple of otherwise unreasonable situations. One is this: if the changes occurring in our planet are the result of mere carelessness—a more or less random thing, carelessness—then how come nobody is being careless in a way that benefits the environment? Strike that. I promised, no ecology lessons. Rephrase: how come all these carelessnesses promote a change and not a preservation?

"Next question: What is the direction of the change? You've seen speculative writing about 'terra-forming'—altering other planets to make them habitable by humans. Suppose an effort were being made to change this planet to suit someone else? Suppose they wanted more water and were willing to melt the polar caps by the greenhouse effect? Increase the oxides of sulfur, eliminate certain marine forms from plankton to whales? Reduce the population by increases in lung cancer, emphysema, heart attacks and even war?"

Both men found themselves looking down at the sleeping face in the coffin. Karl said softly, "Look what he was into—petro-chemicals, fossil fuels, food processing, advertising, all the things that made the changes or helped the changers—"

"You're not blaming him for all of it."

"Certainly not. He found willing helpers by the million."

"You don't think he was trying to change a whole planet just so he could be comfortable in it."

"No, I don't think so—and that's the central point I have to make. I don't know if there are any more around like him and Epstein, but I can suppose this: If the changes now going on keep on—and accelerate—then we can expect them."

Wheeler said, "So what would you like to do? Mobilize the world against the invader?"

"Nothing like that. I think I'd slowly and quietly reverse the changes. If this planet is normally unsuitable to them, then I'd keep it so. I don't think they'd have to be driven back. I think they just wouldn't come."

"Or they'd try some other way."

"I don't think so," said Karl. "Because they tried this one. If they thought they could do it with fleets of spaceships and super-zap guns, they'd be doing it. No—this is their way and if it doesn't work, they can try somewhere else."

Wheeler began pulling thoughtfully at his lip. Karl said softly, "All it would take is someone who knew what he was doing, who could command enough clout and who had the wit to make it pay. They might even arrange a man's life—to get the kind of man they need."

And before Wheeler could answer, Karl took up his scalpel.

"I want you to do something for me," he said sharply in a new, commanding tone—actually, Wheeler's own. "I want you to do it because I've done it and I'll be damned if I want to be the only man in the world who has."

Leaning over the head of the casket, he made an incision along the hairline from temple to temple. Then, bracing his elbows against the edge of the box and steadying one hand with the other, he drew the scalpel straight down the center of the forehead and down onto the nose, splitting it exactly in two. Down he went through the upper lip and then the lower, around the point of the chin and under it to the throat. Then he stood up.

"Put your hands on his cheeks," he ordered. Wheeler

frowned briefly (how long had it been since anyone had spoken to him that way?), hesitated, then did as he was told.

"Now press your hands together and down."

The incision widened slightly under the pressure, then abruptly the flesh gave and the entire skin of the face slipped off. The unexpected lack of resistance brought Wheeler's hands to the bottom of the coffin and he found himself face to face, inches away, with the corpse.

Like the lungs and kidneys, the eyes—eye?—passed the median, very slightly reduced at the center. The pupil was oval, its long axis transverse. The skin was pale lavender with yellow vessels and in place of a nose was a thread-fringed hole. The mouth was circular, the teeth not quite radially placed; there was little chin.

Without moving, Wheeler closed his eyes, held them shut for one second, two, and then courageously opened them again. Karl whipped around the end of the coffin and got an arm around Wheeler's chest. Wheeler leaned on it heavily for a moment, then stood up quickly and brushed the arm away.

"You didn't have to do that."

"Yes, I did," said Karl. "Would you want to be the only man in the world who'd gone through that—with nobody to tell it to?"

And after all, Wheeler could laugh. When he had finished he said, "Push that button."

"Hand me that cover."

Most obediently Cleveland Wheeler brought the coffin lid and they placed it.

Karl pushed the button and they watched the coffin slide into the square of flame. Then they left.

Joe Trilling had a funny way of making a living. It was a good living, but of course he didn't make anything like the bundle he could have made in the city. On the other hand, he lived in the mountains a half-mile away from a picturesque village, in clean air and piney-birchy woods along with lots of mountain laurel and he was his own boss. There wasn't much competition for what he did.

What he did was to make simulacra of medical specimens, mostly for the armed forces, although he had plenty of or-

ders from medical schools, film producers and an occasional individual, no questions asked. He could make a
model of anything inside, affixed to or penetrating a body
or any part of it. He could make models to be looked at,
models to be felt, smelled and palpated. He could give you
gangrene that stunk or dewy thyroids with real dew on
them. He could make one-of-a-kind or he could set up a production line. Dr. Joe Trilling was, to put it briefly, the best
there was at what he did.

"The clincher," Karl told him (in much more relaxed circumstances than their previous ones; daytime now, with
beer), "the real clincher was the face bit. God, Joe, that
was a beautiful piece of work."

"Just nuts and bolts. The beautiful part was your idea
—his hands on it."

"How do you mean?"

"I've been thinking back to that," Joe said. "I don't think
you yourself realize how brilliant a stroke that was. It's
all very well to set up a show for the guy, but to make him
put his hands as well as his eyes and brains on it—that
was the stroke of genius. It's like—well, I can remember
when I was a kid coming home from school and putting
my hand on a fence rail and somebody had spat on it."
He displayed his hand, shook it. "All these years I can remember how that felt. All these years couldn't wear it
away, all those scrubbings couldn't wash it away. It's more
than a cerebral or psychic thing, Karl—more than the
memory of an episode. I think there's a kind of memory
mechanism in the cells themselves, especially on the hands,
that can be invoked. What I'm getting to is that no matter how long he lives, Cleve Wheeler is going to feel that
skin slip under his palms, and that is going to bring him
nose to nose with that face. No, you're the genius, not me."

"Na. You knew what you were doing. I didn't."

"Hell you didn't." Joe leaned far back in his lawn chaise
—so far he could hold up his beer and look at the sun
through it from the underside. Watching the receding bubbles defy perspective (because they swell as they rise), he
murmured, "Karl?"

"Yuh."

"Ever hear of Occam's Razor?"

"Um. Long time back. Philosophical principle. Or logic

or something. Let's see. Given an effect and a choice of possible causes, the simplest cause is always the one most likely to be true. Is that it?"

"Not too close, but close enough," said Joe Trilling lazily. "Hm. You're the one who used to proclaim that logic is sufficient unto itself and need have nothing to do with truth."

"I still proclaim it."

"Okay. Now, you and I know that human greed and carelessness are quite enough all by themselves to wreck this planet. We didn't think that was enough for the likes of Cleve Wheeler, who can really do something about it, so we constructed him a smog-breathing extra-terrestrial. I mean, he hadn't done anything about saving the world for our reasons, so we gave him a whizzer of a reason of his own. Right out of our heads."

"Dictated by all available factors. Yes. What are you getting at, Joe?"

"Oh—just that our complicated hoax is simple, really, in the sense that it brought everything down to a single cause. Occam's Razor slices things down to simplest causes. Single causes have a fair chance of being right."

Karl put down his beer with a bump. "I never thought of that. I've been too busy to think of that. *Suppose we were right?*"

They looked at each other, shaken.

At last Karl said, "What do we look for now, Joe—space ships?"

THE QUEEN OF AIR AND DARKNESS

Poul Anderson

If there's such a thing as a Renaissance man in science fiction today, it would have to be Poul Anderson, a writer with perception, style, knowledgeability and good sense. He's written just about every type of science fiction and fantasy story there is, plus some very good mystery novels. If I had any complaint at all about his work, I suppose it would be that he uses his gifts for poetic imagery too seldom. But in this tale he blends *all* of his skills to produce a haunting, beautiful picture of an alien planet where magic and science meet in battle.

The last glow of the last sunset would linger almost until midwinter. But there would be no more day, and the northlands rejoiced. Blossoms opened, flamboyance on firethorn trees, steel-flowers rising blue from the brok and rainplant that cloaked all hills, shy whiteness of kiss-me-never down in the dales. Flitteries darted among them on iridescent wings; a crownbuck shook his horns and bugled. Between horizons the sky deepened from purple to sable. Both moons were aloft, nearly full, shining frosty on leaves and molten on waters. The shadows they made were blurred by an aurora, a great blowing curtain of light across half heaven. Behind it the earliest stars had come out.

A boy and a girl sat on Wolund's Barrow just under
the dolmen it upbore. Their hair, which streamed halfway
down their backs, showed startlingly forth, bleached as it
was by summer. Their bodies, still dark from that season,
merged with earth and bush and rock, for they wore only
garlands. He played on a bone flute and she sang. They
had lately become lovers. Their age was about sixteen,
but they did not know this, considering themselves Outlings
and thus indifferent to time, remembering little or nothing
of how they had once dwelt in the lands of men.

His notes piped cold around her voice:

"Cast a spell,
weave it well
of dust and dew
and night and you."

A brook by the grave mound, carrying moonlight down to
a hill-hidden river, answered with its rapids. A flock of hell-
bats passed black beneath the aurora.

A shape came bounding over Cloudmoor. It had two
arms and two legs, but the legs were long and claw-footed
and feathers covered it to the end of a tail and broad wings.
The face was half human, dominated by its eyes. Had Ayoch
been able to stand wholly erect, he would have reached to
the boy's shoulder.

The girl rose. "He carries a burden," she said. Her vision
was not meant for twilight like that of a northland creature born, but she had learned how to use every sign her
senses gave her. Besides the fact that ordinarily a pook
would fly, there was a heaviness to his haste.

"And he comes from the south." Excitement jumped in
the boy, sudden as a green flame that went across the con-
stellation Lyrth. He sped down the mound. "Ohoi, Ayoch!"
he called. "Me here, Mistherd!"

"And Shadow-of-a-Dream," the girl laughed, following.

The pook halted. He breathed louder than the soughing
in the growth around him. A smell of bruised yerba lifted
where he stood.

"Well met in winterbirth," he whistled. "You can help
me bring this to Carheddin."

He held out what he bore. His eyes were yellow lanterns
above. It moved and whimpered.

"Why, a child," Mistherd said.

"Even as you were, my son, even as you were. Ho, ho, what a snatch!" Ayoch boasted. "They were a score in yon camp by Fallowwood, armed, and besides watcher engines they had big ugly dogs aprowl while they slept. I came from above, however, having spied on them till I knew that a handful of dazedust—"

"The poor thing." Shadow-of-a-Dream took the boy and held him to her small breasts. "So full of sleep yet, aren't you?" Blindly, he sought a nipple. She smiled through the veil of her hair. "No, I am still too young, and you already too old. But come, when you wake in Carheddin under the mountain, you shall feast."

"Yo-ah," said Ayoch very softly. "She is abroad and has heard and seen. She comes." He crouched down, wings folded. After a moment Mistherd knelt, and then Shadow-of-a-Dream, though she did not let go the child.

The Queen's tall form blocked off the moons. For a while she regarded the three and their booty. Hill and moor sounds withdrew from their awareness until it seemed they could hear the northlights hiss.

At last Ayoch whispered, "Have I done well, Starmother?"

"If you stole a babe from a camp full of engines," said the beautiful voice, "then they were folk out of the far south who may not endure it as meekly as yeomen."

"But what can they do, Snowmaker?" the pook asked. "How can they track us?"

Mistherd lifted his head and spoke in pride. "Also, now they too have felt the awe of us."

"And he is a cuddly dear," Shadow-of-a-Dream said. "And we need more like him, do we not, Lady Sky?"

"It had to happen in some twilight," agreed she who stood above. "Take him onward and care for him. By this sign," which she made, "is he claimed for the Dwellers."

Their joy was freed. Ayoch cartwheeled over the ground till he reached a shiverleaf. There he swarmed up the trunk and out on a limb, perched half hidden by unrestful pale foliage, and crowed. Boy and girl bore the child toward Carheddin at an easy distance-devouring lope which let him pipe and her sing:

"Wahaii, wahaii!
Wayala, laii!
Wing on the wind
high over heaven,
shrilly shrieking,
rush with the rainspears,
tumble through tumult,
drift to the moonhoar trees and the dream-heavy shadows
    beneath them,
and rock in, be one with the clinking wavelets of lakes
    where the starbeams drown."

As she entered, Barbro Cullen felt, through all grief and fury, stabbed by dismay. The room was unkempt. Journals, tapes, reels, codices, file boxes, bescribbled papers were piled on every table. Dust filmed most shelves and corners. Against one wall stood a laboratory setup, microscope and analytical equipment. She recognized it as compact and efficient, but it was not what you would expect in an office, and it gave the air a faint chemical reek. The rug was threadbare, the furniture shabby.

This was her final chance?

Then Eric Sherrinford approached. "Good day, Mrs. Cullen," he said. His tone was crisp, his handclasp firm. His faded gripsuit didn't bother her. She wasn't inclined to fuss about her own appearance except on special occasions. (And would she ever again have one, unless she got back Jimmy?) What she observed was a cat's personal neatness.

A smile radiated in crow's feet from his eyes. "Forgive my bachelor housekeeping. On Beowulf we have—we had, at any rate, machines for that, so I never acquired the habit myself, and I don't want a hireling disarranging my tools. More convenient to work out of my apartment than keep a separate office. Won't you be seated?"

"No, thanks. I couldn't," she mumbled.

"I understand. But if you'll excuse me, I function best in a relaxed position."

He jackknifed into a lounger. One long shank crossed the other knee. He drew forth a pipe and stuffed it from a pouch. Barbro wondered why he took tobacco in so ancient a way. Wasn't Beowulf supposed to have the up-to-date equipment that they still couldn't afford to build on

Roland? Well, of course old customs might survive anyhow. They generally did in colonies, she remembered reading. People had moved starward in the hope of preserving such outmoded things as their mother tongues or constitutional government or rational-technological civilization. . . .

Sherrinford pulled her up from the confusion of her weariness: "You must give me the details of your case, Mrs. Cullen. You've simply told me your son was kidnaped and your local constabulary did nothing. Otherwise, I know just a few obvious facts, such as your being widowed rather than divorced; and you're the daughter of outwayers in Olga Ivanoff Land, who nevertheless kept in close telecommunication with Christmas Landing; and you're trained in one of the biological professions; and you had several years' hiatus in field work until recently you started again."

She gaped at the high-cheeked, beak-nosed, black-haired and gray-eyed countenance. His lighter made a *scrit* and a flare which seemed to fill the room. Quietness dwelt on this height above the city, and winter dusk was seeping through the windows. "How in cosmos do you know that?" she heard herself exclaim.

He shrugged and fell into the lecturer's manner for which he was notorious. "My work depends on noticing details and fitting them together. In more than a hundred years on Roland, tending to cluster according to their origins and thought-habits, people have developed regional accents. You have a trace of the Olgan burr, but you nasalize your vowels in the style of this area, though you live in Portolondon. That suggests steady childhood exposure to metropolitan speech. You were part of Matsuyama's expedition, you told me, and took your boy along. They wouldn't have allowed any ordinary technician to do that; hence, you had to be valuable enough to get away with it. The team was conducting ecological research; therefore, you must be in the life sciences. For the same reason, you must have had previous field experience. But your skin is fair, showing none of the leatheriness one gets from prolonged exposure to this sun. Accordingly, you must have been mostly indoors for a good while before you went on your ill-fated trip. As for widowhood—you never mentioned a husband to me, but you have had a man whom you thought so highly of that you still wear both the wedding and the engagement ring he gave you."

Her sight blurred and stung. The last of those words had brought Tim back; huge, ruddy, laughterful and gentle. She must turn from this other person and stare outward. "Yes," she achieved saying, "you're right."

The apartment occupied a hilltop above Christmas Landing. Beneath it the city dropped away in walls, roofs, archaistic chimneys and lamplit streets, goblin lights of human-piloted vehicles, to the harbor, the sweep of Venture Bay, ships bound to and from the Sunward Islands and remoter regions of the Boreal Ocean, which glimmered like mercury in the afterglow of Charlemagne. Oliver was swinging rapidly higher, a mottled orange disc a full degree wide; closer to the zenith which it could never reach, it would shine the color of ice. Alde, half the seeming size, was a thin slow crescent near Sirius, which she remembered was near Sol, but you couldn't see Sol without a telescope—

"Yes," she said around the pain in her throat, "my husband is about four years dead. I was carrying our first child when he was killed by a stampeding monocerus. We'd been married three years before. Met while we were both at the University—casts from School Central can only supply a basic education, you know— We founded our own team to do ecological studies under contract—you know, can a certain area be settled while maintaining a balance of nature, what crops will grow, what hazards, that sort of question— Well, afterward I did lab work for a fisher co-op in Portolondon. But the monotony, the . . . shut-in-ness . . . was eating me away. Professor Matsuyama offered me a position on the team he was organizing to examine Commissioner Hauch Land. I thought, God help me, I thought Jimmy—Tim wanted him named James, once the tests showed it'd be a boy, after his own father and because of 'Timmy and Jimmy' and —oh, I thought Jimmy could safely come along. I couldn't bear to leave him behind for months, not at his age. We could make sure he'd never wander out of camp. What could hurt him inside it? *I* had never believed those stories about the Outlings stealing human children. I supposed parents were trying to hide from themselves the fact they'd been careless, they'd let a kid get lost in the woods or attacked by a pack of satans or—well, I learned better, Mr. Sherrinford. The guard robots were evaded and the dogs were drugged, and when I woke, Jimmy was gone."

He regarded her through the smoke from his pipe. Barbro Engdahl Cullen was a big woman of thirty or so (Rolandic years, he reminded himself, ninety-five percent of Terrestrial, not the same as Beowulfan years), broad-shouldered, long-legged, full-breasted, supple of stride; her face was wide, straight nose, straight-forward hazel eyes, heavy but mobile mouth; her hair was reddish-brown, cropped below the ears, her voice husky, her garment a plain street robe. To still the writhing of her fingers, he asked skeptically, "Do you now believe in the Outlings?"

"No. I'm just not so sure as I was." She swung about with half a glare for him. "And we have found traces."

"Bits of fossils," he nodded. "A few artifacts of a neolithic sort. But apparently ancient, as if the makers died ages ago. Intensive search has failed to turn up any real evidence for their survival."

"How intensive can search be, in a summer-stormy, winter-gloomy wilderness around the North Pole?" she demanded. "When we are, how many, a million people on an entire planet, half of us crowded into this one city?"

"And the rest crowding this one habitable continent," he pointed out.

"Arctica covers five million square kilometers," she flung back. "The Arctic Zone proper covers a fourth of it. We haven't the industrial base to establish satellite monitor stations, build aircraft we can trust in those parts, drive roads through the damned darklands and establish permanent bases and get to know them and tame them. Good Christ, generations of lonely outwaymen told stories about Graymantle, and the beast was never seen by a proper scientist till last year!"

"Still, you continue to doubt the reality of the Outlings?"

"Well, what about a secret cult among humans, born of isolation and ignorance, lairing in the wilderness, stealing children when they can for—" She swallowed. Her head drooped. "But you're supposed to be the expert."

"From what you told me over the visiphone, the Porto-london constabulary questions the accuracy of the report your group made, thinks the lot of you were hysterical, claims you must have omitted a due precaution, and the child toddled away and was lost beyond your finding."

His dry words pried the horror out of her. Flushing, she snapped, "Like any settler's kid? No. I didn't simply yell. I consulted Data Retrieval. A few too many such cases are recorded for accident to be a very plausible explanation. And shall we totally ignore the frightened stories about reappearances? But when I went back to the constabulary with my facts, they brushed me off. I suspect that was not entirely because they're undermanned. I think they're afraid too. They're recruited from country boys, and Portolondon lies near the edge of the unknown."

Her energy faded. "Roland hasn't got any central police force," she finished drably. "You're my last hope."

The man puffed smoke into twilight, with which it blent, before he said in a kindlier voice than hitherto: "Please don't make it a high hope, Mrs. Cullen. I'm the solitary private investigator on this world, having no resources beyond myself, and a newcomer to boot."

"How long have you been here?"

"Twelve years. Barely time to get a little familiarity with the relatively civilized coastlands. You settlers of a century or more—what do you, even, know about Arctica's interior?"

Sherrinford sighed. "I'll take the case, charging no more than I must, mainly for the sake of the experience," he said. "But only if you'll be my guide and assistant, however painful it will be for you."

"Of course! I dreaded waiting idle. Why me, though?"

"Hiring someone else as well qualified would be prohibitively expensive on a pioneer planet where every hand has a thousand urgent tasks to do. Besides, you have a motive. And I'll need that. As one who was born on another world altogether strange to this one, itself altogether strange to Mother Earth, I am too dauntingly aware of how handicapped we are."

Night gathered upon Christmas Landing. The air stayed mild, but glimmer-lit tendrils of fog, sneaking through the streets, had a cold look, and colder yet was the aurora where it shuddered between the moons. The woman drew closer to the man in this darkening room, surely not aware that she did, until he switched on a fluoropanel. The same knowledge of Roland's aloneness was in both of them.

One light-year is not much as galactic distances go. You could walk it in about 270 million years, beginning at the middle of the Permian Era, when dinosaurs belonged to the remote future, and continuing to the present day when spaceships cross even greater reaches. But stars in our neighborhood average some nine light-years apart, and barely one percent of them have planets which are man-habitable, and speeds are limited to less than that of radiation. Scant help is given by relativistic time contraction and suspended animation en route. These made the journeys seem short, but history meanwhile does not stop at home.

Thus voyages from sun to sun will always be few. Colonists will be those who have extremely special reasons for going. They will take along germ plasm for exogenetic cultivation of domestic plants and animals—and of human infants, in order that population can grow fast enough to escape death through genetic drift. After all, they cannot rely on further immigration. Two or three times a century, a ship may call from some other colony. (Not from Earth. Earth has long ago sunk into alien concerns.) Its place of origin will be an old settlement. The young ones are in no position to build and man interstellar vessels.

Their very survival, let alone their eventual modernization, is in doubt. The founding fathers have had to take what they could get, in a universe not especially designed for man.

Consider, for example, Roland. It is among the rare happy finds, a world where humans can live, breathe, eat the food, drink the water, walk unclad if they choose, sow their crops, pasture their beasts, dig their mines, erect their homes, raise their children and grandchildren. It is worth crossing three quarters of a light-century to preserve certain dear values and strike new roots into the soil of Roland.

But the star Charlemagne is of type F9, forty percent brighter than Sol, brighter still in the treacherous ultraviolet and wilder still in the wind of charged particles that seethes from it. The planet has an eccentric orbit. In the middle of the short but furious northern summer, which includes periastron, total insolation is more than double what Earth gets; in the depth of the long northern winter, it is barely less than Terrestrial average.

Native life is abundant everywhere. But lacking elaborate machinery, not yet economically possible to construct for more than a few specialists, man can only endure the high latitudes. A ten-degree axial tilt, together with the orbit, means that the northern part of the Arctican continent spends half its year in unbroken sunlessness. Around the South Pole lies an empty ocean.

Other differences from Earth might superficially seem more important. Roland has two moons, small but close, to evoke clashing tides. It rotates once in thirty-two hours, which is endlessly, subtly disturbing to organisms evolved through gigayears of a quicker rhythm. The weather patterns are altogether unterrestrial. The globe is a mere 9500 kilometers in diameter; its surface gravity is 0.42×980 cm/sec^2; the sea level air pressure is slightly above one Earth atmosphere. (For actually, Earth is the freak, and man exists because a cosmic accident blew away most of the gas that a body its size ought to have kept, as Venus has done.)

However, Homo can truly be called sapiens when he practices his specialty of being unspecialized. His repeated attempts to freeze himself into an all-answering pattern or culture or ideology, or whatever he has named it, have repeatedly brought ruin. Give him the pragmatic business of making his living and he will usually do rather well. He adapts, within broad limits.

These limits are set by such factors as his need for sunlight and his being, necessarily and forever, a part of the life that surrounds him and a creature of the spirit within.

Portolondon thrust docks, boats, machinery, warehouses into the Gulf of Polaris. Behind them huddled the dwellings of its 5000 permanent inhabitants: concrete walls, storm shutters, high-peaked tile roofs. The gaiety of their paint looked forlorn amidst lamps; this town lay past the Arctic Circle.

Nevertheless Sherrinford remarked, "Cheerful place, eh? The kind of thing I came to Roland looking for."

Barbro made no reply. The days in Christmas Landing, while he made his preparations, had drained her. Gazing out the dome of the taxi that was whirring them downtown from the hydrofoil that brought them, she supposed he meant the lushness of forest and meadows along the road, brilliant hues and phosphorescence of flowers in gardens, clamor of wings overhead. Unlike Terrestrial flora in cold climates, Arctican vegetation spends every daylit hour in frantic growth and energy storage. Not till summer's fever gives place to gentle winter does it bloom and fruit; and estivating animals rise from their dens and migratory birds come home.

The view was lovely, she had to admit: beyond the trees, a spaciousness climbing toward remote heights, silvery-gray under a moon, an aurora, the diffuse radiance from a sun just below the horizon.

Beautiful as a hunting satan, she thought, and as terrible. That wilderness had stolen Jimmy. She wondered if she would at least be given to find his little bones and take them to his father.

Abruptly she realized that she and Sherrinford were at their hotel and that he had been speaking of the town. Since it was next in size after the capital, he must have visited here often before. The streets were crowded and noisy; signs flickered, music blared from shops, taverns, restaurants, sports centers, dance halls; vehicles were jammed down to molasses speed; the several-stories-high office buildings stood aglow. Portolondon linked an enormous hinterland to the outside world. Down the Gloria River came timber rafts, ores, harvest of farms whose owners were slowly making Rolandic life serve them, meat and ivory and furs gathered by rangers in the mountains beyond Troll Scarp. In from the sea came coastwise freighters, the fishing fleet, produce of the Sunward Islands, plunder of whole continents farther south where bold men adventured. It clanged in Portolondon, laughed, blustered, connived, robbed, preached, guzzled, swilled, toiled, dreamed, lusted, built, destroyed, died, was born, was happy, angry, sorrowful, greedy, vulgar, loving, ambitious, human. Neither the sun's blaze elsewhere nor the half year's twilight here—wholly night around midwinter—was going to stay man's hand.

Or so everybody said.

Everybody except those who had settled in the darklands. Barbro used to take for granted that they were evolving curious customs, legends, and superstitions, which would die when the outway had been completely mapped and controlled. Of late, she had wondered. Perhaps Sherrinford's hints, about a change in his own attitude brought about by his preliminary research, were responsible.

Or perhaps she just needed something to think about besides how Jimmy, the day before he went, when she asked him whether he wanted rye or French bread for a sandwich, answered in great solemnity—he was becoming interested in the alphabet—"I'll have a slice of what we people call the F bread."

She scarcely noticed getting out of the taxi, registering, being conducted to a primitively furnished room. But after she unpacked, she remembered Sherrinford had suggested a confidential conference. She went down the hall and knocked on his door. Her knuckles sounded less loud than her heart.

He opened the door, finger on lips, and gestured her toward a corner. Her temper bristled until she saw the image of Chief Constable Dawson in the visiphone. Sherrinford must have chimed him up and must have a reason to keep her out of scanner range. She found a chair and watched, nails digging into knees.

The detective's lean length refolded itself. "Pardon the interruption," he said. "A man mistook the number. Drunk, by the indications."

Dawson chuckled. "We get plenty of those." Barbro recalled his fondness for gabbing. He tugged the beard which he affected, as if he were an outwayer instead of a townsman. "No harm in them as a rule. They only have a lot of voltage to discharge, after weeks or months in the backlands."

"I've gathered that that environment—foreign in a million major and minor ways to the one that created man—I've gathered that it does do odd things to the personality." Sherrinford tamped his pipe. "Of course, you know my practice has been confined to urban and suburban areas. Isolated garths seldom need private investigators. Now that situation appears to have changed. I called to ask you for advice."

"Glad to help," Dawson said. "I've not forgotten what you did for us in the de Tahoe murder case." Cautiously: "Better explain your problem first."

Sherrinford struck fire. The smoke that followed cut

through the green odors—even here, a paved pair of kilometers from the nearest woods—that drifted past traffic rumble through a crepuscular window. "This is more a scientific mission than a search for an absconding debtor or an industrial spy," he drawled. "I'm looking into two possibilities: that an organization, criminal or religious or whatever, has long been active and steals infants; or that the Outlings of folklore are real."

"Huh?" On Dawson's face Barbro read as much dismay as surprise. "You can't be serious!"

"Can't I?" Sherrinford smiled. "Several generations' worth of reports shouldn't be dismissed out of hand. Especially not when they become more frequent and consistent in the course of time, not less. Nor can we ignore the documented loss of babies and small children, amounting by now to over a hundred, and never a trace found afterward. Nor the finds which demonstrate that an intelligent species once inhabited Arctica and may still haunt the interior."

Dawson leaned forward as if to climb out of the screen. "Who engaged you?" he demanded. "That Cullen woman? We were sorry for her, naturally, but she wasn't making sense, and when she got downright abusive—"

"Didn't her companions, reputable scientists, confirm her story?"

"No story to confirm. Look, they had the place ringed with detectors and alarms, and they kept mastiffs. Standard procedure in country where a hungry sauroid or whatever might happen by. Nothing could've entered unbenownst."

"On the ground. How about a flyer landing in the middle of camp?"

"A man in a copter rig would've roused everybody."

"A winged being might be quieter."

"A living flyer that could lift a three-year-old boy? Doesn't exist."

"Isn't in the scientific literature, you mean, Constable. Remember Graymantle; remember how little we know about Roland, a planet, an entire world. Such birds do exist on Beowulf—and on Rustum, I've read. I made a calculation from the local ratio of air density to gravity, and, yes, it's marginally possible here too. The child could have been carried off for a short distance before wing muscles were exhausted and the creature must descend."

Dawson snorted. "First it landed and walked into the tent where mother and boy were asleep. Then it walked away, toting him, after it couldn't fly further. Does that sound like a bird of prey? And the victim didn't cry out, the dogs didn't bark!"

"As a matter of fact," Sherrinford said, "those inconsistencies are the most interesting and convincing features of the whole account. You're right, it's hard to see how a human kidnaper could get in undetected, and an eagle type of creature wouldn't operate in that fashion. But none of this applies to a winged intelligent being. The boy could have been drugged. Certainly the dogs showed signs of having been."

"The dogs showed signs of having overslept. Nothing had disturbed them. The kid wandering by wouldn't do so. We don't need to assume one damn thing except, first, that he got restless and, second, that the alarms were a bit sloppily rigged—seeing as how no danger was expected from inside camp—and let him pass out. And, third, I hate to speak this way, but we must assume the poor tyke starved or was killed."

Dawson paused before adding: "If we had more staff, we could have given the affair more time. And would have, of course. We did make an aerial sweep, which risked the lives of the pilots, using instruments which would've spotted the kid anywhere in a fifty-kilometer radius, unless he was dead. You know how sensitive thermal analyzers are. We drew a complete blank. We have more important jobs than to hunt for the scattered pieces of a corpse."

He finished brusquely. "If Mrs. Cullen's hired you, my advice is you find an excuse to quit. Better for her, too. She's got to come to terms with reality."

Barbro checked a shout by biting her tongue.

"Oh, this is merely the latest disappearance of the series," Sherrinford said. She didn't understand how he could maintain his easy tone when Jimmy was lost. "More thoroughly recorded than any before, thus more suggestive. Usually an outwayer family has given a tearful but undetailed account of their child who vanished and must have been stolen by the Old Folk. Sometimes, years later, they'd tell about glimpses of what they swore must have been the grown child, not really human any longer, flitting past in murk or peering through a window or working mischief upon them. As you say, neither the authorities nor the scientists have had personnel or resources to mount a proper investigation. But as I say, the matter appears to be worth investigating. Maybe a private party like myself can contribute."

"Listen, most of us constables grew up in the outway. We don't just ride patrol and answer emergency calls; we go back there for holidays and reunions. If any gang of . . . of human sacrificers was around, we'd know."

"I realize that. I also realize that the people you came from have a widespread and deep-seated belief in non-human beings with supernatural powers. Many actually go through rites and make offerings to propitiate them."

"I know what you're leading up to," Dawson fleered. "I've heard it before, from a hundred sensationalists. The aborigines are the Outlings. I thought better of you. Surely you've visited a museum or three, surely you've read literature from planets which do have natives—or damn and blast, haven't you ever applied that logic of yours?"

He wagged a finger. "Think," he said. "What have we in fact discovered? A few pieces of worked stone; a few megaliths that might be artificial; scratchings on rock that seem to show plants and animals, though not the way any human culture would ever have shown them; traces of fires and broken bones; other fragments of bone that seem as if they might've belonged to thinking creatures, as if they might've been inside fingers or around big brains. If so, however, the owners looked nothing like men. Or angels, for that matter. Nothing! The most anthropoid reconstruction I've seen shows a kind of two-legged crocagator."

"Wait, let me finish. The stories about the Outlings—oh, I've heard them too, plenty of them. I believed them when I was a kid—the stories tell how there're different kinds, some winged, some not, some half human, some completely human except maybe for being too handsome— It's fairyland from ancient Earth all over again. Isn't it? I got interested once and dug into the Heritage Library microfiles, and be damned if I didn't find almost the identical yarns, told by peasants centuries before spaceflight.

"None of it squares with the scanty relics we have, if

they are relics, or with the fact that no area the size of Arctica could spawn a dozen different intelligent species, or . . . hellfire, man, with the way your common sense tells you aborigines would behave when humans arrived!"

Sherrinford nodded. "Yes, yes," he said. "I'm less sure than you that the common sense of nonhuman beings is precisely like our own. I've seen so much variation within mankind. But, granted, your arguments are strong. Roland's too few scientists have more pressing tasks than tracking down the origins of what is, as you put it, a revived medieval superstition."

He cradled his pipe bowl in both hands and peered into the tiny hearth of it. "Perhaps what interests me most," he said softly, "is why—across that gap of centuries, across a barrier of machine civilization and its utterly antagonistic world-view—no continuity of tradition whatsoever—why have hard-headed, technologically organized, reasonably well-educated colonists here brought back from its grave a belief in the Old Folk?"

"I suppose eventually, if the University ever does develop the psychology department they keep talking about, I suppose eventually somebody will get a thesis out of your question." Dawson spoke in a jagged voice, and he gulped when Sherrinford replied:

"I propose to begin now. In Commissioner Haunch Land, since that's where the latest incident occurred. Where can I rent a vehicle?"

"Uh, might be hard to do—"

"Come, come. Tenderfoot or not, I know better. In an economy of scarcity, few people own heavy equipment. But since it's needed, it can always be rented. I want a camper bus with a ground-effect drive suitable for every kind of terrain. And I want certain equipment installed which I've brought along, and the top canopy section replaced by a gun turret controllable from the driver's seat. But I'll supply the weapons. Besides rifles and pistols of my own, I've arranged to borrow some artillery from Christmas Landing's police arsenal."

"Hoy? Are you genuinely intending to make ready for . . . a war . . . against a myth?"

"Let's say I'm taking out insurance, which isn't terribly expensive, against a remote possibility. Now, besides the bus, what about a light aircraft carried piggyback for use in surveys?"

"No." Dawson sounded more positive than hitherto. "That's asking for disaster. We can have you flown to a base camp in a large plane when the weather report's exactly right. But the pilot will have to fly back at once, before the weather turns wrong again. Meteorology's underdeveloped on Roland; the air's especially treacherous this time of year, and we're not tooled up to produce aircraft that can outlive every surprise." He drew breath. "Have you no idea of how fast a whirly-whirly can hit, or what size hailstones might strike from a clear sky, or—? Once you're there, man, you stick to the ground." He hesitated. "That's an important reason our information is so scanty about the outway, and its settlers are so isolated."

Sherrinford laughed ruefully. "Well, I suppose if details are what I'm after, I must creep along anyway."

"You'll waste a lot of time," Dawson said. "Not to mention your client's money. Listen, I can't forbid you to chase shadows, but—"

The discussion went on for almost an hour. When the screen finally blanked, Sherrinford rose, stretched, and walked toward Barbro. She noticed anew his peculiar gait. He had come from a planet with a fourth again of Earth's gravitational drag, to one where weight was less that half Terrestrial. She wondered if he had flying dreams.

"I apologize for shuffling you off like that," he said. "I didn't expect to reach him at once. He was quite truthful about how busy he is. But having made contact, I didn't want to remind him overmuch of you. He can dismiss my project as a futile fantasy which I'll soon give up. But he might have frozen completely, might even have put up obstacles before us, if he'd realized through you how determined we are."

"Why should he care?" she asked in her bitterness.

"Fear of consequences, the worse because it is unadmitted—fear of consequences, the more terrifying because they are unguessable." Sherrinford's gaze went to the screen, and thence out the window to the aurora pulsing in glacial blue and white immensely far overhead. "I suppose you saw I was talking to a frightened man. Down underneath his

conventionality and scoffing, he believes in the Outlings—
oh, yes, he believes."

The feet of Mistherd flew over yerba and outpaced wind-
blown driftweed. Beside him, black and misshapen, hulked
Nagrim the nicor, whose earthquake weight left a swath of
crushed plants. Behind, luminous blossoms of a firethorn
shone through the twining, trailing outlines of Morgarel the
wraith.

Here Cloudmoor rose in a surf of hills and thickets. The
air lay quiet, now and then carrying the distance-muted howl
of a beast. It was darker than usual at winterbirth, the
moons being down and aurora a wan flicker above mountains on the northern world-edge. But this made the stars
keen, and their numbers crowded heaven, and Ghost Road
shone among them as if it, like the leafage beneath,
were paved with dew.

"Yonder!" bawled Nagrim. All four of his arms pointed.
The party had topped a ridge. Far off glimmered a spark.
"Hoah, hoah! 'Ull we right off stamp dem flat, or pluck dem
apart slow?"

We shall do nothing of the sort, bonebrain, Morgarel's
answer slid through their heads. *Not unless they attack us,
and they will not unless we make them aware of us, and
her command is that we spy out their purposes.*

"Gr-r-rum-m-m. I know deir aim. Cut down trees, stick
plows in land, sow deir cursed seed in de clods and in deir
shes. 'Less we drive dem into de bitterwater, and soon, soon,
dey'll wax too strong for us."

"Not too strong for the Queen!" Mistherd protested,
shocked.

Yet they do have new powers, it seems, Morgarel reminded him. *Carefully must we probe them.*

"Den carefully can we step on dem?" asked Nagrim.

The question woke a grin out of Mistherd's own uneasiness. He slapped the scaly back. "Don't talk, you," he
said. "It hurts my ears. Nor think; that hurts your head.
Come, run!"

Ease yourself, Morgarel scolded. *You have too much life
in you, human-born.*

Mistherd made a face at the wraith, but obeyed to the
extent of slowing down and picking his way through what

cover the country afforded. For he traveled on behalf of the Fairest, to learn what had brought a pair of mortals questing hither.

Did they seek that boy whom Ayoch stole? (He continued to weep for his mother, though less and less often as the marvels of Carheddin entered him.) Perhaps. A birdcraft had left them and their car at the now-abandoned campsite, from which they had followed an outward spiral. But when no trace of the cub had appeared inside a reasonable distance, they did not call to be flown home. And this wasn't because weather forbade the farspeaker waves to travel, as was frequently the case. No, instead the couple set off toward the mountains of Moonhorn. Their course would take them past a few outlying invader steadings and on into realms untrodden by their race.

So this was no ordinary survey. Then what was it?

Mistherd understood now why she who reigned had made her adopted mortal children learn, or retain, the clumsy language of their forebears. He had hated that drill, wholly foreign to Dweller ways. Of course, you obeyed her, and in time you saw how wise she had been. . . .

Presently he left Nagrim behind a rock—the nicor would only be useful in a fight—and crawled from bush to bush until he lay within man-lengths of the humans. A rainplant drooped over him, leaves soft on his bare skin, and clothed him in darkness. Morgarel floated to the crown of a shiverleaf, whose unrest would better conceal his flimsy shape. He'd not be much help either. And that was the most troublous, the almost appalling thing here. Wraiths were among those who could not just sense and send thought, but cast illusions. Morgarel had reported that this time his power seemed to rebound off an invisible cold wall around the car.

Otherwise the male and female had set up no guardian engines and kept no dogs. Belike they supposed none would be needed, since they slept in the long vehicle which bore them. But such contempt of the Queen's strength could not be tolerated, could it?

Metal sheened faintly by the light of their campfire. They sat on either side, wrapped in coats against a coolness that Mistherd, naked, found mild. The male drank smoke. The female stared past him into a dusk which her flame-dazzled eyes must see as thick gloom. The dancing glow brought her vividly forth. Yes, to judge from Ayoch's tale, she was the dam of the new cub.

Ayoch had wanted to come too, but the Wonderful One forbade. Pooks couldn't hold still long enough for such a mission.

The man sucked on his pipe. His cheeks thus pulled into shadow while the light flickered across nose and brow, he looked disquietingly like a shearbill about to stoop on prey.

"—No, I tell you again, Barbro, I have no theories," he was saying. "When facts are insufficient, theorizing is ridiculous at best, misleading at worst."

"Still, you must have some idea of what you're doing," she said. It was plain that they had threshed this out often before. No Dweller could be as persistent as she or as patient as he. "That gear you packed—that generator you keep running—"

"I have a working hypothesis or two, which suggested what equipment I ought to take."

"Why won't you tell me what the hypotheses are?'

"They themselves indicate that that might be inadvisable at the present time. I'm still feeling my way into the labyrinth. And I haven't had a chance yet to hook everything up. In fact, we're really only protected against so-called telepathic influence—"

"What?" She started. "Do you mean . . . those legends about how they can read minds too—" Her words trailed off and her gaze sought the darkness beyond his shoulders.

He leaned forward. His tone lost its clipped rapidity, grew earnest and soft. "Barbro, you're racking yourself to pieces. Which is no help to Jimmy if he's alive, the more so when you may well be badly needed later on. We've a long trek before us, and you'd better settle into it."

She nodded jerkily and caught her lip between her teeth for moment before she answered, "I'm trying."

He smiled around his pipe. "I expect you'll succeed. You don't strike me as a quitter or a whiner or an enjoyer of misery."

She dropped a hand to the pistol at her belt. Her voice changed; it came out of her throat like knife from sheath.

"When we find them, they'll know what I am. What humans are."

"Put anger aside also," the man urged. "We can't afford emotions. If the Outlings are real, as I told you I'm provisionally assuming, they're fighting for their homes." After a short stillness he added: "I like to think that if the first explorers had found live natives, men would not have colonized Roland. But it's too late now. We can't go back if we wanted to. It's a bitter-end struggle, against an enemy so crafty that he's even hidden from us the fact that he is waging war."

"Is he? I mean, skulking, kidnaping an occasional child—"

"That's part of my hypothesis. I suspect those aren't harassments; they're tactics employed in a chillingly subtle strategy."

The fire sputtered and sparked. The man smoked awhile, brooding, until he went on:

"I didn't want to raise your hopes or excite you unduly while you had to wait on me, first in Christmas Landing, then in Portolondon. Afterward we were busy satisfying ourselves that Jimmy had been taken farther from camp than he could have wandered before collapsing. So I'm only now telling you how thoroughly I studied available material on the . . . Old Folk. Besides, at first I did it on the principle of eliminating every imaginable possibility, however absurd. I expected no result other than final disproof. But I went through everything, relics, analyses, histories, journalistic accounts, monographs; I talked to outwayers who happened to be in town and to what scientists we have who've taken any interest in the matter. I'm a quick study. I flatter myself I became as expert as anyone—though God knows there's little to be expert on. Furthermore, I, a comparative stranger to Roland, maybe looked on the problem with fresh eyes. And a pattern emerged for me.

"If the aborigines had become extinct, why hadn't they left more remnants? Arctica isn't enormous, and it's fertile for Rolandic life. It ought to have supported a population whose artifacts ought to have accumulated over millennia. I've read that on Earth, literally tens of thousands of paleolithic hand axes were found, more by chance than archeology.

"Very well. Suppose the relics and fossils were deliberately removed, between the time the last survey party left and the first colonizing ships arrived. I did find some support for that idea in the diaries of the original explorers. They were too preoccupied with checking the habitability of the planet to make catalogues of primitive monuments. However, the remarks they wrote down indicate they saw much more than later arrivals did. Suppose what we have found is just what the removers overlooked or didn't get around to.

"That argues a sophisticated mentality, thinking in long-range terms, doesn't it? Which in turn argues that the Old Folk were not mere hunters or neolithic farmers."

"But nobody ever saw buildings or machines or any such thing," Barbro objected.

"No. Most likely the natives didn't go through our kind of metallurgic-industrial evolution. I can conceive of other paths to take. Their full-fledged civilization might have begun, rather than ended, in biological science and technology. It might have developed potentialities of the nervous system, which might be greater in their species than in man. We have those abilities to some degree ourselves, you realize. A dowser, for instance, actually senses variations in the local magnetic field caused by a water table. However, in us, these talents are maddeningly rare and tricky. So we took our business elsewhere. Who needs to be a telepath, say, when he has a visiphone? The Old Folk may have seen it the other way around. The artifacts of their civilization may have been, may still be unrecognizable to men."

"They could have identified themselves to the men, though," Barbro said. "Why didn't they?"

"I can imagine any number of reasons. As, they could have had a bad experience with interstellar visitors earlier in their history. Ours is scarcely the sole race that has spaceships. However, I told you I don't theorize in advance of the facts. Let's say no more than that the Old Folk, if they exist, are alien to us."

"For a rigorous thinker, you're spinning a mighty thin thread."

"I've admitted this is entirely provisional." He squinted at her through a roil of campfire smoke. "You came to me, Barbro, insisting in the teeth of officialdom that your boy had been stolen, but your own talk about cultists kidnapers was ridiculous. Why are you reluctant to admit the reality of nonhumans?"

"In spite of the fact that Jimmy's being alive probably depends on it," she sighed. "I know."

A shudder. "Maybe I don't dare admit it."

"I've said nothing thus far that hasn't been speculated about in print," he told her. "A disreputable speculation, true. In a hundred years, nobody has found valid evidence for the Outlings being more than a superstition. Still, a few people have declared it's at least possible that intelligent natives are at large in the wilderness."

"I know," she repeated. "I'm not sure, though, what has made you, overnight, take those arguments seriously."

"Well, once you got me started thinking, it occurred to me that Roland's outwayers are not utterly isolated medieval crofters. They have books, telecommunications, power tools, motor vehicles; above all, they have a modern science-oriented education. Why *should* they turn superstitious? Something must be causing it." He stopped. "I'd better not continue. My ideas go further than this; but if they're correct, it's dangerous to speak them aloud."

Mistherd's belly muscles tensed. There was danger for fair, in that shearbill head. The Garland Bearer must be warned. For a minute he wondered about summoning Nagrim to kill these two. If the nicor jumped them fast, their firearms might avail them naught. But no. They might have left word at home, or— He came back to his ears. The talk had changed course. Barbro was murmuring, "—why you stayed on Roland."

The man smiled his gaunt smile. "Well, life on Beowulf held no challenge for me. Heorot is—or was; this was decades past, remember—Heorot was densely populated, smoothly organized, boringly uniform. That was partly due to the lowland frontier, a safety valve that bled off the dissatisfied. But I lack the carbon dioxide tolerance necessary to live healthily down there. An expedition was being readied to make a swing around a number of colony worlds, especially those which didn't have the equipment to keep in laser contact. You'll recall its announced purpose, to seek out new ideas in science, arts, sociology, philosophy, whatever might prove valuable. I'm afraid they found little on Roland relevant to Beowulf. But I, who had wangled a berth,

I saw opportunities for myself and decided to make my home here."

"Were you a detective back there, too?"

"Yes, in the official police. We had a tradition of such work in our family. Some of that may have come from the Cherokee side of it, if the name means anything to you. However, we also claimed collateral descent from one of the first private inquiry agents on record, back on Earth before spaceflight. Regardless of how true that may be, I found him a useful model. You see, an archetype—"

The man broke off. Unease crossed his features. "Best we go to sleep," he said. "We've a long distance to cover in the morning."

She looked outward. "Here is no morning."

They retired. Mistherd rose and cautiously flexed limberness back into his muscles. Before returning to the Sister of Lyrth, he risked a glance through a pane in the car. Bunks were made up, side by side, and the humans lay in them. Yet the man had not touched her, though hers was a bonny body, and nothing that had passed between them suggested he meant to do so.

Eldritch, humans. Cold and clay-like. And they would overrun the beautiful wild world? Mistherd spat in disgust. It must not happen. It would not happen. She who reigned had vowed that.

The lands of William Irons were immense. But this was because a barony was required to support him, his kin and cattle, on native crops whose cultivation was still poorly understood. He raised some Terrestrial plants as well, by summerlight and in conservatories. However, these were a luxury. The true conquest of northern Arctica lay in yerba hay, in bathyrhiza wood, in pericoup and glycophyllon, and eventually, when the market had expanded with population and industry, in chalcanthemum for city florists and pelts of cage-bred rover for city furriers.

That was in a tomorrow Irons did not expect that he would live to see. Sherrinford wondered if the man really expected anyone ever would.

The room was warm and bright. Cheerfulness crackled in the fireplace. Light from fluoropanels gleamed off hand-carven chests and chairs and tables, off colorful draperies and shelved dishes. The outwayer sat solid in his high seat, stoutly clad, beard flowing down his chest. His wife and daughters brought coffee, whose fragrance joined the remnant odors of a hearty supper, to him, his guests, and his sons.

But outside, wind hooted, lightning flared, thunder bawled, rain crashed on roof and walls and roared down to swirl among the courtyard cobblestones. Sheds and barns crouched against hugeness beyond. Trees groaned, and did a wicked undertone of laughter run beneath the lowing of a frightened cow? A burst of hailstones hit the tiles like knocking knuckles.

You could feel how distant your neighbors were, Sherrinford thought. And nonetheless they were the people whom you saw oftenest, did daily business with by visiphone (when a solar storm didn't make gibberish of their voices and chaos of their faces) or in the flesh, partied with, gossiped and intrigued with, intermarried with; in the end, they were the people who would bury you. The lights of the coastal towns were monstrously farther away.

William Irons was a strong man. Yet when now he spoke, fear was in his tone. "You'd truly go over Troll Scarp?"

"Do you mean Hanstein Palisades?" Sherrinford responded, more challenge than question.

"No outwayer calls it anything but Troll Scarp," Barbro said.

And how had a name like that been reborn, light-years and centuries from Earth's Dark Ages?

"Hunters, trappers, prospectors—rangers, you call them—travel in those mountains," Sherrinford declared.

"In certain parts," Irons said. "That's allowed, by a pact once made 'tween a man and the Queen after he'd done well by a jack-o'-the-hill that a satan had hurt. Wherever the plumablanca grows, men may fare, if they leave mangoods on the altar boulders in payment for what they take out of the land. Elsewhere—" one fist clenched on a chair arm and went slack again—" 's not wise to go."

"It's been done, hasn't it?"

"Oh, yes. And some came back all right, or so they claimed, though I've heard they were never lucky afterward. And some didn't; they vanished. And some who returned babbled of wonders and horrors, and stayed witlings the rest of their lives. Not for a long time has anybody been

rash enough to break the pact and overtread the bounds."
Irons looked at Barbro almost entreatingly. His woman and
children stared likewise, grown still. Wind hooted beyond
the walls and rattled the storm shutters. "Don't you."

"I've reason to believe my son is there," she answered.

"Yes, yes, you've told and I'm sorry. Maybe something
can be done. I don't know what, but I'd be glad to, oh, lay a
double offering on Unvar's Barrow this midwinter, and a
prayer drawn in the turf by a flint knife. Maybe they'll
return him." Irons sighed. "They've not done such a thing
in man's memory, though. And he could have a worse lot.
I've glimpsed them myself, speeding madcap through twilight. They seem happier than we are. Might be no kindness,
sending your boy home again."

"Like in the Arvid song," said his wife.

Irons nodded. "M-hm. Or others, come to think of it."

"What's this?" Sherrinford asked. More sharply than before, he felt himself a stranger. He was a child of cities and
technics, above all a child of the skeptical intelligence. This
family *believed*. It was disquieting to see more than a
touch of their acceptance in Barbro's slow nod.

"We have the same ballad in Olga Ivanoff Land," she
told him, her voice less calm than the words. "It's one of
the traditional ones—nobody knows who composed them—
that are sung to set the measure of a ring-dance in a
meadow."

"I noticed a multilyre in your baggage, Mrs. Cullen," said
the wife of Irons. She was obviously eager to get off the ex-
plosive topic of a venture in defiance of the Old Folk. A
songfest could help. "Would you like to entertain us?"

Barbro shook her head, white around the nostrils. The
oldest boy said quickly, rather importantly, "Well, sure, I
can, if our guests would like to hear."

"I'd enjoy that, thank you." Sherrinford leaned back in
his seat and stoked his pipe. If this had not happened spontaneously, he would have guided the conversation toward a
similar outcome.

In the past he had had no incentive to study the folklore
of the outway, and not much chance to read the scanty
references on it since Barbro brought him her trouble. Yet
more and more he was becoming convinced that he must
get an understanding—not an anthropological study, but a

feel from the inside out—of the relationship between Roland's frontiersmen and those beings which haunted them.

A bustling followed, rearrangement, settling down to listen, coffee cups refilled and brandy offered on the side. The boy explained, "The last line is the chorus. Everybody join in, right?" Clearly he too hoped thus to bleed off some of the tension. Catharsis through music? Sherrinford wondered, and added to himself: No; exorcism.

A girl strummed a guitar. The boy sang, to a melody which beat across the storm noise:

"It was the ranger Arvid
rode homeward through the hills
among the shadowy shiverleafs,
along the chiming rills.
  The dance weaves under the firethorn.

"The night wind whispered around him
with scent of brok and rue.
Both moons rose high above him
and hills aflash with dew.
  The dance weaves under the firethorn.

"And dreaming of that woman
who waited in the sun,
he stopped, amazed by starlight,
and so he was undone.
  The dance weaves under the firethorn.

"For there beneath a barrow
that bulked athwart a moon,
the Outling folk were dancing
in glass and golden shoon.
  The dance weaves under the firethorn.

"The Outling folk were dancing
like water, wind, and fire
to frosty-ringing harpstrings,
and never did they tire.
  The dance weaves under the firethorn.

"To Arvid came she striding
from where she watched the dance,

the Queen of Air and Darkness,
with starlight in her glance.
The dance weaves under the firehorn.

"With starlight, love, and terror
in her immortal eye,
the Queen of Air and Darkness—"

"No!" Barbro leaped from her chair. Her fists were
clenched and tears flogged her cheekbones. "You can't—
pretend that—about the things that stole Jimmy!"
She fled from the chamber, upstairs to her guest bedroom.

But she finished the song herself. That was about seventy
hours later, camped in the steeps where rangers dared not
fare.
She and Sherrinford had not said much to the Irons family, after refusing repeated pleas to leave the forbidden country alone. Nor had they exchanged many remarks at first
as they drove north. Slowly, however, he began to draw her
out about her own life. After a while she almost forgot to
mourn, in her remembering of home and old neighbors.
Somehow this led to discoveries—that he, beneath his pro-
fessorial manner, was a gourmet and a lover of opera and
appreciated her femaleness; that she could still laugh and
find beauty in the wild land around her—and she realized,
half guiltily, that life held more hopes than even the recovery
of the son Tim gave her.
"I've convinced myself he's alive," the detective said. He
scowled. "Frankly, it makes me regret having taken you
along, I expected this would be only a fact-gathering trip,
but it's turning out to be more. If we're dealing with real
creatures who stole him, they can do real harm. I ought to
turn back to the nearest garth and call for a plane to fetch
you."
"Like bottommost hell you will, mister," she said. "You
need somebody who knows outway conditions, and I'm a
better shot than average."
"M-m-m . . . it would involve considerable delay too,
wouldn't it? Besides the added distance, I can't put a signal
through to any airport before this current burst of solar
interference has calmed down."

Next "night" he broke out his remaining equipment and set it up. She recognized some of it, such as the thermal detector. Other items were strange to her, copied to his order from the advanced apparatus of his birthworld. He would tell her little about them. "I've explained my suspicion that the ones we're after have telepathic capabilities," he said in apology.

Her eyes widened. "You mean it could be true, the Queen and her people can read minds?"

"That's part of the dread which surrounds their legend, isn't it? Actually there's nothing spooky about the phenomenon. It was studied and fairly well defined centuries ago, on Earth. I daresay the facts are available in the scientific microfiles at Christmas Landing. You Rolanders have simply had no occasion to seek them out, any more than you've yet had occasion to look up how to build power-beamcasters or spacecraft."

"Well, how does telepathy work, then?"

Sherrinford recognized that her query asked for comfort as much as it did for facts, and he spoke with deliberate dryness: "The organism generates extremely longwave radiation which can, in principle, be modulated by the nervous system. In practice, the feebleness of the signals and their low rate of information transmission make them elusive, hard to detect and measure. Our prehuman ancestors went in for more reliable senses, like vision and hearing. What telepathic transceiving we do is marginal at best. But explorers have found extraterrestrial species that got an evolutionary advantage from developing the system further, in their particular environments. I imagine such species could include one which gets comparatively little direct sunlight— in fact, appears to hide from broad day. It could even become so able in this regard that, at short range, it can pick up man's weak emissions and make man's primitive sensitivities resonate to its own strong sendings."

"That would account for a lot, wouldn't it?" Barbro said faintly.

"I've now screened our car by a jamming field," Sherrinford told her, "but it reaches only a few meters past the chassis. Beyond, a scout of theirs might get a warning from your thoughts, if you knew precisely what I'm trying to do. I have a well-trained subconscious which sees to it that I

think about this in French when I'm outside. Communication
has to be structured to be intelligible, you see, and that's a
different enough structure from English. But English is the
only human language on Roland, and surely the Old Folk
have learned it."

She nodded. He had told her his general plan, which was
too obvious to conceal. The problem was to make contact
with the aliens, if they existed. Hitherto, they had only
revealed themselves, at rare intervals, to one or a few back-
woodsmen at a time. An ability to generate hallucinations
would help them in that. They would stay clear of any
large, perhaps unmanageable expedition which might pass
through their territory. But two people, braving all prohibi-
tions, shouldn't look too formidable to approach. And . . .
this would be the first human team which not only worked
on the assumption that the Outlings were real, but possessed
the resources of modern, off-planet police technology.

Nothing happened at that camp. Sherrinford said he hadn't
expected it would. The Old Folk seemed cautious this near
to any settlement. In their own lands they must be bolder.

And by the following "night," the vehicle had gone well
into yonder country. When Sherrinford stopped the engine
in a meadow and the car settled down, silence rolled in like
a wave.

They stepped out. She cooked a meal on the glower while
he gathered wood, that they might later cheer themselves
with a campfire. Frequently he glanced at his wrist. It bore
no watch—instead, a radio-controlled dial, to tell what the
instruments in the bus might register.

Who needed a watch here? Slow constellations wheeled
beyond glimmering aurora. The moon Alde stood above a
snowpeak, turning it argent, though this place lay at a good-
ly height. The rest of the mountains were hidden by the
forest that crowded around. Its trees were mostly shiverleaf
and feathery white plumablanca, ghostly amidst their shadows. A few firethorns glowed, clustered dim lanterns, and the
underbrush was heavy and smelled sweet. You could see
surprisingly far through the blue dusk. Somewhere nearby,
a brook sang and a bird fluted.

"Lovely here," Sherrinford said. They had risen from their
supper and not yet sat down again or kindled their fire.

"But strange," Barbro answered as low. "I wonder if it's really meant for us. If we can really hope to possess it."

His pipestem gestured at the stars. "Man's gone to stranger places than this."

"Has he? I . . . oh, I suppose it's just something left over from my outway childhood, but do you know, when I'm under them I can't think of the stars as balls of gas, whose energies have been measured, whose planets have been walked on by prosaic feet. No, they're small and cold and magical; our lives are bound to them; after we die, they whisper to us in our graves." Barbro glanced downward. "I realize that's nonsense."

She could see in the twilight how his face grew tight. "Not at all," he said. "Emotionally, physics may be a worse nonsense. And in the end, you know, after a sufficient number of generations, thought follows feeling. Man is not at heart rational. He could stop believing the stories of science if those no longer felt right."

He paused. "That ballad which didn't get finished in the house," he said, not looking at her. "Why did it affect you so?"

"I couldn't stand hearing *them,* well, praised. Or that's how it seemed. Sorry for the fuss."

"I gather the ballad is typical of a large class."

"Well, I never thought to add them up. Cultural anthropology is something we don't have time for on Roland, or more likely it hasn't occurred to us, with everything else there is to do. But—now you mention it, yes, I'm surprised at how many songs and stories have the Arvid motif in them."

"Could you bear to recite it?"

She mustered the will to laugh. "Why, I can do better than that if you want. Let me get my multilyre and I'll perform."

She omitted the hypnotic chorus line, though, when the notes rang out, except at the end. He watched her where she stood against moon and aurora.

> "—the Queen of Air and Darkness
> cried softly under sky:
>
> " 'Light down, you ranger Arvid,
> and join the Outling folk.
> You need no more be human,
> which is a heavy yoke.'

"He dared to give her answer:
'I may do naught but run.
A maiden waits me, dreaming
in lands beneath the sun.

" 'And likewise wait me comrades
and tasks I would not shirk,
for what is ranger Arvid
if he lays down his work?

" 'So wreak your spells, you Outling,
and cast your wrath on me.
Though maybe you can slay me,
you'll not make me unfree.'

"The Queen of Air and Darkness
stood wrapped about with fear
and northlight-flares and beauty
he dared not look too near.

"Until she laughed like harpsong
and said to him in scorn:
'I do not need a magic
to make you always mourn.

" 'I send you home with nothing
except your memory
of moonlight, Outling music,
night breezes, dew, and me.

" 'And that will run behind you,
a shadow on the sun,
and that will lie beside you
when every day is done.

" 'In work and play and friendship
your grief will strike you dumb
for thinking what you are—and—
what you might have become.

" 'Your dull and foolish woman
treat kindly as you can.

Go home now, ranger Arvid,
set free to be a man!

"In flickering and laughter
the Outling folk were gone.
He stood alone by moonlight
and wept until the dawn.
The dance weaves under the firethorn."

She laid the lyre aside. A wind rustled leaves. After a long quietness Sherrinford said, "And tales of this kind are part of everyone's life in the outway?"

"Well, you could put it thus," Barbro replied. "Though they're not all full of supernatural doings. Some are about love or heroism. Traditional themes."

"I don't think your particular tradition has arisen of itself." His tone was bleak. "In fact, I think many of your songs and stories were not composed by human beings."

He snapped his lips shut and would say no more on the subject. They went early to bed.

Hours later, an alarm roused them.

The buzzing was soft, but it brought them instantly alert. They slept in gripsuits, to be prepared for emergencies. Skyglow lit them through the canopy. Sherrinford swung out of his bunk, slipped shoes on feet, and clipped gun holster to belt. "Stay inside," he commanded.

"What's here?" Her pulse thuttered.

He squinted at the dials of his instruments and checked them against the luminous telltale on his wrist. "Three animals," he counted. "Not wild ones happening by. A large one, homeothermic, to judge from the infrared, holding still a short ways off. Another . . . hm, low temperature, diffuse and unstable emission, as if it were more like a . . . a swarm of cells coordinated somehow . . . pheromonally? . . . hovering, also at a distance. But the third's practically next to us, moving around in the brush; and that pattern looks human."

She saw him quiver with eagerness, no longer seeming a professor. "I'm going to try to make a capture," he said. "When we have a subject for interrogation—Stand ready to let me back in again fast. But don't risk yourself, whatever happens. And keep this cocked." He handed her a loaded big-game rifle.

His tall frame poised by the door, opened it a crack. Air blew in, cool, damp, full of fragrances and murmurings. The moon Oliver was now also aloft, the radiance of both unreally brilliant, and the aurora seethed in whiteness and ice-blue.

Sherrinford peered afresh at his telltale. It must indicate the directions of the watchers, among those dappled leaves. Abruptly he sprang out. He sprinted past the ashes of the campfire and vanished under trees. Barbro's hand strained on the butt of her weapon.

Racket exploded. Two in combat burst onto the meadow. Sherrinford had clapped a grip on a smaller human figure. She could make out by streaming silver and rainbow flicker that the other was nude, male, long haired, lithe, and young. He fought demoniacally, seeking to use teeth and feet and raking nails, and meanwhile he ululated like a satan.

The identification shot through her: A changeling, stolen in babyhood and raised by the Old Folk. This creature was what they would make Jimmy into.

"Ha!" Sherrinford forced his opponent around and drove stiffened fingers into the solar plexus. The boy gasped and sagged: Sherrinford manhandled him toward the car.

Out from the woods came a giant. It might itself have been a tree, black and rugose, bearing four great gnarly boughs; but earth quivered and boomed beneath its leg-roots, and its hoarse bellowing filled sky and skulls.

Barbro shrieked. Sherrinford whirled. He yanked out his pistol, fired and fired, flat whipcracks through the half-light. His free arm kept a lock on the youth. The troll shape lurched under those blows. It recovered and came on, more slowly, more carefully, circling around to cut him off from the bus. He couldn't move fast enough to evade it unless he released his prisoner—who was his sole possible guide to Jimmy—

Barbro leaped forth. "Don't!" Sherrinford shouted. "For God's sake, stay inside!" The monster rumbled and made snatching motions at her. She pulled the trigger. Recoil slammed her in the shoulder. The colossus rocked and fell. Somehow it got its feet back and lumbered toward her. She retreated. Again she shot, and again. The creature snarled.

Blood began to drip from it and gleam oilily amidst dewdrops. It turned and went off, breaking branches, into the darkness that laired beneath the woods.

"Get to shelter!" Sherrinford yelled. "You're out of the jammer field!"

A mistiness drifted by overhead. She barely glimpsed it before she saw the new shape at the meadow edge. "Jimmy!" tore from her.

"Mother." He held out his arms. Moonlight coursed in his tears. She dropped her weapon and ran to him.

Sherrinford plunged in pursuit. Jimmy flitted away into the brush. Barbro crashed after, through clawing twigs. Then she was seized and borne away.

Standing over his captive, Sherrinford strengthened the fluoro output until vision of the wilderness was blocked off from within the bus. The boy squirmed beneath that colorless glare.

"You are going to talk," the man said. Despite the haggardness in his features, he spoke quietly.

The boy glared through tangled locks. A bruise was purpling on his jaw. He'd almost recovered ability to flee while Sherrinford chased and lost the woman. Returning, the detective had barely caught him. Time was lacking to be gentle, when Outling reinforcements might arrive at any moment. Sherrinford had knocked him out and dragged him inside. He sat lashed into a swivel seat.

He spat. "Talk to you, manclod?" But sweat stood on his skin, and his eyes flickered unceasingly around the metal which caged him.

"Give me a name to call you by."

"And have you work a spell on me?"

"Mine's Eric. If you don't give me another choice, I'll have to call you . . . m-m-m . . . Wuddikins."

"What?" However eldritch, the bound one remained a human adolescent. "Mistherd, then." The lilting accent of his English somehow emphasized its sullenness. "That's not the sound, only what it means. Anyway, it's my spoken name, naught else."

"Ah, you keep a secret name you consider to be real?"

"She does. I don't know myself what it is. She knows the real names of everybody."

Sherrinford raised his brows. "She?"

"Who reigns. May she forgive me, I can't make the reverent sign when my arms are tied. Some invaders call her the Queen of Air and Darkness."

"So." Sherrinford got pipe and tobacco. He let silence wax while he started the fire. At length he said:

"I'll confess the Old Folk took me by surprise. I didn't expect so formidable a member of your gang. Everything I could learn had seemed to show they work on my race— and yours, lad—by stealth, trickery, and illusion."

Mistherd jerked a truculent nod. "She created the first nicors not long ago. Don't think she has naught but dazzlements at her beck."

"I don't. However, a steel-jacketed bullet works pretty well too, doesn't it?"

Sherrinford talked on, softly, mostly to himself: "I do still believe the, ah, nicors—all your half-humanlike breeds —are intended in the main to be seen, not used. The power of projecting mirages must surely be quite limited in range and scope as well as in the number of individuals who possess it. Otherwise she wouldn't have needed to work as slowly and craftily as she has. Even outside our mind-shield, Barbro—my companion—could have resisted, could have remained aware that whatever she saw was unreal . . . if she'd been less shaken, less frantic, less driven by need."

Sherrinford wreathed his head in smoke. "Never mind what I experienced," he said. "It couldn't have been the same as for her. I think the command was simply given us, 'You will see what you most desire in the world, running away from you into the forest.' Of course, she didn't travel many meters before the nicor waylaid her. I'd no hope of trailing them; I'm no Arctican woodsman, and besides, it'd have been too easy to ambush me. I came back to you." Grimly: "You're my link to your overlady."

"You think I'll guide you to Starhaven or Carheddin? Try making me, clod-man."

"I want to bargain."

"I s'pect you intend more'n that." Mistherd's answer held surprising shrewdness. "What'll you tell after you come home?"

"Yes, that does pose a problem, doesn't it? Barbro Cullen and I are not terrified outwayers. We're of the city. We brought recording instruments. We'd be the first of our kind to report an encounter with the Old Folk, and that report would be detailed and plausible. It would produce action."

"So you see I'm not afraid to die," Mistherd declared, though his lips trembled a bit. "If I let you come in and do your manthings to my people, I'd have naught left worth living for."

"Have no immediate fears," Sherrinford said. "You're merely bait." He sat down and regarded the boy through a visor of calm. (Within, it wept in him: *Barbro, Barbro!*) "Consider. Your Queen can't very well let me go back, bringing my prisoner and telling about hers. She has to stop that somehow. I could try fighting my way through—this car is better armed than you know—but that wouldn't free anybody. Instead, I'm staying put. New forces of hers will get here as fast as they can. I assume they won't blindly throw themselves against a machine gun, a howitzer, a fulgurator. They'll parley first, whether their intentions are honest or not. Thus I make the contact I'm after."

"What d' you plan?" The mumble held anguish.

"First, this, as a sort of invitation." Sherrinford reached out to flick a switch. "There. I've lowered my shield against mind-reading and shape-casting. I daresay the leaders, at least, will be able to sense that it's gone. That should give them confidence."

"And next?"

"Next we wait. Would you like something to eat or drink?"

During the time which followed, Sherrinford tried to jolly Mistherd along, find out something of his life. What answers he got were curt. He dimmed the interior lights and settled down to peer outward. That was a long few hours.

They ended at a shout of gladness, half a sob, from the boy. Out of the woods came a band of the Old Folk.

Some of them stood forth more clearly than moons and stars and northlights should have caused. He in the van rode a white crownbuck whose horns were garlanded. His form was manlike but unearthly beautiful, silver-blond hair falling from beneath the antlered helmet, around the proud cold face. The cloak fluttered off his back like living wings. His frost-colored mail rang as he fared.

Behind him, to right and left, rode two who bore swords whereon small flames gleamed and flickered. Above, a flying flock laughed and trilled and tumbled in the breezes. Near them drifted a half-transparent mistiness. Those others who passed among trees after their chieftain were harder to make out. But they moved in quicksilver grace and as it were to a sound of harps and trumpets.

"Lord Luighaid." Glory overflowed in Mistherd's tone. "Her master Knower—himself."

Sherrinford had never done a harder thing than to sit at the main control panel, finger near the button of the shield generator, and not touch it. He rolled down a section of canopy to let voices travel. A gust of wind struck him in the face, bearing odors of the roses in his mother's garden. At his back, in the main body of the vehicle, Mistherd strained against his bonds till he could see the oncoming troop.

"Call to them," Sherrinford said. "Ask if they will talk with me."

Unknown, flutingly sweet words flew back and forth. "Yes," the boy interpreted. "He will, the Lord Luighaid. But I can tell you, you'll never be let go. Don't fight them. Yield. Come away. You don't know what 'tis to be alive till you've dwelt in Carheddin under the mountain."

The Outlings drew nigh.

Jimmy glimmered and was gone. Barbro lay in strong arms, against a broad breast, and felt the horse move beneath her. It had to be a horse, though only a few were kept any longer on the steadings, and they only for special uses or love. She could feel the rippling beneath its hide, hear a rush of parted leafage and the thud when a hoof struck stone; warmth and living scent welled up around her through the darkness.

He who carried her said mildly, "Don't be afraid, darling. It was a vision. But he's waiting for us, and we're bound for him."

She was aware in a vague way that she ought to feel terror or despair or something. But her memories lay behind her—she wasn't sure just how she had come to be here—she was borne along in a knowledge of being loved. At peace, at peace, rest in the calm expectation of joy . . .

After a while the forest opened. They crossed a lea where boulders stood gray-white under the moons, their shadows shifting in the dim hues which the aurora threw across them. Flitteries danced, tiny comets, above the flowers between. Ahead gleamed a peak whose top was crowned in clouds.

Barbro's eyes happened to be turned forward. She saw the horse's head and thought, with quiet surprise: "Why, this is Sambo, who was mine when I was a girl. She looked upward at the man. He wore a black tunic and a cowled cape, which made his face hard to see. She could not cry aloud, here. "Tim," she whispered.

"Yes, Barbro."

"I buried you—"

His smile was endlessly tender. "Did you think we're no more than what's laid back into the ground? Poor torn sweetheart. She who's called us is the All Healer. Now rest and dream."

"Dream," she said, and for a space she struggled to rouse herself. But the effort was weak. Why should she believe ashen tales about . . . atoms and energies, nothing else to fill a gape of emptiness . . . tales she could not bring to mind . . . when Tim and the horse her father gave her carried her on to Jimmy? Had the other thing not been the evil dream, and this her first drowsy awakening from it?

As if he heard her thoughts, he murmured, "They have a song in Outling lands. The Song of the Men:

"The world sails
to an unseen wind.
Light swirls by the bows.
The wake is night.
But the Dwellers have no such sadness."

"I don't understand," she said.

He nodded. "There's much you'll have to understand, darling, and I can't see you again until you've learned those truths. But meanwhile you'll be with our son."

She tried to lift her head and kiss him. He held her down. "Not yet," he said. "You've not been received among the Queen's people. I shouldn't have come for you, except that she was too merciful to forbid. Lie back, lie back."

Time blew past. The horse galloped tireless, never stumbling, up the mountain. Once she glimpsed a troop riding down it and thought they were bound for a last weird battle in the west against . . . who? . . . one who lay cased in iron and sorrow—Later she would ask herself the name of him who had brought her into the land of the Old Truth.

Finally spires lifted splendid among the stars, which are small and magical and whose whisperings comfort us after we are dead. They rode into a courtyard where candles burned unwavering, fountains splashed and birds sang. The air bore fragrance of brok and pericoup, of rue and roses, for not everything that man brought was horrible. The Dwellers waited in beauty to welcome her. Beyond their stateliness, pooks cavorted through the gloaming; among the trees darted children; merriment caroled across music more solemn.

"We have come—" Tim's voice was suddenly, inexplicably, a croak. Barbro was not sure how he dismounted, bearing her. She stood before him and saw him sway on his feet.

Fear caught her. "Are you well?" She seized both his hands. They felt cold and rough. Where had Sambo gone? Her eyes searched beneath the cowl. In this brighter illumination, she sought to have seen her man's face clearly. But it was blurred, it kept changing. "What's wrong, oh, what's happened?"

He smiled. Was that the smile she had cherished? She couldn't completely remember. "I, I must go," he stammered, so low she could scarcely hear. "Our time is not ready." He drew free of her grasp and leaned on a robed form which had appeared at his side. A haziness swirled over both their heads. "Don't watch me go . . . back into the earth," he pleaded. "That's death for you. Till our time returns—There, our son!"

She had to fling her gaze around. Kneeling, she spread wide her arms. Jimmy struck her like a warm, solid cannonball. She rumpled his hair; she kissed the hollow of his neck; she laughed and wept and babbled foolishness; and this was no ghost, no memory that had stolen off when she wasn't looking. Now and again, as she turned her attention to yet another hurt which might have come upon him—hunger, sickness, fear—and found none, she would glimpse their surroundings. The gardens were gone. It didn't matter.

"I missed you so, Mother. Stay?"

"I'll take you home, dearest."

"Stay. Here's fun. I'll show. But you stay."

A sighing went through the twilight. Barbro rose. Jimmy clung to her hand. They confronted the Queen.

Very tall she was in her robes woven of northlights, and her starry crown and her garlands of kiss-me-never. Her countenance recalled Aphrodite of Milos, whose picture Barbro had often seen in the realms of men, save that the Queen's was more fair and more majesty dwelt upon it and in the night-blue eyes. Around her the gardens woke to new reality, the court of the Dwellers and the heaven-climbing spires.

"Be welcome," she spoke, her speaking a song, "forever."

Against the awe of her, Barbro said, "Moonmother, let us go home."

"That may not be."

"To our world, little and beloved," Barbro dreamed she begged, "which we build for ourselves and cherish for our children."

"To prison days, angry nights, works that crumble in the fingers, loves that turn to rot or stone or driftweed, loss, grief, and the only sureness that of the final nothingness. No. You too, Wanderfoot who is to be, will jubilate when the banners of the Outworld come flying into the last of the cities and man is made wholly alive. Now go with those who will teach you."

The Queen of Air and Darkness lifted an arm in summons. It halted, and none came to answer.

For over the fountains and melodies lifted a gruesome growling. Fires leaped, thunders crashed. Her hosts scattered screaming before the steel thing which boomed up the mountainside. The pooks were gone in a whirl of frightened wings. The nicors flung their bodies against the unalive invader and were consumed, until their Mother cried to them to retreat.

Barbro cast Jimmy down and herself over him. Towers wavered and smoked away. The mountain stood bare under icy moons, save for rocks, crags, and farther off a glacier in whose depths the auroral light pulsed blue. A cave mouth darkened a cliff. Thither folk streamed, seeking refuge underground. Some were human of blood, some grotesques like the pooks and nicors and wraiths; but most were lean, scaly, long-tailed, long-beaked, not remotely men or Outlings.

For an instant, even as Jimmy wailed at her breast—perhaps as much because the enchantment had been wrecked as because he was afraid—Barbro pitied the Queen who stood alone in her nakedness. Then that one also had fled, and Barbro's world shivered apart.

The guns fell silent; the vehicle whirred to a halt. From it sprang a boy who called wildly, "Shadow-of-a-Dream, where are you? It's me, Mistherd, oh, come, come!"—before he remembered that the language they had been raised in was not man's. He shouted in that until a girl crept out of a thicket where she had hidden. They stared at each other through dust, smoke, and moonglow. She ran to him.

A new voice barked from the car, "Barbro, hurry!"

Christmas Landing knew day: short at this time of year, but sunlight, blue skies, white clouds, glittering water, salt breezes in busy streets, and the sane disorder of Eric Sherrinford's living room.

He crossed and uncrossed his legs where he sat, puffed on his pipe as if to make a veil, and said, "Are you certain you're recovered? You mustn't risk overstrain."

"I'm fine," Barbro Cullen replied, though her tone was flat. "Still tired, yes, and showing it, no doubt. One doesn't go through such an experience and bounce back in a week. But I'm up and about. And to be frank, I must know what's happened, what's going on, before I can settle down to regain my full strength. Not a word of news anywhere."

"Have you spoken to others about the matter?"

"No. I've simply told visitors I was too exhausted to talk. Not much of a lie. I assumed there's a reason for censorship."

Sherrinford looked relieved. "Good girl. It's at my urging. You can imagine the sensation when this is made public. The authorities agreed they need time to study the facts, think and debate in a calm atmosphere, have a decent policy ready to offer voters who're bound to become rather hysterical at first." His mouth quirked slightly upward. "Furthermore, your nerves and Jimmy's get their chance to heal before the journalistic storm breaks over you. How is he?"

"Quite well. He continues pestering me for leave to go play with his friends in the Wonderful Place. But at his age, he'll recover—he'll forget."

"He may meet them later anyhow."

"What? We didn't—" Barbro shifted in her chair. "I've forgotten too. I hardly recall a thing from our last hours. Did you bring back any kidnaped humans?"

"No. The shock was savage as it was, without throwing them straight into an . . . an institution. Mistherd, who's basically a sensible young fellow, assured me they'd get along, at any rate as regards survival necessities, till arrangements can be made." Sherrinford hesitated. "I'm not sure what the arrangements will be. Nobody is, at our present stage. But obviously they include those people—or many of them, especially those who aren't fullgrown—rejoining the human race. Though they may never feel at home in civilization. Perhaps in a way that's best, since we will need some kind of mutually acceptable liaison with the Dwellers."

His impersonality soothed them both. Barbro became able to say, "Was I too big a fool? I do remember how I yowled and beat my head on the floor."

"Why, no." He considered the big woman and her pride for a few seconds before he rose, walked over and laid a hand on her shoulder. "You'd been lured and trapped by a skillful play on your deepest instincts, at a moment of sheer nightmare. Afterward, as that wounded monster carried you off, evidently another type of being came along, one that could saturate you with close-range neuropsychic forces. On top of this, my arrival, the sudden brutal abolishment of every hallucination, must have been shattering. No wonder if you cried out in pain. Before you did, you competently got Jimmy and yourself into the bus, and you never interfered with me."

"What did you do?"

"Why, I drove off as fast as possible. After several hours, the atmospherics let up sufficiently for me to call Porto-london and insist on an emergency airlift. Not that that was vital. What chance had the enemy to stop us? They didn't even try.—But quick transportation was certainly helpful."

"I figured that's what must have gone on." Barbro caught

his glance. "No, what I meant was, how did you find us in the backlands?"

Sherrinford moved a little off from her. "My prisoner was my guide. I don't think I actually killed any of the Dwellers who'd come to deal with me. I hope not. The car simply broke through them, after a couple of warning shots, and afterward outpaced them. Steel and fuel against flesh wasn't really fair. At the cave entrance, I did have to shoot down a few of those troll creatures. I'm not proud of it."

He stood silent. Presently: "But you were a captive," he said. "I couldn't be sure what they might do to you, who had first claim on me." After another pause: "I don't look for any more violence."

"How did you make . . . the boy . . . co-operate?"

Sherrinford paced from her to the window, where he stood staring out at the Boreal Ocean. "I turned off the mind-shield," he said. "I let their band get close, in full splendor of illusion. Then I turned the shield back on, and we both saw them in their true shapes. As we went northward, I explained to Mistherd how he and his kind had been hood-winked, used, made to live in a world that was never really there. I asked him if he wanted himself and whomever he cared about to go on till they died as domestic animals— yes, running in limited freedom on solid hills, but always called back to the dream-kennel." His pipe fumed furiously. "May I never see such bitterness again. He had been taught to believe he was free."

Quiet returned, above the hectic traffic. Charlemagne drew nearer to setting; already the east darkened.

Finally Barbro asked, "Do you know why?"

"Why children were taken and raised like that? Partly because it was in the pattern the Dwellers were creating; partly in order to study and experiment on members of our species—minds, that is, not bodies; partly because humans have special strengths which are helpful, like being able to endure full daylight."

"But what was the final purpose of it all?"

Sherrinford paced the floor. "Well," he said, "of course the ultimate motives of the aborigines are obscure. We can't do more than guess at how they think, let alone how they feel. But our ideas do seem to fit the data.

"Why did they hide from man? I suspect they, or rather

their ancestors—for they aren't glittering elves, you know; they're mortal and fallible too—I suspect the natives were only being cautious at first, more cautious than human primitives, though certain of those on Earth were also slow to reveal themselves to strangers. Spying, mentally eavesdropping, Roland's Dwellers must have picked up enough language to get some idea of how different man was from them, and how powerful; and they gathered that more ships would be arriving, bringing settlers. It didn't occur to them that they might be conceded the right to keep their lands. Perhaps they're still more fiercely territorial than we. They determined to fight, in their own way. I daresay, once we begin to get insight into that mentality, our psychological science will go through its Copernican revolution."

Enthusiasm kindled in him. "That's not the sole thing we'll learn, either," he went on. "They must have science of their own, a nonhuman science born on a planet that isn't Earth. Because they did observe us as profoundly as we've ever observed ourselves; they did mount a plan against us, one that would have taken another century or more to complete. Well, what else do they know? How do they support their civilization without visible agriculture or aboveground buildings or mines or anything? How can they breed whole new intelligent species to order? A million questions, ten million answers!"

"*Can* we learn from them?" Barbro asked softly. "Or can we only overrun them as you say they fear?"

Sherrinford halted, leaned elbow on mantel, hugged his pipe and replied, "I hope we'll show more charity than that to a defeated enemy. It's what they are. They tried to conquer us and failed, and now in a sense we are bound to conquer them, since they'll have to make their peace with the civilization of the machine rather than see it rust away as they strove for. Still, they never did us any harm as atrocious as what we've inflicted on our fellow men in the past. And, I repeat, they could teach us marvelous things; and we could teach them, too, once they've learned to be less intolerant of a different way of life."

"I suppose we can give them a reservation," she said, and didn't know why he grimaced and answered so roughly:

"Let's leave them the honor they've earned! They fought to save the world they'd always known from that—" he made a chopping gesture at the city—"and just possibly we'd be better off ourselves with less of it."

He sagged a trifle and sighed, "However, I suppose if Elfland had won, man on Roland would at last—peacefully, even happily—have died away. We live with our archetypes, but can we live in them?"

Barbro shook her head. "Sorry, I don't understand."

"What?" He looked at her in a surprise that drove out melancholy. After a laugh: "Stupid of me. I've explained this to so many politicians and scientists and commissioners and Lord knows what, these past days, I forgot I'd never explained to you. It was a rather vague idea of mine, most of the time we were traveling, and I don't like to discuss ideas prematurely. Now that we've met the Outlings and watched how they work, I do feel sure."

He tamped down his tobacco. "In limited measure," he said, "I've used an archetype throughout my own working life. The rational detective. It hasn't been a conscious pose —much—it's simply been an image which fitted my personality and professional style. But it draws an appropriate response from most people, whether or not they've ever heard of the original. The phenomenon is not uncommon. We meet persons who, in varying degrees, suggest Christ or Buddha or the Earth Mother or, say, on a less exalted plane, Hamlet or d'Artagnan. Historical, fictional, and mythical, such figures crystallize basic aspects of the human psyche, and when we meet them in our real experience, our reaction goes deeper than consciousness."

He grew grave again: "Man also creates archetypes that are not individuals. The Anima, the Shadow—and, it seems, the Outworld. The world of magic, of glamour—which originally meant enchantment—of half-human beings, some like Ariel and some like Caliban, but each free of mortal frailties and sorrows—therefore, perhaps, a little carelessly cruel, more than a little tricksy; dwellers in dusk and moonlight, not truly gods but obedient to rulers who are enigmatic and powerful enough to be—Yes, our Queen of Air and Darkness knew well what sights to let lonely people see, what illusions to spin around them from time to time, what songs and legends to set going among them. I wonder how much she and her underlings gleaned from human fairy tales, how much they made up themselves, and how much men created all over again, all unwittingly, as the sense of living on the edge of the world entered them."

Shadows stole across the room. It grew cooler and the traffic noises dwindled. Barbro asked mutedly, "But what could this do?"

"In many ways," Sherrinford answered, "the outwayer *is* back in the Dark Ages. He has few neighbors, hears scanty news from beyond his horizon, toils to survive in a land he only partly understands, that may any night raise unforeseeable disasters against him, and is bounded by enormous wildernesses. The machine civilization which brought his ancestors here is frail at best. He could lose it as the Dark Ages nations had lost Greece and Rome, as the whole of Earth seems to have lost it. Let him be worked on, long, strongly, cunningly, by the archetypical Outworld, until he has come to believe in his bones that the magic of the Queen of Air and Darkness is greater than the energy of engines; and first his faith, finally his deeds will follow her. Oh, it wouldn't happen fast. Ideally, it would happen too slowly to be noticed, especially by self-satisfied city people. But when in the end a hinterland gone back to the ancient way turned from them, how could they keep alive?"

Barbro breathed, "She said to me, when their banners flew in the last of our cities, we would rejoice."

"I think we would have, by then," Sherrinford admitted. "Nevertheless, I believe in choosing one's destiny."

He shook himself, as if casting off a burden. He knocked the dottle from his pipe and stretched, muscle by muscle. "Well," he said, "it isn't going to happen."

She looked straight at him. "Thanks to you."

A flush went up his thin cheeks. "In time, I'm sure, somebody else would have— What matters is what we do next, and that's too big a decision for one individual or one generation to make."

She rose. "Unless the decision is personal, Eric," she suggested, feeling heat in her own face.

It was curious to see him shy. "I was hoping we might meet again."

"We will."

Ayoch sat on Wolund's Barrow. Aurora shuddered so brilliant, in such vast sheafs of light, as almost to hide the waning moons. Firethorn blooms had fallen; a few still glowed around the tree roots, amidst dry brok which crackled underfoot and smelled like woodsmoke. The air remained warm, but no gleam was left on the sunset horizon.

"Farewell, fare lucky," the pook called. Mistherd and Shadow-of-a-Dream never looked back. It was as if they didn't dare. They trudged on out of sight, toward the human camp whose lights made a harsh new star in the south.

Ayoch lingered. He felt he should also offer good-by to her who had lately joined him that slept in the dolmen. Likely none would meet here again for loving or magic. But he could only think of one old verse that might do. He stood and trilled:

> "Out of her breast
> a blossom ascended.
> The summer burned it.
> The song is ended."

Then he spread his wings for the long flight away.

IN ENTROPY'S JAWS

Robert Silverberg

I don't think Bob Silverberg has ever written a better novelette than this one: a subtle, fluid, fascinating and complex story about a man trying to pick up the pieces of his shattered life—and finding that they are, indeed, only pieces. It all depends on how you arrange them.

Static crackles from the hazy golden cloud of airborne loudspeakers drifting just below the ceiling of the spaceliner cabin. A hiss: Communications filters are opening. An impending announcement from the bridge, no doubt. Then the captain's bland, mechanical voice: "We are approaching the Panama Canal. All passengers into their bottles until the all-clear after insertion. When we come out the far side, we'll be traveling at eighty lights toward the Perseus relay booster. Thank you." In John Skein's cabin the warning globe begins to flash, dousing him with red, yellow, green light, going up and down the visible spectrum, giving him some infra- and ultra- too. Not everybody who books passage on this liner necessarily has human sensory equipment. The signal will not go out until Skein is safely in his bottle. Go on, it tells him. Get in. Get in. Panama Canal coming up.

Obediently he rises and moves across the narrow cabin toward the tapering dull-skinned steel container, two and a half meters high, that will protect him against the dimensional stresses of canal insertion. He is a tall, angular man with thin lips, a strong chin, glossy black hair that clings close to his high-vaulted skull. His skin is deeply tanned but his eyes are those of one who has been in winter for some time. This is the fiftieth year of his second go-round. He is traveling alone toward a world of the Abbondanza system, perhaps the last leg on a journey that has occupied him for several years.

The passenger bottle swings open on its gaudy rhodium-jacketed hinge when its sensors, picking up Skein's mass and thermal output, tell it that its protectee is within entry range. He gets in. It closes and seals, wrapping him in a seamless magnetic field. "Please be seated," the bottle tells him softly. "Place your arms through the stasis loops and your feet in the security platens. When you have done this the pressor fields will automatically be activated and you will be fully insulated against injury during the coming period of turbulence." Skein, who has had plenty of experience with faster-than-light travel, has anticipated the instructions and is already in stasis. The bottle closes. "Do you wish music?" it asks him. "A book? A vision spool? Conversation?"

"Nothing, thanks," Skein says, and waits.

He understands waiting very well by this time. Once he was an impatient man, but this is a thin season in his life, and it has been teaching him the arts of stoic acceptance. He will sit here with the Buddha's own complacency until the ship is through the canal. Silent, alone, self-sufficient. If only there will be no fugues this time. Or, at least—he is negotiating the terms of his torment with his demons—at least let there be no flashforwards. If he must break loose again from the matrix of time, he prefers to be cast only into his yesterdays, never into his tomorrows.

"We are almost into the canal now," the bottle tells him pleasantly.

"It's all right. You don't need to look after me. Just let me know when it's safe to come out."

He closes his eyes. Trying to envision the ship: a fragile glimmering purple needle squirting through clinging blackness, plunging toward the celestial vortex just ahead, the maelstrom of clashing forces, the soup of contravariant tensors. The Panama Canal, so-called. Through which the liner will shortly rush, acquiring during its passage such a garland of borrowed power that it will rip itself free of the standard fourspace; it will emerge on the far side of the canal into a strange, tranquil pocket of the universe where the speed of light is the downside limiting velocity, and no one knows where the upper limit lies.

Alarms sound in the corridor, heavy, resonant: clang, clang, clang. The dislocation is beginning. Skein is braced. What does it look like out there? Folds of glowing black velvet, furry swatches of the disrupted continuum, wrapping themselves around the ship? Titanic lightnings hammering on the hull? Laughing centaurs flashing across the twisted heavens? Despondent masks, fixed in tragic grimaces, dangling between the blurred stars? Streaks of orange, green, crimson: sick rainbows, limp, askew? In we go. *Clang, clang, clang.* The next phase of the voyage now begins. He thinks of his destination, holding an image of it rigidly in mind. The picture is vivid, though this is a world he has visited only in spells of temporal fugue. Too often; he has been there again and again in these moments of disorientation in time. The colors are wrong on that world. Purple sand. Blue-leaved trees. Too much manganese? Too little copper? He will forgive it its colors if it will grant him his answers. And then. Skein feels the familiar ugly throbbing at the base of his neck, as if the tip of his spine is swelling like a balloon. He curses. He tries to resist. As he feared, not even the bottle can wholly protect him against these stresses. Outside the ship the universe is being wrenched apart; some of that slips in here and throws him into a private epilepsy of the time-line. Space-time is breaking up for him. He will go into fugue. He clings, fighting, knowing it is futile. The currents of time buffet him, knocking him a short distance into the future, then a reciprocal distance into the past, as if he is a bubble of insect spittle glued loosely to a dry reed. He cannot hold on much longer. Let it not be flashforward, he prays, wondering who it is to whom he prays. Let it not be flashforward. And he loses his grip. And shatters. And is swept in shards across time.

Of course, if x *is before* y *then it remains eternally before* y, *and nothing in the passage of time can change this. But the peculiar position of the "now" can be easily expressed simply because our language has tenses. The future* will be, *the present is, and the past was; the light will be red, it is now yellow, and it was green. But do we, in these terms, really describe the "processional" character of time? We sometimes say that an event is future, then it is present, and finally it is past; and by this means we seem to dispense with tenses, yet we portray the passage of time. But this is really not the case; for all that we have done is to translate our tenses into the words "then" and "finally," and into the order in which we state our clauses. If we were to omit these words or their equivalents, and mix up the clauses, our sentences would no longer be meaningful. To say that the future, the present, and the past are in some sense is to dodge the problem of time by resorting to the tenseless language of logic and mathematics. In such an atemporal language it would be meaningful to say that Socrates is mortal because all men are mortal and Socrates is a man, even though Socrates has been dead many centuries. But if we cannot describe time either by a language containing tenses or by a tenseless language, how shall we symbolize it?*

He feels the curious doubleness of self, the sense of having been here before, and knows it is flashback. Some comfort in that. He is a passenger in his own skull, looking out through the eyes of John Skein on an event that he has already experienced, and which he now is powerless to alter.

His office. All its gilded magnificence. A crystal dome at the summit of Kenyatta Tower. With the amplifiers on he can see as far as Serengeti in one direction, Mombasa in another. Count the fleas on an elephant in Tsavo Park. A wall of light on the east-southeast face of the dome, housing his data-access units. No one can stare at that wall more than thirty seconds without suffering intensely from a surfeit of information. Except Skein; he drains nourishment from it, hour after hour.

As he slides into the soul of that earlier Skein he takes a brief joy in the sight of his office, like Aeneas relishing a vision of unfallen Troy, like Adam looking back into Eden. How good it was. That broad sweet desk with its subtle components dedicated to his service. The gentle psycho-sensitive carpet, so useful and so beautiful. The undulating ribbon-sculpture gliding in and out of the dome's skin, undergoing molecular displacement each time and forever exhibiting the newest of its infinity of possible patterns. A rich man's office; he was unabashed in his pursuit of elegance. He had earned the right to luxury through the intelligent use of his innate skills. Returning now to that lost dome of wonders, he quickly seizes his moment of satisfaction, aware that shortly some souring scene of subtraction will be replayed for him, one of the stages in the darkening and withering of his life. But which one?

"Send in Coustakis," he hears himself say, and his words give him the answer. That one. He will again watch his own destruction. Surely there is no further need to subject him to this particular re-enactment. He has been through it at least seven times; he is losing count. An endless spiraling track of torment.

Coustakis is bald, blue-eyed, sharp-nosed, with the desperate look of a man who is near the end of his first go-round and is not yet sure that he will be granted a second. Skein guesses that he is about seventy. The man is unlikable: he dresses coarsely, moves in aggressive blurting little strides, and shows in every gesture and glance that he seethes with envy of the opulence with which Skein surrounds himself. Skein feels no need to like his clients, though. Only to respect. And Coustakis is brilliant; he commands respect.

Skein says, "My staff and I have studied your proposal in great detail. It's a cunning scheme."

"You'll help me?"

"There are risks for me," Skein points out. "Nissenson has a powerful ego. So do you. I could get hurt. The whole concept of synergy involves risk for the Communicator. My fees are calculated accordingly."

"Nobody expects a Communicator to be cheap," Coustakis mutters.

"I'm not. But I think you'll be able to afford me. The question is whether I can afford you."

"You're very cryptic, Mr. Skein. Like all oracles."

Skein smiles. "I'm not an oracle, I'm afraid. Merely a conduit through whom connections are made. I can't foresee the future."

"You can evaluate probabilities."

"Only concerning my own welfare. And I'm capable of arriving at an incorrect evaluation."

Coustakis fidgets. "Will you help me or won't you?"

"The fee," Skein says, "is half a million down, plus an equity position of fifteen percent in the corporation you'll establish with the contacts I provide."

Coustakis gnaws at his lower lip. "So much?"

"Bear in mind that I've got to split my fee with Nissenson. Consultants like him aren't cheap."

"Even so. Ten percent."

"Excuse me, Mr. Coustakis. I really thought we were past the point of negotiation in this transaction. It's going to be a busy day for me, and so—" Skein passes his hand over a black rectangle on his desk and a section of the floor silently opens, uncovering the dropshaft access. He nods toward it. The carpet reveals the colors of Coustakis' mental processes: black for anger, green for greed, red for anxiety, yellow for fear, blue for temptation, all mixed together in the hashed pattern betraying the calculations now going on in his mind. Coustakis will yield. Nevertheless Skein proceeds with the charade of standing, gesturing toward the exit, trying to usher his visitor out. "All right," Coustakis says explosively, "fifteen percent!"

Skein instructs his desk to extrude a contract cube. He says, "Place your hand here, please," and as Coustakis touches the cube he presses his own palm against its opposite face. At once the cube's sleek crystalline surface darkens and roughens as the double sensory output bombards it. Skein says, "Repeat after me. I, Nicholas Coustakis, whose handprint and vibration pattern are being imprinted in this contract as I speak—"

"I, Nicholas Coustakis, whose handprint and vibration pattern are being imprinted in this contract as I speak—"

"—do knowingly and willingly assign to John Skein Enterprises, as payment for professional services to be rendered, an equity interest in Coustakis Transport Ltd. or any successor corporation amounting to—"

"—do knowingly and willingly assign—"

They drone on in turns through a description of Coustakis' corporation and the irrevocable nature of Skein's part ownership in it. Then Skein files the contract cube and says, "If you'll phone your bank and put your thumb on the cash part of the transaction, I'll make contact with Nissenson and you can get started."

"Half a million?"

"Half a million."

"You know I don't have that kind of money."

"Let's not waste time, Mr. Coustakis. You have assets. Pledge them as collateral. Credit is easily obtained."

Scowling, Coustakis applies for the loan, gets it, transfers the funds to Skein's account. The process takes eight minutes; Skein uses the time to review Coustakis' ego profile. It displeases Skein to have to exert such sordid economic pressures; but the service he offers does, after all, expose him to dangers, and he must cushion the risk by high guarantees, in case some mishap should put him out of business.

"Now we can proceed," Skein says, when the transaction is done.

Coustakis has almost invented a system for the economical instantaneous transportation of matter. It will not, unfortunately, ever be useful for living things, since the process involves the destruction of the material being shipped and its virtually simultaneous reconstitution elsewhere. The fragile entity that is the soul cannot withstand the withering blast of Coustakis' transmitter's electron beam. But there is tremendous potential in the freight business; the Coustakis transmitter will be able to send cabbages to Mars, computers to Pluto, and, given the proper linkage facilities, it should be able to reach the inhabited extrasolar planets.

However, Coustakis has not yet perfected his system. For five years he has been stymied by one impassable problem: keeping the beam tight enough between transmitter and receiver. Beam-spread has led to chaos in his experiments; marginal straying results in the loss of transmitted information, so that that which is being sent invariably arrives incomplete. Coustakis has depleted his resources in the unsuccessful search for a solution, and thus has been forced to the desperate and costly step of calling in a Communicator.

For a price, Skein will place him in contact with someone who can solve his problem. Skein has a network of consultants on several worlds, experts in technology and finance and philology and nearly everything else. Using his own mind as the focal nexus, Skein will open telepathic communion between Coustakis and a consultant.

"Get Nissenson into a receptive state," he orders his desk.

Coustakis, blinking rapidly, obviously uneasy, says, "First let me get it clear. This man will see everything that's in my mind? He'll get access to my secrets?"

"No. No. I filter the communion with great care. Nothing will pass from your mind to his except the nature of the problem you want him to tackle. Nothing will come back from his mind to yours except the answer."

"And if he doesn't have the answer?"

"He will."

Skein gives no refunds in the event of failure, but he has never had a failure. He does not accept jobs that he feels will be inherently impossible to handle. Either Nissenson will see the solution Coustakis has been overlooking, or else he will make some suggestion that will nudge Coustakis toward finding the solution himself. The telepathic communion is the vital element. Mere talking would never get anywhere. Coustakis and Nissenson could stare at blueprints together for months, pound computers side by side for years, debate the difficulty with each other for decades, and still they might not hit on the answer. But the communion creates a synergy of minds that is more than a doubling of the available brainpower. A union of perceptions, a heightening, that always produces that mystic flash of insight, that leap of the intellect.

"And if he goes into the transmission business for himself afterward?" Coustakis asks.

"He's bonded," Skein says curtly. "No chance of it. Let's go, now. Up and together."

The desk reports that Nissenson, half the world away in São Paulo, is ready. Skein's power does not vary with distance. Quickly he throws Coustakis into the receptive condition, and swings around to face the brilliant lights of his data-access units. Those sparkling, shifting little blazes kindle his gift, jabbing at the electrical rhythms of his brain until he is lifted into the energy level that permits the opening of a communion. As he starts to go up, the other Skein who is watching, the time-displaced prisoner behind his forehead, tries frenziedly to prevent him from entering the fatal linkage. *Don't. Don't. You'll overload. They're too strong for you.* Easier to halt a planet in its orbit, though. The course of the past is frozen; all this has already happened; the Skein who cries out in silent anguish is merely an observer, necessarily passive, here to view the maiming of his earlier self.

Skein reaches forth one tendril of his mind and engages Nissenson. With another tendril he snares Coustakis. Steadily, now, he draws the two tendrils together.

There is no way to predict the intensity of the forces that will shortly course through his brain. He has done what he could, checking the ego profiles of his client and the consultant, but that really tells him little. What Coustakis and Nissenson may be as individuals hardly matters; it is what they may become in communion that he must fear. Synergic intensities are unpredictable. He has lived for a lifetime and a half with the possibility of a burnout.

The tendrils meet.

Skein the observer winces and tries to armor himself against the shock. But there is no way to deflect it. Out of Coustakis' mind flows a description of the matter transmitter and a clear statement of the beam-spread problem; Skein shoves it along to Nissenson, who begins to work on a solution. But when their minds join it is immediately evident that their combined strength will be more than Skein can control. This time the synergy will destroy him. But he cannot disengage; he has no mental circuitbreaker. He is caught, trapped, impaled. The entity that is Coustakis/Nissenson will not let go of him, for that would mean its own destruction. A wave of mental energy goes rippling and dancing along the vector of communion from Coustakis to Nissenson and goes bouncing back, pulsating and gaining strength, from Nissenson to Coustakis. A fiery oscillation is set up. Skein sees what is happening; he has become the amplifier of his own doom. The torrent of energy continues to gather power each time it reverberates from Coustakis to Nissenson, from Nissenson to Coustakis. Powerless, Skein watches the energy-pumping effect building up a mighty charge. The discharge is bound to come soon, and he will be the one who must receive it. How long? How long? The juggernaut fills the corridors of his mind. He ceases to know which end of the circuit is Nissenson, which is Coustakis; he perceives only two shining walls of mental power, between which he is stretched ever thinner, a twanging wire of ego, heating up, heating up, glowing now, emitting a searing blast of heat, particles of identity streaming away from him like so many liberated ions—

Then he lies numb and dazed on the floor of his office, grinding his face into the psychosensitive carpet, while Coustakis barks over and over, "Skein? Skein? Skein? Skein?"

Like any other chronometric device, our inner clocks are subject to their own peculiar disorders and, in spite of the substantial concordance between private and public time, discrepancies may occur as the result of sheer inattention. Mach noted that if a doctor focuses his attention on the patient's blood, it may seem to him to squirt out before the lancet enters the skin and, for similar reasons, the feebler of two stimuli presented simultaneously is usually perceived later. . . . Normal life requires the capacity to recall experiences in a sequence corresponding, roughly at least, to the order in which they actually occurred. It requires in addition that our potential recollections should be reasonably accessible to consciousness. These potential recollections mean not only a perpetuation within us of representations of the past, but also a ceaseless interplay between such representations and the uninterrupted input of present information from the external world. Just as our past may be at the service of our present, so the present may be remotely controlled by our past: in the words of Shelley, "Swift as a Thought by the snake Memory stung."

"Skein? Skein? Skein? Skein?"

His bottle is open and they are helping him out. His cabin is full of intruders. Skein recognizes the captain's robot, the medic, and a couple of passengers, the little swarthy man from Pingalore and the woman from Globe Fifteen. The cabin door is open and more people are coming in. The medic makes a cuff-shooting gesture and a blinding haze of metallic white particles wraps itself about Skein's head. The little tingling prickling sensations spur him to wakefulness. "You didn't respond when the bottle told you it was all right," the medic explains. "We're through the canal."

"Was it a good passage? Fine. Fine. I must have dozed."

"If you'd like to come to the infirmary—a routine check, only—put you through the diagnostat—"

"No. No. Will you all please go? I assure you, I'm quite all right."

Reluctantly, clucking over him, they finally leave. Skein gulps cold water until his head is clear. He plants himself flatfooted in midcabin, trying to pick up some sensation of forward motion. The ship now is traveling at something like fifteen million miles a second. How long is fifteen million miles? How long is a second? From Rome to Naples it was a morning's drive on the autostrada. From Tel Aviv to Jerusalem was the time between twilight and darkness. San Francisco to San Diego spanned lunch to dinner by superpod. As I slide my right foot two inches forward we traverse fifteen million miles. From where to where? And why? He has not seen Earth in twenty-six months. At the end of this voyage his remaining funds will be exhausted. Perhaps he will have to make his home in the Abbondanza system; he has no return ticket. But of course he can travel to his heart's discontent within his own skull, whipping from point to point along the time-line in the grip of the fugues.

He goes quickly from his cabin to the recreation lounge.

The ship is a second-class vessel, neither lavish nor seedy. It carries about twenty passengers, most of them, like him, bound outward on one-way journeys. He has not talked directly to any of them, but he has done considerable eavesdropping in the lounge, and by now can tag each one of them with the proper dull biography. The wife bravely joining her pioneer husband, whom she has not seen for half a decade. The remittance man under orders to place ten thousand light-years, at the very least, between himself and his parents. The glittery-eyed entrepreneur, a Phoenician merchant sixty centuries after his proper era, off to carve an empire as a middleman's middleman. The tourists. The bureaucrat. The colonel. Among this collection Skein stands out in sharp relief; he is the only one who has not made an effort to know and be known, and the mystery of his reserve tantalizes them.

He carries the fact of his crackup with him like some wrinkled dangling yellowed wen. When his eyes meet those of any of the others he says silently, You see my deformity? I am my own survivor. I have been destroyed and lived to look back on it. Once I was a man of wealth and power, and look at me now. But I ask for no pity. Is that understood?

Hunching at the bar, Skein pushes the node for filtered rum. His drink arrives, and with it comes the remittance man, handsome, young, insinuating. Giving Skein a confidential wink, as if to say, *I* know. You're on the run, too.

"From Earth, are you?" he says to Skein.

"Formerly."

"I'm Pid Rocklin."

"John Skein."

"What were you doing there?"

"On Earth?" Skein shrugs. "A Communicator. I retired four years ago."

"Oh." Rocklin summons a drink. "That's good work, if you have the gift."

"I had the gift," Skein says. The unstressed past tense is as far into self-pity as he will go. He drinks and pushes for another one. A great gleaming screen over the bar shows the look of space: empty, here beyond the Panama Canal, although yesterday a million suns blazed on that ebony rectangle. Skein imagines he can hear the whoosh of hydrogen molecules scraping past the hull at eighty lights. He sees them as blobs of brightness millions of miles long, going *zip!* and *zip!* and *zip!* as the ship spurts along. Abruptly a purple nimbus envelopes him and he drops into a flash-forward fugue so quickly there is not even time for the usual futile resistance. "Hey, what's the matter?" Pid Rocklin says, reaching for him. "Are you all—" and Skein loses the universe.

He is on the world that he takes to be Abbondanza VI, and his familiar companion, the skull-faced man, stands beside him at the edge of an oily orange sea. They appear to be having the debate about time once again. The skull-faced man must be at least a hundred twenty years old; his skin lies against his bones with, seemingly, no flesh at all under it, and his face is all nostrils and burning eyes. Bony sockets, sharp shelves for cheekbones, a bald dome of a skull. The neck no more than wrist-thick, rising out of shriveled shoulders. Saying, "Won't you ever come to see that causality is merely an illusion, Skein? The notion that there's a consecutive series of events is nothing but a fraud. We impose form on our lives, we talk of time's arrow, we say that there's a flow from A through G and Q to Z, we make believe everything is nicely linear. But it isn't, Skein. It isn't."

"So you keep telling me."

"I feel an obligation to awaken your mind to the truth. G can come before A, and Z before both of them. Most of us don't like to perceive it that way, so we arrange things in what seems like a more logical pattern, just as a novelist will put the motive before the murder and the murder before the arrest. But the universe isn't a novel. We can't make nature imitate art. It's all random, Skein, random, random! Look there. You see what's drifting on the sea?"

On the orange waves tosses the bloated corpse of a shaggy blue beast. Upturned saucery eyes, drooping snout, thick limbs. Why is it not waterlogged by now? What keeps it afloat?

The skull-faced man says, "Time is an ocean, and events come drifting to us as randomly as dead animals on the waves. We filter them. We screen out what doesn't make sense and admit them to our consciousness in what seems to be the right sequence." He laughs. "The grand delusion! The past is nothing but a series of films slipping unpredictably into the future. And vice versa."

"I won't accept that," Skein says stubbornly. "It's a demonic, chaotic, nihilistic theory. It's idiocy. Are we graybeards before we're children? Do we die before we're born? Do trees devolve into seeds? Deny linearity all you like. I won't go along."

"You can say that after all you've experienced?"

Skein shakes his head. "I'll go on saying it. What I've been going through is a mental illness. Maybe I'm deranged, but the universe isn't."

"Contrary. You've only recently become sane and started to see things as they really are," the skull-faced man insists. "The trouble is that you don't want to admit the evidence you've begun to perceive. Your filters are down, Skein! You've shaken free of the illusion of linearity! Now's your chance to show your resilience. Learn to live with the real reality. Stop this silly business of imposing an artificial order on the flow of time. Why *should* effect follow cause? Why *shouldn't* the seed follow the tree? Why must you persist in holding tight to a useless, outworn, contemptible system of false evaluations of experience when you've managed to break free of the—"

"Stop it! Stop it! Stop it! Stop it!"

"—right, Skein?"

"What happened?"

"You started to fall off your stool," Pid Rocklin says. "You turned absolutely white. I thought you were having some kind of a stroke."

"How long was I unconscious?"

"Oh, three, four seconds, I suppose. I grabbed you and propped you up, and your eyes opened. Can I help you to your cabin? Or maybe you ought to go to the infirmary."

"Excuse me," Skein says hoarsely, and leaves the lounge.

When the hallucinations began, not long after the Coustakis overload, he assumed at first that they were memory disturbances produced by the fearful jolt he had absorbed. Quite clearly most of them invoked scenes of his past, which he would relive, during the moments of fugue, with an intensity so brilliant that he felt he had actually been thrust back into time. He did not merely recollect, but rather he experienced the past anew, following a script from which he could not deviate as he spoke and felt and reacted. Such strange excursions into memory could be easily enough explained: His brain had been damaged, and it was heaving old segments of experience into view in some kind of attempt to clear itself of debris and heal the wounds. But while the flashbacks were comprehensible, the flashforwards were not, and he did not recognize them at all for what they actually were. Those scenes of himself wandering alien worlds, those phantom conversations with people he had never met, those views of spaceliner cabins and transit booths and unfamiliar hotels and passenger terminals, seemed merely to be fantasies, random fictions of his injured brain. Even when he started to notice that there was a consistent pattern to these feverish glimpses of the unknown, he still did not catch on. It appeared as though he was seeing himself performing a sort of quest, or perhaps a pilgrimage; the slices of unexperienced experience that he was permitted to see began to fit into a coherent structure of travel and seeking. And certain scenes and conversations recurred, yes, sometimes several times the same day, the script always the same, so that he began to learn a few of the scenes word for word. Despite the solid texture of these episodes, he persisted in thinking of them as mere brief flickering segments of nightmare. He could not imagine why the injury to his brain was causing him to have these waking dreams of long space voyages and unknown planets, so vivid and so momentarily real, but they seemed no more frightening to him than the equally vivid flashbacks.

Only after a while, when many months had passed since the Coustakis incident, did the truth strike him. One day he found himself living through an episode that he considered to be one of his fantasies. It was a minor thing, one that he had experienced, in whole or in part, seven or eight times. What he had seen, in fitful bursts of uninvited delusion, was himself in a public garden on some hot spring morning, standing before an immense baroque building while a grotesque group of non-human tourists filed past him in a weird creaking, clanking procession of inhalator suits and breather-wheels and ion-disperser masks. That was all. Then it happened that a harrowing legal snarl brought him to a city in North Carolina about fourteen months after the overload, and after having put in his appearance at the courthouse, he set out on a long walk through the grimy, decayed metropolis and came, as if by an enchantment, to a huge metal gate behind which he could see a dark sweep of lavish forest, oaks and rhododendrons and magnolias, laid out in an elegant formal manner. It was, according to a sign posted by the gate, the estate of a nineteenth-century millionaire, now open to all and preserved in its ancient state despite the encroachments of the city on its borders. Skein bought a ticket and went in, on foot, hiking for what seemed like miles through cool leafy glades, until abruptly the path curved and he emerged into the bright sunlight and saw before him the great gray bulk of a colossal mansion, hundreds of rooms topped by parapets and spires, with a massive portico from which vast columns of stairs descended. In wonder he moved toward it, for this was the building of his frequent fantasy, and as he approached he beheld the red and green and purple figures crossing the portico, those coiled and gnarled and looping shapes he had seen before, the eerie horde of alien travelers here to take in the wonders of Earth. Heads without eyes, eyes without heads, multiplicities of limbs and absences of limbs, bodies like tumors and tumors like bodies, all the universe's imagination on display in these agglomerated life-forms, so strange and yet not at all strange to him. But this time it was no fantasy. It fit smoothly into the sequence of the events of the day, rather than dropping, dreamlike, intrusive, into that sequence. Nor did it fade after a few moments; the scene remained sharp, never leaving him to plunge back into "real" life. This was reality itself, and he had experienced it before.

Twice more in the next few weeks things like that happened to him, until at last he was ready to admit the truth to himself about his fugues: that he was experiencing flashforwards as well as flashbacks, that he was being subjected to glimpses of his own future.

T'ang, the high king of the Shang, asked Hsia Chi saying, "In the beginning, were there already individual things?" Hsia Chi replied, "If there were no things then, how could there be any now? If later generations should pretend that there had been no things in our time, would they be right?" T'ang said, "Have things then no before and no after?" To which Hsia Chi replied, "The ends and the origins of things have no limit from which they began. The origin of one thing may be considered the end of another; the end of one may be considered the origin of the next. Who can distinguish accurately between these cycles? What lies beyond all things, and before all events, we cannot know."

They reach and enter the Perseus relay booster, which is a whirling celestial anomaly structurally similar to the Panama Canal but not nearly so potent, and it kicks the ship's velocity to just above a hundred lights. That is the voyage's final acceleration; the ship will maintain this rate for two and a half days, until it clocks in at Scylla, the main deceleration station for this part of the galaxy, where it will be seized by a spongy web of forces twenty light-minutes in diameter and slowed to sublight velocities for the entry into the Abbondanza system.

Skein spends nearly all of this period in his cabin, rarely eating and sleeping very little. He reads almost constantly, obsessively dredging from the ship's extensive library a wide and capricious assortment of books. Rilke. Kafka. Eddington, *The Nature of the Physical World*. Lowry, *Hear Us O Lord From Heaven Thy Dwelling Place*. Elias. Razhuminin. Dickey. Pound. Fraisse, *The Psychology of Time*. Greene, *Dream and Delusion*. Poe. Shakespeare. Marlowe. Tourneur. *The Waste Land*. *Ulysses*. *Heart of Darkness*. Bury, *The Idea of Progress*. Jung. Büchner. Pirandello. *The Magic Mountain*. Ellis, *The Rack*. Cervantes. Blenheim. Fierst. Keats. Nietzsche. His mind swims with images and bits of verse, with floating sequences of dialogue, with unscaffolded dialectics. He dips into each work briefly, magpielike, seeking bright scraps. The words form a scaly impasto on the inner surface of his skull. He finds that this heavy verbal overdose helps, to some slight extent, to fight off the fugues; his mind is weighted, perhaps, bound by this leaden clutter of borrowed genius to the moving line of the present, and during his debauch of reading he finds himself shifting off that line less frequently than in the recent past. His mind whirls. *Man is a rope stretched between the animal and the Superman—A rope over an abyss*. My patience is exhausted. *See, see where Christ's blood streams in the firmament! One drop would save my soul*. I had not thought death had undone so many. These fragments I have shored against my ruins. *Hoogspanning. Levensgevaar. Peligro de Muerte. Electricidad. Danger*. Give me my spear. *Old father, old artificer, stand me now and ever in good stead*. You like this garden? Why is it yours? We evict those who destroy! *And then went down to the ship, set keel to breakers, forth on the godly sea*. There is no "official" theory of time, defined in creeds or universally agreed upon among Christians. Christianity is not concerned with the purely scientific aspects of the subject nor, within wide limits, with its philosophical analysis, except insofar as it is committed to a fundamentally realist view and could not admit, as some Eastern philosophies have done, that temporal existence is mere illusion. *A shudder in the loins engenders there the broken wall, the burning roof and tower and Agamemnon dead*. Stately, plump Buck Mulligan came from the stairhead, bearing a bowl of lather on which a mirror and a razor lay crossed. *In what distant deeps or skies burnt the fire of thine eyes? On what wings dare he aspire? What the hand dare seize the fire?* These fragments I have shored against my ruins. Hieronymo's mad againe. *Then felt I like some watcher of the skies when a new planet swims into his ken.* It has also lately been postulated that the physical concept of information is identical with a phenomenon of reversal of entropy. The psychologist must add a few remarks here: It does not seem convincing to me that information is *eo ipso* identical with a *pouvoir d'organisation* which undoes entropy. *Datta. Dayadhvam. Damyata. Shantih shantih shantih*

Nevertheless, once the ship is past Scylla and slowing toward the Abbondanza planets, the periods of fugue become frequent once again, so that he lives entrapped, shuttling between the flashing shadows of yesterday and tomorrow.

After the Coustakis overload he tried to go on in the old way as best he could. He gave Coustakis a refund without even being asked, for he had been of no service, nor could he ever be. Instantaneous transportation of matter would have to wait. But Skein took other clients. He could still make the communion, after a fashion, and when the nature of the task was sufficiently low-level he could even deliver a decent synergetic response.

Often his work was unsatisfactory, however. Contacts would break at awkward moments, or, conversely, his filter mechanism would weaken and he would allow the entire contents of his client's mind to flow into that of his consultant. The results of such disasters were chaotic, involving him in heavy medical expenses and sometimes in damage suits. He was forced to place his fees on a contingency basis: no synergy, no pay. About half the time he earned nothing for his output of energy. Meanwhile his overhead remained the same as always: the domed office, the network of consultants, the research staff, and the rest. His effort to remain in business was eating rapidly into the bank accounts he had set aside against just such a time of storm.

They could find no organic injury to his brain. Of course, so little was known about a Communicator's gift that it was impossible to determine much by medical analysis. If they could not locate the center from which a Communicator powered his communions, how could they detect the place where he had been hurt? The medical archives were of no value; there had been eleven previous cases of overload, but each instance was physiologically unique. They told him he would eventually heal, and sent him away. Sometimes the doctors gave him silly therapies: counting exercises, rhythmic blinkings, hopping on his left leg and then his right, as if he had had a stroke. But he had not had a stroke.

For a time he was able to maintain his business on the momentum of his reputation. Then, as word got around that he had been hurt and was no longer any good, clients stopped coming. Even the contingency basis for fees failed to attract them. Within six months he found that he was lucky to find a client a week. He reduced his rates, and that seemed only to make things worse, so he raised them to something not far below what they had been at the time of the overload. For a while the pace of business increased, as if people were getting the impression that Skein had recovered. He gave such spotty service, though. Blurred and wavering communions, unanticipated positive feedbacks, filtering problems, information deficiencies, redundancy surpluses—"You take your mind in your hands when you go to Skein," they were saying now.

The fugues added to his professional difficulties.

He never knew when he would snap into hallucination. It might happen during a communion, and often did. Once he dropped back to the moment of the Coustakis-Nissenson hookup and treated a terrified client to a replay of his overload. Once, although he did not understand at the time what was happening, he underwent a flashforward and carried the client with him to a scarlet jungle on a formaldehyde world, and when Skein slipped back to reality the client remained in the scarlet jungle. There was a damage suit over that one, too.

Temporal dislocation plagued him into making poor guesses. He took on clients whom he could not possibly serve, and wasted his time on them. He turned away people whom he might have been able to help to his own profit. Since he was no longer anchored firmly to his timeline, but drifted in random oscillations of twenty years or more in either direction, he forfeited the keen sense of perspective on which he had previously founded his professional judgments. He grew haggard and lean, also. He passed through a tempest of spiritual doubts that amounted to total submission and then total rejection of faith within the course of four months. He changed lawyers almost weekly. He liquidated assets with invariably catastrophic timing to pay his cascading bills.

A year and a half after the overload, he formally renounced his registration and closed his office. It took six months more to settle the remaining damage suits. Then, with what was left of his money, he bought a spaceliner ticket and set out to search for a world with purple sand and blue-leaved trees, where, unless his fugues had played him false, he might be able to arrange for the repair of his broken mind.

Now the ship has returned to the conventional fourspace and dawdles planetward at something rather less than half the speed of light. Across the screens there spreads a necklace of stars; space is crowded here. The captain will point out Abbondanza to anyone who asks: a lemon-colored sun, bigger than that of Earth, surrounded by a dozen bright planetary pips. The passengers are excited. They buzz, twitter, speculate, anticipate. No one is silent except Skein. He is aware of many love affairs; he has had to reject several offers just in the past three days. He has given up reading and is trying to purge his mind of all he has stuffed into it. The fugues have grown worse. He has to write notes to himself, saying things like *You are a passenger aboard a ship heading for Abbondanza VI, and will be landing in a few days,* so that he does not forget which of his three entangled time-lines is the true one.

Suddenly he is with Nilla on the island in the Gulf of Mexico, getting aboard the little excursion boat. Time stands still here; it could almost be the twentieth century. The frayed, sagging cords of the rigging. The lumpy engine inefficiently converted from internal combustion to turbines. The mustachioed Mexican bandits who will be their guides today. Nilla, nervously coiling her long blonde hair, saying, "Will I get seasick, John? The boat rides right in the water, doesn't it? It won't even hover a little bit?"

"Terribly archaic," Skein says. "That's why we're here."

The captain gestures them aboard. Juan, Francisco, Sebastián. Brothers. *Los hermanos.* Yards of white teeth glistening below the drooping mustaches. With a terrible roar the boat moves away from the dock. Soon the little town of crumbling pastel buildings is out of sight and they are heading jaggedly eastward along the coast, green shoreward water on their left, the blue depths on the right. The morning sun coming up hard. "Could I sunbathe?" Nilla asks. Unsure of herself; he has never seen her this way, so hesitant, so abashed. Mexico has robbed her of her New York assurance. "Go ahead," Skein says. "Why not?" She drops her robe. Underneath she wears only a waist-strap; her heavy breasts look white and vulnerable in the tropic glare, and the small nipples are a faded pink. Skein sprays her with protective sealant and she sprawls out on the deck. *Los hermanos* stare hungrily and talk to each other in low rumbling tones. Not Spanish. Mayan, perhaps? The natives have never learned to adopt the tourists' casual nudity here. Nilla, obviously still uneasy, rolls over and lies face down. Her broad smooth back glistens.

Juan and Francisco yell. Skein follows their pointing fingers. Porpoises! A dozen of them, frisking around the bow, keeping just ahead of the boat, leaping high and slicing down into the blue water. Nilla gives a little cry of joy and rushes to the side to get a closer look. Throwing her arm self-consciously across her bare breasts. "You don't need to do that," Skein murmurs. She keeps herself covered. "How lovely they are," she says softly. Sebastián comes up beside them. "*Amigos*," he says. "They are. My friends." The cavorting porpoises eventually disappear. The boat bucks bouncily onward, keeping close to the island's beautiful empty palmy shore. Later they anchor, and he and Nilla swim masked, spying on the coral gardens. When they haul themselves on deck again it is almost noon. The sun is terrible. "Lunch?" Francisco asks. "We make you good lunch now?" Nilla laughs. She is no longer hiding her body. "I'm starved!" she cries.

"We make you good lunch," Francisco says, grinning, and he and Juan go over the side. In the shallow water they are clearly visible near the white sand of the bottom. They have spear-guns; they hold their breaths and prowl.

Too late Skein realizes what they are doing. Francisco hauls a fluttering spiny lobster out from behind a rock. Juan impales a huge pale crab. He grabs three conchs also, surfaces, dumps his prey on the deck. Francisco arrives with the lobster. Juan, below again, spears a second lobster. The animals are not dead; they crawl sadly in circles on the deck as they dry. Appalled, Skein turns to Sebastián and says, "Tell them to stop. We're not that hungry." Sebastián, preparing some kind of salad, smiles and shrugs. Francisco has brought up another crab, bigger than the first. "Enough," Skein says. *"Basta! Basta!"* Juan, dripping, tosses down three more conchs. "You pay us good," he says. "We give you good lunch." Skein shakes his head. The deck is becoming a slaughterhouse for ocean life. Sebastián now energetically splits conch shells, extracts the meat, drops it into a vast bowl to marinate in a yellow-green fluid. *"Basta!"* Skein yells. Is that the right word in Spanish? He knows it's right in Italian. *Los hermanos* look amused. The sea is full of life, they seem to be telling him. We give you good lunch. Suddenly Francisco erupts from the water, bearing something immense. A turtle! Forty, fifty pounds! The joke has gone too far. "No," Skein says. "Listen, I have to forbid this. Those turtles are almost extinct. Do you understand that? *Muerto. Perdido. Desaparecido.* I won't eat a turtle. Throw it back. Throw it back." Francisco smiles. He shakes his head. Deftly he binds the turtle's flippers with rope. Juan says, "Not for lunch, *señor*. For us. For to sell. *Mucho dinero.*" Skein can do nothing. Francisco and Sebastián have begun to hack up the crabs and lobsters. Juan slices peppers into the bowl where the conchs are marinating. Pieces of dead animals litter the deck. "Oh, I'm *starving*," Nilla says. Her waist-strap is off too, now. The turtle watches the whole scene, beady-eyed. Skein shudders. Auschwitz, he thinks. Buchenwald. For the animals it's Buchenwald every day.

Purple sand, blue-leaved trees. An orange sea gleaming not far to the west under a lemon sun. "It isn't much farther," the skull-faced man says. "You can make it. Step by step by step is how."

"I'm winded," Skein says. "Those hills—"

"I'm twice your age, and I'm doing fine."

"You're in better shape. I've been cooped up on space-ships for months and months."

"Just a short way on," says the skull-faced man. "About a hundred meters from the shore."

Skein struggles on. The heat is frightful. He has trouble getting a footing in the shifting sand. Twice he trips over black vines whose fleshy runners form a mat a few centimeters under the surface; loops of the vines stick up here and there. He even suffers a brief fugue, a seven-second flashback to a day in Jerusalem. Somewhere at the core of his mind he is amused by that: a flashback within a flash-forward. Encapsulated concentric hallucinations. When he comes out of it, he finds himself getting to his feet and brushing sand from his clothing. Ten steps onward the skull-faced man halts him and says, "There it is. Look there, in the pit."

Skein sees a funnel-shaped crater right in front of him, perhaps five meters in diameter at ground level and dwindling to about half that width at its bottom, some six or seven meters down. The pit strikes him as a series of perfect circles making up a truncated cone. Its sides are smooth and firm, almost glazed, and the sand has a brown tinge. In the pit, resting peacefully on the flat floor, is something that looks like a golden amoeba the size of a large cat. A row of round blue-black eyes crosses the hump of its back. From the perimeter of its body comes a soft green radiance.

"Go down to it," the skull-faced man says. "The force of its power falls off with the cube of the distance; from up here you can't feel it. Go down. Let it take you over. Fuse with it. Make communion, Skein, make communion!"

"And will it heal me? So that I'll function as I did before the trouble started?"

"If you let it heal you, it will. That's what it wants to do. It's a completely benign organism. It thrives on repairing broken souls. Let it into your head; let it find the damaged place. You can trust it. Go down."

Skein trembles on the edge of the pit. The creature below flows and eddies, becoming first long and narrow, then high and squat, then resuming its basically circular form. Its color deepens almost to scarlet, and its radiance shifts toward yellow. As if preening and stretching itself. It seems to be waiting for him. It seems eager. This is what he has sought so long, going from planet to wearying planet. The skull-faced man, the purple sand, the pit, the creature. Skein slips his sandals off. *What have I to lose?* He sits for a moment on the pit's rim; then he shimmies down, sliding part of the way, and lands softly, close beside the being that awaits him. And immediately feels its power.

He enters the huge desolate cavern that is the cathedral of Haghia Sophia. A few Turkish guides lounge hopefully against the vast marble pillars. Tourists shuffle about, reading to each other from cheap plastic guidebooks. A shaft of light enters from some improbable aperture and splinters against the Moslem pulpit. It seems to Skein that he hears the tolling of bells and feels incense prickling at his nostrils. But how can that be? No Christian rites have been performed here in a thousand years. A Turk looms before him. "Show you the mosyics?" he says. *Mosyics.* "Help you understand this marvelous building? A dollar. No? Maybe change money? A good rate. Dollars, marks, Eurocredits, what? You speak English? Show you the mosyics?" The Turk fades. The bells grow louder. A row of bowed priests in white silk robes files past the altar, chanting in—what? Greek? The ceiling is encrusted with gems. Gold plate gleams everywhere. Skein senses the terrible complexity of the cathedral, teeming now with life, a whole universe engulfed in this gloom, a thousand chapels packed with worshippers, long lines waiting to urinate in the crypts, a marketplace in the balcony, jeweled necklaces changing hands with low murmurs of negotiation, babies being born behind the alabaster sarcophagi, the bells tolling, dukes nodding to one another, clouds of incense swirling toward the dome, the figures in the mosaics alive, making the sign of the Cross, smiling, blowing kisses, the pillars moving now, becoming fat-middled as they bend from side to side, the entire colossal structure shifting and flowing and melting. And a ballet of Turks. "Show you the mosyics?" "Change money?" "Postcards? Souvenir of Istanbul?" A plump, pink American face: "You're John Skein, aren't you? The Communicator? We worked together on the big fusion-chamber merger in '53." Skein shakes his head. "It must be that you are mistaken," he says, speaking in Italian. "I am not he. Pardon. Pardon." And joins the line of chanting priests.

Purple sand, blue-leaved trees. An orange sea under a lemon sun. Looking out from the top deck of the terminal, an hour after landing, Skein sees a row of towering hotels rising along the nearby beach. At once he feels the wrongness: There should be no hotels. The right planet has no such towers; therefore this is another of the wrong ones.

He suffers from complete disorientation as he attempts to place himself in sequence. *Where am I?* Aboard a liner heading toward Abbondanza VI. *What do I see?* A world I have previously visited. *Which one?* The one with the hotels. The third out of seven, isn't it?

He has seen this planet before, in flashforwards. Long before he left Earth to begin his quest he glimpsed those hotels, that beach. Now he views it in flashback. That perplexes him. He must try to see himself as a moving point traveling through time, viewing the scenery now from this perspective, now from that.

He watches his earlier self at the terminal. Once it was his future self. How confusing, how needlessly muddling! "I'm looking for an old Earthman," he says. "He must be a hundred, hundred twenty years old. A face like a skull—no flesh at all, really. A brittle man. No? Well, can you tell me, does this planet have a life-form about this big, a kind of blob of golden jelly, that lives in pits down by the seashore, and—No? No? Ask someone else, you say? Of course. And perhaps a hotel room? As long as I've come all this way."

He is getting tired of finding the wrong planets. What folly this is, squandering his last savings on a quest for a world seen in a dream! He would have expected planets with purple sand and blue-leaved trees to be uncommon; but no, in an infinite universe one can find a dozen of everything, and now he has wasted almost half his money and close to a year, visiting two planets and this one and not finding what he seeks.

He goes to the hotel they arrange for him.

The beach is packed with sunbathers, most of them from Earth. Skein walks among them. "Look," he wants to say. "I have this trouble with my brain, an old injury, and it gives me these visions of myself in the past and future, and one of the visions I see is a place where there's a skull-faced man who takes me to a kind of amoeba in a pit that can heal me, do you follow? And it's a planet with purple sand and blue-leaved trees, just like this one, and I figure if I keep going long enough I'm bound to find it and the skull-face and the amoeba, do you follow me? And maybe this is the planet after all, only I'm in the wrong part of it. What should I do? What hope do you think I really have?" This is the third world. He knows that he must visit a number of wrong ones before he finds the right one. But how many? How many? And when will he know that he has the right one?

Standing silent on the beach, he feels confusion come over him, and drops into fugue, and is hurled to another world. Purple sand, blue-leaved trees. A fat, friendly Pingalorian consul. "A skull-faced man? No, I can't say I know of any." Which world is this, Skein wonders? One that I have already visited, or one that I have not yet come to? The manifold layers of illusion dazzle him. Past and future and present lie like a knot around his throat. Shifting planes of reality; intersecting films of event. Purple sand, blue-leaved trees. Which planet is this? Which one? Which one? He is back on the crowded beach. A lemon sun. An orange sea. He is back in his cabin on the space-liner. He sees a note in his own handwriting: *You are a passenger aboard a ship heading for Abbondanza VI, and will be landing in a few days.* So everything was a vision. Flashback? Flashforward? He is no longer able to tell. He is baffled by these identical worlds. Purple sand. Blue-leaved trees. He wishes he knew how to cry.

Instead of a client and a consultant for today's communion, Skein has a client and a client. A man and a woman, Michaels and Miss Schumpeter. The communion is of an unusually intimate kind. Michaels has been married six times, and several of the marriages apparently have been dissolved under bitter circumstances. Miss Schumpeter, a woman of some wealth, loves Michaels but doesn't entirely trust him; she wants a peep into his mind before she'll put her thumb to the marital cube. Skein will oblige. The fee has already been credited to his account. Let me not to the marriage of true minds admit impediments. If she does not like what she finds in her beloved's soul, there may not be any marriage, but Skein will have been paid.

A tendril of his mind goes to Michaels, now. A tendril to Miss Schumpeter. Skein opens his filters. "Now you'll meet for the first time," he tells them. Michaels flows to her. Miss Schumpeter flows to him. Skein is merely the conduit. Through him pass the ambitions, betrayals, failures, vanities, deteriorations, disputes, treacheries, lusts, generosities, shames, and follies of these two human beings. If he wishes, he can examine the most private sins of Miss Schumpeter and the darkest yearnings of her future husband. But he does not care. He sees such things every day. He takes no pleasure in spying on the psyches of these two. Would a surgeon grow excited over the sight of Miss Schumpeter's Fallopian tubes or Michaels' pancreas? Skein is merely doing his job. He is no voyeur, simply a Communicator. He looks upon himself as a public utility.

When he severs the contact, Miss Schumpeter and Michaels both are weeping.

"I love you!" she wails.

"Get away from me!" he mutters.

Purple sand. Blue-leaved trees. Oily orange sea.

The skull-faced man says, "Won't you ever come to see that causality is merely an illusion, Skein? The notion that there's a consecutive series of events is nothing but a fraud. We impose form on our lives, we talk of time's arrow, we say that there's a flow from A through G and Q to Z, we make believe everything is nicely linear. But it isn't, Skein. It isn't."

"So you keep telling me."

"I feel an obligation to awaken your mind to the truth. G can come before A, and Z before both of them. Most of us don't like to perceive it that way, so we arrange things in what seems like a more logical pattern, just as a novelist will put the motive before the murder and the murder before the arrest. But the universe isn't a novel. We can't make nature imitate art. It's all random, Skein, random, random!"

"Half a million?"

"Half a million."

"You know I don't have that kind of money."

"Let's not waste time, Mr. Coustakis. You have assets. Pledge them as collateral. Credit is easily obtained." Skein waits for the inventor to clear his loan. "Now we can proceed," he says, and tells his desk, "Get Nissenson into a receptive state."

Coustakis says, "First let me get it clear. This man will see everything that's in my mind? He'll get access to my secrets?"

"No. No. I filter the communion with great care. Nothing will pass from your mind to his except the nature of the problem you want him to tackle. Nothing will come back from his mind to yours except the answer."

"And if he doesn't have the answer?"

"He will."

"And if he goes into the transmission business for himself afterward?"

"He's bonded," Skein says curtly. "No chance of it. Let's go, now. Up and together."

"Skein? Skein? Skein? Skein?"

The wind is rising. The sand, blown aloft, stains the sky gray. Skein clambers from the pit and lies by its rim, breathing hard. The skull-faced man helps him get up.

Skein has seen this series of images hundreds of times.

"How do you feel?" the skull-faced man asks.

"Strange. Good. My head seems so clear!"

"You had communion down there?"

"Oh, yes. Yes."

"And?"

"I think I'm healed," Skein says in wonder. "My strength is back. Before, you know, I felt cut down to the bone, a minimum version of myself. And now. And now." He lets a tendril of consciousness slip forth. It meets the mind of the skull-faced man. Skein is aware of a glassy interface; he can touch the other mind, but he cannot enter it. "Are you a Communicator too?" Skein asks, awed.

"In a sense. I feel you touching me. You're better, aren't you?"

"Much. Much. Much."

"As I told you. Now you have your second chance, Skein. Your gift has been restored. Courtesy of our friend in the pit. They love being helpful."

"Skein? Skein? Skein? Skein?"

*We conceive of time either as flowing or as enduring.
The problem is how to reconcile these concepts. From a
purely formalistic point of view there exists no difficulty,
as these properties can be reconciled by means of the concept of a* duratio successiva. *Every unit of time measure
has this characteristic of a flowing permanence: an hour
streams by while it lasts and so long as it lasts. Its flowing
is thus identical with its duration. Time, from this point of
view, is transitory;* but its passing away lasts.

In the early months of his affliction he experienced a great
many scenes of flashforward while in fugue. He saw himself
outside the nineteenth-century mansion, he saw himself in a
dozen lawyers' offices, he saw himself in hotels, terminals,
spaceliners, he saw himself discussing the nature of time
with the skull-faced man, he saw himself trembling on the
edge of the pit, he saw himself emerging healed, he saw
himself wandering from world to world, looking for the
right one with purple sand and blue-leaved trees. As time
unfolded most of these flashforwards duly entered the flow of
the present; he *did* come to the mansion, he *did* go to those
hotels and terminals, he *did* wander those useless worlds.
Now, as he approaches Abbondanza VI, he goes through a
great many flashbacks and a relatively few flashforwards,
and the flashforwards seem to be limited to a fairly narrow
span of time, covering his landing on Abbondanza VI, his
first meeting with the skull-faced man, his journey to the pit,
and his emergence, healed, from the amoeba's lair. Never
anything beyond that final scene. He wonders if time is going
to run out for him on Abbondanza VI.

The ship lands on Abbondanza VI half a day ahead of
schedule. There are the usual decontamination procedures
to endure, and while they are going on Skein rests in his
cabin, counting minutes to liberty. He is curiously confident
that this will be the world on which he finds the skull-faced
man and the benign amoeba. Of course, he has felt that
way before, looking out from other spaceliners at other
planets of the proper coloration, and he has been wrong. But
the intensity of his confidence is something new. He is
sure that the end of his quest lies here.

"Debarkation beginning now," the loudspeakers say.

He joins the line of outgoing passengers. The others smile, embrace, whisper; they have found friends or even mates on this voyage. He remains apart. No one says goodbye to him. He emerges into a brightly lit terminal, a great cube of glass that looks like all the other terminals scattered across the thousands of worlds that man has reached. He could be in Chicago or Johannesburg or Beirut: The scene is one of porters, reservations clerks, customs officials, hotel agents, taxi drivers, guides. A blight of sameness spreading across the universe. Stumbling through the customs gate, Skein finds himself set upon. Does he want a taxi, a hotel room, a woman, a man, a guide, a homestead plot, a servant, a ticket to Abbondanza VII, a private car, an interpreter, a bank, a telephone? The hubbub jolts Skein into three consecutive ten-second fugues, all flashbacks: He sees a rainy day in Tierra del Fuego, he conducts a communion to help a maker of sky-spectacles perfect the plot of his latest extravaganza, and he puts his palm to a cube in order to dictate contract terms to Nicholas Coustakis. Then Coustakis fades, the terminal reappears, and Skein realizes that someone has seized him by the left arm just above the elbow. Bony fingers dig painfully into his flesh. It is the skull-faced man. "Come with me," he says. "I'll take you where you want to go."

"This isn't just another flashforward, is it?" Skein asks, as he has watched himself ask so many times in the past. "I mean, you're really here to get me."

The skull-faced man says, as Skein has heard him say so many times in the past, "No, this time it's no flashforward. I'm really here to get you."

"Thank God. Thank God. Thank God."

"Follow along this way. You have your passport handy?"

The familiar words. Skein is prepared to discover he is merely in fugue, and expects to drop back into frustrating reality at any moment. But no. The scene does not waver. It holds firm. It holds. At last he has caught up with this particular scene, overtaking it and enclosing it, pearl-like, in the folds of the present. He is on the way out of the terminal. The skull-faced man helps him through the formalities. How withered he is! How fiery the eyes, how gaunt the face! Those frightening orbits of bone jutting through the skin of the forehead. That parched cheek. Skein listens

for a dry rattle of ribs. One sturdy punch and there would
be nothing left but a cloud of white dust, slowly settling.

"I know your difficulty," the skull-faced man says. "You've
been caught in entropy's jaws. You're being devoured. The
injury to your mind—it's tipped you into a situation you
aren't able to handle. You *could* handle it, if you'd only
learn to adapt to the nature of the perceptions you're getting now. But you won't do that, will you? And you want
to be healed. Well, you can be healed here, all right. More
or less healed. I'll take you to the place."

"What do you mean, I could handle it if I'd only learn
to adapt?"

"Your injury has liberated you. It's shown you the truth
about time. But you refuse to see it."

"What truth?" Skein asks flatly.

"You still try to think that time flows neatly from alpha
to omega, from yesterday through today to tomorrow,"
the skull-faced man says as they walk slowly through the
terminal. "But it doesn't. The idea of the forward flow of
time is a deception we impose on ourselves in childhood.
An abstraction, agreed upon by common convention, to
make it easier for us to cope with phenomena. The truth
is that events are random, that chronological flow is only
our joint hallucination, that if time can be said to flow
at all, it flows in all 'directions' at once. Therefore—"

"Wait," Skein says. "How do you explain the laws of
thermodynamics? Entropy increases; available energy constantly diminishes; the universe heads toward ultimate stasis."

"Does it?"

"The second law of thermodynamics—"

"Is an abstraction," the skull-faced man says, "which unfortunately fails to correspond with the situation in the true
universe. It isn't a divine law. It's a mathematical hypothesis
developed by men who weren't able to perceive the real
situation. They did their best to account for the data within
a framework they could understand. Their laws are formu-
lations of probability, based on conditions that hold within
closed systems, and given the right closed system the second
law is useful and illuminating. But in the universe as a
whole it simply isn't true. There *is* no arrow of time. Entropy does *not* necessarily increase. Natural processes *can*
be reversible. Causes do *not* invariably precede effects. In

fact, the concepts of cause and effect are empty. There are neither causes nor effects, but only events, spontaneously generated, which we arrange in our minds in comprehensible patterns of sequence."

"No," Skein mutters. "This is insanity!"

"There are no patterns. Everything is random."

"No."

"Why not admit it? Your brain has been injured; what was destroyed was the center of temporal perception, the node that humans use to impose this unreal order on events. Your time filter has burned out. The past and the future are as accessible to you as the present, Skein: you can go where you like, you can watch events drifting past as they really do. Only you haven't been able to break up your old habits of thought. You still try to impose the conventional entropic order on things, even though you lack the mechanism to do it, now, and the conflict between what you perceive and what you think you perceive is driving you crazy. Eh?"

"How do you know so much about me?"

The skull-faced man chuckles. "I was injured in the same way as you. I was cut free from the time-line long ago, through the kind of overload you suffered. And I've had years to come to terms with the new reality. I was as terrified as you were, at first. But now I understand. I move about freely. I know things, Skein." A rasping laugh. "You need rest, though. A room, a bed. Time to think things over. Come. There's no rush now. You're on the right planet; you'll be all right soon."

Further, the association of entropy increase with time's arrow is in no sense circular; rather, it tells us something both about what will happen to natural systems in time, and about what the time order must be for a series of states of a system. Thus, we may often establish a time order among a set of events by use of the time-entropy association, free from any reference to clocks and magnitudes of time intervals from the present. In actual judgments of before-after we frequently do this on the basis of our experience (even though without any explicit knowledge of the law of entropy increase): we know, for example, that for iron in air the state of pure metal must have been be-

fore that of a rusted surface, or that the clothes will be dry after, not before, they have hung in the hot sun.

A tense, humid night of thunder and temporal storms. Lying alone in his oversized hotel room, five kilometers from the purple shore, Skein suffers fiercely from fugue.

"Listen, I have to forbid this. Those turtles are almost extinct. Do you understand that? *Muerto. Perdido. Desaparecido.* I won't eat a turtle. Throw it back. Throw it back."

"I'm happy to say your second go-round has been approved, Mr. Skein. Not that there was ever any doubt. A long and happy new life to you, sir."

"Go down to it. The force of its power falls off with the cube of the distance; from up here you can't feel it. Go down. Let it take you over. Fuse with it. Make communion, Skein, make communion!"

"Show you the mosyics? Help you understand this marvelous building? A dollar. No? Maybe change money? A good rate."

"First let me get it clear. This man will see everything that's in my mind? He'll get access to my secrets?"

"I love you."
"Get away from me!"

"Won't you ever come to see that causality is merely an illusion, Skein? The notion that there's a consecutive series of events is nothing but a fraud. We impose form on our lives, we talk of time's arrow, we say that there's a flow from A through G and Q to Z, we make believe everything is nicely linear. But it isn't, Skein. It isn't."

Breakfast on a leafy veranda. Morning light out of the west, making the trees glow with an ultramarine glitter. The skull-faced man joins him. Skein secretly searches the parched face. Is everything an illusion? Perhaps *he* is an illusion.

They walk toward the sea. Well before noon they reach the shore. The skull-faced man points to the south, and they follow the coast; it is often a difficult hike, for in places the sand is washed out and they must detour inland, scrambling over quartzy cliffs. The monstrous old man is indefatigable. When they pause to rest, squatting on a timeless purple strand made smooth by the recent tide, the debate about time resumes, and Skein hears words that have been echoing in his skull for four years and more. It is as though everything up till now has been a rehearsal for a play, and now at last he has taken the stage.

"Won't you ever come to see that causality is merely an illusion, Skein?"

"I feel an obligation to awaken your mind to the truth."

"Time is an ocean, and events come drifting to us as randomly as dead animals on the waves."

Skein offers all the proper cues.

"I won't accept that! It's a demonic, chaotic, nihilistic theory."

"You can say that after all you've experienced?"

"I'll go on saying it. What I've been going through is a mental illness. Maybe I'm deranged, but the universe isn't."

"Contrary. You've only recently become sane and started to see things as they really are. The trouble is that you don't want to admit the evidence you've begun to perceive. Your filters are down, Skein! You've shaken free of the illusion of linearity! Now's your chance to show your resilience. Learn to live with the real reality. Stop this silly business of imposing an artificial order on the flow of time. Why *should* effect follow cause? Why *shouldn't* the seed follow the tree? Why must you persist in holding tight to a useless, outworn, contemptible system of false evaluations of experience when you've managed to break free of the——"

"Stop it! Stop it! Stop it! Stop it!"

By early afternoon they are many kilometers from the hotel, still keeping as close to the shore as they can. The terrain is uneven and divided, with rugged fingers of rock running almost to the water's edge, and Skein finds the journey even more exhausting than it had seemed in his visions of it. Several times he stops, panting, and has to be urged to go on.

"It isn't much farther," the skull-faced man says. "You can make it. Step by step is how."

"I'm winded. Those hills——"

"I'm twice your age, and I'm doing fine."

"You're in better shape. I've been cooped up on space-ships for months and months."

"Just a short way on," says the skull-faced man. "About a hundred meters from the shore."

Skein struggles on. The heat is frightful. He trips in the sand; he is blinded by sweat; he has a momentary flash-back fugue. "There it is," the skull-faced man says, finally. "Look there, in the pit."

Skein beholds the conical crater. He sees the golden amoeba.

"Go down to it," the skull-faced man says. "The force of its power falls off with the cube of the distance; from up here you can't feel it. Go down. Let it take you over. Fuse with it. Make communion, Skein, make communion!"

"And will it heal me? So that I'll function as I did before the trouble started?"

"If you let it heal you, it will. That's what it wants to do. It's a completely benign organism. It thrives on repairing broken souls. Let it into your head; let it find the damaged place. You can trust it. Go down."

Skein trembles on the edge of the pit. The creature below flows and eddies, becoming first long and narrow, then high and squat, then resuming its basically circular form. Its color deepens almost to scarlet, and its radiance shifts toward yellow. As if preening and stretching itself. It seems to be waiting for him. It seems eager. This is what he has sought so long, going from planet to wearying planet. The skull-faced man, the purple sand, the pit, the creature. Skein slips his sandals off. *What have I to lose?* He sits for a moment on the pit's rim; then he shimmies down, sliding part of the way, and lands softly, close beside the being that awaits him. And immediately feels its power. Something brushes against his brain. The sensation reminds him of the training sessions of his first go-round, when the in-structors were showing him how to develop his gift. The

fingers probing his consciousness. Go on, enter, he tells
them. I'm open. I'm open. And he finds himself in contact with the being of the pit. Wordless. A two-way flow
of unintelligible images is the only communon; shapes drift
from and into his mind. The universe blurs. He is no longer
sure where the center of his ego lies. He has thought of
his brain as a sphere with himself at its center, but now
it seems extended, elliptical, and an ellipse has no center,
only a pair of foci, here and here, one focus in his own
skull and one—where?—within that fleshy amoeba. And
suddenly he is looking at himself through the amoeba's eyes.
The large biped with the bony body. How strange, how grotesque! Yet it suffers. Yet it must be helped. It is injured.
It is broken. We go to it with all our love. We will heal.
And Skein feels something flowing over the bare folds and
fissures of his brain. But he can no longer remember whether
he is the human or the alien, the bony one or the bone-
less. Their identities have mingled. He goes through fugues
by the scores, seeing yesterdays and tomorrows, and everything is formless and without content; he is unable to recognize himself or to understand the words being spoken.
It does not matter. All is random. All is illusion. Release
the knot of pain you clutch within you. Accept. Accept.
Accept. Accept.

He accepts.

He releases.

He merges.

He casts away the shreds of ego, the constricting exo-
skeleton of self, and placidly permits the necessary adjust-
ments to be made.

*The possibility, however, of genuine thermodynamic en-
tropy decrease for an isolated system—no matter how rare
—does raise an objection to the definition of time's direction in terms of entropy. If a large, isolated system did
by chance go through an entropy decrease as one state
evolved from another, we would have to say that time
"went backward" if our definition of time's arrow were
basically in terms of entropy increase. But with an ultimate
definition of the forward direction of time in terms of the
actual occurrence of states, and measured time intervals
from the present, we can readily accommodate the entropy*

decrease; it would become merely a rare anomaly in the
physical processes of the natural world.

The wind is rising. The sand, blown aloft, stains the sky
gray. Skein clambers from the pit and lies by its rim,
breathing hard. The skull-faced man helps him get up.

Skein has seen this series of images hundreds of times.

"How do you feel?" the skull-faced man asks.

"Strange. Good. My head seems so clear!"

"You had communion down there?"

"Oh, yes. Yes."

"And?"

"I think I'm healed," Skein says in wonder. "My strength
is back. Before, you know, I felt cut down to the bone,
a minimum version of myself. And now. And now." He
lets a tendril of consciousness slip forth. It meets the mind
of the skull-faced man. Skein is aware of a glassy interface; he can touch the other mind, but he cannot enter
it. "Are you a Communicator too?" Skein asks, awed.

"In a sense. I feel you touching me. You're better, aren't
you?"

"Much. Much. Much."

"As I told you. Now you have your second chance, Skein.
Your gift has been restored. Courtesy of our friend in the
pit. They love being helpful."

"What shall I do now? Where shall I go?"

"Anything. Anywhere. Anywhen. You're free to move
along the time-line as you please. In a state of controlled,
directed fugue, so to speak. After all, if time is random, if
there is no rigid sequence of events—"

"Yes."

"Then why not choose the sequence that appeals to you?
Why stick to the set of abstractions your former self has
handed you? You're a free man, Skein. Go. Enjoy. Undo
your past. Edit it. Improve on it. It isn't your past, any
more than this is your present. It's all one, Skein, all *one*.
Pick the segment you prefer."

He tests the truth of the skull-faced man's words. Cautiously Skein steps three minutes into the past and sees himself struggling up out of the pit. He slides four minutes
into the future and sees the skull-faced man, alone, trudging

northward along the shore. Everything flows. All is fluidity. He is free. He is free.

"You see, Skein?"

"Now I do," Skein says. He is out of entropy's jaws. He is time's master, which is to say he is his own master. He can move at will. He can defy the imaginary forces of determinism. Suddenly he realizes what he must do now. He will assert his free will; he will challenge entropy on its home ground. Skein smiles. He cuts free of the time-line and floats into what others would call the past.

"Get Nissenson into a receptive state," he orders his desk.

Coustakis, blinking rapidly, obviously uneasy, says, "First let me get it clear. This man will see everything that's in my mind? He'll get access to my secrets?"

"No. No. I filter the communion with great care. Nothing will pass from your mind to his except the nature of the problem you want him to tackle. Nothing will come back from his mind to yours except the answer."

"And if he doesn't have the answer?"

"He will."

"And if he goes into the transmission business for himself afterward?" Coustakis asks.

"He's bonded," Skein says curtly. "No chance of it. Let's go, now. Up and together."

The desk reports that Nissenson, half the world away in São Paulo, is ready. Quickly Skein throws Coustakis into the receptive condition, and swings around to face the brilliant lights of his data-access units. Here is the moment when he can halt the transaction. Turn again, Skein. Face Coustakis, smile sadly, inform him that the communion will be impossible. Give him back his money, send him off to break some other Communicator's mind. And live on, whole and happy, ever after. It was at this point, visiting this scene endlessly in his fugues, that Skein silently and hopelessly cried out to himself to stop. Now it is within his power, for this is no fugue, no illusion of time-shift. He has shifted. He is here, carrying with him the knowledge of all that is to come, and he is the only Skein on the scene, the operative Skein. Get up, now. Refuse the contract.

He does not. Thus he defies entropy. Thus he breaks the chain.

He peers into the sparkling, shifting little blazes until they kindle his gift, jabbing at the electrical rhythms of his brain until he is lifted into the energy level that permits the opening of a communion. He starts to go up. He reaches forth one tendril of his mind and engages Nissenson. With another tendril he snares Coustakis. Steadily, now, he draws the two tendrils together. He is aware of the risks, but believes he can surmount them.

The tendrils meet.

Out of Coustakis' mind flows a description of the matter transmitter and a clear statement of the beam-spread problem; Skein shoves it along to Nissenson, who begins to work on a solution. The combined strength of the two minds is great, but Skein deftly lets the excess charge bleed away, and maintains the communion with no particular effort, holding Coustakis and Nissenson together while they deal with their technical matters. Skein pays little attention as their excited minds rush toward answers. *If you. Yes, and then. But if. I see, yes. I could. And. However, maybe I should. I like that. It leads to. Of course. The inevitable result. Is it feasible, though? I think so. You might have to. I could. Yes. I could. I could.*

"I thank you a million times," Coustakis says to Skein. "It was all so simple, once we saw how we ought to look at it. I don't begrudge your fee at all. Not at all."

Coustakis leaves, glowing with delight. Skein, relieved, tells his desk, "I'm going to allow myself a three-day holiday. Fix the schedule to move everybody up accordingly."

He smiles. He strides across his office, turning up the amplifiers, treating himself to the magnificent view. The nightmare undone. The past revised. The burnout avoided. All it took was confidence. Enlightenment. A proper understanding of the processes involved.

He feels the sudden swooping sensations of incipient temporal fugue. Before he can intervene to regain control, he swings off into darkness and arrives instantaneously on a planet of purple sand and blue-leaved trees. Orange waves lap at the shore. He stands a few meters from a deep conical pit. Peering into it, he sees an amoebalike creature lying beside a human figure; strands of the alien's jellylike substance are wound around the man's body. He recognizes the man to be John Skein. The communion in the pit ends; the man begins to clamber from the pit. The wind is rising. The sand, blown aloft, stains the sky gray. Patiently he watches his younger self struggling up from the pit. Now he understands. The circuit is closed; the knot is tied; the identity loop is complete. He is destined to spend many years on Abbondanza VI, growing ancient and withered. He is the skull-faced man.

Skein reaches the rim of the pit and lies there, breathing hard. He helps Skein get up.

"How do you feel?" he asks.

THE SLICED-CROSSWISE ONLY-ON-TUESDAY WORLD

Philip José Farmer

Phil Farmer wields one of the most flamboyant and joyous imaginations in science fiction. Consider the question of overpopulation, for instance: Assuming there's really no way to reduce the number of people sharing our spaceship Earth, might there not be some way we could each have some elbow room anyway? Farmer has come up with an answer, one that could work at least as easily as the programs now being proposed to deal with the problem. Of course, his answer could also pose new problems. . . .

Getting into Wednesday was almost impossible. Tom Pym had thought about living on other days of the week. Almost everybody with any imagination did. There were even TV shows speculating on this. Tom Pym had even acted in two of these. But he had no genuine desire to move out of his own world. Then his house burned down.

This was on the last day of the eight days of spring. He awoke to look out the door at the ashes and the firemen. A man in a white asbestos suit motioned for him to stay inside. After fifteen minutes, another man in a suit gestured that it was safe. He pressed the button by the door, and it swung open. He sank down in the ashes to his ankles; they were a trifle warm under the inch-thick coat of water-soaked crust.

There was no need to ask what had happened, but he did anyway.

The fireman said, "A short-circuit, I suppose. Actually, we don't know. It started shortly after midnight, between the time that Monday quit and we took over."

Tom Pym thought that it must be strange to be a fireman or a policeman. Their hours were so different, even though they were still limited by the walls of midnight.

By then the others were stepping out of their stoners or "coffins" as they were often called. That left sixty still occupied.

They were due for work at 08:00. The problem of getting new clothes and a place to live would have to be put off until off-hours, because the TV studio where they worked was behind in the big special it was due to put on in 144 days.

They ate breakfast at an emergency center. Tom Pym asked a grip if he knew of any place he could stay. Though the government would find one for him, it might not look very hard for a convenient place.

The grip told him about a house only six blocks from his former house. A makeup man had died, and as far as he knew the vacancy had not been filled. Tom got onto the phone at once, since he wasn't needed at that moment, but the office wouldn't be open until ten, as the recording informed him. The recording was a very pretty girl with red hair, tourmaline eyes, and a very sexy voice. Tom would have been more impressed if he had not known her. She had played in some small parts in two of his shows, and the maddening voice was not hers. Neither was the color of her eyes.

At noon he called again, got through after a ten-minute wait, and asked Mrs. Bellefield if she would put through a request for him. Mrs. Bellefield reprimanded him for not having phoned sooner; she was not sure that anything could be done today. He tried to tell her his circumstances and then gave up. Bureaucrats! That evening he went to a public emergency place, slept for the required four hours while the inductive fields speeded up his dreaming, woke up, and got into the upright cylinder of eternium. He stood for ten seconds, gazing out through the transparent door at other cylinders with their still figures, and then he pressed the button. Approximately fifteen seconds later he became unconscious.

He had to spend three more nights in the public stoner. Three days of fall were gone; only five left. Not that that mattered in California so much. When he had lived in Chicago, winter was like a white blanket being shaken by a madwoman. Spring was a green explosion. Summer was a bright roar and a hot breath. Fall was the topple of a drunken jester in garish motley.

The fourth day, he received notice that he could move into the very house he had picked. This surprised and pleased him. He knew of a dozen who had spent a whole year—forty-eight days or so—in a public station while waiting. He moved in the fifth day, with three days of spring to enjoy. But he would have to use up his two days off to shop for clothes, bring in groceries and other goods, and get acquainted with his housemates. Sometimes he wished he had not been born with the compulsion to act. TV'ers worked five days at a stretch, sometimes six, while a plumber, for instance, only put in three days out of seven.

The house was as large as the other, and the six extra blocks to walk would be good for him. It held eight people per day, counting himself. He moved in that evening, introduced himself, and got Mabel Curta, who worked as a secretary for a producer, to fill him in on the household routine. After he made sure that his stoner had been moved into the stoner room, he could relax somewhat.

Mabel Curta had accompanied him into the stoner room, since she had appointed herself his guide. She was a short, overly curved woman of about thirty-five (Tuesday time). She had been divorced three times, and marriage was no more for her unless, of course, Mr. Right came along. Tom was between marriages himself, but he did not tell her so.

"We'll take a look at your bedroom," Mabel said. "It's small but it's soundproofed, thank God."

He started after her, then stopped. She looked back through the doorway and said, "What is it?"

"This girl . . ."

There were sixty-three of the tall gray eternium cylinders.

He was looking through the door of the nearest at the girl within.

"Wow! Really beautiful!"

If Mabel felt any jealousy, she suppressed it.

"Yes, isn't she!"

The girl had long, black, slightly curly hair, a face that could have launched him a thousand times times a thousand times, a figure that had enough but not too much, and long legs. Her eyes were open; in the dim light they looked a purplish-blue. She wore a thin silvery dress.

The plate by the top of the door gave her vital data. Jennie Marlowe. Born 2031 A.D., San Marino, California. She would be twenty-four years old. Actress. Unmarried. Wednesday's child.

"What's the matter?" Mabel said.

"Nothing."

How could he tell her that he felt sick in his stomach from a desire that could never be satisfied? Sick from beauty?

> For will in us is over-ruled by fate.
> Who ever loved, that loved not at first sight?

"What?" Mabel said, and then, after laughing, "You must be kidding?"

She wasn't angry. She realized that Jennie Marlowe was no more competition than if she were dead. She was right. Better for him to busy himself with the living of this world. Mabel wasn't too bad; cuddly, really, and, after a few drinks, rather stimulating.

They went downstairs afterward after 18:00 to the TV room. Most of the others were there, too. Some had their ear plugs in; some were looking at the screen but talking. The newscast was on, of course. Everybody was filling up on what had happened last Tuesday and today. The Speaker of the House was retiring after his term was up. His days of usefulness were over, and his recent ill health showed no signs of disappearing. There was a shot of the family graveyard in Mississippi with the pedestal reserved for him. When science someday learned how to rejuvenate, he would come out of stonerment.

"That'll be the day!" Mabel said. She squirmed on his lap.

"Oh, I think they'll crack it," he said. "They're already on the track; they've succeeded in stopping the aging of rabbits."

"I don't mean that," she said. "Sure, they'll find out how to rejuvenate people. But then what? You think they're going to bring them all back? With all the people they got now, and then they'll double, maybe triple, maybe quadruple the population? You think they won't just leave them standing out there?" She giggled, and said, "What would the pigeons do without them?"

He squeezed her waist. At the same time, he had a vision of himself squeezing *that* girl's waist. Hers would be soft enough but with no hint of fat.

Forget about her. Think of now. Watch the news.

A Mrs. Wilder had stabbed her husband and then herself with a kitchen knife. Both had been stonered immediately after the police arrived, and they had been taken to the hospital. An investigation of a work slowdown in the county government offices was taking place. The complaints were that Monday's people were not setting up the computers for Tuesday's. The case was being referred to the proper authorities of both days. The Ganymede base reported that the Great Red Spot of Jupiter was emitting weak but definite pulses that did not seem to be random.

The last five minutes of the program was a precis devoted to outstanding events of the other days. Mrs. Cuthmar, the housemother, turned the channel to a situation comedy with no protests from anybody.

Tom left the room, after telling Mabel that he was going to bed early—alone, and to sleep. He had a hard day tomorrow.

He tiptoed down the hall and the stairs and into the stoner room. The lights were soft, there were many shadows, and it was quiet. The sixty-three cylinders were like ancient granite columns of an underground chamber of a buried city. Fifty-five faces were white blurs behind the clear metal. Some had their eyes open; most had closed them while waiting for the field radiated from the machine in the base. He looked through Jennie Marlowe's door. He felt sick again. Out of his reach; never for him. Wednesday was only a day away. No, it was only a little less than four and a half hours away.

He touched the door. It was slick and only a little cold. She stared at him. Her right forearm was bent to hold the strap of a large purse. When the door opened, she would step out, ready to go. Some people took their showers and fixed their faces as soon as they got up from their sleep and then went directly into the stoner. When the field was automatically radiated at 05:00, they stepped out a minute later, ready for the day.

He would like to step out of his "coffin," too, at the same time.

But he was barred by Wednesday.

He turned away. He was acting like a sixteen-year-old kid. He had been sixteen about one hundred and six years ago, not that that made any difference. Physiologically, he was thirty.

As he started up to the second floor, he almost turned around and went back for another look. But he took himself by his neck-collar and pulled himself up to his room. There he decided he would get to sleep at once. Perhaps he would dream about her. If dreams were wish-fulfillments, they would bring her to him. It still had not been "proved" that dreams always expressed wishes, but it had been proved that man deprived of dreaming did go mad. And so the somniums radiated a field that put man into a state in which he got all the sleep, and all the dreams, that he needed within a four-hour period. Then he was awakened and a little later went into the stoner where the field suspended all atomic and subatomic activity. He would remain in that state forever unless the activating field came on.

He slept, and Jennie Marlowe did not come to him. Or, if she did, he did not remember. He awoke, washed his face, went down eagerly to the stoner, where he found the entire household standing around, getting in one last smoke, talking, laughing. Then they would step into their cylinders, and a silence like that at the heart of a mountain would fall.

He had often wondered what would happen if he did not go into the stoner. How would he feel? Would he be panicked? All his life, he had known only Tuesdays. Would

Wednesday rush at him, roaring, like a tidal wave? Pick him up and hurl him against the reefs of a strange time?

What if he made some excuse and went back upstairs and did not go back down until the field had come on? By then, he could not enter. The door to his cylinder would not open again until the proper time. He could still run down to the public emergency stoners only three blocks away. But if he stayed in his room, waiting for Wednesday?

Such things happened. If the breaker of the law did not have a reasonable excuse, he was put on trial. It was a felony second only to murder to "break time," and the unexcused were stonered. All felons, sane or insane, were stonered. Or *mañanaed*, as some said. The *mañanaed* criminal waited in immobility and unconsciousness, preserved unharmed until science had techniques to cure the insane, the neurotic, the criminal, the sick. *Mañana*.

"What was it like in Wednesday?" Tom had asked a man who had been unavoidably left behind because of an accident.

"How would I know? I was knocked out except for about fifteen minutes. I was in the same city, and I had never seen the faces of the ambulance men, of course, but then I've never seen them here. They stonered me and left me in the hospital for Tuesday to take care of."

He must have it bad, he thought. Bad. Even to think of such a thing was crazy. Getting into Wednesday was almost impossible. Almost. But it could be done. It would take time and patience, but it could be done.

He stood in front of his stoner for a moment. The others said, "See you! So long! Next Tuesday!" Mabel called, "Good night, lover!"

"Good night," he muttered.

"What?" she shouted.

"Good night!"

He glanced at the beautiful face behind the door. Then he smiled. He had been afraid that she might hear him say good night to a woman who called him lover.

He had ten minutes left. The intercom alarms were whooping. Get going, everybody! Time to take the six-day trip! Run! Remember the penalties!

He remembered, but he wanted to leave a message. The recorder was on a table. He activated it and said, "Dear

Miss Jennie Marlowe. My name is Tom Pym, and my stoner is next to yours. I am an actor, too; in fact, I work at the same studio as you. I know this is presumptuous of me, but I have never seen anybody so beautiful. Do you have a talent to match your beauty? I would like to see some run-offs of yours shows. Would you please leave some in room five? I'm sure the occupant won't mind. Yours, Tom Pym."

He ran it back. It was certainly bald enough, and that might be just what was needed. Too flowery or too pressing would have made her leery. He had commented on her beauty twice but not overstressed it. And the appeal to her pride in her acting would be difficult to resist. Nobody knew better than he about that.

He whistled a little on his way to the cylinder. Inside, he pressed the button and looked at his watch. Five minutes to midnight. The light on the huge screen above the computer in the police station would not be flashing for him. Ten minutes from now, Wednesday's police would step out of their stoners in the precinct station, and they would take over their duties.

There was a ten-minute hiatus between the two days in the police station. All hell could break loose in these few minutes and it sometimes did. But a price had to be paid to maintain the walls of time.

He opened his eyes. His knees sagged a little and his head bent. The activation was a million microseconds fast —from eternium to flesh and blood almost instantaneously, and the heart never knew that it had been stopped for such a long time. Even so, there was a little delay in the muscles' response to a standing position.

He pressed the button, opened the door, and it was as if his button had launched the day. Mabel had made herself up last night so that she looked dawn-fresh. He complimented her and she smiled happily. But he told her he would meet her for breakfast. Halfway up the staircase he stopped, and waited until the hall was empty. Then he sneaked back down and into the stoner room. He turned on the recorder.

A voice, husky but also melodious, said, "Dear Mister Pym. I've had a few messages from other days. It was fun to talk back and forth across the abyss between the worlds, if you don't mind my exaggerating a little. But there is really no sense in it, once the novelty has worn off. If you become interested in the other person, you're frustrating yourself. That person can only be a voice in a recorder and a cold waxy face in a metal coffin. I wax poetic. Pardon me. If the person doesn't interest you, why continue to communicate? There is no sense in either case. And I *may* be beautiful. Anyway, I thank you for the compliment, but I am also sensible.

"I should have just not bothered to reply. But I want to be nice; I didn't want to hurt your feelings. So please don't leave any more messages."

He waited while silence was played. Maybe she was pausing for effect. Now would come a chuckle or a low honey-throated laugh, and she would say, "However, I don't like to disappoint my public. The run-offs are in your room."

The silence stretched out. He turned off the machine and went to the dining room for breakfast.

Siesta time at work was from 14:40 to 14:45. He lay down on the bunk and pressed the button. Within a minute he was asleep. He did dream of Jennie this time; she was a white shimmering figure solidifying out of the darkness and floating toward him. She was even more beautiful than she had been in her stoner.

The shooting ran overtime that afternoon, so that he got home just in time for supper. Even the studio would not dare keep a man past his supper hour, especially since the studio was authorized to serve food only at noon.

He had time to look at Jennie for a minute before Mrs. Cuthmar's voice screeched over the intercom. As he walked down the hall, he thought, "I'm getting barnacled on her. It's ridiculous. I'm a grown man. Maybe . . . maybe I should see a psycher."

Sure, make your petition, and wait until a psycher has time for you. Say about three hundred days from now, if you are lucky. And if the psycher doesn't work out for you, then petition for another, and wait six hundred days.

Petition. He slowed down. Petition. What about a request, not to see a psycher, but to move? Why not? What did he have to lose? It would probably be turned down, but he could at least try.

Even obtaining a form for the request was not easy. He spent two nonwork days standing in line at the Center

City Bureau before he got the proper forms. The first time, he was handed the wrong form and had to start all over again. There was no line set aside for those who wanted to change their days. There were not enough who wished to do this to justify such a line. So he had had to queue up before the Miscellaneous Office counter of the Mobility Section of the Vital Exchange Department of the Interchange and Cross Transfer Bureau. None of these titles had anything to do with emigration to another day.

When he got his form the second time, he refused to move from the office window until he had checked the number of the form and asked the clerk to double-check it. He ignored the cries and the mutterings behind him. Then he went to one side of the vast room and stood in line before the punch machines. After two hours, he got to sit down at a small rolltop desk-shaped machine, above which was a large screen. He inserted the form into the slot, looked at the projection of the form, and punched buttons to mark the proper spaces opposite the proper questions. After that, all he had to do was to drop the form into a slot and hope it did not get lost. Or hope he would not have to go through the same procedure because he had improperly punched the form.

That evening, he put his head against the hard metal and murmured to the rigid face behind the door, "I must really love you to go through all this. And you don't even know it. And worse, if you did, you might not care one bit."

To prove to himself that he had kept his gray stuff, he went out with Mabel that evening to a party given by Sol Voremwolf, a producer. Voremwolf had just passed a civil service examination giving him an A-13 rating. This meant that, in time, with some luck and the proper pull, he would become an executive vice-president of the studio.

The party was a qualified success. Tom and Mabel returned about half an hour before stoner time. Tom had managed to refrain from too many blowminds and liquor, so he was not tempted by Mabel. Even so, he knew that when he became unstonered he would be half-loaded and he'd have to take some dreadful counter-actives. He would look and feel like hell at work, since he had missed his sleep.

He put Mabel off with an excuse and went down to the stoner room ahead of the others. Not that that would do him any good if he wanted to get stonered early. The stoners only activated within narrow time limits.

He leaned against the cylinder and patted the door. "I tried not to think about you all evening. I wanted to be fair to Mabel; it's not fair to go out with her and think about you all the time."

All's fair in love . . .

He left another message for her, then wiped it out. What was the use? Besides, he knew that his speech was a little thick. He wanted to appear at his best for her.

Why should he? What did she care for him?

The answer was, he did care, and there was no reason or logic connected with it. He loved this forbidden, untouchable, far-away-in-time, yet-so-near woman.

Mabel had come in silently. She said, "You're sick!"

Tom jumped away. Now why had he done that? He had nothing to be ashamed of. Then why was he so angry with her? His embarrassment was understandable but his anger was not.

Mabel laughed at him, and he was glad. Now he could snarl at her. He did so, and she turned away and walked out. But she was back in a few minutes with the others. It would soon be midnight.

By then he was standing inside the cylinder. A few seconds later he left it, pushed Jennie's backward on its wheels, and pushed his around so that it faced hers. He went back in, pressed the button, and stood there. The double doors only slightly distorted his view. But she seemed even more removed in distance, in time, and in unattainability.

Three days later, well into winter, he received a letter. The box inside the entrance hall buzzed just as he entered the front door. He went back and waited until the letter was printed and had dropped out from the slot. It was the reply to his request to move to Wednesday.

Denied. Reason: He had no reasonable reason to move.

That was true. But he could not give his real motive. It would have been even less impressive than the one he had given. He had punched the box opposite No. 12. REASON:

TO GET INTO AN ENVIRONMENT WHERE MY TALENTS WILL
BE MORE LIKELY TO BE ENCOURAGED.

He cursed and he raged. It was his human, his civil right
to move into any day he pleased. That is, it should be his
right. What if a move did cause much effort? What if it
required a transfer of his I.D. and all the records connected with him from the moment of his birth? What if . . . ?

He could rage all he wanted to, but it would not change
a thing. He was stuck in the world of Tuesday.

Not yet, he muttered. Not yet. Fortunately, there is no
limit to the number of requests I can make in my own
day. I'll send out another. They think they can wear me
out, huh? Well, I'll wear them out. Man against the machine. Man against the system. Man against the bureaucracy
and the hard cold rules.

Winter's twenty days had sped by. Spring's eight days
rocketed by. It was summer again. On the second day of
the twelve days of summer, he received a reply to his second
request.

It was neither a denial nor an acceptance. It stated that if
he thought he would be better off psychologically in Wednesday because his astrologer said so, then he would have to
get a psycher's critique of the astrologer's analysis. Tom
Pym jumped into the air and clicked his sandaled heels
together. Thank God that he lived in an age that did not
classify astrologers as charlatans! The people—the masses
—had protested that astrology was a necessity and that
it should be legalized and honored. So laws were passed,
and because of that, Tom Pym had a chance.

He went down to the stoner room and kissed the door
of the cylinder and told Jennie Marlowe the good news. She
did not respond, though he thought he saw her eyes
brighten just a little. That was, of course, only his imagination, but he liked his imagination.

Getting a psycher for a consultation and getting through
the three sessions took another year, another forty-eight
days. Doctor Sigmund Traurig was a friend of Doctor Stelhela, the astrologer, and so that made things easier for
Tom.

"I've studied Doctor Stelhela's chart carefully and analyzed carefully your obsession for this woman," he said. "I
agree with Doctor Stelhela that you will always be unhappy

in Tuesday, but I don't quite agree with him that you will be happier in Wednesday. However, you have this thing going for this Miss Marlowe, so I think you should go to Wednesday. But only if you sign papers agreeing to see a psycher there for extended therapy."

Only later did Tom Pym realize that Doctor Traurig might have wanted to get rid of him because he had too many patients. But that was an uncharitable thought.

He had to wait while the proper papers were transmitted to Wednesday's authorities. His battle was only half-won. The other officials could turn him down. And if he did get to his goal, then what? She could reject him without giving him a second chance.

It was unthinkable, but she could.

He caressed the door and then pressed his lips against it. "Pygmalion could at least touch Galatea," he said. "Surely, the gods—the big dumb bureaucrats—will take pity on me, who can't even touch you. Surely."

The psycher had said that he was incapable of a true and lasting bond with a woman, as so many men were in this world of easy-come-easy-go liaisons. He had fallen in love with Jennie Marlowe for several reasons. She may have resembled somebody he had loved when he was very young. His mother, perhaps? No? Well, never mind. He would find out in Wednesday—perhaps. The deep, the important, truth was that he loved Miss Marlowe because she could never reject him, kick him out, or become tiresome, complain, weep, yell, insult, and so forth. He loved her because she was unattainable and silent.

"I love her as Achilles must have loved Helen when he saw her on top of the walls of Troy," Tom said.

"I wasn't aware that Achilles was ever in love with Helen of Troy," Doctor Traurig said drily.

"Homer never said so, but I *know* that he must have been! Who could see her and *not* love her?"

"How the hell would I know? I never saw her! If I had suspected these delusions would intensify . . ."

"I am a poet!" Tom said.

"Overimaginative, you mean! Hmmm. She must be a douser! I don't have anything particular to do this evening. I'll tell you what . . . my curiosity is aroused . . . I'll come down to your place tonight and take a look at this fabulous beauty, your Helen of Troy."

Doctor Traurig appeared immediately after supper, and Tom Pym ushered him down the hall and into the stoner room at the rear of the big house as if he were a guide conducting a famous critic to a just-discovered Rembrandt.

The doctor stood for a long time in front of the cylinder. He hmmmed several times and checked her vital-data plate several times. Then he turned and said, "I see what you mean, Mr. Pym. Very well. I'll give the go-ahead."

"Ain't she something?" Tom said on the porch. "She's out of this world, literally and figuratively, of course."

"Very beautiful. But I believe that you are facing a great disappointment, perhaps heartbreak, perhaps, who knows, even madness, much as I hate to use that unscientific term."

"I'll take the chance," Tom said. "I know I sound nuts, but where would we be if it weren't for nuts? Look at the man who invented the wheel, at Columbus, at James Watt, at the Wright brothers, at Pasteur, you name them."

"You can scarcely compare these pioneers of science with their passion for truth with you and your desire to marry a woman. But, as I have observed, she is strikingly beautiful. Still, that makes me exceedingly cautious. Why isn't she married? What's wrong with her?"

"For all I know, she may have been married a dozen times!" Tom said. "The point is, she isn't now! Maybe she's disappointed and she's sworn to wait until the right man comes along. Maybe . . ."

"There's no maybe about it; you're neurotic," Traurig said. "But I actually believe that it would be more dangerous for you *not* to go to Wednesday than it would be *to* go."

"Then you'll say yes!" Tom said, grabbing the doctor's hand and shaking it.

"Perhaps. I have some doubts."

The doctor had a faraway look. Tom laughed and released the hand and slapped the doctor on the shoulder. "Admit it! You were really struck by her! You'd have to be dead not to!"

"She's all right," the doctor said. "But you must think this over. If you do go there and she turns you down, you might go off the deep end, much as I hate to use such a poetical term."

"No, I won't. I wouldn't be a bit the worse off. Better off, in fact. I'll at least get to see her in the flesh."

Spring and summer zipped by. Then, a morning he would never forget, the letter of acceptance. With it, instructions on how to get to Wednesday. These were simple enough. He was to make sure that the technicians came to his stoner sometime during the day and readjusted the timer within the base. He could not figure out why he could not just stay out of the stoner and let Wednesday catch up to him, but by now he was past trying to fathom the bureaucratic mind.

He did not intend to tell anyone at the house, mainly because of Mabel. But Mabel found out from someone at the studio. She wept when she saw him at supper time, and she ran upstairs to her room. He felt badly, but he did not follow to console her.

That evening, his heart beating hard, he opened the door to his stoner. The others had found out by then; he had been unable to keep the business to himself. Actually, he was glad that he had told them. They seemed happy for him, and they brought in drinks and had many rounds of toasts. Finally Mabel came downstairs, wiping her eyes, and she said she wished him luck, too. She had known that he was not really in love with her. But she did wish someone would fall in love with her just by looking inside her stoner.

When she found out that he had gone to see Doctor Traurig, she said, "He's a very influential man. Sol Voremwolf had him for his analyst. He says he's even got influence on other days. He edits the *Psyche Crosscurrents*, you know, one of the few periodicals read by other people."

Other, of course, meant those who lived in Wednesdays through Mondays.

Tom said he was glad he had gotten Traurig. Perhaps he had used his influence to get the Wednesday authorities to push through his request so swiftly. The walls between the worlds were seldom broken, but it was suspected that the very influential did it when they pleased.

Now, quivering, he stood before Jennie's cylinder again.

The last time, he thought, that I'll see her stonered. Next time, she'll be warm, colorful, touchable flesh.

"*Ave atque vale!*" he said aloud. The others cheered. Mabel said, "How corny!" They thought he was addressing them, and perhaps he had included them.

He stepped inside the cylinder, closed the door, and pressed the button. He would keep his eyes open, so that . . .

And today was Wednesday. Though the view was exactly the same, it was like being on Mars.

He pushed open the door and stepped out. The seven people had faces he knew and names he had read on their plates. But he did not know them.

He started to say hello, and then he stopped.

Jennie Marlowe's cylinder was gone.

He seized the nearest man by the arm.

"Where's Jennie Marlowe?"

"Let go. You're hurting me. She's gone. To Tuesday."

"*Tuesday! Tuesday?*"

"Sure. She'd been trying to get out of here for a long time. She had something about this day being unlucky for her. She was unhappy, that's for sure. Just two days ago, she said her application had finally been accepted. Apparently, some Tuesday psycher had used his influence. He came down and saw her in her stoner and that was it, brother."

The walls and the people and the stoners seemed to be distorted. Time was bending itself this way and that. He wasn't in Wednesday; he wasn't in Tuesday. He wasn't in *any* day. He was stuck inside himself at some crazy date that should never have existed.

"She can't do that!"

"Oh, no! She just did that!"

"But . . . you can't transfer more than once!"

"That's her problem."

It was his, too.

"I should never have brought him down to look at her!" Tom said. "The swine! The unethical swine!"

Tom Pym stood there for a long time, and then he went into the kitchen. It was the same environment, if you discounted the people. Later, he went to the studio and got a part in a situation play which was, really, just like all those in Tuesday. He watched the newscaster that night.

The President of the U.S.A. had a different name and face, but the words of his speech could have been those of Tuesday's President. He was introduced to a secretary of a producer; her name wasn't Mabel, but it might as well have been.

The difference here was that Jennie was gone, and oh, what a world of difference it made to him.

A MEETING WITH MEDUSA

Arthur C. Clarke

> When science fiction people fall to classifying sf writers into this school and that, one of the basic dividing lines is between the science-oriented writers (Hal Clement, Larry Niven) and those more concerned with the aesthetics of the human condition (Ray Bradbury, Theodore Sturgeon). Like all dividing lines, though, this one wanders, and there are writers who contrive to work both sides of the line. Foremost among these is Arthur C. Clarke, whose abiding delight in the wonders of science never overrides his fascination with humanity. Here is a fine example of Clarke writing in vivid detail about a probe into Jupiter . . . and about the man who makes that probe.

A DAY TO REMEMBER

The Queen Elizabeth was five kilometers above the Grand Canyon, dawdling along at a comfortable 180, when Howard Falcon spotted the camera platform closing in from the right. He had been expecting it—nothing else was cleared to fly at this altitude—but he was not too happy to have company. Although he welcomed any signs of public interest, he also wanted as much empty sky as he could get. After all, he was the first man in history to navigate a ship half a kilometer long.

So far, this first test flight had gone perfectly; ironically enough, the only problem had been the century-old aircraft carrier Chairman Mao, borrowed from the San Diego naval museum for support operations. Only one of Mao's four nuclear reactors was still operating, and the old battlewagon's top speed was barely 30 knots. Luckily, wind speed at sea level had been less than half this, so it had not been too difficult to maintain still air on the flight deck. Though there had been a few anxious moments during gusts, when the mooring lines had been dropped, the great dirigible had risen smoothly, straight up into the sky, as if on an invisible elevator. If all went well, Queen Elizabeth IV would not meet Chairman Mao for another week.

Everything was under control; all test instruments gave normal readings. Commander Falcon decided to go upstairs and watch the rendezvous. He handed over to his second officer and walked out into the transparent tubeway that led through the heart of the ship. There, as always, he was overwhelmed by the spectacle of the largest space ever enclosed by man.

The ten spherical gas cells, each more than 100 meters across, were ranged one behind the other like a line of gigantic soap bubbles. The tough plastic was so clear that he could see through the whole length of the array and make out details of the elevator mechanism almost half a kilometer from his vantage point. All around him, like a three-dimensional maze, was the structural framework of the ship—the great longitudinal girders running from nose to tail, the 15 hoops that were the ribs of this skyborne colossus, whose varying sizes defined its graceful, streamlined profile.

At this low speed, there was very little sound—merely the soft rush of wind over the envelope and an occasional creak of metal as the pattern of stresses changed. The shadowless light from the rows of lamps far overhead gave the whole scene a curiously submarine quality, and to Falcon this was enhanced by the spectacle of translucent gasbags. He had once encountered a squadron of large but harmless jellyfish, pulsing their mindless way above a shallow tropical reef, and the plastic bubbles that gave

Queen Elizabeth her lift often reminded him of these—especially when changing pressures made them crinkle and scatter new patterns of light.

He walked 50 meters down the axis of the ship, until he came to the forward elevator, between gas cells one and two. Riding up to the observation deck, he noticed that it was uncomfortably hot and dictated a brief memo to himself on his pocket recorder. The Queen obtained almost a quarter of her buoyancy from the unlimited amounts of waste heat produced by her fusion power plant; on this lightly loaded flight, indeed, only six of the ten gas cells contained helium and the remaining four were full of air; yet she still carried 200 tons of water as ballast. However, running the cells at high temperatures did produce problems in refrigerating the accessways; it was obvious that a little more work would have to be done here.

A refreshing blast of cooler air hit him in the face when he stepped out onto the observation deck and into the dazzling sunlight streaming through the Plexiglas roof. Half a dozen workmen, with an equal number of superchimp assistants, were busily laying the partly completed dance floor, while others were installing electric wiring and fixing furniture. It was a scene of controlled chaos, and Falcon found it hard to believe that everything would be ready for the maiden voyage, only four weeks ahead. Well, that was not *his* problem, thank goodness. He was merely the captain, not the cruise director.

The human workers waved to him and the simps flashed toothy smiles as he walked through the confusion into the already completed sky lounge. This was his favorite place in the whole ship, and he knew that once she was operating, he would never again have it all to himself. He would allow himself just five minutes of private enjoyment.

He called the bridge, checked that everything was still in order, and relaxed into one of the comfortable swivel chairs. Below, in a curve that delighted the eye, was the unbroken silver sweep of the ship's envelope. He was perched at the highest point, surveying the whole immensity of the largest vehicle ever built. And when he had tired of *that* —all the way out to the horizon was the fantastic wilderness carved by the Colorado River in half a billion years of time.

Apart from the camera platform (it had now fallen back and was filming from amidships), he had the sky to himself. It was blue and empty, clear down to the horizon. In his grandfather's day, Falcon knew, it would have been streaked with vapor trails and stained with smoke. Both had gone; the aerial garbage had vanished with the primitive technologies that spawned it, and the long-distance transportation of this age arced too far beyond the stratosphere for any sight or sound of it to reach Earth. Once again, the lower atmosphere belonged to the birds and the clouds—and now to Queen Elizabeth IV.

It was true, as the old pioneers had said at the beginning of the 20th Century; this was the only way to travel—in silence and luxury, breathing the air around you and not cut off from it, near enough to the surface to watch the ever-changing beauty of land and sea. The subsonic jets of the 1980s, packed with hundreds of passengers seated ten abreast, could not even begin to match such comfort and spaciousness.

Of course, the Q. E. would never be an economic proposition; and even if her projected sister ships were built, only a few of the world's quarter of a billion inhabitants would ever enjoy this silent gliding through the sky. But a secure and prosperous global society could afford such follies and, indeed, needed them for its novelty and entertainment. There were at least 1,000,000 men on Earth whose discretionary income exceeded 1000 new dollars a year, so the Queen would not lack for passengers.

Falcon's pocket communicator beeped; the copilot was calling from the bridge.

"OK for rendezvous, Captain? We've got all the data we need from this run, and the TV people are getting impatient."

Falcon glanced at the camera platform, now matching his speed a quarter of a kilometer away.

"OK," he replied. "Proceed as arranged. I'll watch from here."

He walked back through the busy chaos of the observation deck, so that he could have a better view amidships. As he did so, he could feel the change of vibration underfoot; by the time he had reached the rear of the lounge, the ship had come to rest. Using his master key, he let himself out onto the small external platform flaring from the end of the deck; half a dozen people could stand there, with only low guardrails separating them from the vast sweep of the envelope—and from the ground, thousands of meters below. It was an exciting place to be and perfectly safe even when the ship was traveling at speed, for it was in the dead air behind the huge dorsal blister of the observation deck. Nevertheless, it was not intended that the passengers would have access to it; the view was a little too vertiginous.

The covers of the forward cargo hatch had already opened like giant trap doors, and the camera platform was hovering above them, preparing to descend. Along this route, in the years to come, would travel thousands of passengers and tons of supplies; only on rare occasions would the Queen drop down to sea level and dock with her floating base.

A sudden gust of crosswind slapped Falcon's cheek and he tightened his grip on the guardrail. The Grand Canyon was a bad place for turbulence, though he did not expect much at this altitude. Without any real anxiety, he focused his attention on the descending platform, now about 50 meters above the ship. He knew that the highly skilled operator who was flying the remotely controlled vehicle had performed this very simple maneuver a dozen times already; it was inconceivable that he would have any difficulties.

Yet he seemed to be reacting rather sluggishly; that last gust had drifted the platform almost to the edge of the open hatchway. Surely the pilot could have corrected before this . . . did he have a control problem? It was very unlikely; these remotes had multiple-redundancy, fail-safe take-overs and any number of backup systems. Accidents were almost unheard of.

But there he went again, off to the left. Could the pilot be *drunk?* Improbable though that seemed, Falcon considered it seriously for a moment. Then he reached for his microphone switch.

Once again, without warning, he was slapped violently in the face. He hardly felt it, for he was staring in horror at the camera platform. The distant operator was fighting for control, trying to balance the craft on its jets—but he was only making matters worse. The oscillations increased—20 degrees, 40, 60, 90. . . .

"Switch to automatic, you fool!" Falcon shouted uselessly into his microphone. "Your manual control's not working!"

The platform flipped over onto its back; the jets no longer supported it but drove it swiftly downward. They had suddenly become allies of the gravity they had fought until this moment.

Falcon never heard the crash, though he felt it; he was already inside the observation deck, racing for the elevator that would take him down to the bridge. Workmen shouted at him anxiously, asking what had happened. It would be many months before he knew the answer to that question.

Just as he was stepping into the elevator cage, he changed his mind. What if there were a power failure? Better be on the safe side, even if it took longer and time was of the essence. He began to run down the spiral stairway enclosing the shaft.

Halfway down, he paused for a second to inspect the damage. That damned platform had gone clear through the ship, rupturing two of the gas cells as it did so. They were still collapsing slowly, in great falling veils of plastic. He was not worried about the loss of lift—the ballast could easily take care of that, as long as eight cells remained intact. Far more serious was the possibility of structural damage; already he could hear the great latticework around him groaning and protesting under its abnormal loads. It was not enough to have sufficient lift; unless it was properly distributed, the ship would break her back.

He was just resuming his descent when a superchimp, shrieking with fright, came racing down the elevator shaft, moving with incredible speed hand over hand along the *outside* of the latticework. In its terror, the poor beast had torn off its company uniform, perhaps in an unconscious attempt to regain the freedom of its ancestors.

Falcon, still descending as swiftly as he could, watched its approach with some alarm; a distraught simp was a powerful and potentially dangerous animal, especially if fear overcame its conditioning. As it overtook him, it started to call out a string of words, but they were all jumbled together, and the only one he could recognize was a plaintive, frequently repeated "Boss." Even now, Falcon realized, it looked toward humans for guidance; he felt sorry for the creature, involved in a man-made disaster beyond its comprehension and for which it bore no responsibility.

It stopped opposite him, on the other side of the lattice; there was nothing to prevent it from coming through the open framework if it wished. Now its face was only inches from his and he was looking straight into the terrified eyes. Never before had he been so close to a simp and able to study its features in such detail; he felt that strange mingling of kinship and discomfort that all men experience when they gaze thus into the mirror of time.

His presence seemed to have calmed the creature; Falcon pointed up the shaft, back toward the observation deck, and said very clearly and precisely: "Boss—boss—*go.*" To his relief, the simp understood; it gave him a grimace that might have been a smile and at once started to race back the way it had come. Falcon had given it the best advice he could; if any safety remained aboard the Queen, it was in that direction. But his duty lay in the other.

He had almost completed his descent when, with a sound of rending metal, the vessel pitched nose down and the lights went out. But he could still see quite well, for a shaft of sunlight streamed through the open hatch and the huge tear in the envelope. Many years ago, he had stood in a great cathedral nave, watching the light pouring through the stained-glass windows and forming pools of multicolored radiance on the ancient flagstones. The dazzling shaft of sunlight through the ruined fabric high above reminded him of that moment. He was in a cathedral of metal, falling down the sky.

When he reached the bridge and was able for the first time to look outside, he was horrified to see how close the ship was to the ground. Only 1000 meters below were the beautiful and deadly pinnacles of rock and the red rivers of mud that were still carving their way down into the past. There was no level area anywhere in sight where a ship as large as the Queen could come to rest on an even keel.

A glance at the display board told him that all the ballast had gone. However, rate of descent had been reduced to a few meters a second; they still had a fighting chance.

Without a word, Falcon eased himself into the pilot's seat and took over such control as remained. The instrument board showed him everything he wished to know;

speech was superfluous. In the background, he could hear the communications officer giving a running report over the radio. By this time, all the news channels of Earth would have been preempted, and he could imagine the utter frustration of the program controllers. One of the most spectacular wrecks in history was occurring—without a single camera to record it. The last moments of the Queen would never fill millions with awe and terror, as had those of the Hindenburg a century and a half before.

Now the ground was only half a kilometer away, still coming up slowly. Though he had full thrust, he had not dared use it, lest the weakened structure collapse; but now he realized that he had no choice. The wind was taking them toward a fork in the canyon, where the river was split by a wedge of rock, like the prow of some gigantic, fossilized ship of stone. If she continued on her present course, the Queen would straddle that triangular plateau and come to rest with at least a third of her length jutting out over nothingness; she would snap like a rotten stick.

From far away, above the sound of straining metal and escaping gas, came the familiar whistle of the jets as Falcon opened up the lateral thrusters. The ship staggered and began to slew to port. The shriek of tearing metal was now almost continuous—and the rate of descent had started to increase ominously. A glance at the damage-control board showed that cell number five had just gone.

The ground was only meters away; even now, he could not tell whether his maneuver would succeed or fail. He switched the thrust vectors over to vertical, giving maximum lift to reduce the force of impact.

The crash seemed to last forever. It was not violent—merely prolonged and irresistible. It seemed that the whole universe was falling about them.

The sound of crunching metal came nearer, as if some great beast were eating its way through the dying ship.

Then floor and ceiling closed upon him like a vise.

"BECAUSE IT'S THERE"

"Why do you want to go to Jupiter?"

"As Springer said when he lifted for Pluto—because it's there."

"Thanks. Now we've got *that* out of the way—the real reason." Howard Falcon smiled, though only those who knew him well could have interpreted the slight, leathery grimace. Webster was one of them; for more than 20 years, they had been involved in each other's projects. They had shared triumphs and disasters—including the greatest disaster of all.

"Well, Springer's cliché is still valid. We've landed on all the terrestrial planets but none of the gas giants. They are the only real challenge left in the Solar System."

"An expensive one. Have you worked out the cost?"

"As well as I can; here are the estimates. But remember —this isn't a one-shot mission but a transportation system. Once it's proved out, it can be used over and over again. And it will open up not merely Jupiter but *all* the giants."

Webster looked at the figures and whistled.

"Why not start with an easier planet—Uranus, for example? Half the gravity and less than half the escape velocity. Quieter weather, too—if that's the right word for it."

Webster had certainly done his homework. But that, of course, was why he was head of Long Range Planning.

"There's very little saving, when you allow for the extra distance and the logistics problems. For Jupiter, we can use the facilities on Ganymede. Beyond Saturn, we'd have to establish a new supply base."

Logical, thought Webster; but he was sure that it was not the important reason. Jupiter was lord of the Solar System; Falcon would be interested in no lesser challenge.

"Besides," Falcon continued, "Jupiter is a major scientific scandal. It's more than a hundred years since its radio storms were discovered, but we still don't know what causes them —and the Great Red Spot is as big a mystery as ever. That's why I can get matching funds from the Bureau of Astronautics. Do you know how many probes they have dropped into that atmosphere?"

"A couple of hundred, I believe."

"*Three* hundred and twenty-six, over the past fifty years— about a quarter of them total failures. Of course, they've learned a hell of a lot, but they've barely scratched the planet. Do you realize how *big* it is?"

"More than ten times the size of Earth."

"Yes, yes—but do you know what that really means?" Falcon pointed to the large globe in the corner of Webster's office.

"Look at India—how small it seems. Well, if you skinned Earth and spread it out on the surface of Jupiter, it would look about as big as India does here."

There was a long silence while Webster contemplated the equation: Jupiter is to Earth as Earth is to India. Falcon had —deliberately, of course—chosen the best possible example. . . .

Was it already ten years ago? Yes, it must have been. The crash lay seven years in the past (*that* date was engraved on his heart) and those initial tests had taken place three years before the first and last flight of the Queen Elizabeth.

Ten years ago, then, Commander (no, Lieutenant) Falcon had invited him to a preview—a three-day drift across the northern plains of India, within sight of the Himalayas. "Perfectly safe," he had promised. "It will get you away from the office—and will teach you what this whole thing is about."

Webster had not been disappointed. Next to his first journey to the Moon, it had been the most memorable experience of his life. And yet, as Falcon had assured him, it had been perfectly safe and quite uneventful.

They had taken off from Srinagar just before dawn, with the huge silver bubble of the balloon already catching the first light of the Sun. The ascent had been made in total silence; there were none of the roaring propane burners that had lifted the hot-air balloons of an earlier age. All the heat they needed came from the little pulsed-fusion reactor, weighing only 100 kilograms, hanging in the open mouth of the envelope. While they were climbing, its laser was zapping ten times a second, igniting the merest whiff of deuterium fuel; once they had reached altitude, it would fire only a few times a minute, making up for the heat lost through the great gasbag overhead.

And so, even while they were a kilometer above the ground, they could hear dogs barking, people shouting, bells ringing. Slowly the vast, Sun-smitten landscape expanded around them; two hours later, they had leveled out at five kilometers and were taking frequent draughts of oxygen. They could relax and admire the scenery; the on-board instrumentation was doing all the work—gathering the information that would be required by the designers of the still-unnamed liner of the skies.

It was a perfect day; the southwest monsoon would not break for another month, and there was hardly a cloud in the sky. Time seemed to have come to a stop; they resented the hourly radio reports that interrupted their reverie. And all around, to the horizon and far beyond, was that infinite, ancient landscape drenched with history—a patchwork of villages, fields, temples, lakes, irrigation canals.

With a real effort, Webster broke the hypnotic spell of that ten-year-old memory. It had converted him to lighter-than-air flight—and it had made him realize the enormous size of India, even in a world that could be circled within 90 minutes. And yet, he repeated to himself, Jupiter is to Earth as Earth is to India.

"Granted your argument," he said, "and supposing the funds are available, there's another question you have to answer. Why should you do better than the—what is it—three hundred and twenty-six robot probes that have already made the trip?"

"I am better qualified than they were—as an observer and as a pilot. *Especially* as a pilot; don't forget—I've more experience of lighter-than-air flight than anyone in the world."

"You could still serve as controller and sit safely on Ganymede."

"But that's just the point! They've already done that. Don't you remember what killed the Queen?"

Webster knew perfectly well, but he merely answered, "Go on."

"Time lag—*time lag!* That idiot of a platform controller thought he was using a local radio circuit. But he'd been accidentally switched through a satellite—oh, maybe it wasn't his fault, but he should have noticed. That's a half-second time lag for the round trip. Even then it wouldn't have mattered, flying in calm air. It was the turbulence over the Grand Canyon that did it. When the platform tipped and he corrected for that—it had already tipped the other way. Ever tried to drive a car over a bumpy road with a half-second delay in the steering?"

"No, and I don't intend to try. But I can imagine it."

"Well, Ganymede is more than a million kilometers from Jupiter. That means a round-trip delay of six seconds. No, you need a controller on the spot—to handle emergencies in real time. Let me show you something. Mind if I use this?"

"Go ahead."

Falcon picked up a postcard that was lying on Webster's desk; they were almost obsolete on Earth, but this one showed a 3-D view of a Martian landscape and was decorated with exotic and expensive stamps. He held it so that it dangled vertically.

"This is an old trick, but it helps make my point. Place your thumb and finger on either side, not quite touching. That's right."

Webster put out his hand, almost but not quite gripping the card.

"Now catch it."

Falcon waited for a few seconds; then, without warning, he let go of the card. Webster's thumb and fingers closed on empty air.

"I'll do it again, just to show there's no deception. You see?"

Once again, the falling card slipped through Webster's fingers.

"Now you try it on me."

This time, Webster grasped the card and dropped it without warning. It had scarcely moved before Falcon had caught it; Webster almost imagined he could hear a click, so swift was the other's reaction.

"When they put me together again," Falcon remarked in an expressionless voice, "the surgeons made some improvements. This is one of them—and there are others. I want to make the most of them. Jupiter is the place where I can do it."

Webster stared for long seconds at the fallen card, absorbing the improbable colors of the Trivium Charontis Escarpment. Then he said quietly, "I understand. How long do you think it will take?"

"With your help, plus the bureau, plus all the science

foundations we can drag in—oh, three years. Then a year for trials—we'll have to send in at least two test models. So with luck—five years."

"That's about what I thought. I hope you get your luck; you've earned it. But there's one thing I won't do."

"What's that?"

"Next time you go ballooning, don't expect *me* as passenger."

THE WORLD OF THE GODS

The fall from Jupiter V to Jupiter itself takes only three and a half hours; few men could have slept on so awesome a journey. Sleep was a weakness that Howard Falcon hated, and the little he still required brought dreams that time had not yet been able to exorcise. But he could expect no rest in the three days that lay ahead and must seize what he could during the long fall down into that ocean of clouds, 100,000 kilometers below.

As soon as Kon-Tiki had entered her transfer orbit and all the computer checks were satisfactory, he prepared for the last sleep he might ever know. It seemed appropriate that at almost the same moment Jupiter eclipsed the bright and tiny Sun, he swept into the monstrous shadow of the planet. For a few minutes a strange, golden twilight enveloped the ship; then a quarter of the sky became an utterly black hole in space, while the rest was a blaze of stars. No matter how far one traveled across the Solar System, *they* never changed; these same constellations now shone on Earth, half a billion kilometers away. The only novelties here were the small pale crescents of Callisto and Ganymede; doubtless there were a dozen other moons up there in the sky, but they were all much too tiny and too distant for the unaided eye to pick them out.

"Closing down for two hours," he reported to the mother ship, hanging 1000 kilometers above the desolate rocks of Jupiter V, in the radiation shadow of the tiny satellite. If it never served any other useful purpose, Jupiter V was a cosmic bulldozer perpetually sweeping up the charged particles that made it unhealthy to linger close to Jupiter. Its wake was almost free of radiation, and here a ship could park in perfect safety while death sleeted invisibly all around.

Falcon switched on the sleep inducer and consciousness faded swiftly out as the electric pulses surged gently through his brain. While Kon-Tiki fell toward Jupiter, gaining speed second by second in that enormous gravitational field, he slept without dreams. They always came when he awoke; and he had brought his nightmares with him from Earth.

Yet he never dreamed of the crash itself, though he often found himself again face to face with that terrified superchimp, as he descended the spiral stairway between the collapsing gasbags. None of the simps had survived; those that were not killed outright were so badly injured that they had been painlessly euthed. He sometimes wondered why he dreamed only of this doomed creature, which he had never met before the last minutes of its life—and not of the friends and colleagues he had lost aboard the dying Queen.

The dreams he feared most always began with his first return to consciousness. There had been little physical pain; in fact, there had been no sensation of any kind. He was in darkness and silence and did not even seem to be breathing. And—strangest of all—he could not locate his limbs. He could move neither his hands nor his feet, because he did not know where they were.

The silence had been the first to yield. After hours or days, he had become aware of a faint throbbing, and eventually, after long thought, he deduced that this was the beating of his own heart. That was the first of his many mistakes.

Then there had been faint pinpricks, sparkles of light, ghosts of pressures upon still unresponsive limbs. One by one his senses had returned, and pain had come with them. He had had to learn everything anew, recapitulating babyhood and infancy. Though his memory was unaffected and he could understand words that were spoken to him, it was months before he was able to answer except by the flicker of an eyelid. He could still remember the moments of triumph when he had spoken the first word, turned the page of a book—and, finally, learned to move under his own power. *That* was a victory, indeed, and it had taken him almost two years to prepare for it. A hundred times he had envied that dead superchimp, but *he* had been given no choice. The doctors had made their decision—and now, 12 years later, he was where no human being had ever traveled before and moving faster than any man in history.

Kon-Tiki was just emerging from shadow, and the Jovian dawn bridged the sky ahead in a titanic bow of light, when the persistent buzz of the alarm dragged Falcon up from sleep. The inevitable nightmares (he had been trying to summon a nurse but did not even have the strength to push the button) swiftly faded from consciousness; the greatest—and perhaps last—adventure of his life was before him.

He called Mission Control, now 100,000 kilometers away and falling swiftly below the curve of Jupiter, to report that everything was in order. His velocity had just passed 50 kilometers a second (*that* was one for the books) and in half an hour, Kon-Tiki would hit the outer fringes of the atmosphere, as he started on the most difficult entry in the entire Solar System. Although scores of probes had survived this flaming ordeal, they had been tough, solidly packed masses of instrumentation, able to withstand several hundred gravities of drag. Kon-Tiki would hit peaks of 30 *g* and would average more than ten before she came to rest in the upper reaches of the Jovian atmosphere. Very carefully and thoroughly, Falcon began to attach the elaborate system of restraints that anchored him to the walls of the cabin. When he had finished, he was virtually a part of the ship's structure.

The clock was counting backward; 100 seconds to entry. For better or worse, he was committed. In a minute and a half, he would graze the Jovian atmosphere and would be caught irrevocably in the grip of the giant.

The countdown was three seconds late—not at all bad, considering the unknowns involved. Beyond the walls of the capsule came a ghostly sighing that rose steadily to a high-pitched, screaming roar. The noise was quite different from that of a re-entry on Earth or Mars; in this thin atmosphere of hydrogen and helium, all sounds were transformed a couple of octaves higher. On Jupiter, even thunder would have falsetto overtones.

With the rising scream came also mounting weight; within seconds he was completely immobilized. His field of vision contracted until it embraced only the clock and the accelerometer; 15 *g*, and 480 seconds to go.

He never lost consciousness; but then, he had not expected to. Kon-Tiki's trail through the Jovian atmosphere must be really spectacular—by this time, thousands of kilometers long. Five hundred seconds after entry, the drag began to taper off: ten *g*, five *g*, two. . . . Then weight vanished almost completely; he was falling free, all his enormous orbital velocity destroyed.

There was a sudden jolt as the incandescent remnants of the heat shield were jettisoned. It had done its work and would not be needed again; Jupiter could have it now. He released all but two of the restraining buckles and waited for the automatic sequencer to start the next and most critical series of events.

He did not see the first drogue parachute pop out, but he could feel the slight jerk, and the rate of fall diminished immediately. Kon-Tiki had lost all her horizontal speed and was going straight down at 1000 kilometers an hour. Everything depended on the next 60 seconds.

There went the second drogue. He looked up through the overhead window and saw, to his immense relief, that clouds of glittering foil were billowing out behind the falling ship. Like a great flower unfurling, the thousands of cubic meters of the balloon spread out across the sky, scooping up the thin gas until it was fully inflated. Kon-Tiki's rate of fall dropped to a few kilometers an hour and remained constant. Now there was plenty of time; it would take him days to fall all the way down to the surface of Jupiter.

But he would get there eventually, if he did nothing about it; the balloon overhead was merely acting as an efficient parachute. It was providing no lift, nor could it do so while the gas inside and out was the same.

With its characteristic and rather disconcerting crack, the fusion reactor started up, pouring torrents of heat into the envelope overhead. Within five minutes, the rate of fall had become zero; within six, the ship had started to rise. According to the radar altimeter, it had leveled out at 430 kilometers above the surface—or whatever passed for a surface on Jupiter.

Only one kind of balloon will work in an atmosphere of hydrogen, which is the lightest of all gases—and that is a hot-hydrogen balloon. As long as the fusor kept ticking over, Falcon could remain aloft, drifting across a world that could hold a hundred Pacifics. After traveling more than half a billion kilometers, Kon-Tiki had at last begun to justify her name. She was an aerial raft, adrift upon the currents of the Jovian atmosphere.

Though a whole new world was lying around him, it was more than an hour before Falcon could examine the view. First he had to check all the capsule's systems and test its response to the controls. He had to learn how much extra heat was necessary to produce a desired rate of ascent and how much gas he must vent in order to descend. Above all, there was the question of stability. He must adjust the length of the cables attaching his capsule to the huge, pear-shaped balloon, to damp out vibrations and get the smoothest possible ride. So far, he was lucky; at this level, the wind was steady and the Doppler reading on the invisible surface gave him a ground speed of 350 kilometers an hour. For Jupiter, that was modest; winds of up to 1000 had been observed. But mere speed, of course, was unimportant; the real danger was turbulence. If he ran into that, only skill and experience and swift reaction could save him—and these were not matters that could yet be programmed into a computer.

Not until he was satisfied that he had got the feel of this strange craft did Falcon pay any attention to Mission Control's pleadings. Then he deployed the booms carrying the instrumentation and the atmospheric samplers; the capsule now resembled a rather untidy Christmas tree but still rode smoothly down the Jovian winds, while it radioed up its torrents of information to the recorders on the ship 100,000 kilometers above. And now, at last, he could look around.

His first impression was unexpected and even a little disappointing. As far as the scale of things was concerned, he might have been ballooning over an ordinary cloudscape on Earth. The horizon seemed at a normal distance; there was no feeling at all that he was on a world 11 times the diameter of his own. Then he looked at the infrared radar, sounding the layers of atmosphere beneath him—and knew how badly his eyes had been deceived.

That layer of clouds, apparently five kilometers away, was really 60 kilometers below. And the horizon, whose distance he would have guessed at 200, was actually 3000 kilometers from the ship.

The crystalline clarity of the hydrohelium atmosphere and the enormous curvature of the planet had fooled him completely. It was even harder to judge distances here than on the Moon; everything he saw must be multiplied by ten.

It was a simple matter and he should have been prepared for it. Yet somehow it disturbed him profoundly. He did not feel that Jupiter was huge but that *he* had shrunk— to a tenth of his normal size. Perhaps, with time, he would grow accustomed to the inhuman scale of this world; yet as he stared toward that unbelievably distant horizon, he felt as if a wind colder than the atmosphere around him was blowing through his soul. Despite all his arguments, this might never be a place for man. He could well be both the first and the last to descend through the clouds of Jupiter.

The sky above was almost black, except for a few wisps of ammonia cirrus perhaps 20 kilometers overhead. It was cold up there on the fringes of space, but both pressure and temperature increased rapidly with depth. At the level where Kon-Tiki was drifting now, it was 50 degrees centigrade below zero and the pressure was five atmospheres. A hundred kilometers farther down, it would be as warm as equatorial Earth—and the pressure about the same as at the bottom of one of the shallower seas. Ideal conditions for life.

A quarter of the brief Jovian day had already gone; the Sun was halfway up the sky, but the light on the unbroken cloudscape below had a curious mellow quality. That extra half billion kilometers had robbed the Sun of all its power; though the sky was clear, Falcon found himself continually thinking that it was a heavily overcast day. When night fell, the onset of darkness would be swift, indeed; though it was still morning, there was a sense of autumnal twilight in the air. But autumn, of course, was something that never came to Jupiter. There were no seasons here.

Kon-Tiki had come down in the exact center of the Equatorial Zone—the least colorful part of the planet. The sea of clouds that stretched out to the horizon was tinted a pale salmon; there were none of the yellows and pinks and even reds that banded Jupiter at higher latitudes. The Great Red Spot itself—most spectacular of all the planet's features—lay thousands of kilometers to the south. It had been a temptation to descend there, but the South Tropical Disturbance was unusually active, with currents reaching 1500 kilometers an hour. It would have been asking for trouble to head into that maelstrom of unknown forces. The Great Red Spot and its mysteries would have to wait for future expeditions.

The Sun, moving across the sky twice as swiftly as it did on Earth, was now nearing the zenith and had become eclipsed by the great silver canopy of the balloon. Kon-Tiki was still drifting swiftly, smoothly westward at a steady 350, but only the radar gave any indication of this. Was it always as calm here? Falcon asked himself. The scientists who had talked learnedly of the Jovian doldrums and had predicted that the equator would be the quietest place seemed to know what they were talking about, after all. He had been profoundly skeptical of all such forecasts and had agreed with one unusually modest researcher who had told him bluntly, "There are *no* experts on Jupiter." Well, there would be at least one by the end of this day.

If he managed to survive until then.

THE VOICES OF THE DEEP

That first day, the Father of the Gods smiled upon him. It was as calm and peaceful here on Jupiter as it had been, years ago, when he was drifting with Webster across the plains of northern India. Falcon had time to master his new skills, until Kon-Tiki seemed an extension of his own body. Such luck was more than he had dared hope, and he began to wonder what price he might have to pay for it.

The five hours of daylight were almost over; the clouds below were full of shadows, which gave them a massive solidity they had not possessed when the Sun was higher. Color was swiftly draining from the sky, except in the west itself, where a band of deepening purple lay along the horizon. Above this band was the thin crescent of a closer moon, pale and bleached against the utter blackness beyond.

With a speed perceptible to the eye, the Sun went straight down over the edge of Jupiter, 3000 kilometers away. The stars came out in their legions—and there was the beautiful evening star of Earth, on the very frontier of twilight, reminding him how far he was from home. It followed the Sun down into the west; man's first night on Jupiter had begun.

With the onset of darkness, Kon-Tiki started to sink. The balloon was no longer heated by the feeble sunlight and was losing a small part of its buoyancy. Falcon did nothing to increase lift; he had expected this and was planning to descend.

The invisible cloud deck was still 50 kilometers below and he would reach it about midnight. It showed up clearly on the infrared radar, which also reported that it contained a vast array of complex carbon compounds, as well as the usual hydrogen, helium and ammonia. The chemists were dying for samples of that fluffy, pinkish stuff; though some atmospheric probes had already gathered a few grams, that had only whetted their appetites. Half the basic molecules of life were here, floating high above the surface of Jupiter. And where there was food, could life be far away? That was the question that, after more than 100 years, no one had been able to answer.

The infrared was blocked by the clouds, but the microwave radar sliced right through and showed layer after layer, all the way down to the hidden surface more than 400 kilometers below. That was barred to him by enormous pressures and temperatures; not even robot probes had ever reached it intact. It lay in tantalizing inaccessibility at the bottom of the radar screen, slightly fuzzy and showing a curious granular structure that his equipment could not resolve.

An hour after sunset, he dropped his first probe. It fell swiftly for 100 kilometers, then began to float in the denser atmosphere, sending back torrents of radio signals, which he relayed up to Mission Control. Then there was nothing else to do until sunrise, except to keep an eye on the rate of descent, monitor the instruments, and answer occasional queries. While she was drifting in this steady current, Kon-Tiki could look after herself.

Just before midnight, a woman controller came on watch and introduced herself with the usual pleasantries. Ten minutes later she called again, her voice at once serious and excited.

"Howard! Listen in on channel forty-six—high gain."

Channel 46? There were so many telemetering circuits that he knew the numbers of only those that were critical; but as soon as he threw the switch, he recognized this one.

He was plugged into the microphone on the probe, floating 130 kilometers below him in an atmosphere now almost as dense as water.

At first, there was only a soft hiss of whatever strange winds stirred down in the darkness of that unimaginable world. And then, out of the background noise, there slowly emerged a booming vibration that grew louder and louder, like the beating of a gigantic drum. It was so low that it was felt as much as heard, and the beats steadily increased their tempo, though the pitch never changed. Now it was a swift, almost infrasonic throbbing—and then, suddenly, in mid-vibration, it stopped, so abruptly that the mind could not accept the silence, but memory continued to manufacture a ghostly echo in the deepest caverns of the brain.

It was the most extraordinary sound that Falcon had ever heard, even among the multitudinous noises of Earth. He could think of no natural phenomenon that could have caused it, nor was it like the cry of any animal, not even one of the great whales.

It came again, following exactly the same pattern. Now that he was prepared for it, he estimated the length of the sequence; from first faint throb to final crescendo, it lasted just over ten seconds.

And this time, there was a real echo, very faint and far away. Perhaps it came from one of the many reflecting layers deeper in this stratified atmosphere; perhaps it was another more distant source. Falcon waited for a second echo, but it never came.

Mission Control reacted quickly and asked him to drop another probe at once. With two microphones operating, it would be possible to find the approximate location of the sources. Oddly enough, none of Kon-Tiki's own external mikes could detect anything except wind noises; the boomings, whatever they were, must have been trapped and channeled beneath an atmospheric reflecting layer far below.

They were coming, it was soon discovered, from a cluster of sources about 2000 kilometers away. The distance gave no indication of their power; in Earth's oceans, quite feeble sounds could travel equally far. And as for the obvious assumption that living creatures were responsible, the chief exobiologist quickly ruled that out.

"I'll be very disappointed," said Dr. Brenner, "if there

are no microorganisms or plants here. But nothing like animals, because there's no free oxygen. All biochemical reactions on Jupiter must be low-energy ones—there's just no way an active creature could generate enough power to function."

Falcon wondered if this were true; he had heard the argument before and reserved judgment.

"In any case," continued Brenner, "some of those sound waves are a hundred meters long! Even an animal as big as a whale couldn't produce them. They *must* have a natural origin."

Yes, that seemed plausible, and probably the physicists would be able to come up with an explanation. What would a blind alien make. Falcon wondered, of the sounds he might hear when standing beside a stormy sea or a geyser or a volcano or a waterfall? He might well attribute them to some huge beast.

About an hour before sunrise, the voices of the deep died away and Falcon began to busy himself with preparation for the dawn of his second day. Kon-Tiki was now only five kilometers above the nearest cloud layer; the external pressure had risen to ten atmospheres and the temperature was a tropical 30 degrees. A man could be comfortable here with no more equipment than a breathing mask and the right grade of heliox mixture.

"We've some good news for you," Mission Control reported soon after dawn. "The cloud layer's breaking up. You'll have partial clearing in an hour—but watch out for turbulence."

"I've already noticed some," Falcon answered. "How far down will I be able to see?"

"At least twenty kilometers, down to the second thermocline. *That* cloud deck is solid—it never breaks."

And it's out of my reach, Falcon told himself; the temperature down there must be over 100 degrees. This was the first time that any balloonist had ever had to worry not about his ceiling but about his—basement?

Ten minutes later, he could see what Mission Control had already observed from its superior vantage point. There was a change in color near the horizon, and the cloud layer had become ragged and humpy, as if something had torn it open. He turned up his little nuclear furnace and gave Kon-Tiki another five kilometers of altitude so that he could get a better view.

The sky below was clearing rapidly—completely, as if something was dissolving away the solid overcast. An abyss was opening up before his eyes; a moment later, he sailed out over the edge of a cloud canyon 20 kilometers deep and 1000 kilometers wide.

A new world lay spread beneath him; Jupiter had stripped away one of its many veils. The second layer of clouds, unattainably far below, was much darker in color than the first. It was almost salmon pink and curiously mottled with little islands of brick red. They were all oval-shaped, with their long axes pointing east-west, in the direction of the prevailing wind. There were hundreds of them, all about the same size, and they reminded Falcon of puffy little cumulus clouds in the terrestrial sky.

He reduced buoyancy, and Kon-Tiki began to drop down the face of the dissolving cliff. It was then that he noticed the snow.

White flakes were forming in the air and drifting slowly downward. Yet it was much too warm for snow—and, in any event, there was scarcely a trace of water at this altitude. Moreover, there was no glitter nor sparkle about these flakes as they went cascading down into the depths; when, presently, a few landed on an instrument boom outside the main viewing port, he saw that they were a dull, opaque white—not crystalline at all—and quite large, several centimeters across. They looked like wax, and Falcon guessed that this was precisely what they were. Some chemical reaction was taking place in the atmosphere around him, condensing out the hydrocarbons floating in the Jovian air.

A hundred kilometers ahead, a disturbance was taking place in the cloud layer. The little red ovals were being jostled around and were beginning to form a spiral—the familiar cyclonic pattern so common in the meteorology of Earth. The vortex was emerging with astonishing speed; if that was a storm ahead, Falcon told himself, he was in big trouble.

And then his concern changed to wonder—and to fear. For what was developing in his line of flight was not a storm at all. Something enormous—something scores of kilometers across—was rising through the clouds.

The reassuring thought that it, too, might be a cloud—a thunderhead boiling up from the lower levels of the atmosphere—lasted only a few seconds. No; this was *solid*. It shouldered its way through the pink-and-salmon overcast like an iceberg rising from the deeps.

An *iceberg*, floating on hydrogen? That was impossible, of course; but perhaps it was not too remote an analogy. As soon as he focused the telescope upon the enigma, Falcon saw that it was a whitish mass, threaded with streaks of red and brown. It must be, he decided, the same stuff as the "snowflakes" falling around him—a mountain range of wax. And it was not, he soon realized, as solid as he had thought; around the edges, it was continually crumbling and re-forming.

"I know what it is," he radioed Mission Control, which for the past few minutes had been asking anxious questions. "It's a mass of bubbles—some kind of foam. Hydrocarbon froth. Get the chemists working on—*just a minute!*"

"What is it?" called Mission Control. "What is it?"

He ignored the frantic pleas from space and concentrated all his mind upon the image in the telescope field. He had to be sure; if he made a mistake, he would be the laughingstock of the Solar System.

Then he relaxed, glanced at the clock, and switched off the nagging voice from Jupiter V.

"Hello, Mission Control," he said very formally. "This is Howard Falcon aboard Kon-Tiki, Ephemeris Time Nineteen Hours Twenty One Minutes Fifteen Seconds. Latitude Zero Degrees Five Minutes North. Longitude One Hundred Five Degrees Forty Two Minutes, System One.

"Tell Dr. Brenner that there is life on Jupiter. And it's *big*."

THE WHEELS OF POSEIDON

"I'm very happy to be proved wrong," Dr. Brenner radioed back cheerfully. "Nature always has something up her sleeve. Keep the long-focus camera on target and give us the steadiest pictures you can."

The things moving up and down those waxen slopes were still too far away for Falcon to make out many details, and they must have been very large to be visible at all at such a distance. Almost black and shaped like arrowheads, they maneuvered by slow undulations of their entire bodies, so that they looked rather like giant manta rays swimming above some tropical reef.

Perhaps they were sky-borne cattle browsing on the cloud pastures of Jupiter, for they seemed to be feeding along the dark, red-brown streaks that ran like dried-up river beds down the flanks of the floating cliffs. Occasionally, one of them would dive headlong into the mountain of foam and disappear completely from sight.

Kon-Tiki was moving only slowly with respect to the cloud layer below; it would be at least three hours before she was above those ephemeral hills. She was in a race with the Sun; Falcon hoped that darkness would not fall before he could get a good view of the mantas, as he had christened them, as well as the fragile landscape over which they flapped their way.

It was a long three hours; during the whole time, he kept the external microphones on full gain, wondering if here was the source of that booming in the night. The mantas were certainly large enough to have produced it; when he could get an accurate measurement, he discovered that they were almost 100 meters across the wings. That was three times the length of the largest whale—though he doubted if they could weigh more than a few tons.

Half an hour before sunset, Kon-Tiki was almost above the "mountains."

"No," said Falcon, answering Mission Control's repeated questions about the mantas. "They're still showing no reaction to me. I don't think they're intelligent—they look like harmless vegetarians. And even if they try to chase me— I'm sure they can't reach my altitude."

Yet he was a little disappointed when the mantas showed not the slightest interest in him as he sailed high above their feeding ground. Perhaps they had no way of detecting his presence; when he examined and photographed them through the telescope, he could see no signs of any sense organs. The creatures were merely huge black deltas rippling over hills and valleys that, in reality, were little more substantial than the clouds of Earth. Though they looked so solid. Falcon knew that anyone who stepped on those white mountains would go crashing through them as if they were made of tissue paper.

At close quarters, he could see the myriads of cellules or bubbles from which they were formed. Some of these were quite large—a meter or so in diameter—and Falcon wondered in what witch's caldron of hydrocarbons they had been brewed. There must be enough petrochemicals deep down in the atmosphere of Jupiter to supply all Earth's needs for 1,000,000 years.

The short day had almost gone when he passed over the crest of the waxen hills, and the light was fading rapidly along their lower slopes. There were no mantas on this western side, and for some reason, the topography was very different. The foam was sculpted into long, level terraces, like the interior of a lunar crater. He could almost imagine that they were gigantic steps leading down to the hidden surface of the planet.

And on the lowest of those steps, just clear of the swirling clouds that the mountain had displaced when it came surging skyward, was a roughly oval mass two or three kilometers across. It was difficult to see, being only a little darker than the gray-white foam on which it rested. Falcon's first reaction was that he was looking at a forest of pallid trees, like gaint mushrooms that had never seen the Sun.

Yes, it must be a forest—he could see hundreds of thin trunks springing from the white, waxy froth in which they were rooted. But the trees were packed astonishingly close together; there was scarcely any space between them. Perhaps it was not a forest after all but a single enormous tree —like one of the giant, multiple-trunked banyans of the East. He had once seen, in Java, a banyan tree 200 meters across; this monster was at least ten times that size.

The light had almost gone; the cloudscape had turned purple with refracted sunlight, and in a few seconds that, too, would have vanished. In the very last light of his second day on Jupiter, Howard Falcon saw—or thought he saw—something that cast the very gravest doubts on his interpretation of the white oval.

Unless the dim light had totally deceived him, those hundreds of thin trunks were beating back and forth, in perfect synchronism, like fronds of kelp rocking in the surge.

And the tree was no longer in the place where he had first seen it.

"Sorry about this," said Mission Control soon after sunset, "but we think Source Beta is going to blow within the next hour. Probability seventy percent."

Falcon glanced quickly at the chart. Beta—Jupiter latitude 140 degrees—was 30,000 kilometers away and well below his horizon. Even though major eruptions ran as high as ten megatons, he was much too far away for the shock wave to be a serious danger. The radio storm that it would trigger was, however, quite a different matter.

The decameter outbursts that sometimes made Jupiter the most powerful radio source in the whole sky had been discovered back in the 1950s, to the utter astonishment of the astronomers. Now, more than a century later, their real cause was still a mystery. Only the symptoms were understood; the explanation was completely unknown.

The "volcano" theory had best stood the test of time—although no one imagined that this word had the same meaning on Jupiter as on Earth. At frequent intervals—often several times a day—titanic eruptions occurred in the lower depths of the atmosphere, probably on the hidden surface of the planet itself. A great column of gas, more than 1000 kilometers high, would start boiling upward, as if determined to escape into space.

Against the most powerful gravitational field of all the planets, it had no chance. Yet some traces—a mere few million tons—usually managed to reach the Jovian ionosphere; and when they did, all hell broke loose.

The radiation belts surrounding Jupiter completely dwarf the feeble Van Allen belts of Earth. When they are short-circuited by an ascending column of gas, the result is an electrical discharge millions of times more powerful than any terrestrial flash of lightning; it sends a colossal thunderclap of radio noise flooding across the entire Solar System —and on out to the stars.

It had been discovered that these radio outbursts came from four main areas of the planet; perhaps there were weaknesses here that allowed the fires of the interior to break out from time to time. The scientists on Ganymede, largest of Jupiter's many moons, now thought that they could predict the onset of a decameter storm; their accuracy was about as good as a weather forecaster's of the early 1900s.

Falcon did not know whether to welcome or to fear a radio storm; it would certainly add to the value of the mission—if he survived it. His course had been planned to keep as far as possible from the main centers of disturbance, especially the most active one, Source Alpha. As luck would have it, the threatening Beta was the closest to him; he hoped that 30,000 kilometers—almost the circumference of Earth—was a safe enough distance.

"Probability ninety percent," said Mission Control with a distinct note of urgency. "And forget that hour. Ganymede says it may be any moment."

The radio had scarcely fallen silent when the reading on the magnetic-field-strength meter started to shoot upward. Before it could go off-scale, it reversed and began to drop as rapidly as it had risen. Far away and thousands of kilometers below, something had given the planet's molten core a titanic jolt.

"There she blows!" called Mission Control.

"Thanks—I already know. When will the storm hit me?"

"You can expect onset in five minutes. Peak in ten."

Far round the curve of Jupiter, a funnel of gas as wide as the Pacific Ocean was climbing spaceward at thousands of kilometers an hour. Already, the thunderstorms of the lower atmosphere would be raging around it—but they were as nothing to the fury that would explode when the radiation belt was reached and it began dumping its surplus electrons onto the planet. Falcon began to retract all the instrument booms that were extended out from the capsule; there were no other precautions he could take. It would be four hours before the atmospheric shock wave reached him—but the radio blast, traveling at the speed of light, would be here in a tenth of a second once the discharge had been triggered.

The radio monitor, scanning back and forth across the spectrum, still showed nothing unusual—just the normal mush of background static. Then Falcon noticed that the noise level was slowly creeping upward. The explosion was gathering its strength.

At such a distance, he had never expected to *see* anything. But suddenly a flicker as of far-off heat lightning danced along the eastern horizon. Simultaneously, half the circuit breakers jumped out of the main switchboard, the lights failed and all communications channels went dead.

He tried to move but was completely unable to do so. The paralysis that gripped him was not merely psychological; he seemed to have lost all control of his limbs and could feel a painful tingling sensation over his entire body. It was impossible that the electric field could have penetrated into this shielded cabin—yet there was a flickering glow over the instrument board, and he could hear the unmistakable crackle of a brush discharge.

With a series of sharp bangs, the emergency systems operated and the overloads reset themselves. The lights flickered on again and Falcon's paralysis disappeared as swiftly as it had come. After glancing at the board to make sure that all circuits were back to normal, he moved quickly to the viewing ports.

There was no need to switch on the inspection lamps—the cables supporting the capsule seemed to be on fire. Lines of light, glowing an electric blue against the darkness, stretched upward from the main lift ring to the equator of the giant balloon; and rolling slowly along several of them were dazzling balls of fire.

The sight was so strange and so beautiful that it was hard to read any menace in it. Few people, Falcon knew, had ever seen ball lightning from such close quarters—and certainly none had survived if they were riding a hydrogen-filled balloon back in the atmosphere of Earth. He remembered the flaming death of the Hindenburg, destroyed by a stray spark when she docked at Lakehurst in 1937; as it had done so often in the past, the horrifying old newsreel film flashed through his mind. But at least that could not happen here, though there was more hydrogen above his head than had ever filled the last of the zeppelins. It would be a few billion years yet before anyone could light a fire in the atmosphere of Jupiter.

With a sound like briskly frying bacon, the speech circuit came back to life.

"Hello, Kon-Tiki—are you receiving? Are you receiving?"

The words were chopped and badly distorted but intelligible. Falcon's spirits lifted; he had resumed contact with the world of men.

"I receive you," he said. "Quite an electrical display, but no damage—so far."

"Thanks—thought we'd lost you. Please check telemetry channels three, seven, twenty-six. Also gain on camera two. And we don't quite believe the readings on the external ionization probes."

Reluctantly, Falcon tore his gaze away from the fascinating pyrotechnic display around Kon-Tiki, though from time to time he kept glancing out the windows. The ball lightning disappeared first, the fiery globes slowly expanding until they reached a critical size, at which point they vanished in a gentle explosion. But for an hour later there were still faint glows around all the exposed metal on the outside of the capsule; and the radio circuits remained noisy until well after midnight.

The remaining hours of darkness were completely uneventful—until just before dawn. Because it came from the east, Falcon assumed that he was seeing the first faint hint of sunrise. Then he realized that it was still 20 minutes too early for it—and the glow that had appeared along the horizon was moving toward him even as he watched. It swiftly detached itself from the arch of stars that marked the invisible edge of the planet, and he saw that it was a relatively narrow band, quite sharply defined. The beam of an enormous searchlight appeared to be swinging beneath the clouds.

Perhaps 100 kilometers behind the first racing bar of light came another, parallel to it and moving at the same speed. And beyond that another, and another—until all the sky flickered with alternating sheets of light and darkness.

By this time, Falcon thought, he had been inured to wonders, and it seemed impossible that this display of pure, soundless luminosity could present the slightest danger. But it was so astonishing and so inexplicable that he felt cold naked fear gnawing at his self-control. No man could look upon such a sight without feeling a helpless pygmy, in the presence of forces beyond his comprehension. Was it possible that, after all, Jupiter carried not only life but intelligence? And, perhaps, an intelligence that only now was beginning to react to his alien presence.

"Yes, we see it," said Mission Control in a voice that

echoed his own awe. "We've no idea what it is. Stand by—we're calling Ganymede."

The display was slowly fading; the bands racing in from the far horizon were much fainter, as if the energies that powered them were becoming exhausted. In five minutes, it was all over; the last faint pulse of light flickered along the western sky and then was gone. Its passing left Falcon with an overwhelming sense of relief. The sight was so hypnotic and so disturbing that it was not good for any man's peace of mind to contemplate it too long.

He was more shaken than he cared to admit. The electrical storm was something that he could understand, but *this* was totally incomprehensible.

Mission Control was still silent. Falcon knew that the information banks up on Ganymede were now being searched, while men and computers turned their minds to the problem. If no answer could be found there, it would be necessary to call Earth; that would mean a delay of almost an hour. The possibility that even Earth might be unable to help was one that Falcon did not care to contemplate.

He had never before been so glad to hear the voice of Mission Control as when Dr. Brenner finally came on the circuit. The biologist sounded relieved—yet subdued, like a man who had just come through some great intellectual crisis.

"Hello, Kon-Tiki. We've solved your problem, but we can still hardly believe it.

"What you've been seeing is bioluminescence—very similar to that produced by microorganisms in the tropical seas of Earth. Here they're in the atmosphere, not the ocean, but the principle is the same."

"But the pattern," protested Falcon. "It was so regular—so *artificial*. And it was hundreds of kilometers across!"

"It was even larger than you imagine—you observed only a small part of it. The whole pattern was five thousand kilometers wide and looked like a revolving wheel. You merely saw the spokes, sweeping past you at about a kilometer a second——"

"A *second*," Falcon could not help interjecting. "No animals could move that fast!"

"Of course not—let me explain. What you saw was triggered by the shock wave from Source Beta, moving at the speed of sound."

"But what about the pattern?" Falcon insisted.

"That's the surprising part. It's a very rare phenomenon, but identical wheels of light—except that they're a thousand times smaller—have been observed in the Persian Gulf and the Indian Ocean. Listen to this: British India Company's Patna, Persian Gulf, May 1880, eleven-thirty P.M.—'An enormous luminous wheel, whirling round, the spokes of which appeared to brush the ship along. The spokes were two hundred or three hundred yards long . . . each wheel contained about sixteen spokes. . . .' And here's one from the Gulf of Oman, dated 23 May, 1906: 'The intensely bright luminescence approached us rapidly, shooting sharply defined light rays to the west in rapid succession, like the beam from the searchlight of a warship. . . . To the left of us, a gigantic fiery wheel formed itself, with spokes that reached as far as one could see. The whole wheel whirled around for two or three minutes.' The archive computer on Ganymede dug up about five hundred cases—it would have printed out the lot if we hadn't stopped it in time."

"I'm convinced—but still baffled."

"I don't blame you; the full explanation wasn't worked out until late in the 20th Century. It seems that these luminous wheels are the results of submarine earthquakes and always occur in shallow waters, where the shock waves can be reflected and cause standard wave patterns. Sometimes bars—sometimes rotating wheels—the 'Wheels of Poseidon,' they've been called. The theory was finally proved by making underwater explosions and photographing the results from a satellite. No wonder sailors used to be superstitious. Who would have believed a thing like *this?*"

So that was it, Falcon told himself. When Source Beta blew its top, it must have sent shock waves in all directions —through the compressed gas of the lower atmosphere, through the solid body of Jupiter itself. Meeting and criss-crossing, those waves must have canceled here, reinforced there; the whole planet must have rung like a bell.

Yet the explanation did not destroy the sense of wonder and awe; he would never be able to forget those flickering bands of light racing through the unattainable depths of the Jovian atmosphere. He felt that he was not merely on a strange planet but in some magical realm between myth and reality.

This was a world where absolutely *anything* could happen, and no man could possibly guess what the future would bring.

And he still had a whole day to go.

MEDUSA

When the true dawn finally arrived, it brought a sudden change of weather. Kon-Tiki was moving through a blizzard; waxen snowflakes were falling so thickly that visibility was reduced to zero. Falcon began to worry about the weight that might be accumulating on the envelope; then he noticed that any flakes settling outside the windows quickly disappeared. Kon-Tiki's continuous outpouring of heat was evaporating them as swiftly as they arrived.

If he had been ballooning on Earth, he would also have worried about the possibility of collision. That, at least, was no danger here; any Jovian mountains were several hundred kilometers below him. And as for the floating islands of foam, hitting them would probably be like plowing into slightly hardened soap bubbles.

Nevertheless, he switched on the horizontal radar, which until now had been completely useless; only the vertical beam, giving his distance from the invisible surface, so far had been of any value. And then he had another surprise.

Scattered across a huge sector of the sky ahead were dozens of large and brilliant echoes. They were completely isolated from one another and hung apparently unsupported in space. Falcon suddenly remembered a phrase that the earliest aviators had used to describe one of the hazards of their profession—"clouds stuffed with rocks." That was a perfect description of what seemed to lie in the track of Kon-Tiki.

It was a disconcerting sight; then Falcon again reminded himself that nothing *really* solid could possibly hover in this atmosphere. Perhaps it was some strange meteorological phenomenon—and, in any case, the nearest echo was over 200 kilometers away.

He reported to Mission Control, which could provide no

explanation. But it gave the welcome news that he would be clear of the blizzard in another 30 minutes.

It did not warn him, however, of the violent cross wind that abruptly grabbed Kon-Tiki and swept it almost at right angles to its previous track. Falcon needed all his skill and the maximum use of what little control he had over his ungainly vehicle to prevent it from being capsized. Within minutes, he was racing northward at 500 kilometers an hour; then, as suddenly as it had started, the turbulence ceased; he was still moving at high speed but in smooth air. He wondered if he had been caught in the Jovian equivalent of a jet stream.

Then the snowstorm suddenly dissolved, and he saw what Jupiter had been preparing for him.

Kon-Tiki had entered the funnel of a gigantic whirlpool, at least 300 kilometers across. The balloon was being swept along a curving wall of cloud; overhead, the Sun was shining in a clear sky, but far beneath, this great hole in the atmosphere drilled down to unknown depths, until it reached a misty floor where lightning flickered almost continuous.

Though the vessel was being dragged downward so slowly that it was in no immediate danger, Falcon increased the flow of heat into the envelope, until Kon-Tiki hovered at a constant altitude. Not until then did he abandon the fantastic spectacle outside and consider again the problem of the radar.

The nearest echo was now only 40 kilometers away— and all of them, he quickly realized, were distributed along the wall of the vortex; they were moving with it, apparently caught in the whirlpool like Kon-Tiki itself. He aimed the telescope along the radar bearing and found himself looking at a curious mottled cloud that almost filled the field of view.

It was not easy to see, being only a little darker than the whirling wall of mist that formed its background. Not until he had been staring for several minutes did Falcon realize that he had met it once before.

The first time, it had been crawling across the drifting mountains of foam and he had mistaken it for a giant, many-trunked tree. Now at last he could appreciate its real size and complexity and he could give it a better name to fix its image in his mind. It did not resemble a tree at all but a jellyfish—a medusa, such as might be met trailing its tentacles as it drifted along the warm eddies of the Gulf Stream.

This medusa was two kilometers across, and its scores of dangling tentacles were hundreds of meters long. They swayed slowly back and forth in perfect unison, taking more than a minute for each complete undulation—almost as if the creature were clumsily rowing itself through the sky.

The other echoes were more distant medusae; Falcon turned the telescope on half a dozen and could see no variations in shape or size. They all seemed to be of the same species, and he wondered just why they were drifting lazily around in this 1000-kilometer orbit. Perhaps they were feeding upon the aerial plankton sucked in by the whirlpool—as Kon-Tiki itself had been.

"Do you realize, Howard," said Dr. Brenner when he had recovered from his initial astonishment, "that this thing is about a hundred thousand times as large as the biggest whale? And even if it's only a gasbag, it must still weigh a million tons! I can't even guess at its metabolism; it must generate megawatts of heat to maintain its buoyancy."

"But if it's just a gasbag, why is it such a damn good radar reflector?"

"I haven't the faintest idea. Can you get any closer?"

Brenner's question was not an idle one; if Falcon changed altitude to take advantage of the differing wind velocities, he could approach the medusa as closely as he wished. At the moment, he preferred his present 40 kilometers and said so, firmly.

"I see what you mean," Brenner answered a little reluctantly. "Let's stay where we are for the present." That "we" gave Falcon a certain wry amusement; an extra 100,000 kilometers made a considerable difference to one's point of view.

For the next two hours, Kon-Tiki drifted uneventfully in the gyre of the great whirlpool, while Falcon experimented with filters and camera contrast, trying to get a clear view of the medusa. He began to wonder if its elusive coloration were some kind of camouflage; perhaps, like many animals of Earth, it was trying to lose itself against its background. That was a trick used both by hunters and by the hunted.

In which category was the medusa? That was a question

he could hardly expect to have answered in the short time that was left to him. Yet just before noon, without the slightest warning, the answer came.

Like a squadron of antique jet fighters, five mantas came sweeping through the wall of mist that formed the funnel of the vortex. They were flying in a V formation, directly toward the pallid gray cloud of the medusa—and there was no doubt in Falcon's mind that they were on the attack. He had been quite wrong to assume that they were harmless vegetarians.

Yet everything happened at such a leisurely pace that it was like watching a slow-motion film. The mantas undulated along at perhaps 50 kilometers an hour; it seemed ages before they reached the medusa, which continued to paddle imperturbably along at an even slower speed. Huge though they were, the mantas looked tiny beside the monster they were approaching; when they flapped down onto its back, they appeared about as large as birds landing on a whale.

Could the medusa defend itself? Falcon wondered. As long as they avoided those huge, clumsy tentacles, he did not see how the attacking mantas could be in any danger. And perhaps their host was not even aware of them; they could be insignificant parasites, as tolerated as fleas upon a dog.

But now it was obvious that the medusa was in distress. With agonizing slowness, it began to tip over, like a capsizing ship. After ten minutes, it had tilted 45 degrees; it was also rapidly losing altitude. It was impossible not to feel a sense of pity for the beleaguered monster, and to Howard Falcon the sight brought bitter memories. In a grotesque way, the fall of the medusa was almost a parody of the dying Queen's last moments.

Yet he knew that his sympathies were on the wrong side. High intelligence could only develop among predators—not among the drifting browsers of either sea or air. The mantas were far closer to him than was this monstrous bag of gas; and anyway, who could *really* sympathize with a creature 100,000 times larger than a whale?

Then he noticed that the medusa's tactics seemed to be having some effect. The mantas had been disturbed by its slow roll and were flapping heavily away from its back—like gorged vultures interrupted at mealtime. But they did not move very far, continuing to hover a few meters from the still capsizing monster.

There was a sudden, blinding flash of light, synchronized with a crash of static over the radio. One of the mantas, slowly twisting end over end, was plummeting straight downward. As it fell, it trailed behind it a smoky black plume. Though there could be no fire, the resemblance to an aircraft going down in flames was quite uncanny.

In unison, the remaining mantas dived steeply away from the medusa, gaining speed by losing altitude. Within minutes, they had vanished back into the wall of cloud from which they had emerged. And the medusa, no longer falling, began to roll back toward the horizontal. Soon it was sailing along once more on an even keel, as if nothing had happened.

"Beautiful!" said Dr. Brenner after a moment of stunned silence. "It's developed electric defenses—like some of our eels and rays. But that must have been about a million volts! Can you see any organs that might produce the discharge? Anything looking like electrodes?"

"No," Falcon answered, after switching to the highest power of the telescope. "But here's something odd. Do you see this pattern? Check back on the earlier images—I'm sure it wasn't there before."

A broad, mottled band had appeared along the side of the medusa. It formed a startlingly regular checkerboard, each square of which was itself speckled in a complex subpattern of short horizontal lines. They were spaced equal distances apart, in a geometrically perfect array of rows and columns.

"You're right," said Dr. Brenner, and now there was something very much like awe in his voice. "That's just appeared. And I'm afraid to tell you what I think it is."

"Well, I have no reputation to lose—at least as a biologist. Shall I give my guess?"

"Go ahead."

"That's a large meter-band radio array. The sort of thing they used back at the beginning of the 20th Century."

"I was afraid you'd say that. Now we know why it gave such a massive echo."

"But why has it just appeared?"

"Probably an aftereffect of the discharge."

"I've just had another thought," said Falcon rather slowly. "Do you suppose it's *listening* to us?"

"On this frequency? I doubt it. Those are meter—no, *decameter* antennas, judging by their size. Hmm . . . that's an idea!"

Dr. Brenner fell silent, obviously contemplating some new line of thought. Presently, he continued: "I bet they're tuned to the radio outbursts! That's something nature never got round to doing on Earth. We have animals with sonar and even electric senses, but nothing ever developed a radio sense. Why bother, where there was so much light?

"But it's different here. Jupiter is *drenched* with radio energy. It's worth while using it—maybe even tapping it. That thing could be a floating power plant!"

A new voice cut into the conversation.

"Mission Commander here. This is all very interesting— but there's a much more important matter to settle. *Is it intelligent?* If so, we've got to consider the First Contact directives."

"Until I came here," said Dr. Brenner somewhat ruefully, "I would have sworn that anything that can make a short-wave antenna system *must* be intelligent. Now I'm not sure. This could have evolved naturally. I suppose it's no more fantastic than the human eye."

"Then we have to play safe and assume intelligence. For the present, therefore, this expedition comes under all the clauses of the Prime Directive."

There was a long silence while everyone on the radio circuit absorbed the implications of this. For the first time in the history of space flight, the rules that had been established through more than a century of argument might have to be applied. Man had—it was hoped—profited from his mistakes on Earth. Not only moral considerations but his own self-interest demanded that he should not repeat them among the planets. It could be disastrous to treat a superior intelligence as the American settlers had treated the red Indians or as almost everyone had treated the Africans.

The first rule was: Keep your distance—make no attempt to approach nor even to communicate until "they" have had plenty of time to study you. Exactly what was meant by plenty of time no one had ever been able to decide; it was left to the discretion of the man on the spot.

A responsibility of which he had never dreamed had descended upon Howard Falcon. In the few hours that remained to him on Jupiter, he might become the first ambassador of the human race.

And *that* was an irony so delicious that he almost wished the surgeons had restored to him the power of laughter.

PRIME DIRECTIVE

It was growing darker, but Falcon scarcely noticed as he strained his eyes toward that living cloud in the field of the telescope. The wind that was still sweeping Kon-Tiki steadily around the funnel of the great whirlpool had now brought him within 20 kilometers of the creature; if he got much closer than ten, he would take evasive action. Though he felt certain that the medusa's electric weapons were short-ranged, he did not wish to put the matter to the test. That would be a problem for future explorers, and he wished them luck.

Now it was quite dark in the capsule—and that was strange, because sunset was still hours away. Automatically, he glanced at the horizontally scanning radar, as he had done every few minutes. Apart from the medusa he was studying, there was no other object within 100 kilometers of him.

Suddenly, with startling power, he heard the sound that had come booming out of the Jovian night—the throbbing beat that grew more and more rapid, then stopped mid-crescendo. The whole capsule vibrated with it, like a pea in a kettledrum.

Howard Falcon realized two things almost simultaneously during the sudden, aching silence. *This* time, the sound was not coming from thousands of kilometers way, over a radio circuit. It was in the very atmosphere around him.

The second thought was even more disturbing. He had quite forgotten—it was inexcusable, but there had been other apparently more important things on his mind—that most of the sky above him was completely blanked out by Kon-Tiki's gasbag. Being lightly silvered to conserve its heat, the great balloon was an effective shield both to radar and to vision.

He had known this, of course; it had been a minor defect

of the design, tolerated because it did not appear important. It seemed very important to Howard Falcon now—as he saw that fence of gigantic tentacles, thicker than the trunks of any tree, descending all around the capsule.

He heard Brenner yelling: "Remember the Prime Directive! Don't alarm it!" Before he could make an appropriate answer, that overwhelming drumbeat started again and drowned all other sounds.

The sign of a really skilled test pilot is how he reacts not to foreseeable emergencies but to ones that nobody could have anticipated. Falcon did not hesitate for more than a second to analyze the situation; then, in a lightning-swift movement, he pulled the rip cord.

That word was an archaic survival from the days of the first hydrogen balloons; on Kon-Tiki, the rip cord did not tear open the gasbag but merely operated a set of louvers round the upper curve of the envelope. At once, the hot gas started to rush out; Kon-Tiki, deprived of her lift, began to fall swiftly in this gravity field two and a half times as strong as Earth's.

Falcon had a momentary glimpse of great tentacles whipping upward and away; he had just time to note that they were studded with large bladders or sacs, presumably to give them buoyancy, and that they ended in multitudes of thin feelers like the roots of a plant. He half expected a bolt of lightning, but nothing happened.

His precipitous rate of descent was slackening as the atmosphere thickened and the deflated envelope acted as a parachute. Kon-Tiki had dropped more than three kilometers; it should be safe to close the louvers again. By the time he had restored buoyancy and was in equilibrium once more, he had lost another two kilometers of altitude and was getting dangerously near his safety limit.

He peered anxiously through the overhead windows, though he did not expect to see anything except the obscuring bulk of the balloon. But he had side-slipped during his descent, and part of the medusa was just visible a couple of kilometers above him. It was much closer than he expected —and it was still coming down, faster than he would have believed possible.

Mission Control was calling anxiously; he shouted, "I'm OK—but it's still coming after me. I can't go any deeper."

That was not quite true. He could go a lot deeper—about 300 kilometers. But it would be a one-way trip, and most of the journey would be of little interest to him.

Then, to his great relief, he saw that the medusa was leveling off about a kilometer above him. Perhaps it had decided to approach this strange intruder with caution—or perhaps it, too, found this deeper layer uncomfortably hot. The temperature was over 50 degrees, and Falcon wondered how much longer his life-support system could handle matters.

Dr. Brenner was back on the circuit, still worrying about the Prime Directive.

"Remember—it may only be inquisitive!" he cried without much conviction. "Try not to frighten it!"

Falcon was getting rather tired of this advice and recalled a TV discussion he had once seen between a space lawyer and an astronaut. After the full implications of the Prime Directive had been carefully spelled out, the incredulous spacer had exclaimed: "So if there were no alternative, I must sit still and let myself be eaten?" The lawyer had not even cracked a smile when he answered: "That's an *excellent* summing up."

It had seemed funny at the time; it was not at all amusing now.

And then Falcon saw something that made him even more unhappy. The medusa was still hovering a kilometer above him—but one of its tentacles was becoming incredibly elongated and was stretching down toward Kon-Tiki, thinning out at the same time. As a boy, he had once seen the funnel of a tornado descending from a storm cloud over the Kansas plains; the thing coming toward him now evoked vivid memories of that black, twisting snake in the sky.

"I'm rapidly running out of options," he reported to Mission Control. "I now have only a choice between frightening it and giving it a bad stomach-ache. I don't think it will find Kon-Tiki very digestible, if that's what it has in mind."

He waited for comments from Brenner, but the biologist remained silent.

"Very well—it's twenty-seven minutes ahead of time, but I'm starting the ignition sequencer. I hope I'll have enough reserve to correct my orbit later."

He could no longer see the medusa; it was directly overhead once more. But he knew that the descending tentacle must now be very close to the balloon. It would take almost five minutes to bring the reactor up to full thrust.

The fusor was primed. The orbit computer had not rejected the situation as wholly impossible. The air scoops were open, ready to gulp in tons of the surrounding hydrohelium on demand. Even under optimum conditions, this would have been the moment of truth—for there had been no way of testing how a nuclear ram jet would *really* work in the strange atmosphere of Jupiter.

Very gently, something rocked Kon-Tiki. Falcon tried to ignore it.

Ignition had been planned ten kilometers higher than this, in an atmosphere of less than a quarter of the density— and 30 degrees cooler. Too bad.

What was the shallowest dive he could get away with for the air scoops to work? When the ram ignited, he'd be heading *toward* Jupiter, with two and a half g to help him get there. Could he possibly pull out in time?

A large, heavy hand patted the balloon. The whole vessel bobbed up and down, like one of the yo-yos that had just become the craze back on Earth.

Of course, Brenner *might* be perfectly right. Perhaps it was just trying to be friendly. Maybe he should try to talk to it over the radio. Which should it be: "Pretty pussy"? "Down, Fido!"? or "Take me to your leader"?

The tritium-deuterium ratio was correct. He was ready to light the candle, with a 100,000,000-degree match.

The thin tip of the tentacle came slithering round the edge of the balloon, only 20 meters away. It was about the size of an elephant's trunk and, by the delicate way it was moving, appeared to be almost as sensitive. There were little palps at its very end, like questing mouths. He was sure that Dr. Brenner would be fascinated.

This seemed about as good a time as any. He gave a swift scan of the entire control board, started the final four-second ignition count, broke the safety seal, and pressed the JETTISON switch.

There was a sharp explosion and an instant loss of weight. Kon-Tiki was falling freely, nose down. Overhead, the discarded balloon was racing upward, dragging the inquisitive tentacle with it. Falcon had no time to see if the gasbag actually hit the medusa, because at that moment the ram jet fired and he had other matters to think about.

A roaring column of hot hydrohelium was pouring out of the reactor nozzles, swiftly building up thrust—but *toward* Jupiter, not away from it. He could not pull out yet, for vector control was too sluggish. Unless he could gain complete control and achieve horizontal flight within the next five seconds, the vehicle would dive too deeply into the atmosphere and would be destroyed.

With agonizing slowness—those five seconds seemed like 50—he managed to flatten out, then pull the nose upward. He glanced back only once and caught a final glimpse of the medusa many kilometers away. Kon-Tiki's discarded gasbag had apparently escaped from its grasp, for he could see no sign of it.

Now he was master once more—no longer drifting helplessly on the winds of Jupiter but riding his own column of atomic fire back to the stars. The ram jet would steadily give him velocity and altitude, until he had reached near orbital speed at the fringes of the atmosphere. Then, with a brief burst of pure rocket power, he would regain the freedom of space.

Halfway to orbit, he looked south and saw the tremendous enigma of the Great Red Spot—that floating island twice the size of Earth—coming up over the horizon. He stared into its mysterious beauty until the computer warned him that conversion to rocket thrust was only 60 seconds ahead, then tore his gaze reluctantly away.

"Some other time," he murmured.

"What's that?" said Mission Control. "What did you say?"

"It doesn't matter," he replied.

BETWEEN TWO WORLDS

"You're a hero now, Howard," said Webster, "not just a celebrity. You've given them something to think about—injected some excitement into their lives. Not one in a million will actually travel to the Outer Giants—but the whole human race will go in imagination. And that's what counts."

"I'm glad to have made your job a little easier."

Webster was too old a friend to take offense at the note of irony. Yet it surprised him; this was not the first change in Howard that he had noticed since the return from Jupiter.

The administrator pointed to the famous sign on his desk, borrowed from an impresario of an earlier age: ASTONISH ME!

"I'm not ashamed of my job. New knowledge, new resources—they're all very well. But men also need novelty and excitement. Space travel has become routine; you've made it a great adventure once more. It will be a long, long time before we get Jupiter pigeonholed. And maybe longer still before we understand those medusae. I still think that one *knew* where your blind spot was. Anyway, have you decided on your next move? Saturn, Uranus, Neptune—you name it."

"I don't know. I've thought about Saturn, but I'm not really needed there. It's only one gravity, not two and a half like Jupiter. So men can handle it."

Men, thought Webster. He said men. He's never done that before. And when did I last hear him use the word we? He's changing—slipping away from us.

"Well," he said aloud, rising from his chair to conceal his slight uneasiness. "Let's get the conference started. The cameras are all set up and everyone's waiting. You'll meet a lot of old friends."

He stressed the last word, but Howard showed no response; the leathery mask of his face was becoming more and more difficult to read. Instead, he rolled back from the administrator's desk, unlocked his undercarriage so that it no longer formed a chair, and rose on his hydraulics to his full seven feet of height. It had been good psychology on the part of the surgeons to give him that extra 12 inches as some compensation for all else that he had lost when the Queen had crashed.

He waited until Webster had opened the door, then pivoted neatly on his balloon tires and headed for it at a smooth and silent 30 kilometers an hour. The display of speed and precision was not flaunted arrogantly; already, it was quite unconscious.

Howard Falcon, who had once been a man and could still pass for one over a voice circuit, felt a calm sense of achievement—and, for the first time in years, something like peace of mind. Since his return from Jupiter, the nightmares had ceased. He had found his role at last.

He knew now why he had dreamed about that superchimp aboard the doomed Queen Elizabeth. Neither man nor beast, it was between two worlds; and so was he.

He alone could travel unprotected on the lunar surface; the life-support system inside the metal cylinder that had replaced his fragile body functioned equally well in space or under water. Gravity fields ten times that of Earth were an inconvenience, but nothing more. And no gravity was best of all.

The human race was becoming more remote from him, the ties of kinship more tenuous. Perhaps these air-breathing, radiation-sensitive bundles of unstable carbon compounds had no right beyond the atmosphere; they should stick to their natural homes—Earth, Moon, Mars.

Someday, the real masters of space would be machines, not men—and he was neither. Already conscious of his destiny, he took a somber pride in his unique loneliness— the first immortal, midway between two orders of creation.

He would, after all, be an ambassador; between the old and the new—between the creatures of carbon and the creatures of metal who must one day supersede them.

Both would have need of him in the troubled centuries that lay ahead.

THE FRAYED STRING ON THE STRETCHED FOREFINGER OF TIME

Lloyd Biggle, Jr.

Here's a delightful blending of science fiction and mystery writing: a story about a future where murderers are stopped by the police *before* they commit their crimes, and of one potential murderer who poses a problem no one had foreseen. As science provides new ways of lengthening life, so does it offer new ways of ending it: *sic transit in excelsis.*

Inspector-Commander J. Harwell Graham sat at the center of his complex police web like a massive, bespectacled spider, alertly poised for frenzied action at the faintest electronic quiver—but Graham's actions were mental, and he *thought* his prey into entangling cocoons fashioned of their own intended misdeeds. The inspector-commander was a brain that plugged itself into the world during duty hours, and then, because he found defiance of the law in all men, withdrew defeated.

He finished his afternoon dictation with an intimidating glance at the clock. The dictowriter spat the final memorandum onto his desk. Graham scrutinized it, signed his name, fed it back to the machine for copying and distribution.

"Ten minutes to tour's end," he informed the box. "Let's see what Pre-Murder has picked up."

177

"Ready to roll, sir," his secretary answered immediately.

Graham thumbed a control, settled himself comfortably against yielding pneumatic contours, and watched the day's accumulation of Pre-Murder information flash across the wall screen.

Newly appointed Assistant Inspector-Commander Roger Proller gaped at it. It was his second day on the job, and already he was stripped of illusions. The inspector-commander suspected that Higher Authority appointed assistants in the hope that one would prove capable of snatching his job. He treated them brutally and used up four a year, and for the wrong reason. Higher Authority considered the inspector-commander irreplaceable. The assistants were told frankly: Guard him, save his energy whenever possible, and preserve him from failure at all cost because failure could destroy him.

Words and numbers flicked past so rapidly that Proller could only snatch at disconnected phrases: . . . WILL LUNCH IN LONDON TOMORROW WITH . . . CASE 2936 NO REPORT . . . HER ORDER FOR SEVENTEEN . . . CASE 3162 . . . FAILED TO ATTEND . . . ACTIVITY ROUTINE . . . NO REPORT . . . CASE 3299 . . . WILL NOT RETURN UNTIL . . . The inspector-commander, who not only read this minutiae but also memorized it and filed it away in his labyrinthine brain, would, as soon as the run was completed, mercilessly examine Proller's memory and find it wanting.

A red star flashed into view, and the blurred procession of words slowed to a halt. CLINGMAN, WALTER, CASE PM 3497. PLACED ORDER FOR TWO DOZEN MANNEQUINS. DOCTOR STILTER AGAIN RECOMMENDS CLOSING FILE.

Proller consulted his notebook. Pre-Murder suspects were always odd, but this one seemed spectacularly so. He had invested a small fortune in plastic, life-sized images of a business rival, and he arranged them in various postures about his estate and each evening strolled around throwing knives at them. The doctors thought this a healthy purge of murderous impulses. The inspector-commander had a hunch that Clingman wasn't purging himself of anything; he was just having target practice.

"Clingman, Walter, Case PM 3497," Graham's voice rasped. "Medical recommendation declined. Continue surveillance."

Words and numbers flickered again, picked up speed. . . .
3545 ACTION ROUTINE . . . DISCHARGED THREE EMPLOYEES
. . . CASE 3601 . . . VISITED LAW AGENT . . . RETURNED
YESTERDAY'S PURCHASES . . .

Another red star, STAMITZ, CHRISTOPHER. CASE PM
3742. FELIX MANELLOW CALLED AT SUSPECT'S OFFICE AT
14:36 THIS DATE. LEFT AT 15:10. IMMEDIATELY APPRE-
HENDED FOR QUESTIONING, CLAIMED HIS VISIT CONCERNED
A PRIVATE BUSINESS MATTER, REFUSED FURTHER COMMENT.

Graham snarled at the box. "Sergeant Ryan! Immediately!"

Ryan appeared *almost* immediately. He had dived into the
nulgrav shaft, and he floated into view head first. Graham
kept his eyes on the screen while Ryan righted himself and
came to a salute.

"Sit down, Ryan. So Stamitz has acquired a hand weapon."

"It's possible, sir. They should have searched Manellow
before he saw Stamitz, but neither of the men on duty recognized him until he was leaving."

Graham gestured impatiently. "Manellow hasn't delivered
a weapon personally for years. He learned not to the hard
way. How much money did he have?"

"One hundred, three fifteens, and a seven. Two and a
half in small change. He couldn't have collected more than a
token down payment."

"Or a token last payment." Graham turned to the box. "I
want a financial survey on Christopher Stamitz, PM 3742.
Specifically, I want to know if he's been diverting money to
an illegal account. He'll have been planning this for at least
five years." He leaned back and fixed his gaze on Ryan. "Fif-
teen-ten. Stamitz has the weapon by now."

"The men are being very alert, sir."

"Correction. He has access to the weapon by now. Neither Manellow nor Stamitz are fools. The weapon will have
been left at the place agreed upon. That constitutes delivery."
Graham meditated for a moment, brow furrowed, plump
fingers tapping his desk. "I'm a bit disappointed in Stamitz,"
he announced. "He's a scientific genius and the most brilliant Pre-Murder suspect we've ever had. I never suspected
that he'd resort to a clumsy hand weapon." He pivoted toward Ryan. "Has Bryling been notified?"

"Yes, sir. He was offered full-time protection. He refused,

of course. Made a joke of it. Not afraid of Stamitz, hand weapon or no. The usual."

"But he has his protection anyway? Good. Excuse me while I finish the Pre-Murder run."

When the screen finally darkened, Graham tilted to a half recline, eyes closed, and a moment later he pushed himself to his feet. "I'll have to see Stamitz. It may be premature, but I have no choice."

Proller bounded forward anxiously. "Couldn't I do it, sir?

The inspector-commander thought this unworthy of comment. He said, "Come along. Both of you."

It was a street of old, old buildings of real brick, and odd, esoteric businesses: a furrier who brashly asserted that the trimmings on the garments he sold came "direct from the animal to you"; a natural food firm that claimed to have real coffee and sugar in stock, which puzzled Proller less than the implication that someone might want them; an old-fashioned medical doctor whose faded M.D. sign creaked in the slight breeze beside that of the inevitable apothecary who sold the concoctions the doctor foisted onto his unsuspecting patients; two antique shops, one catering to a clientele that had nostalgic yearnings for articles fashioned of plastic. None of the buildings had roof parking, and they had to walk from the nearest public arena. Graham set a waddling pace that belied his weight and age, and Proller, perspiring, watched him with concern.

Stamitz's business was as shabby and as esoteric as the others, but it looked to the future rather than the past. Sus-AN, the sign read, and it was Stamitz's fumbling attempt to compete with John Bryling's plush studio that displayed its multifaceted facade in the next commercial ward, LIFE SUSPENSION UNLIMITED. Sus-AN's display window contained only a few dusty pamphlets, but Graham paused to study them. Proller wondered if his chief was uncertain of how to proceed. An interview was the most touchy part of a Pre-Murder investigation. Handled properly and with correct timing, nine out of ten Pre-Murderers were jolted back to normality. Handled ineptly, months of solid police work could be ruined.

A buzzer sounded when Graham opened the door and cut off when Ryan closed it behind them. Stamitz sat at a desk in one corner of the room—a small, untidy, sad-looking person with too much hair on his head and not enough on his face. Few would accord him a second glance, many would overlook him entirely, but Graham had called him brilliant. Proller studied him curiously, wondering if this withered remembrance of a man was indeed capable of secreting his own web and watching it with the invincible patience of genius.

He scrambled to his feet and offered his hands, which Graham touched perfunctorily. "Christopher Stamitz," Stamitz said softly.

Graham quickly pronounced introductions and placed his credentials on the desk. Stamitz blinked at them and then regarded Graham with eyebrows arched innocently. "Really? Has one of your suspects popped himself into suspension?"

Graham scowled at him. "I beg your pardon?"

"Please sit down," Stamitz said apologetically and dropped into his own chair. Graham and Proller occupied the two worn visitor's chairs; Sergeant Ryan was left standing. The only other item of furniture was a low table carelessly stacked with the same pamphlets they'd seen in the window.

"I've wondered about it," Stamitz went on. "Man commits a crime, puts himself into suspension until the statute of limitations expires. The way the present law is drawn, there's nothing that could be done. A legal suspension can't be cut short except for medical reasons, and in the single instance where a medical problem did develop, the suspendee was already dead. I take every reasonable precaution, but I have neither the time nor the money to properly investigate my customers. On the other hand, since suspension requires the presence of two medical technicians, an application certified by a registered law agent, and approval by a district justice, most criminals might think it a risky venture."

"The justice normally orders a police investigation before approving an application," Graham said. "That's not my problem, though. I head the Pre-Detection Squad."

"Ah! You work on crimes before they're committed. Yes, I suppose it would be possible for someone to make all the arrangements for a suspension and then commit a crime on his way to the lab. He might be under before anyone knew there'd been a crime."

"Interesting idea," Graham murmured. "I'll look into it. Specifically, I'm investigating the pre-murder of John Bryling."

"Bryling? Bryling has been—"

"Not 'has been.' Is going to be. Naturally I intend to stop it."

"Naturally," Stamitz echoed, "but I don't understand—"

"Of course you do." Graham passed around his pack of smoke capsules, popped one into his own mouth, bit the seal, and puffed deeply. Stamitz blew a slender thread of smoke at the ceiling and turned an innocent gaze on Graham.

"I'm sympathetic," Graham said. "Morally, Bryling is a monster, but he's a law-abiding monster. He stole your company and your scientific processes, maneuvered you into bankruptcy, got you fined and imprisoned for doing private research on the processes you developed yourself, ruined your family in ways too obnoxious to mention—and he did all of that without breaking a single law. Now you have to lease the processes he stole from you in order to operate this scruffy enterprise, and lately he's been indulging in price cutting in an attempt to ruin you again: I haven't been able to figure out why. Have you?"

Stamitz smiled wistfully. "I think he's afraid of me—afraid I'll devise some scientific sleight-of-hand that will let me do unto him something of what he's done unto me." He smiled again. "I believe in a Higher Justice, Inspector-Commander. That's the only reason I've survived."

Graham said dryly, "In spite of its many conspicuous failures, the only justice I have faith in is that defined by law. I have to protect Bryling, and by extension I have to prevent you from ruining what remains of your life. Are you willing to submit to hypnotic analysis?"

Stamitz blurted bewilderedly, "But why?"

"To expose the details of your plot against John Bryling."

Stamitz chuckled. "If I have a plot against Bryling, it's buried so deeply that I know nothing about it. I'd be as interested as you in finding out what it is. Of course I'll submit to your hypnotic analysis."

"When?"

Stamitz shrugged. "At your convenience. No, let's say at our mutual convenience. I can't afford to neglect the little business that I have."

"Tomorrow afternoon?"

Stamitz opened an appointment book and held it up to show a blank page. "Any time tomorrow."

"How about this evening?"

Stamitz turned a page. "I have two suspensions scheduled. My biggest day in months. But any time tomorrow—"

Graham scribbled on a card and handed it to him. "My office in Police Central. I'll make the necessary arrangements."

As they left the building and turned toward the arena, Proller observed, "He seems cooperative enough."

"He'll be cooperative enough *tomorrow*," Graham rasped savagely. "That was what I had to find out. He'll be cooperative tomorrow because he intends to murder Bryling tonight."

Higher Authority, more commonly known as Commissioner Eustace Jevan, glared at Proller and said testily, "If the inspector-commander says Stamitz is plotting murder, then you can take it that Stamitz is plotting murder."

"It seems so incredible," Proller protested. "Who can say why Manellow went to see Stamitz? Maybe he was getting an estimate on a suspension. The inspector-commander didn't even bother to ask Stamitz about that."

"In all of his long tenure, this jurisdiction has never had a premeditated murder," Higher Authority said coldly. "He intends to make certain that this case is no exception, and you make certain that he succeeds."

The private lake was ringed with tinted lights, their reflections rippling halos in the choppy water. The underground mansion's terrace was a square blotch of light on the dark expanse of forest. A police patrol guided Proller to a landing near the command van, which was parked in a small clearing.

The unit captain greeted Proller sourly. "Do *you* know what's going on?"

"Inspector-Commander Graham is preventing a murder."

"*He's* preventing a murder! Then what are *we* doing out in this wilderness?"

"Bryling is going to be murdered by a suspended animation expert named Stamitz," Proller said. "At this moment

Stamitz is at his place of business in the central city, along with two medical technicians, a law agent, and a deputized clerk of the district justice. Stamitz is preparing two clients for suspension. Bryling, as you know, is at home entertaining friends. Neither of them will be going anywhere soon, but Stamitz has a hand weapon and could be plotting a proxy crime. Your job is to make certain that *no one* comes near Bryling tonight."

"Including his guests, I suppose," the captain said bitterly. "If I had four times as many men, I could do a sort of job —maybe. Headquarters made the assignment on the standard meters-per-man formula, and headquarters has never heard of trees. I'm using every man I have; they'll have to spend the night out there without relief, and when I spaced them along Bryling's fence, they were so far apart that anyone with an infra detector could have walked right between them. The undergrowth is so thick that a man can see about as far as he can reach. I just ordered the men up to the clearing around the house, which means that they're trespassing, and Bryling will have all of us in court tomorrow. It's impossible to walk through that mess quietly, and every third step one of my men trips and falls with a crash, and Bryling and his guests jump up and spill their drinks. I'm surprised he hasn't called the police."

"The object is to have him alive tomorrow—in or out of court. What is it?"

"The inspector-commander wants to talk with you."

Graham's voice snapped at Proller. "Come on in. I've just canceled the watch on Bryling's estate."

"But why?"

"Aren't you fools in communication with the men on watch? Bryling took off in his private craft five minutes ago. He's headed for the central city. Stamitz placed a call to him, and Bryling left immediately, which is what we've been expecting. He's going to see Stamitz."

"Why did you expect that?"

"Because Stamitz was so smugly confident. He knew we could easily keep him away from Bryling, but he also knew there'd be no possible way for us to keep Bryling away from him if Bryling wanted to meet him. Obviously he was certain he had a way to make Bryling want to meet him."

"What did he say to him?

"We'll never know. Bryling's viewer is equipped with a classified scrambler, and Stamitz is evidently using one he built himself. The lab won't even try to decode it."

"Then there's nothing more to be done here?"

"No," Graham said. "Come on in. If Bryling can leave Stamitz's office alive, he won't need protection at home."

The old buildings seemed curiously shapeless at night. Only Stamitz's establishment was lighted; the closest reflector was a mile away, and the half moon, when the clouds did not cover it, provided almost as much light.

Proller crouched in the doorway of the furrier, watching Stamitz's windows and wishing Graham would hurry. The inspector-commander had gone looking for a justice from whom he might be able to coax a preventive-arrest order. He had nothing to offer in evidence except his own insights, and the prospect was not promising.

Bryling had arrived long before Proller, and he was followed shortly by a man whom the watch detail identified as his law agent. There was now a conference in progress in Stamitz's office: Bryling, Bryling's law agent, the two medical technicians Stamitz had hired for his other cases, Stamitz's law agent, and the justice clerk were engaged in a long and apparently complicated discussion. Stamitz seemed to be playing no part in it, and when it finally concluded, with much flourishing and endorsing of papers, none of the papers were passed to him.

Stamitz waited, politely patient, until Bryling's law agent had ceremoniously folded the papers and tucked them into his folio. Then he produced his own stack of papers and the two law agents began to scrutinize them.

Two dim figures waddled along the shadowed street: Inspector-Commander Graham and a portly, petulant justice. "Justice Klinger," Graham said, performing introductions. "He wants to see the evidence himself before he issues an order."

Proller described what he had witnessed. The justice snorted. "Sounds as if Bryling is taking a suspension. Naturally there'd be a lot of papers—when a multimillionaire undergoes suspension, there are multitudinous contingencies to be provided for."

"With a competitor?" Graham demanded. "With his worst enemy?"

Even in the shadows the justice's massive shrug was visible. "Stamitz is the acknowledged authority, and a man of his professional stature is not likely to let personal considerations affect his work."

"In ordinary relationships, perhaps not," Graham agreed, "but when you ruin a man, common sense should tell you not to entrust your life to him."

"The law is not conceived as an instrument to force a man to act with common sense," the justice said dryly. "Let's go in."

They walked in on an array of blank faces that quickly sorted into contrasting expressions: irritation for the specialists, fury for Bryling, and mild amusement for Stamitz. Proller muttered to Graham, "He expected this."

Graham nodded.

Stamitz said mildly, "Our appointment is for tomorrow afternoon, sir."

"That was based on the assumption that Bryling would be alive tomorrow afternoon," Graham growled.

Bryling flushed and said angrily, "I told your men earlier today—when I want the police meddling in my affairs, I'll ask for them."

Justice Klinger waved for silence. "The inspector-commander has made a grave charge," he announced. "He wants a preventive-arrest order issued for Christopher Stamitz, attested reason being the protection of the life of John Bryling. Are you here of your own free choice, Mr. Bryling?"

"Certainly."

"Do you consider that your life is in danger?"

"Certainly not!"

"The assumption is that you're here to undergo suspension. For what term?"

"The maximum. Five hundred years."

"I now ask the witnesses: Is it your opinion that John Bryling is at this place and pursuing this action of his own free will?"

They nodded gravely and answered in chorus. "Yes."

The justice fixed the clerk in a stern gaze. "Are you prepared to certify that the subject's action is both legal and voluntary?"

"I have already done so."

The justice turned to Graham. "One of the witnesses is his own law agent. You may examine."

"When did you make this voluntary decision?" Graham asked Bryling.

"I've been considering it for years. Everyone connected with our profession does."

"You didn't answer my question. When did you finally decide?"

"This evening."

"This evening, in the middle of a party at which you were the host, you suddenly decided to take a suspension, and you contacted your business rival—"

"He contacted me. He said he was processing two cases; he had the necessary witnesses on hand and could do three as easily as two, and he reminded me that I'd told him long ago that someday—"

"What inducement did he offer?"

Bryling did not answer.

"What threat did he make?"

"None," Bryling said. "It was my own decision."

"There is no legal basis for interference," Justice Klinger announced.

"I have one request," Graham said. "I'd like to place the department's own medical expert as an observer."

"At whose expense?" Stamitz demanded.

"The department's."

"Then I have no objection. If he can get here within an hour, he can observe or take part or whatever he wishes."

"Is this satisfactory to you?" the justice asked Bryling.

"I don't see that it makes any difference," Bryling said.

"Very well. With the department's medical technician in attendance, the suspension can proceed. I so rule."

He nodded perfunctorily at Graham and waddled away.

"And that," Graham muttered, "is the best that I can do. Tomorrow, when Stamitz comes in for his hypnotic analysis, we'll find out what really happened."

The law agent was firm and politely contemptuous. "In return for his cooperation with the incredible whimsies of your department, inspector-commander, my client was subjected to an outrageous and illegal harassment. I have here a justice order forbidding further interference with his lawful private and professional activities. Christopher Stamitz will *not* appear for hypnotic analysis, and you are commanded to abandon all surveillance of his person and property."

"I have a Pre-Murder authorization approved by three justices," Graham said stiffly.

"Since the alleged victim has taken a suspension, he hardly needs further protection from your department."

"Present your order to my secretary, and he will make the necessary arrangements," Graham said. The law agent departed, and Graham slumped forward in his chair and muttered, "Beaten!"

"Three medical technicians certified that the suspension proceeded normally," Proller observed.

Graham shook his head. "Bryling is dead."

"The postsuspension examinations have indicated that the subject took the suspension very well."

"No. He's dead."

Higher Authority glared at Proller. "Your only order," Commissioner Jevan remarked coldly, "was to make certain that he did not fail. Did I need to explain that you were also to make certain that he did not *think* he had failed?"

"No, sir," Proller said, "but at this moment all anyone *knows* is that something very peculiar happened. The inspector-commander's instinct calls it murder. The tests and procedures of the medical technicians show that Bryling took a normal suspension and is in perfect health. All I want is a requisition for lab work so I can find out the truth."

"If your tests are negative, nothing will be proved or disproved, and the inspector-commander will continue to think that he's failed. If your tests are positive, he'll *know* that he's failed. Kindly explain to me what these tests could possibly contribute to the carrying out of your assignment."

"But sir—"

"The inspector-commander has prevented hundreds of murders. He'll prevent more if only his career isn't terminated by this one ridiculous case. Your assignment, Proller, is to save the inspector-commander's career."

"Yes, sir."

Stamitz scowled. "You're Graham's assistant. I obtained a justice order—"

Proller waved his hand indifferently. "I'm not harassing you. I just stopped by to offer my sympathy."

"For what?"

Proller said soothingly, "After all Bryling had done to you, it must have been a terrible feeling to have to preside over a suspension that would take him completely beyond the reach of justice. He'll be laughing at you when he revives."

"Your sympathy is wasted," Stamitz said. "I have no feeling at all about Bryling except that I'm grateful for the business he gave me. A maximum-term suspension is a highly profitable operation."

"I can't help wondering what he'll think when he opens his eyes five hundred years from now. 'I escaped! I have my millions compounded and Stamitz has been dust for hundreds of years and can't touch me!' What do you think he'll think?"

"I have no feeling about Bryling," Stamitz said again. "Like I told you before, I believe in a Higher Justice. I'm satisfied to leave Bryling to that."

"Does Higher Justice have a reach five hundred years long?" Proller asked.

Stamitz did not answer.

Proller burst into Graham's office and exclaimed, "Stamitz has confessed!"

"I doubt that," Graham said flatly. "Why would he?"

"To save his neck. He just took a suspension, and if that doesn't amount to a confession—"

"Stamitz? Took a suspension?"

"Yes, sir. Obviously he was afraid we'd find out what he did; so he popped himself completely out of reach of the statute of limitations."

"How far out of reach?"

"Four hundred ninety-nine years and eight months."

"You blithering idiot!" Graham leaped to his feet and paced the floor excitedly. "That's not a confession, that's an admission of failure! It proves the suspension was perfectly in order. Stamitz will be out just long enough ahead of Bryling to plan a murder. Since he invented the suspension process, the gullible scientists of the future will no

doubt let him study its results, and he'll have great fun working with the team reviving Bryling!"

"Then—you were wrong about Bryling being murdered?"

"I was, and it's the kind of mistake I don't mind making," Graham said jubilantly. "I want you to place official information with Stamitz's medical records. The technicians who revive him should notify the authorities that Stamitz underwent suspension in order to commit murder. And you can close our file."

"Yes, sir. For what official reason?"

Graham smiled. "The principals are no longer in this jurisdiction."

The lab technician held only a grade-two rank, and he was torn between a desire to pull off a complicated analysis all by himself and a fear that he'd be skinned for unauthorized use and/or waste of government property. He said, "I ran all the tests again. It's got to be mercury-base compound M 4939."

"If it's an industrial compound, where would stamitz get a hold of it?"

"A research chemist of his stature could manufacture it in his sleep, and he had all the necessary chemicals."

Proller nodded thoughtfully. "He had the chemicals, and because that compound was once in common use, there'd be a quantity of medical literature concerning its toxic effects."

"For anything as complicated as a suspension, he'd need specific information."

"In the past two years he's used large numbers of experimental animals," Proller said. "He was licensed for work on a new suspension process."

"So how did he manage to fool three medical technicians and not you?"

"The technicians ran their own tests on each batch of fix as it was prepared. I swiped a few of Stamitz's test tubes, and when he wasn't looking, I took samples of each batch *after* he'd pumped it into Bryling. The poison was in the final batch. Obviously he managed to add it after the technicians completed their tests."

"So we have a murder to report."

"There hasn't been a murder," Proller said. "The contrary—Bryling is in perfect health."

"His life is in danger, then. Someone ought to do something."

Proller shook his head. "As long as he's in suspension, he's perfectly safe. When he's revived, whenever it is, he'll have only a few minutes to live after his bodily processes start again, and most of it will be excruciating."

"Then someone should get a justice order and have him pumped out."

"He's in deep freeze. You can't pump out any of him unless you thaw out all of him, and that means reviving him. It wouldn't help anyway—the poison has already reached his vital organs, and he went under just before the effects could be detected. Didn't I tell you Stamitz experimented with animals for two years? When he's revived, he'll live just long enough to die—painfully."

"How the devil did Stamitz get Bryling into his shop in the first place?"

Proller smiled wryly. "He had help—from us! He paid Manellow to make a social call, and Inspector-Commander Graham took the bait against his better judgment, which he had to do, and gave Bryling massive protection against the hand weapon Manellow didn't sell and Stamitz wouldn't have used anyway. All the protection accomplished was to scare Bryling half to death. Then Stamitz placed a scrambled call to Bryling and said, 'I have a quantity of hand weapons and men who can use them. They're watching you right now.' And Bryling, who had just been listening to four companies of police clomp around in the forest near his terrace, probably came close to expiring on the spot. Stamitz gave him a choice of coming in at once for a maximum-term suspension or dying immediately."

"Sure," the technician said. "Why didn't he just run for cover?"

"The assassins in the forest would have shot him before he got to the house. He did just what Stamitz told him to —stayed in sight and made no false moves while notifying his law agent and ordering out his craft. Then he flew straight to Stamitz's office because Stamitz told him he'd be followed, and of course he was—by a whole police fleet. Once he got there, he knew weapons would be pointing at him from concealment; so even when the police came, he made no attempt to escape. He's been deathly afraid of Stamitz for years—it shows in everything he did. He'd be certain Stamitz would use a hand weapon if he had one, and the police told him Stamitz had one. He thought the only alternative to instant death was a suspension, and once he'd accepted that, of course he took the suspension voluntarily. He wanted it as quickly as possible."

"Why'd Stamitz take a suspension?"

"To have the supreme pleasure of watching Bryling die. Why else? For a time I thought I'd talked him into it, but that was before you finished your analysis. You've done a splendid piece of work, and I'm sorry I have to tear it up; but if Inspector-Commander Graham sees it, he'll know he's had his first Pre-Murder failure."

"We ought to do *something,*" the technician said stubbornly.

Proller shook his head. "No. Nothing at all, and I'm ignoring Graham's order to place information with Stamitz's medical records. Look, we don't know—yet—what the natural mortality may be on long suspensions. Neither man may survive to be revived."

"That's so," the technician agreed.

"And either man may die shortly after revival due to the after-effects of the five-hundred-year suspension."

"Maybe so, but a man was murdered, or is being murdered, or is going to be murdered. Shouldn't Commissioner Jevan decide something like this?"

"He already has. He gave me my orders, and I'm following them. I'm also thinking that the inspector-commander himself called Bryling a monster. He stole Stamitz's company and his scientific processes, maneuvered him into bankruptcy, got him fined and imprisoned for doing private research on the processes he developed himself, and ruined his family in ways too obnoxious to mention—all without breaking a law. He even made Stamitz lease back his own stolen processes in order to operate a marginal business, and then Bryling tried to ruin him a second time by price-cutting. All that, and the law is still on Bryling's side. What do *you* think?"

"I get you. A murder five hundred years in the future is nothing to lose sleep over, especially when the victim is a skunk like Bryling. In this case you and I will be the Higher Authority and tear up the records."

"Not 'Higher Authority,'" Proller said with a smile. "Higher Justice."

HOW CAN WE SINK WHEN WE CAN FLY?

Alexei Panshin

This story was written for a volume of four original novelettes based on themes supplied by Isaac Asimov, and right away the author ran into a difficulty common to people working with ideas not of their own making: he didn't quite believe things would work out that way. How he came to terms with someone else's idea of the future makes a story within the story—a beautifully written, memorable account of how our present looks to someone from tomorrow.

(Alexei Panshin, a Nebula award-winning novelist, lives on a farm in Pennsylvania with his wife Cory, just as he describes it in the story. Other characters are real too, though their names are changed. The story becomes an exercise in the meeting of fantasy and autobiography.)

In the final analysis civilization can be saved only if we are willing to change our ways of life. We have to invent utopias not necessarily to make them reality but to help us formulate worthwhile human goals.

René Dubos

1

Endings of stories come easy. It is the beginnings, when anything is still possible, that come hard.

To think yourself into somewhere strange and someone new, and then to live it, takes the nerve of a revolutionary or a bride. If writers had that kind of nerve, they wouldn't be writers. They would be starting revolutions and getting married, like everyone else. As it is, we tend to cultivate our gardens and mull a lot.

When the beginnings come harder than usual and when the only news that penetrates the Pennsylvania outback is of lost causes and rumors of lost causes, I give a call to Rob to grab whoever he can find between Springfield, Massachusetts, and here, and come on down for the weekend. The people around here are good people, but all they know is what they hear on the evening news. And they can't talk shop. Rob talks good shop, and he has a completely unique set of rumors. His news is no better, but it isn't the common line.

It does him good to come, too. Springfield is no place to live. In a sense I feel responsible for Rob. Springfield was founded by William Pynchon, who was an ancestor of mine. He wrote a book in Greek called *The Meritorious Price of Our Redemption,* which was burned on Boston Common in 1650 as religiously unsound, and he went back to England. He stayed long enough to found Springfield and a branch of my mother's family, and make me responsible for Rob.

If I ever meet Thomas Pynchon, who wrote *V.,* I intend to ask him how he feels about Springfield, Mass. In the meantime Rob has some leeway with me, which he takes advantage of on occasion.

I was expecting Rob and Leigh, but when we picked them up on Friday morning at the lunch-counter bus stop across the river in New Jersey, they had a kid with them. Leigh is in her thirties, good silent strong plain people. She writes Westerns. Rob had collected her in New York. Where he'd gotten the kid I didn't know.

"This is Juanito," Rob said.

The kid was blond as Maytime, dressed in worn blue jeans and a serape. He was wishing for a beard. I didn't know him, but he looked like a member of the tribe.

"I'm Alex and this is Cory," I said, and he nodded. Then the five of us headed for our 1951 Plymouth, our slow beast.

"I'm just as glad to get out of here," Rob said, looking back as we headed onto the bridge to Pennsylvania. "It reminds me of Springfield."

It is a depressing battered little town. A good place to leave behind.

Cory said, "And you know, there are people who commute to work in New York from here every day. Two hours each way."

"It's a long way to come for flaking paint and tumble-down houses," Rob said, "But I suppose if that's the way you like to live . . ."

He turned to look at the brighter prospect of the Pennsylvania hills. "Well," he said, "let's get going. Bring on your sheep and geese and cats."

I said, "There are a couple of ducks now, and Gemma had three kittens."

The only part of the livestock that belongs to us is two of the cats. There are two stray tomcats on the place and some independent bullfrogs. The sheep and their lambs are the farmer's. The rest belongs to our landlady up in the big house.

Leigh said, "How old are the kittens?"

Cory turned and said over the seat back, "They haven't even got their eyes open."

Across the Delaware in Pennsylvania we passed a broad field full of dead auto bodies rusting into the land, crossed the shortest covered bridge in the county, and headed up into the hills.

"Well," said Rob. "How badly are you stuck?"

"Stuck," I said. "I'm doing a story based on an idea by Isaac Asimov for an anthology of new stories."

"You're a hack," said Rob. "You work for money."

"Right," I said. "I work to live, and live to work. No, my problem is that I want to respect Asimov's idea without following it to the letter. I guess the problem is that I can't see any way to get from our now to his future. When

I listen to the news, I wonder about any future at all. So I sit in front of the typewriter, but I don't write. I'll find the story, I'll see the way, but right now I'm still trying to find my beginning."

"Don't brood about it," said Leigh. "Sit down and write it the simplest way." Kind advice, because in spite of what Leigh may sometimes say about her own work, that's not the way she writes.

"Seen any movies lately?" Rob asked. Not an idle question.

"None," I said. The movies they've been bringing around here haven't been the ones I'm planning to catch. Not Anthony Quinn and Ingrid Bergman in a love story for the ages. Besides, I couldn't take the chance of getting that far from the typewriter. Not with the birth of a story imminent.

"Hey, you had a sale?" Automatic question.

"My first this year, and just in time, too. We need the money. They're supposed to pay at the end of the month, and today is already the tenth."

"What about letters?" Rob asked. "Have you really been answering your mail?"

"Letters? I'm busy. All my time goes to writing—that is, not writing."

"Travel? Have you been anyplace recently?"

The size of a mental block can be fairly estimated by the writer's list of austerities. It is less a matter of income than an inability to put anything ahead of writing—that is, not writing. If a writer does nothing whatsoever but sit very very still and pretend to think, you know he is up the creek without a paddle.

Cory answered that one. "Not since Christmas," she said.

"Fine," said Rob, like any doctor in possession of a juicy symptom. "Are you able to read?"

"I never stop reading," I said. "I've never been that petrified."

"Name a good novel you read recently."

"Does it have to be good?"

"Name a novel," Rob said. "It doesn't have to be good."

"All right," I said. "I'm not reading fiction. *Creative Mythology*, the fourth volume of *The Masks of God*."

"Is that as heavy as it sounds?"

Cory said, "I lost momentum half through it."

"That one is for inspiration," I said. "Then *Personal Knowledge,* by Polanyi. That's food for thought. And *Heroes and Heretics: A Social History of Dissent*. That's for the times. I pick one or the other up in the morning, read a paragraph or a page, and then I think about the Asimov story."

"Oh, you lucky writers," Leigh said. "Your time is your own."

Rob finally let me off the hook. "Let me see what Asimov wrote when we get to your place. Maybe we can talk it out."

A deer suddenly flashed onto the road ahead of us, showed tail, and bounded off through the wooded hillside. Only Cory and I in the front and Juanito in the back got a good look. Leigh caught just a glimpse, and Rob missed it entirely. I try to bring people by the scenic route, but they have to be prepared to look at things fast. Rob never bothers.

"Nice," said Leigh.

"We sat at sunset over on Geigel Hill Road the other week and watched a whole herd—twelve or more, and even more down in the draw—cross the road and stream up the long open hillside," I said. "And when our landlady's daughter was here for Easter from England, she said there was a herd in the woods on the State Park land just behind the farm."

"Just behind the farm?" Leigh said. "How far would it be?"

Cory said, "Not far. A ten-minute walk. We could go up this afternoon and look."

Rob said, "Not me. I've been up for thirty hours. I need sack time."

"I'll go," said Juanito.

This Pennsylvania countryside offers you just about anything you want. We've been here the better part of a year and still discover surprises within five miles, and even within one, or within three hundred yards: wild onion, wild strawberries, poison ivy. In the space of a mile on a single road you can find high-speed intersection, three-hundred-year-old farmstead, random suburbia, crossroad community, and and woodland in any order and combination you like, strung across little valleys, hidden in hollows, up and over hills. There are even pockets of industry.

"What is that?" Juanito asked.

It's part of the scenery, but you have to be particularly quick to see it. If you could see more of it, perhaps it would have been closed down sooner.

I stopped our old Plymouth tank and backed up the hill to the curve. In early April, with the trees still bare or only barely budding, you can see it from one vantage on the road. Tinny prefab buildings and the half a dozen chemical lagoons perched overlooking the creek, with blue and yellow gullies staining the hillside.

"Every time it rains there's overflow," I said. "That's the Revere Chemicals dump. It was put in in 1965, and the State Health people said at the time that it was going to do this, and it took them five years to close it down. Now it just sits there and leaks. The manager is trying to start a new operation in the next township."

"I hope the deer doesn't drink from that stream," Leigh said.

"He has to take his chances the same as the rest of us," Rob said. Growing up in Springfield has left Rob with more than a little sourness.

When we got to the farm, I stopped the car at the head of the long gravel drive. "Somebody hop out and check the mailbox," I said.

Rob made no move. I said, "Rob, it's your side."

"I've been up for thirty hours," he said.

Juanito said, "I'll look."

He dropped the door on the big white mailbox with the blue and red hex sign matching the white hexes on the barn. I could see that it was empty—and the mail truck not in sight yet.

Juanito hesitated in order to let a semi pass, the wind by-blow whipping his hair and his serape, and then he came back to the car. He had a nonreturnable beer bottle in his hand, one of the little squat ones. It had been on the roadside long enough for the label to wash free, but then it has been a wet spring.

"What about this?" he said.

I was irritated. I had expected the mail to be there when we got back from the run to Frenchtown.

"Oh, throw it back!" I said. "Unless you mean to pick up all the trash along the frontage. Start with the chrome and the broken headlights up at the second phone pole."

The kid looked slightly bewildered at my vehemence. I was immediately sorry.

I switched the engine off, set the brake, and hopped out. "I'll tell you what," I said. "We'll strike a blow."

I walked to the back of the car and opened up the humpback trunk. Then I said, "Throw your bottle in there," and the kid did.

I stepped down into the front field and picked up the black and raddled truck-tire carcass I'd been meaning to police up ever since it was abandoned there. I lugged it up the grade and slung it into the trunk.

"There," I said.

The geese set up their automatic clank and clatter when we drove into the yard. Phoebe is the goose, Alexander the gander. Alexander is the main squawk of the barnyard, Phoebe just the harmony, but when they trudge around the farm, it is Phoebe who leads and Alexander who walks behind attempting to look impressive.

Fang skirted the geese and came skittering past us, tail briefly raised in acknowledgment, a miniature panther in penguin clothes. We followed her into the house for lunch.

The house was once a carriage house. The original beams, marked with the holes and gouges of the gear used to raise and lower carriages, cross the twelve-foot ceiling of the living room, and a glass chandelier hangs from the lowest beam. The kitchen behind and the bedrooms upstairs in the original building and the library and study in the addition are cut to less heroic proportion. It's a tidy small house with an overwhelming living room. It has all the charms of Frank Lloyd Wright without the dim constricted little hallways Wright insisted on designing.

During lunch Cory took me aside and said, "We're going to need more bacon and a dozen eggs."

"I'll go to the Elephant this afternoon," I said.

"Get a couple of half gallons of milk, too." Then she said, "Who is this boy, Alexei? He keeps looking around, but he doesn't say much."

I said, "He seems within the normal range of Rob's friends."

"Well, Rob's strange."

"True. I don't suppose I'd want to put this Juanito to a vote of the neighbors."

Then Cory said, "Alexei, what are we going to do about the taxes if the money doesn't come?"

I said, "We know it's coming. If worse comes to worst, I'll mail our check and we can deposit Henry's check as soon as it comes. Don't brood."

I don't worry about the money except when I absolutely have to. I juggle without thinking, and the money usually comes from somewhere when it has to be found. If I worried about money, I'd be too busy to stare at my typewriter.

After lunch, Rob said, "All right. Let me have a look at that Asimov idea before I collapse."

Cory and Leigh and Juanito went walking back toward the State Park land to look for the deer herd. Two lambs clowning in the plowed lands went ducking urgently under the wire fencing looking for mama at the passage of the people.

Rob and I went back inside the house and into the study. It's a small room. The people before us used it for a nursery. Now it holds our desks, two small armchairs, three small bookcases of reference books, including our prize, the eleventh-edition *Britannica* we bought for $50 in Doylestown, and a catbox in the closet to keep us humble.

I scooped Wolf, our lesser cat, out of my easy chair. She's a tortoiseshell, pine needles and shadow, with an orange nose and a wide black greasepaint moustache. She keeps me company when I write. At five months, she is still small enough to curl up to sleep in my typing-paper box like a mouse tucked up for winter inside a Swiss cheese. I sat down with her on my lap.

Rob said, "How's the collaboration with Cory coming?"

Cory and I have a contract for a fantasy novel in four books.

I said, "Cory has just been reading the novel I did at eighteen to give herself encouragement. She found it very encouraging."

"It's pretty bad?"

"I don't remember it too well, fortunately. Cory says it's about an incredibly narrow and suspicious young man whose only distinguishing feature is that he wants a way to leave."

"That's all?"

"That's all. I made the story up as I went along. I remember that much."

That wasn't all, but that's the way I talk to Rob. I remember there was a galactic empire in the story that did nasty things, and my hero wanted a way to leave it. If I were writing the story now, I suppose he'd try to change it.

"Hmm," said Rob. He wrote a novel at eighteen, too, making it up as he went along. The difference is that his was published and mine wasn't, so he has more to regret. "Let me see what Asimov has to say."

I searched through the clutter on the right-hand corner of my desk. While I was searching, Rob looked through the books on the opposite corner. He came up with *Personal Knowledge* by Michael Polanyi and began to thumb it.

"You weren't kidding about this, were you?" he said. "What do you get out of all of this?" It's a crabbed book in small type with heavy footnotes.

"I don't generally recommend it," I said. "It's epistemology. The nature and limits of knowledge."

"What have you gotten out of it?"

"The power of mind to shape the world. The need for responsible belief," I said. "Not that the idea is new. One of my ancestors . . ."

"I know. One of your ancestors founded Springfield." Rob isn't too sure whether I'm lying in whole or in part about William Pynchon. We do work at misleading each other. I like to tell the truth so that it comes out sounding like a lie for the pure artistic beauty of doing it, and I don't know how much to make of the stories Rob tells me.

"I was about to say, one of my ancestors was the brother of Hosea Ballou, who founded the Universalists. 'The Father of American Universalim.' "

"What's that?"

"They amalgamated with the Unitarians. They're all Unitarian Universalists now. And another ancestor was a cousin of Sam Adams. The point is, they were men of conscience."

"For whatever that means."

"For whatever that means." I handed him the Asimov proposal. "Here, read. This is the relevant part."

Rob read it several times. It said:

> *The Child as Young God.* In this one we picture the society as possessing few children. If the average life expectancy has reached five hundred years, let us suppose, then the percentage of children should be, say, one-twentieth what it is now. In such a society biologic parenthood gives a person immense social prestige but no special rights in the child one has created. All children are children of society in general, with everyone anxious to share in the rights of mothering and fathering. The child is the Golden Boy/Girl of the neighborhood, and there is considerable distress if one of these children approaches adulthood without another child being born to take its place. This story can be poignant and young, for I see it told from the viewpoint of a child who is approaching adulthood and who doesn't want to lose the Goldenness of his position and is perhaps jealous of another child on the way: sibling rivalry on a grand scale.

I stroked Wolf while Rob read. Wolf was purring but not lying quietly. She batted at my hand. I picked up a pipe cleaner and wrapped it into a coil around my little finger and dropped it on the floor. Wolf pushed off my lap, seized the little woolly spring in her jaws, growled fiercely, and ran out of the study. When she isn't batting them under the bookcases in the library and then fishing them out again, she loves to run from room to room with a pipe cleaner in her mouth, growling all the while. She's very fierce.

Rob finished reading, looked up, and said, "It's like something you've done, isn't it?"

"What's that?"

"*Rite of Passage.*"

Rite of Passage was my first novel. It's about a girl, a bright superchild on the verge of adulthood in a low-population future society. Otherwise it's not much the same.

"Hmm. I guess I see what you mean, but I don't think the similarity has to be close enough to be any problem.

The thought of repeating myself is not what's hanging me up. What do you think of the proposal?"

"Well," said Rob, "when did you say the story is supposed to take place?"

I flipped to the front page of the proposal to check. "The next century. The only date mentioned is 2025. After 2025, I guess."

"Fifty years from now? Where do all the five-hundred-year-olds come from?"

I waved that aside. "I'm willing to make it one hundred or one hundred and fifty plus great expectations."

"These people would have to be alive now," Rob said.

"True," I said. "It's something to think about."

It was a good point, just the sort of thing I wanted Rob to come up with. It raised possibilities.

"Are there any restrictions on what you write?"

"Fifteen thousand words and no nasty language."

"What about nasty ideas?"

"Nothing said about that, but I don't suppose they are worried. Everybody knows I never had a nasty idea in my life."

"Oh, yes. Um-hmm," said Rob. "Look, I know this is a radical suggestion, but what's wrong with writing the idea as it stands? There is a story there."

"I know," I said. "I thought of writing it for a long time, but then when I tried I just couldn't do it. That's where I got hung up. I like the opening phrase. I like it—'the child as young god.' That's provocative. It speaks to me. But what a distance to come for nothing. Sibling rivalry? Sibling rivalry? Why write it as science fiction? Why write it at all?"

"What's the matter, Alex?" Rob said. "Are you yearning for relevance again?"

It's a point of philosophical contention between us. Rob believes that all a story has to do is be entertaining.

I said, "Just read this." And I picked the *Whole Earth Catalog* off Cory's desk. I showed him their statement of purpose:

> We *are* as gods and might as well get good at it. So far, remotely done power and glory—as via government, big business, formal education, church—has succeeded to

the point where gross defects obscure actual gains. In response to this dilemma and to these gains a realm of intimate personal power is developing—power of the individual to conduct his own education, find his own inspiration, shape his own environment, and share his adventure with whoever is interested. Tools that aid this process are sought and promoted by the *Whole Earth Catalog.*

"I'd like to speak to that," I said. "I don't have any final solutions. In fifteen thousand words I'm not going to lay out a viable and functioning and uncriticizable utopia, but for God's sake, Rob, shouldn't I at least try to say something relevant? As it is, I don't think the chances are overwhelming that any of us are going to be alive in twenty years, let alone live to five hundred."

"I know. You've said that before."

"Not in print. If the society has solved the problems Asimov says—and we're going to have to—that's what I ought to write about, isn't it? At the price of being relevant and not just entertaining. There is a story in the Asimov proposal that I want to write. Somewhere. And it isn't about a kid who doesn't want to grow up. I just have to find it."

Rob said, "How do you propose to do it?"

"Sit and stare at the typewriter until it comes to me, I guess. Or putter in the garden."

"Do you really have a garden?"

"Of course," I said. "Tom Disch tells me that a half hour in the garden every day keeps the soul pure." Tom's another writer. We tend to pass basic tips like this around our little circles. "I'm going to try it and see what good it does me."

"You do that," said Rob. "And good luck. But I've got to hit the sack now. I'm about to drop off."

I turned off my desk lamp. As I got up, I said, "By the way, just who is this kid, Juanito?"

Rob said, "He's no kid. He's your age."

I wouldn't have thought it. I'm pushing thirty. I said, "Who is he?"

"Who is he?" Rob grinned. He grins like that when he is about to say something that's more entertaining than relevant. "He's Juanito the Watcher. He's your test of relevance. He's watching and assessing. If you're okay, that's cool. But if you aren't right, he'll split without a word. Take your chances."

"Thanks a lot, friend," I said.

Rob went upstairs to flake out, and I walked down to the road to see if the mail had come. It had. My check hadn't. Junk mail.

I sorted the mail as I walked up the long gravel drive to the farm, and I stopped off at the main house to leave Mrs. S. her share of the bills and fliers. I collected ducklings and a spade and set to work on the garden.

I was unhappy about the check not coming, so I lit into the work with a vengeance, turning sod and earth. The ducklings, twice their Easter morning size but still clothed in yellow down, went *reep-a-cheep* and *peep-a-deep* around my heels and gobbled happily when I turned up worms for their benefit. They knew there was someone looking out for their welfare. I was wishing I knew as much.

Spring this year was wet and late, and the only thing in bloom was the weeping willow in the back yard, with its trailing yellow catkins. The trees spread over the running hills to the next farm were still winter sticks. The day was cool enough for a light jacket in spite of the work, and the sky was partly overcast. Gardening was an act of faith that the seasons would change and warmth and flower come. Gardening is an act of faith. I'm a pessimist, but still I garden.

It's much like the times.

Our society is imperfect. That's what we say, and we shrug and let it go at that. Societies change in their own good time, and there isn't much that individuals can do to cause change or direct it. Most people don't try. They have a living to make, and whatever energies are left over they know how to put to good use. They leave politics to politicians.

But let's be honest. Our society is not just imperfect. Our society is an unhappy shambles. And leaving politics to politicians is proving to be a dangerous a business as leaving science to scientists, war to generals, and profits to profiteers.

I read. I watch. I listen. And I judge by my own experience.

The best of us are miserable. We all take drugs—alcohol, tobacco, and pills by the handful. We do work in order to live and live in order to work—an endless unsatisfying round. The jobs are no pleasure. Employers shunt us from one plastic paradise to another. One quarter of the country moves each year. No roots, no stability.

We live our lives in public, with less and less opportunity to know each other. To know anybody.

Farmers can't make a living farming. Small businessmen can't make a living anymore, either. Combines and monoliths take them over or push them out. And because nobody questions the ways of a monolith and stays or rises in one, the most ruthless monoliths survive, run by the narrowest and hungriest and most self-satisfied among us.

The results: rivers that stink of sewage, industrial waste, and dead fish. City air that's the equivalent of smoking two packs of cigarettes a day. Countryside turned to rubble. Chemical lagoons left to stain hillsides with their overflow. Fields of rusting auto bodies.

And all the while, the population is growing. Progress. New consumers. But when I was born, in 1940, there were 140 million people in this country, and now there are more than 200 million, half of them born since 1940. Our institutions are less and less able to cope with the growth. Not enough houses. Not enough schools. Not enough doctors or teachers or jobs. Not enough room at the beach. Not enough beaches.

Not enough food. The world is beginning to starve, and for all the talk of Green Revolutions, we no longer have surplus food. We are importing lamb from Australia and beef from Argentina now. How soon before we all start pulling our belts a notch tighter?

And our country acts like one more self-righteous monolith. Policing the world in the name of one ideal or another. In practice, supporting dictators, suppressing people who want fresh air to breathe as much as any of us, with just as much right. In practice, taking, taking, taking, with both hands. Our country has 6 percent of the world's population. We consume 50 percent of the world's production. How long will we be allowed to continue? Who will we kill to continue?

And as unhappiness rises, crime rises. Women march.

Blacks burn their slums and arm themselves. Kids confront. And nobody is sure of his safety. I'm not sure of mine.

All of us are police, or demonstrators, or caught in between. And there is more of the same to come.

Our society may be worse than a shambles. Certainly, in spite of the inventions, the science, the progress, the magic at our command, our problems are not growing less. Each year is more chaotic than the one before. Marches. Demonstrations. Riots. Assassinations. Crime. Frustration. Malaise. General inability to cope.

We are in a hell of a mess. And nobody has any solutions.

Head-beatings and suppression are not solutions. Barricades are no solution. Bloody revolutions merely exchange one set of power brokers for another.

But the problems we have are real and immediate. Those who are hungry, unskilled, jobless, homeless, or simply chronically unhappy, cannot be told to shut up. The 100 million of us who are young cannot be told to go away. The 100 million of us who are old cannot be ignored. The 20 million of us who are black cannot be killed, deported, or subjugated longer at any cost short of our total ruin as human beings. And so far we have no solutions. Merely the same old knee-jerk reactions of confrontation and suppression.

There may in fact be no solutions.

We may be on the one-way trip to total destruction. These may be the last years of the human race, or the last bearable ones that any of us will know.

In times like these, gardening is an act of faith. That the seasons will change and warmth and flower come. But it is the best thing I know to do. We do garden.

So I worked and thought—and thought about my story. And how we might get from this now of ours to a brighter future. I'd like to believe in one.

And so I worked. As wet as the spring had been, the ground I was turning was muddy, and I was up to my knees in it. And down on my knees. And up to my elbows. Finding worms for the ducklings when I could. Some of the mud—or its cousin—appears on the fourth page of this manuscript. If our printer is worth his salt, I trust it will appear in true and faithful reproduction when you read this. When and wherever you read this, a touch of garden.

After a time, Alexander the gander came waddling over to investigate us, me and the ducklings. There is truth to the adage "cross as a goose." There is also truth to the adage "loose as a goose," but that is of no moment. Alexander lowers his head, opens his beak, and hisses like an angry iguana. He and I have struck a truce. When he acts like an iguana, I act like an iguana back, and I am bigger than he is, so Alexander walks away.

The ducklings don't have my advantages, and Alexander began to run them around in circles. They peeped and ran, peeped and ran. Alexander was doing them no harm, but he was upsetting them mightily. They were too upset to eat worms, and that is upset.

After a few minutes of this I put down my spade and grabbed an armful of disgruntled goose. I held Alexander upside down and began to stroke his belly feathers. Stroke. Stroke. Stroke. After a moment he became less angry. He ceased to hiss. His eyes glazed and he began to tick, every few seconds a wave passing through like the wake behind a canoe. At last I set him back on his feet and Alexander walked dazedly away. He seemed bewildered, not at all certain of what had happened to him. He shook his little head and then reared back and flapped his wings as though he were stretching for the morning. At last he found a place in the middle of the gravel drive and stood there like a sentinel, muttering to himself in goose talk.

It's what I call Upgraded Protective Reaction. I'd like to try it on our so-called leaders.

A sudden stampede of lambs back under the fence announced the return of Cory, Leigh, and Juanito from their walk to the State Park.

"Hello, love," I said. "Did you see anything?"

Cory smiled widely. "We set up the whole herd down by Three Mile Run. They bounded across the valley, and then one last one like an afterthought trying to catch up."

"Oh, fine," I said in appreciation.

Leigh nodded, smiling too. She doesn't talk a lot. She isn't verbal. I am, so we talk some, just as Rob and I talk. But when she and Rob talk, she gestures and he nods, and then he gestures and she nods. She found a worm in

my well-turned mud and held it at a dangle for the smaller
duckling, who gobbled it down.

Cory said, "We're going to have a look at Gemma's kittens."

"Good," I said. "I think I've put in my half hour here.
I'll come along."

"Have you gone to the Elephant yet?"

"Oh," I said. "It slipped my mind. I checked on the
mail, though. The mail came."

"What?"

"Nothing good," I said. "Juanito, want to go to the Elephant with me?"

He really didn't look my age. But then I don't look my
age, either.

"All right," he said.

Cory and Leigh walked off toward the main house to
have their look at the kittens. The ducklings hesitated and
then went pell-melling after them wagging their beam ends
faster than a boxer puppy.

"Now's our chance," I said.

But when Juanito and I got to the car, I remembered
the truck tire.

"Just a minute," I said, and took it out of the trunk.
"Let me put this away while I think of it. Grab your bottle."

He fished the beer bottle from behind the spare tire
where it had rolled. Then he followed me as I hefted the
tire and carried it through the machine shop and into the
tractor shed. I dumped the tire by the great heavy trash
cans.

"Bottle there," I said, pointing to a can, and Juanito
set it on top of the trash like a careful crown.

"What's going to happen to it?" he asked.

"When the ground dries, the farmer will take it all down
and dump it in the woods." Out of sight, out of mind.

"Oh," he said.

We lumbered off to the Elephant in the old Plymouth.
It was once a hotel, a wayside inn. Now it's a crossroads
store and bar. We shop there when we need something in a
hurry. It's a mile down the road. Everything else is five
miles or more. Mostly more.

Juanito said, "Do you drive alone much?"

"Not much," I said. "Cory can't drive yet, so we go shopping together about twice a week." I'm conscious of the trips to Doylestown and Quakertown because they so often cut into my writing.

"Whereabouts you from, Juanito?" I asked.

"Nowhere in particular these days," he said. "I pretty much keep on the move. I stay for a while, and then I move on to the next place."

"Always an outside agitator?" I asked, maneuvering to avoid a dead possum in the road. Possums like to take evening walks down the center of the highway.

"Something like that, I guess," he said.

"I couldn't do it," I said. "I hitched across the country when I was eighteen, but I couldn't take the uncertainty of always being on the move. I couldn't work without roots and routine."

On our right as we drove up the winding hill to the Elephant was a decaying set of grandstands.

"What is that?" asked Juanito.

"The Vargo Dragway," I said. "On a Sunday afternoon you could hear them winding up and gearing down all the way back at the farm. They finally got it shut down last year. It took five years. It always seems to take them five years."

I swung into the gravel parking lot beside the bar. They kept the bacon, eggs, and milk in the refrigerator behind the bar, so we went inside there rather than around to the store. There were two men drinking, but there was no one behind the bar, so we waited. Behind the bar are pictures and an old sign that says, "Elephant Hotel—1848," around the silhouette of an elephant.

One of the drinkers looked us over. A wrinkled pinchface in working clothes.

He said in a loud voice to no one in particular, "Hippies! I don't like 'em. Dirty hippies. Ruining the country. We don't want 'em moving in around here. Bums."

The man sitting at the other end of the bar seemed acutely uncomfortable and looked away from him. I leaned back against the pool table. This sort of thing doesn't happen to me often enough that I know what to do about it.

The drinker kept up the comments. At last I took two steps toward him and said something inane like, "Look, do you want everybody to dress and think like you?" It was inane because he and I were dressed much the same.

He threw his hands up in front of his face and said anxiously, "Get away from me! Get away from me!"

So I stopped and shut up and moved back to the pool table. And he returned to his comments to no one.

"Creeps! Making trouble."

From the doorway to the store, Mrs. Lokay said, "Mr. Pinchen," and I turned, grateful for the interruption. She hasn't got my name straight and she knows nothing of William Pynchon or *The Meritorious Price of Our Redemption*, but at times when I've come in for the Sunday *New York Times* and found no change in my jeans, they've put me down in the book on trust.

We followed her into the store. She said, "Don't mind him. He's mad about his stepson. He shouldn't talk to you that way. Thank you for not making trouble. We'll talk to him."

I shrugged and said, "That's all right," because I didn't know what else to say. I was calm, but I was upset.

Juanito and I waited in the store while Mrs. Lokay went back into the bar for our order. I carried the sack all the way around the building rather than walk back through and set him off again.

I don't really like trouble much, and I'll go out of my way to avoid violence. I clutched the wheel tightly. Instead of driving directly home, I turned off into East Rockhill where the farm country plays out and the woods take over. I set my jaw and drove and thought about all the things I might have said.

I could have said, "That's all right, buddy. I've got a license to look like this. They call it the Constitution."

I could have said, "Have you seen Lyndon Johnson's hair hanging over his collar lately?"

I could have said, "What's the matter? Can't you tell a simple country boy when you see one?"

But I hadn't.

Juanito said, "What you ought to do is get a big plastic sack with a zipper and rig it up. You have two controls. One for warm saline solution, the other for your air line. Spend the night in that. It's very calming."

I said, "It sounds like what I've read about Barry Goldwater falling asleep on the bottom of his swimming pool. Never mind, I have something as good."

I stopped the car, pulling it off to the side of the road. On that side were woods. On the other were fountains, fieldstone walkways, planting, dogwoods, and two scaled-down pyramids, one six feet tall, the other twenty.

"What's this place?" Juanito asked.

"It's the Rosicrucian Meditation Garden," I said, and got out of the car.

The signs say it is open from 8:30 every morning. I've never seen anyone else walking there, but no one has ever come out to ask me to prove that I was meditating.

After I walked around for a time and looked at the tad-poles swimming in the pool around the smaller pyramid—just like the Great Pyramid in Egypt—I got a grip on myself. Thank the Rosicrucians.

As we drove back to the farm, we passed the rock quarry. "Rock quarry," I said in answer to Juanito's question. They don't call it East Rockhill for nothing.

"It won't always be that ugly," I said. "When they have the dam in, all this will be under water. Until the valley silts up, all we'll have to worry about is an invasion and speedboats."

They don't have lakes in this part of Pennsylvania, so they propose to make them.

"I know about that," Juanito said. "Cory mentioned it."

The lake will run through the State Park land. Where the deer herd is now. I don't relish the trade. Ah, but progress.

After dinner, after dark, we all gathered in the living room. Cory collected me from the study where I was taking ten minutes after dinner to stare at my typewriter.

"Are you getting anywhere?" she asked.

I shook my head. "Nothing written. Great and fleeting ideas only."

"Alexei, what are we going to do about the money?"

I said, "Henry said he mailed the check. We just have to trust it to come."

I opened my desk drawer and took out the checkbook with the undernourished balance. I wrote a check out to Internal Revenue for $371.92—more than we had to our name.

"Here," I said. "Put this in the envelope with the return. We'll mail it when the check comes from Henry or on the fifteenth, whichever comes sooner."

Cory tucked the check under the flap of the envelope, but left it unsealed. She set it on top of the phonograph speaker by the front door.

When we came into the living room, Rob said, "Oh, hey. I almost forgot. I brought something for you."

He fished in his bag while I waited. I like presents, even if I don't lie awake on Christmas Eve in anticipation anymore. He came up with a paperback and handed it to me. It was *The Tales of Hoffman,* portions of the transcript of the Chicago Eight trial.

"Thank you," I said. "I'll read it tomorrow."

It was just the book for Rob to give me. His idea of the most pressing urgency in this country is court reform. Which is needed, as anybody who has been through the agonies of waiting in jails and courtrooms can attest. I'm more bothered by the debasement of thought and language starting with calling the War Department the Department of Defense and proceeding down the line from there. One thumbing of the book told me Rob and I had a common meeting ground.

Rob said, "What about your story?"

I said, "I'll read the book in the bathtub."

"Are you going to spend the day in the bathtub?"

"If I have to."

We turned off the lights except for the chandelier, dim and yellow, and Cory brought out a candle and set it to pulsing in its wine-colored glass. Four of us sat on the floor around the candle, and Leigh sat in the easy chair. The light from the chandelier played off the dark veneer and outlined the carriage beams. The candlelight made the rug glow like autumn.

We talked of one thing and another, and I played records. Great Speckled Bird. Crosby, Stills, Nash and Young. The new Baez. Rob pulled out *Highway 61 Revisited,* and I got into it as I never had before.

Wolf and Fang went freaking in the candlelight, chasing each other round and round the room. I put on Quicksilver Messenger Service, the first album, and when "The Fool" reached its peak, Wolf went dashing in and out of the room, ending on the deep window ledge with the last bent note.

And sitting there into the night, we speculated.

Rob, sitting tailor-fashion, said, the conversation having carried him there in some drifting fashion, "Is there really a Mafia?"

"I don't know," I said. "You're closer to it than I am."

"I'm in daily contact with people who think there is," he said thoughtfully. "They think they belong. I could get myself killed. But what I'm asking is, is there *really* a Mafia? Or are there only a lot of people pretending?"

It's a good question. Is there really such a thing as the United States, or just a lot of people pretending?

I said, "Is there really a Revolution?"

Last summer, just before Cory and I left Cambridge to move down here, in fact the day before we moved, I got a call from William James Heckman. Bill had been my roommate my senior year in prep school, and I hadn't heard from him since the day we graduated. He and I had never been friends and never seen much of interest in each other. But I told him sure, come on over.

I was curious. In the spring, eleven years after we graduated, they'd gotten around to throwing a tenth reunion of my class. I'd had a book to finish and had to miss it, and been sorry. I'd been an outsider at Mount Hermon, and I was curious to know what had become of all the Golden People. I like to know the ending to stories, and eleven years later is a good place to put a period to high school. Bill hadn't been Golden People, either, but under the circumstances I was willing to let him serve as a substitute for the reunion.

Bill had changed. Fair enough—I've changed, too. His hair was starting to thin. He wore a moustache with droopy ends, sideburns, and a candystripe shirt.

We traded neutralities and ate chips and dip. He was in Cambridge to visit his former wife. He was studying theater at Cornell. He'd taken a course from Joanna Russ, a writer friend of mine, and mentioned that he had known me, and she had given him my address.

We spoke about relevance. He said that he wanted to do more than just entertain, too.

Then, in the hallway as he was leaving, he said suddenly

and with more than a little pride, "I'm really a revolutionary. I'm working for the Revolution."

"So am I," I said. As he disappeared around the curve in the hallway, I called, with a certain sense of joy, "So are we all."

Is there really a Revolution, or are there just a lot of people pretending? What will happen when enough people pretend hard enough, long enough?

The five of us and the two cats gathered around our candle late on a spring night. If there really is a Revolution, are we its leaders? What if we pretended to be long enough, hard enough?

And I wondered in how many other rooms people were gathered around a flame thinking the same things, dreaming the same dreams. There have to be new ways, there have to be better ways, and we all know it.

Later that night, when we were in bed, Cory said, "Did you find out anything about Juanito? I asked Leigh while you were gone and Rob was sleeping, but she didn't know anything. He was with Rob when Rob showed up."

I said, "All I got from Rob was a put-on." And I told her about it. We laughed and we fell asleep.

But when we got up in the morning, Juanito was gone. Rob was still sleeping on the couch. Leigh was asleep in the second bedroom. And Juanito was gone.

I went outside to look for him. There was a full-grown ewe nibbling on the rosebush by the barn, and I waved my arms and stampeded her back under the wire, kneeling and humping to get through and leaving wool behind. But no Juanito.

There was a trash can by the front door that I hadn't left there. It was full of beer cans, soft-drink cans, rusty oil tins riddled by shot, beer bottles, plastic ice-cream dishes and spoons, cigarette butts, cigarette packs, a partly decayed magazine, and plastic, glass, and chrome from the last auto accident.

I hauled the trash can away, thinking. Cory was standing by the front door when I came back.

"I've got my story," I said. "I've got my story."

"At last," she said.

2

At the age of thirty Little John was still a child, with a child's impatience to be grown. More than anything— more than the long study and the slow ripening that his Guide assured him were the true road to his desires, as indeed they were, in part—he wished to be finished now, matured now, set free from the eternal lessons of the past now. He was a child, one of the chosen few, favored, petted, and loved just for living. On the one hand, he accepted it as his proper due; on the other, he found it a humiliation. It meant he was still only one of the Chosen, only a boy, and he wished to be a grown-up god like everyone else.

It was not that he lacked talent for it. People even more ordinary than he had made Someone of themselves. He simply hadn't yet gotten the idea. Chosen, but not yet called.

He conceived progress in his lessons to be his road to grace. It was what Samantha had taught him to believe, and believing it, he was impatient to gulp down one lesson and be on to the next. He had been led to believe that sheer accumulation was sufficient in itself, and he had closets full of notes. He had also been taught not to believe everything he was told and to think for himself, but this information was lost somewhere on note cards in one of his closets.

Impatient though he was, he tried to conceal his impatience from Samantha. He was awed by his Guide. He was awed by her age, by her reputation, by her impenetrability, and by the sheer living distance between the two of them, her and him. At the same time he accepted as right and proper that someone like her should be his Guide, for, after all, he was one of the Chosen.

Samantha encouraged his awe. Awe, like impatience, was a mark of his greenness, a measure of the distance he had to travel to reach the insight that lessons are to be applied, not merely amassed—that one thing in all the world that she could not tell him but could only leave him to discover for himself in his own time. Behind her impenetrable expression, however, she sighed at his awe, shook her head at his pride in advancement, and smiled at his wriggling impatience. And then tried his patience all the harder.

When he returned from his trip to 1381, she gave him a week to think about the experience before they began to discuss it.

"I could live in 1381 and be a god," Little John said. "It wouldn't be easy, but I saw enough. It takes endurance. That's the chief thing."

They talked about it for a month, day after day. The problems of being a peasant in those times, and still a god, relating as a god should to his fellow men. The problems of overcoming ignorance. And all the while, Little John visibly eager to be done and on to the next trip.

At last she sent him on one. She sent him back to 1381 for another look from a new perspective. It is, after all, one problem to be a powerless peasant courting godhood, and quite another, as Buddha knew, to be a noble aiming for the same end. Little John didn't really see that. All he recognized was 1381 come 'round again when he felt he ought to be off to a new time and new problems of godhood. As though godliness could be measured in trips and not in what was made of them.

So he said again, "I could live in 1381 and be a god. Endurance. That's the main thing. Isn't it?"

She told him to think it over. So they talked about it for another month. And in time he finally said something about the psychological difficulty of shedding power when power is held to be a birthright.

He said, "You could give your money and property to the Church. That's a way."

"Is it a godly way?"

"Well, it could be," he said. "They thought it could."

"Do you think so?"

"I met a very decent Franciscan."

"Organized godliness?"

So they talked further about the times and how it might have been possible to live well in them when your fellow wolves were ready to stay wolves until they died and ready to die to stay wolves. And Little John saw that it was indeed a very different problem than being the godly victim of wolves.

He felt that the last juice had been squeezed from the trip and was ready for the next long before Samantha was ready to send him. And when that trip was back to 1381 again for a stay in a monastery, he felt—well, not cheated, but distinctly disappointed. And he took nothing away from the experience, except for the usual stack of notes.

And after a week of discussion his impatience finally got the better of him.

He said, "Keats died at twenty-five. Masaccio died at twenty-seven, and so did Henry Gwyn-Jeffreys Moseley." He had memorized a long series of people like that, from Emily Brontë to Mikhail Yurievich Lermontov. "I'm nearly thirty. I want to do what I have to do and be done, and be out in the world."

He didn't understand the point. If you are going to do, you do. Those who wait for freedom are never free.

And Samantha, who had a reputation for tartness, said, "Yes, and Christopher Marlowe died at twenty-nine and still wrote all of Shakespeare. Do you think forty or fifty years are too many to spend in preparation for a life as long as you have ahead of you?"

"Oh, no," he said. "Oh, no." But in his heart he did. "It's just that I'm tired of 1381. It's easy to be a god then. It's too easy. I want something harder. Send me to 1970. I'm ready. Really I am."

1970 had a reputation. If you could be a god then, you could be a god anytime. Little John looked on it as a final examination of sorts, and he wanted nothing more than to go.

"Do you believe you're ready to handle 1970?" Samantha asked.

"Oh, yes," he said. "Please."

He was sitting cross-legged before her. They were on the hilltop circle standing high above the community buildings and the flowering fields. The outdoor theater was here, and convocation when decisions had to be made. It was a good place to watch sunset and moonrise. His walks with Samantha often brought them here.

He was more than a little apprehensive at making his request, and he watched Samantha's face closely as she considered, anxious for the least sign of the nature of her answer, impatient for the first clue. And, as usual, her face was composed and gave him no hint.

Little John waited so long and her face was so still that he was half afraid she would fall asleep. He tried to make a still center of himself no less than three times before she spoke, and each time fell victim to wonder and lost the thread. He managed silence and reasonable stillness, and that was all.

At last, she said, "This is not a matter for haste. I think we've spoken enough for today. Walk, meditate, consider your lessons."

"And then?"

"Why, come tomorrow to my chambers at the regular time." And she gave him the sign of dismissal.

So he rose, and gathered his notes, and went down the hill, leaving Samantha still sitting. He turned for a look where the stony path made a corner, and she was still sitting, looking over the valley.

Shelley Anne Fenstermacher, the other Chosen, who was ten years old and half his size and used him as a signpost as he had used Hope Saltonstall when he was younger, was waiting for him. She emptied her bucket of garbage into the hog trough, climbed down from the fence, and came running.

"Did you ask? Did you ask? What did she say?"

"She said I was to walk and meditate," said Little John.

"What do you think it means?"

"I don't know."

He went into his room and got his latest notes from the closet. He didn't know what Samantha had in mind, but if it made the slightest difference, he meant to follow her advice. He always followed her advice to the best of his understanding.

"Can I come?" Shelley asked when he came outside.

"Not today," he said. "Today I'd better walk alone."

"Oh," she said.

"I'm sorry."

So he walked in the woods and meditated and read his note cards, anxious to stuff the least and last of it into his head. If it made a difference, if she quizzed him, he meant to be ready. He had every word she had said to him down on paper. Ask him anything, he'd show he was ready.

And the next day when he and Samantha met, he was ready, that is, ready for anything except what he received, which was nothing. Samantha acted as though he had never spoken. She took up the discussion where he had broken it the day before, and they walked and they talked as usual and she never said a word about his request.

And Little John, afraid to speak, said never a word, either. He did wriggle a lot, though.

At the end of the two hours, however, she said, "A fruitful session, was it not?"

And dumbly, he nodded. And then he said, "Please ma'am, have you made a decision?"

"Yes," she said. "I brought you something." She reached into her pants pocket and brought out an embroidered pouch. "It's a present. Take this grass up on Roundtop tonight, and when the moon is two full hands above the horizon, smoke it and meditate."

That night he sat up on Roundtop on his favorite log. He watched the sun set and he watched the moon rise. And he measured with his hands. When the moon was two full hands above the horizon, he filled his pipe and smoked. And he thought, and his thoughts filled the night to its conclusion. They were good thoughts, but they were all of 1970 and of graduation to godhood. It was good grass.

In gratitude he brought Samantha the best apple he could pick. He searched the whole orchard before he made a choice.

His teacher was pleased with the apple. "Thank you, Little John," she said. She ate it as they walked and wrapped up the core for the pigs.

"What conclusions did you come to last night?" she asked.

His thoughts had been ineffable, so what he said was, "Novalis died at twenty-eight."

"So he did," Samantha said.

They walked on in silence. They walked in silence for two hours. For someone her age Samantha was a brisk and sturdy walker. They circled Roundtop. The day was heavy and hot. There was a skyhawk wheeling high overhead, drifting on the current, and Little John envied it. He wanted to fly free, too.

When they reached home, walking up the lane between the ripe fields, Samantha finally spoke. "Spend the night in Mother," she said. "Then see me tomorrow."

"Without Tempus?" he asked.

"Yes, without Tempus."

"But I've never done that."

She said, "We had Mother before we had Tempus. Try it and see."

"Yes, ma'am," he said.

He had kept Shelley Anne apprised of his progress. When she sought him out after dinner, sitting on the porch in the warm and quiet of the evening, he told her what Samantha wished him to do.

"Really?" she said. "I never heard of that. Does she expect you to change your mind?"

"I don't know," he said. "But I have to do it if she wants me to."

While they were talking, Lenny came out on the porch. "Hi, children," he said. "Are you going to the convo tonight?"

Shelley Anne said she was. Little John said he was busy and had other plans. When Lenny left, Shelley Anne went with him, and Little John was left alone in the evening. He could see the fire up on Roundtop and hear the voices.

At last he went inside and set up Mother, just as though he were going on a trip, but without the drug. He checked the air line. He checked the solution line. And he set the alarm to rouse himself.

He undressed himself and kicked his clothes into the corner. It was something he'd been known to do since he had decided that it wasn't necessarily ungodlike. He picked them up himself sometime, and as long as he did that eventually he figured it was all right.

Then he unzipped Mother and climbed inside. It was overcool on his bare skin until he got used to it, like settling down on a cold toilet seat. He fitted the mouthpiece of the air line into place. He didn't close the bag until he was breathing comfortably.

As the warm saline solution rose in the bag, he cleared his mind. He basked and floated. He had never used Mother except on official trips and had never thought to wonder why it was called Mother. Now he leaned back, drifted and dreamed in Mother's warm arms, and she was very good to him.

Strange undirected dreams flitted through his mind. Pleasant dreams. He saw Shelley Anne Fenstermacher as an old woman, and she nodded, smiled and said, "Hi," just like she always did. He saw Samantha as a ten-year-old with a doll in her arms. He saw his old friends in the monastery in 1381, making their cordials and happily sampling them. And he wheeled through the blue skies along with his friend the skyhawk, coasting on the summer breeze high above the temperate world.

And then he passed beyond dreams.

In the morning, the cool, calm morning, he sat in the slanting sunlight listening to the song of a mockingbird shift and vary, and tried to pick it out with his eye in the leaf-cloaked branches of a walnut tree. At last Samantha came out to join him. He thought he could see the ten-year-old in her, even without the doll.

She said, "How did the night pass?"

Though his skin was prunish, he didn't think to mention it. "Well," he said. "I never spent a night like that before." But already he planned to again. "It was very soothing."

"Ah, was it?" And then, without further preamble, she said, "Do you still want to travel to 1970?"

"Yes, ma'am," he said. "I'm ready for it. I'll show you I am. What else do you want me to do first?"

"Nothing. If you still want to go, if you're still determined to go, I'll send you."

Little John nearly jumped up and gave her a hug, but awe restrained him. If Samantha had been asked, perhaps she would have had him retain that much awe.

So Little John got his trip to 1970, his chance to graduate. Mother was readied again, not for general wandering, but for a directed dream. Samantha calculated the mix of Tempus herself.

She said, "This won't be like any other time you've been."

"Oh, I know that," he said.

"Do you? I almost remember it myself, and it wasn't like now."

"I can handle it."

"Let us hope," she said. "I'm going to see that you are in good hands. Nothing too serious should happen to you."

"Please," he said. "Don't make it too easy."

"Say that again after you've returned. I'm going to give you a mnemonic. If you want to abort the trip and come back before the full period, then concentrate on the mnemonic. Do you understand?"

"I understand," he said.

She checked him out on all points, once, twice, and then again before she was satisfied. Then, at last, he climbed inside Mother and drank the draft she handed him.

"Have a good trip," she said.

"Oh, I will, ma'am. Don't worry about that," Little John said as the sack filled and he drifted away from her, back in time, back in his mind. "I expect to have a *good* time."

That's what he said. Nothing hard about being a god in 1970. They had had all the materials, and by now he had had experience in godhood. He was ready.

But he came back early. And he didn't have a *good* time.

In fact, he was heartsick, subdued, drained. He wouldn't speak to Shelley Anne Fenstermacher. And without prompting by Samantha or anyone he disappeared into the woods to be by himself, and he didn't come back for two days.

He spent the whole time thinking, trying to make sense of what he had seen, and he wasn't able to do it. He missed two whole sessions with Samantha. And when he did turn up at last, he didn't apologize for being missing.

"You were right," he said simply. "I wasn't ready. Send me back to 1381 again. Please."

"Perhaps," Samantha said.

"I don't understand. I don't understand. I knew things weren't right then, but I didn't think they would be like that. Taxes was what they cared about. They didn't even see what was going on. Not really. And it was just before the Revolution. Are things always that bad before they change?"

"Yes," she said. "Always. The only difference this time is the way things changed. And you didn't see the worst of it. Not by half, Little John."

"I didn't?" he said in surprise. "I thought it must be."

She was too kind to laugh. "No."

"But it was so awful. So ruthless. So destructive."

Samantha said, "Those people weren't so bad. As it happens, they were my parents."

"Oh, I'm sorry, ma'am," he said.

"And your grandparents weren't so different. And they did learn better. That's the important thing to remember. If you take away nothing else, remember that. If they hadn't changed, none of us would be here now."

He cried out, "But they had so much power. They all had the power of gods, and they used it so badly."

Little John may have been stupid, abysmally stupid, he may have been green, and he may have had more years ahead of him than little Shelley Anne Fenstermacher before he was fit to be let out in the world, but there were some things he was able to recognize. Some things are writ plain.

3

Endings of stories come easy. It is the beginnings, when anything is still possible, that come hard.

Start now.

NO DIRECTION HOME

Norman Spinrad

Norman Spinrad became the *cause celebre* of science fiction a few years ago with the publication of his controversial sf novel *Bug Jack Barron*. Here, in a more subdued and thoughtful tone, he returns with a speculation on the future of our burgeoning drug industry, both legal and underground—and what he has to say makes surprising sense.

How does it feel
To be on your own?
With no direction home . . .
Like a complete unknown.
Like a rolling stone."
—Bob Dylan, *Like A Rolling Stone*

"But I once *did* succeed in stuffing it all back in Pandora's box," Richardson said, taking another hit. "You remember Pandora Deutchman, don't you, Will? Everybody in the biochemistry department stuffed it all in Pandora's box at one time or another. I seem to vaguely remember one party when you did it yourself."

"Oh you're a real comedian, Dave," Goldberg said, stubbing out his roach and jamming a cork into the glass vial which he had been filling from the petcock at the end of the apparatus' run. "Any day now, I expect you to start slipping strychnine into the goods. That'd be pretty good for a yock, too."

"You know, I never thought of that before. Maybe you got something there. Let a few people go out with a smile, satisfaction guaranteed. Christ Will, we could tell them exactly what it was and still sell some of the stuff."

"That's not funny, man," Goldberg said, handing the vial to Richardson, who carefully snugged it away with the others in the excelsior-packed box. "It's not funny because it's true."

"Hey, you're not getting an attack of morals, are you? Don't move, I'll be right back with some methalin—that oughta get your head straight."

"My head is straight already. Canabinolic acid, our own invention."

"*Canabinolic acid?* Where did you get that, in a drugstore? We haven't bothered with it for three years."

Goldberg placed another empty vial in the rack under the petcock and opened the valve. "Bought it on the street for kicks," he said. "Kids are brewing it in their bathtubs now." He shook his head, almost a random gesture. "Remember what a bitch the original synthesis was?"

"Science marches on!"

"Too bad we couldn't have patented the stuff," Goldberg said as he contemplated the thin stream of clear green liquid entering the open mouth of the glass vial. "We could've retired off the royalties by now."

"If we had the Mafia to collect for us."

"That might be arranged."

"Yeah, well maybe I should look into it," Richardson said as Goldberg handed him another full vial. "We shouldn't be pigs about it, though. Just about ten percent off the top at the manufacturing end. I don't believe in stifling private enterprise."

"No really, Dave," Goldberg said, "maybe we made a mistake in not trying to patent the stuff. People *do* patent combo psychedelics, you know."

"You don't mean *people*, man, you mean outfits like American Marijuana and Psychedelics, Inc. They can afford the lawyers and grease. They can work the FDA's head. We can't."

Goldberg opened the petcock valve. "Yeah, well at least

it'll be six months or so before the Dope Industry or anyone else figures out how to synthesize this new crap, and by that time I think I'll have just about licked the decay problem in the cocanol extraction process. We should be one step ahead of the squares for at least another year."

"You know what I think, Will?" Richardson said, patting the side of the half-filled box of vials. "I think we got a holy mission, is what. I think we're servants of the evolutionary process. Every time we come up with a new psychedelic, we're advancing the evolution of human consciousness. We develop the stuff and make our bread off it for a while, and then the Dope Industry comes up with our synthesis and mass produces it, and then we gotta come up with the next drug out so we can still set our tables in style. If it weren't for the Dope Industry and the way the drug laws are set up, we could stand still and become bloated pluto-crats just by putting out the same old dope year after year. This way, we're doing some good in the world, we're doing something to further human evolution."

Goldberg handed him another full vial. "Screw human evolution," he said. "What has human evolution ever done for us?"

"As you know, Dr. Taller, we're having some unforeseen side-effects with eucomorfamine," General Carlyle said, stuffing his favourite Dunhill with rough-cut burley. Taller took out a pack of Golds, extracted a joint, and lit it with a lighter bearing an Air Force rather than a Psychedelics, Inc. insignia. Perhaps this had been a deliberate gesture, perhaps not.

"With a psychedelic as new as eucomorfamine, General," Taller said, "no side-effects can quite be called 'unforeseen.' After all, even Project Groundhog itself is an experiment."

Carlyle lit his pipe and sucked in a mouthful of smoke which was good and carcinogenic; the General believed that a good soldier should cultivate at least one foolhardy minor vice. "No word-games, please, doctor," he said. "Eucomorfamine is supposed to help our men in the Ground-hog moonbase deal with the claustrophobic conditions; it is not supposed to promote faggotry in the ranks. The reports I've been getting indicate that the drug is doing both. The Air Force does not want it to do both. Therefore, by definition, eucomorfamine has an undesirable side-effect. Therefore, your contract is up for review."

"General, General, psychedelics are not uniforms, after all. You can't expect us to tailor them to order. You asked for a drug that would combat claustrophobia without impairing alertness or the sleep cycle or attention-span or initiative. You think this is easy? Eucomorfamine produces claustrophilia without any side-effect but a raising of the level of sexual energy. As such, I consider it one of the minor miracles of psychedelic science."

"That's all very well, Taller, but surely you can see that we simply cannot tolerate violent homosexual behaviour among our men in the moonbase."

Taller smiled, perhaps somewhat fatuously. "But you can't very well tolerate a high rate of claustrophobic breakdown, either," he said. "You have only four obvious alternatives, General Carlyle: continue to use eucomorfamine and accept a certain level of homosexual incidents, discontinue eucomorfamine and accept a very high level of claustrophobic breakdown, or cancel Project Groundhog. *Or . . .*"

It dawned upon the General that he had been the object of a rather sophisticated sales pitch. "Or go to a drug that would cancel out the side-effect of eucomorfamine," he said. "Your company just wouldn't happen to have such a drug in the works, would it?"

Dr. Taller gave him a we're-all-men-of-the-world grin. "Psychedelics, Inc., *has* been working on a sexual suppressant," he admitted none too grudgingly. "Not an easy psychic spec to fill. The problem is that if you actually decrease sexual energy, you tend to get impaired performance in the higher cerebral centres, which is all very well in penal institutions, but hardly acceptable in Project Groundhogs's case. The trick is to channel the excess energy elsewhere. We decided that the only viable alternative was to siphon it off into mystical fugue-states. Once we worked it out, the biochemistry became merely a matter of detail. We're about ready to bring the drug we've developed—trade name nadabrin—into the production stage."

The General's pipe had gone out. He did not bother to relight it. Instead, he took 5 mg. of lebemil, which seemed more to the point at the moment. "This nadabrin," he said very deliberately, "it bleeds off the excess sexuality into *what?* Fugue-states? Trances? We certainly don't need a drug that makes our men psychotic."

"Of course not. About three hundred micograms of nada-brin will give a man a mystical experience that lasts less than four hours. He won't be much good to you during that time, to be sure, but his sexual energy level will be severely depressed for about a week. Three hundred micrograms to each man on eucomorfamine, say every five days, to be on the safe side."

General Carlyle relit his pipe and ruminated. Things seemed to be looking up. "Sounds pretty good," he finally admitted. "But what about the content of the mystical experiences? Nothing that would impair devotion to duty?"

Taller snubbed out his roach. "I've taken nadabrin myself," he said. "No problems."

"What was it like?"

Taller once again put on his fatuous smile. "That's the best part of nadabrin," he said. "I don't remember what it was like. You don't retain any memories of what happens to you under nadabrin. Genuine fugue-state. So you can be sure the mystical experiences don't have any undesirable content, can't you? Or at any rate, you can be sure that the experience can't impair a man's military performance."

"What the men don't remember can't hurt them, eh?" Carlyle muttered into his pipestem.

"What was that, General?"

"I said I'd recommend that we give it a try."

They sat together in a corner booth back in the smoke, sizing each other up while the crowd in the joint yammered and swirled around them in some other reality, like a Bavarian merrygoround.

"What are you on?" he said, noticing that her hair seemed black and seamless like a beetle's carapace, a dark metal helmet framing her pale face in glory. Wow.

"Peyotadrene," she said, her lips moving like incredibly jeweled and articulated metal flower-petals. "Been up for about three hours. What's your trip?"

"Canabinolic acid," he said, the distortion of his mouth's movement casting his face into an ideogramic pattern which was barely decipherable to her perception as a foreshadow-ing of energy release. Maybe they would make it.

"I haven't tried any of that stuff for months," she said. "I hardly remember what that reality feels like." Her skin luminesced from within, a translucent white china mask over a yellow candle-flame. She was a magnificent artifact, a creation of jaded and sophisticated gods.

"It feels good," he said, his eyebrows forming a set of curves which, when considered as part of a pattern containing the movement of his lips against his teeth, indicated a clear desire to donate energy to the filling of her void. They *would* make it. "Call me old-fashioned maybe, but I still think canabinolic acid is groovy stuff."

"Do you think you could go on a sex-trip behind it?" she asked. The folds and wrinkles of her ears had been carved with microprecision out of pink ivory.

"Well, I suppose so, in a peculiar kind of way," he said, hunching his shoulders forward in a clear gesture of offering, an alignment with the pattern of her movement through space-time that she could clearly perceive as intersecting her trajectory. "I mean, if you want me to ball you, I think I can make it."

The tiny gold hairs on her face were a microscopic field of wheat shimmering in a shifting summer breeze as she said: "That's the most meaningful thing anyone has said to me in hours."

The convergence of every energy configuration in the entire universe toward complete identity with the standing wave pattern of its maximum ideal structure was brightly mirrored for the world to see in the angle between the curves of his lips as he spoke.

Cardinal McGavin, took a peyotadrene-mescamil combo and 5mg. of metadrene an hour and a half before his meeting with Cardinal Rillo; he had decided to try to deal with Rome on a mystical rather than a political level, and that particular prescription made him feel most deeply Christian. And the Good Lord knew that it could become very difficult to feel deeply Christian when dealing with a representative of the Pope.

Cardinal Rillo arrived punctually at three, just as Cardinal McGavin was approaching his mystical peak; the man's punctuality was legend. Cardinal McGavin felt pathos in that: the sadness of a Prince of the Church whose major impact on the souls of his fellows lay in his slavery to the hands of a clock. Because the ascetic-looking old man, with his colourless eyes and pencil-thin lips, was so thoroughly unlovable, Cardinal McGavin found himself cherishing the man for this very existential hopelessness. He sent forth a silent prayer that he, or if not he then at least someone, might be chosen as an instrument through which this poor cold creature might be granted a measure of Divine Grace.

Cardinal Rillo accepted the amenities with cold formality, and in the same spirit agreed to share some claret. Cardinal McGavin knew better than to offer a joint; Cardinal Rillo had been in the forefront of the opposition which had caused the Pope to delay his inevitable encyclical on marijuana for long ludicrous years. That the Pope had chosen such an emissary in this matter was not a good sign.

Cardinal Rillo sipped at his wine in sour silence for long moments while Cardinal McGavin was nearly overcome with sorrow at the thought of the loneliness of the soul of this man, who could not even break the solemnity of his persona to share some Vatican gossip over a little wine with a fellow Cardinal. Finally, the Papal emissary cleared his throat—a dry, archaic gesture—and got right to the point.

"The Pontiff has instructed me to convey his concern at the addition of psychedelics to the composition of the communion host in the Archdiocese of New York," he said, the tone of his voice making it perfectly clear that he wished the Holy Father had given him a much less cautious warning to deliver. But if the Pope had learned anything at all from the realities of this schismatic era, it was caution. Especially when dealing with the American hierarchy, whose allegiance to Rome was based on nothing firmer than nostalgia and symbolic convenience. The Pope had been the last to be convinced of his own fallibility, but in the last few years events seemed to have finally brought the new refinement of Divine Truth home.

"I acknowledge and respect the Holy Father's concern," Cardinal McGavin said. "I shall pray for divine resolution of his doubt."

"I didn't say anything about doubt!" Cardinal Rillo snapped, his lips moving with the crispness of pincers. "How can you impute doubt to the Holy Father?"

Cardinal McGavin's spirit soared over a momentary spark

of anger at the man's pigheadedness; he tried to give Cardinal Rillo's soul a portion of peace. "I stand corrected," he said. "I shall pray for the alleviation of the Holy Father's concern."

But Cardinal Rillo was implacable and inconsolable; his face was a membrane of control over a musculature of rage. "You can more easily relieve the Holy Father's concern by removing the peyotadrene from your hosts!" he said.

"Are those the words of the Holy Father?" Cardinal McGavin asked, knowing the answer.

"Those are my words, Cardinal McGavin," Cardinal Rillo said, "and you would do well to heed them. The fate of your immortal soul may be at stake."

A flash of insight, a sudden small satori, rippled through Cardinal McGavin: Rillo was sincere. For him, the question of a chemically-augmented host was not a matter of Church politics, as it probably was to the Pope; it touched on an area of deep religious conviction. Cardinal Rillo was indeed concerned for the state of his soul, and it behoved him, both as a Cardinal and as a Catholic, to treat the matter seriously on that level. For after all, chemically-augmented communion was a matter of deep religious conviction for him as well. He and Cardinal Rillo faced each other across a gap of existentially-meaningful theological disagreement.

"Perhaps the fate of yours as well, Cardinal Rillo," he said.

"I didn't come here all the way from Rome to seek spiritual guidance from a man who is skating on the edge of heresy, Cardinal McGavin. I came here to deliver the Holy Father's warning that an encyclical may be issued against your position. Need I remind you that if you disobey such an encyclical, you may be excommunicated?"

"Would you be genuinely sorry to see that happen?" Cardinal McGavin asked, wondering how much of the threat was Rillo's wishful thinking, and how much the instructions of the Pope. "Or would you simply feel that the Church had defended itself properly?"

"Both," Cardinal Rillo said without hesitation.

"I like that answer," Cardinal McGavin said, tossing down the rest of his glass of claret. It was a good answer— sincere on both counts. Cardinal Rillo feared both for the

Church and for the soul of the Archbishop of New York, and there was no doubt that he quite properly put the Church first. His sincerity was spiritually refreshing, even though he was thoroughly wrong all round. "But you see, part of the gift of Grace that comes with a scientifically-sound chemical augmentation of communion is a certainty that no one, not even the Pope, can do anything to cut you off from communion with God. In psychedelic communion, one experiences the love of God directly. It's always just a host away; faith is no longer even necessary."

Cardinal Rillo grew somber. "It is my duty to report that to the Pope," he said. "I trust you realize that."

"Who am I talking to, Cardinal Rillo, you or the Pope?"

"You are talking to the Catholic Church, Cardinal Mc-Gavin." Rillo said. "I am an emissary of the Holy Father." Cardinal McGavin felt an instant pang of guilt: His sharpness had caused Cardinal Rillo to imply an untruth out of anger, for surely his Papal mission was far more limited than he had tried to intimate. The Pope was too much of a realist to make the empty threat of excommunication against a Prince of the Church who believed that his power of excommunication was itself meaningless.

But again, a sudden flash of insight illuminated the Cardinal's mind with truth: In the eyes of Cardinal Rillo, in the eyes of an important segment of the Church hierarchy, the threat of excommunication still held real meaning. To accept their position on chemically-augmented communion was to accept the notion that the word of the Pope could withdraw a man from Divine Grace. To accept the sanctity and validity of psychedelic communion was to deny the validity of excommunication.

"You know, Cardinal Rillo," he said. "I firmly believe that if I am excommunicated by the Pope, it will threaten my soul not one iota."

"That's merely cheap blasphemy!"

"I'm sorry," Cardinal McGavin said sincerely, "I meant to be neither cheap nor blasphemous. All I was trying to do was explain that excommunication can hardly be meaningful when God through the psychedelic sciences has seen fit to grant us a means of certain direct experience of his countenance. I believe with all my heart that this is true. You believe with all your heart that it is not."

"I believe that what you experience in your psychedelic communion is nothing less than a masterstroke of Satan, Cardinal McGavin. Evil is infinitely subtle; might not it finally masquerade as the ultimate good? The Devil is not known as the Prince of Liars without reason. I believe that you are serving Satan in what you sincerely believe is the service of God. Is there any way that you can be sure that I am wrong?"

"Can you be sure that *I'm* not right?" Cardinal McGavin said. "If I am, you are attempting to stifle the will of God and wilfully removing yourself from His Grace."

"We cannot both be right . . ." Cardinal Rillo said.

And the burning glare of a terrible and dark mystical insight filled Cardinal McGavin's soul with terror, a harsh illumination of his existential relationship to the Church and to God: They both couldn't be right, but there was no reason why they both couldn't be wrong. Apart from both God and Satan, existed the Void.

Dr. Braden gave Johnny a pat-on-the-head smile and handed him a mango-flavoured lollypop from the supply of goodies in his lower-left desk drawer. Johnny took the lollypop, unwrapped it quickly, popped it into his mouth, leaned back in his chair, and began to suck the sweet avidly, oblivious to the rest of the world. It was a good sign—a preschooler with a proper reaction to a proper basic prescription should focus strongly and completely on the most interesting element in its environment, should be fond of unusual flavours. In the first four years of its life, a child's sensorium should be tuned to accept the widest possible spectrum of sensual stimulation.

Braden turned his attention to the boy's mother, who sat rather nervously on the edge of her chair smoking a joint. "Now, now, Mrs. Lindstrom, there's nothing to worry about," he said. "Johnny has been responding quite normally to his prescription. His attention-span is suitably short for a child of his age, his sensual range slightly exceeds the optimum norm, his sleep pattern is regular and properly deep. And as you requested, he has been given a constant sense of universal love."

"But then why did the school doctor ask me to have his basic prescription changed, Dr. Braden? He said that

Johnny's prescription was giving him the wrong personality pattern for a school-age child."

Dr. Braden was rather annoyed, though of course he would never betray it to the nervous young mother. He knew the sort of failed G.P. who usually occupied a school doctor's position; a faded old fool who knew about as much about psychedelic pediatrics as he did about brain surgery. What he did know was worse than nothing—a smattering of half-assed generalities and pure rubbish that was just enough to convince him that he was an expert. Which entitled him to go around frightening the mothers of other people's patients, no doubt.

"I'm . . . ah, certain you misunderstood what the school doctor said, Mrs. Lindstrom," Dr. Braden said. "At least I hope you did, because if you didn't, then the man is mistaken. You see, modern psychedelic pediatrics recognizes that the child needs to have his consciousness focused in different areas at different stages of his development, if he is to grow up to be a healthy, maximized individual. A child of Johnny's age is in a transitional stage. In order to prepare him for schooling, I'll simply have to alter his prescription so as to increase his attention-span, lower his sensory intensity a shade, and increase his interest in abstractions. Then he'll do fine in school, Mrs. Lindstrom."

Dr. Braden gave the young woman a moderately-stern admonishing frown. "You really should have brought Johnny in for a check-up *before* he started school, you know."

Mrs. Lindstrom puffed nervously on her joint while Johnny continued to suck happily on his lollypop. "Well . . . I was sort of afraid to, Dr. Braden," she admitted. "I know it sounds silly, but I was afraid that if you changed his prescription to what the school wanted, you'd stop the paxum. I didn't want that—I think it's more important for Johnny to continue to feel universal love than increasing his attention-span or any of that stuff. You're not going to stop the paxum, are you?"

"Quite the contrary, Mrs. Lindstrom," Dr. Braden said. "I'm going to increase his dose slightly and give him 10mg. of orodalamine daily. He'll submit to the necessary authority of his teachers with a sense of trust and love, rather than out of fear."

For the first time during the visit, Mrs. Lindstrom smiled.

"Then it all really *is* all right, isn't it?" She radiated happiness born of relief.

Dr. Braden smiled back at her, basking in the sudden surge of good vibrations. This was his peak-experience in pediatrics: feeling the genuine gratitude of a worried mother whose fears he had thoroughly relieved. This was what being a doctor was all about. She trusted him. She put the consciousness of her child in his hands, trusting that those hands would not falter or fail. He was proud and grateful to be a psychedelic pediatrician. He was maximizing human happiness.

"Yes, Mrs. Lindstrom," he said soothingly, "everything is going to be all right."

In the chair in the corner. Johnny Lindstrom sucked on his lollypop, his face transfigured with boyish bliss.

There were moments when Bill Watney got a soul-deep queasy feeling about psychedelic design, and lately he was getting those bad flashes more and more often. He was glad to have caught Spiegelman alone in the designers' lounge; if anyone could do anything for his head, Lennie was it. "I dunno," he said, washing down 15mg. of lebemil with a stiff shot of bourbon, "I'm really thinking of getting out of this business."

Leonard Spiegelman lit a Gold with his 14-Carat gold lighter—nothing but the best for the best in the business—smiled across the coffee-table at Watney, and said quite genially: "You're out of your mind, Bill."

Watney sat hunched slightly forward in his easy chair, studying Spiegelman, the best artist Psychedelics, Inc. had, and envying the older man. Envying not only his talent, but his attitude towards his work. Lennie Spiegelman was not only certain that what he was doing was right, he enjoyed every minute of it. Watney wished he could be like Spiegelman. Spiegelman was happy; he radiated the contented aura of a man who really did have everything he wanted.

Spiegelman opened his arms in a gesture that seemed to make the whole designers' lounge his personal property. "We're the world's best-pampered artists," he said. "We come up with two or three viable drug designs a year, and we can live like kings. And we're practising the world's ultimate artform: creating realities. We're the luckiest mothers alive! Why would anyone with your talent want out of psychedelic design?"

Watney found it difficult to put into words, which was ridiculous for a psychedelic designer, whose work it was to describe new possibilities in human consciousness well enough for the biochemists to develop psychedelics which would transform his specs into styles of reality. It was humiliating to be at a loss for words in front of Lennie Spiegelman, a man he both envied and admired. "I'm getting bad flashes lately," he finally said. "Deep flashes that go through every style of consciousness that I try, flashes that tell me I should be ashamed and disgusted about what I'm doing."

Oh, oh, Lennie Spiegelman thought, the kid is coming up with his first case of designer's cafard. He's floundering around with that no direction home syndrome, and he thinks it's the end of the world. "I know what's bothering you, Bill," he said. "It happens to all of us at one time or another. You feel that designing psychedelic specs is a solipsistic occupation, right? You think there's something morally wrong about designing new styles of consciousness for other people, that we're playing god, that continually altering people's consciousness in ways only we fully understand is a thing that mere mortals have no right to do, like hubris, eh?"

Watney flashed admiration for Spiegelman—his certainty *wasn't* based on a thick ignorance of the existential doubt of their situation. There was hope in that, too. "How can you understand all that, Lennie," he said, "and still dig psychedelic design the way you do?"

"Because it's a load of crap, that's why," Spiegelman said. "Look kid, we're artists, commercial artists at that. We design psychedelics, styles of reality; we don't tell anyone what to think. If people like the realities we design for them, they buy the drugs, and if they don't like our art, they don't. People aren't going to buy food that tastes lousy, music that makes their ears hurt, or drugs that put them in bummer realities. *Somebody* is going to design styles of consciousness for the human race, if not artists like us, then a lot of crummy politicians and power-freaks."

"But what makes us any better than them? Why do we have any more right to play games with the consciousness of the human race than they do?"

The kid is really dense, Spiegelman thought. But then he smiled, remembering that he had been on the same stupid trip when he was Watney's age. "Because we're artists, and they're not," he said. "We're not out to control people. We get our kicks from carving something beautiful out of the void. All we want to do is enrich people's lives. We're creating new styles of consciousness that we think are improved realities, but we're not shoving them down people's throats. We're just laying out our wares for the public—right doesn't even enter into it. We have a compulsion to practise our art. Right and wrong are arbitrary concepts that vary with the style of consciousness, so how on earth can you talk about the right and wrong of psychedelic design? The only way you can judge is by an esthetic criterion—are we producing good art or bad?"

"Yeah, but doesn't *that* vary with the style of consciousness too? Who can judge in an absolute sense whether your stuff is artistically pleasing or not?"

"Jesus Christ, Bill, *I* can judge, can't I?" Spiegelman said. "I know when a set of psychedelic specs is a successful work of art. It either pleases me or it doesn't."

It finally dawned on Watney that that was precisely what was eating at him. A psychedelic designer altered his own reality with a wide spectrum of drugs and then designed other psychedelics to alter other people's realities. Where was anyone's anchor?

"But don't you see, Lennie?" he said. "We don't know what the hell we're doing. We're taking the human race on an evolutionary trip, but we don't know where we're going. We're flying blind."

Spiegelman took a big drag on his joint. The kid was starting to get to him; he was whining too much. Watney didn't want anything out of line—just certainty! "You want me to tell you there's a way you can know when a design is right or wrong in some absolute evolutionary framework, right?" he said. "Well I'm sorry, Bill, there's nothing but us and the void and whatever we carve out of it. We're our own creations, our realities are our own works of art. We're out here all alone."

Watney was living through one of his flashes of dread, and he saw that Spiegelman's words described its content exactly. "But that's exactly what's eating at me!" he said. "Where in hell is our basic reality?"

"There is no basic reality. I thought they taught that in kindergarten these days."

"But what about the basic state? What about the way our reality was before the art of psychedelic design? What about the consciousness-style that evolved naturally over millions of years? Damn it, that was the basic reality, and we've lost it!"

"The hell it was!" Spiegelman said. "Our pre-psychedelic consciousness evolved on a mindless random basis. What makes that reality superior to any other? Just because it was first? We may be flying blind, but natural evolution was worse—it was an idiot process without an ounce of consciousness behind it."

"Goddamn it, you're right all the way down the line, Lennie!" Watney cried in anguish. "But why do you feel so good about it while I feel so rotten? I want to be able to feel the way you do, but I can't."

"Of course you can, Bill," Spiegelman said. He abstractly remembered that he had felt like Watney years ago, but there was no existential reality behind it. What more could a man want than a random universe that was anything he could make of it and nothing else? Who wouldn't rather have a style of consciousness created by an artist than one that was the result of a lot of stupid evolutionary accidents?

He says it with such certainty, Watney thought. Christ, how I want him to be right! How I'd like to face the uncertainty of it all, the void, with the courage of Lennie Spiegelman! Spiegelman had been in the business for fifteen years; maybe he *had* finally figured it all out.

"I wish I could believe that," Watney said.

Spiegelman smiled, remembering what a solemn jerk he had been ten years ago himself. "Ten years ago, I felt just like you feel now," he said. "But I got my head together and now here I am, fat and happy and digging what I'm doing."

"How, Lennie, for chrissakes, *how?*"

"50 mikes of methalin, 40 mg. of lebemil and 20 mg. of peyotadrene daily," Spiegelman said. "It made a new man out of me, and it'll make a new man out of you."

"How do you feel, man?" Kip said, taking the joint out of his mouth and peering intently into Jonesy's eyes. Jonesy looked really weird—pale, manic, maybe a little crazed. Kip was starting to feel glad that Jonesy hadn't talked him into taking the trip with him.

"Oh wow," Jonesy croaked, "I feel strange, I feel *really* strange, and it doesn't feel so good . . ."

The sun was high in the cloudless blue sky; a golden fountain of radiant energy filling Kip's being. The wood-and-bark of the tree against which they sat was an organic reality connecting the skin of his back to the bowels of the earth in an unbroken circuit of protoplasmic electricity. He was a flower of his planet, rooted deep in the rich soil, basking in the cosmic nectar of the sunshine.

But behind Jonesy's eyes was some kind of awful grey vortex. Jonesy looked really bad. Jonesy was definitely floating on the edges of a bummer.

"I don't feel good at all," Jonesy said. "Man, you know the ground is covered with all kinds of hard dead things and the grass is filled with mindless insects and the sun is hot, man, I think I'm burning . . ."

"Take it easy, don't freak, you're on a trip, that's all," Kip said from some asshole superior viewpoint. He just didn't understand, he didn't understand how heavy this trip was, what it felt like to have your head raw and naked out here. Like cut off from every energy flow in the universe—a construction of fragile matter, protoplasmic ooze is all, isolated in an energy-vacuum, existing in relationship to nothing but empty void and horrible mindless matter.

"You don't understand, Kip," he said. "This is reality, the way it really is, and man it's horrible, just a great big ugly machine made up of lots of other machines, you're a machine, I'm a machine, it's all mechanical clockwork. We're just lumps of dead matter run by machinery, kept alive by chemical and electric processes."

Golden sunlight soaked through Kip's skin and turned the core of his being into a miniature stellar phoenix. The wind, through random blades of grass, made love to the bare soles of his feet. What was all this machinery crap? What the hell was Jonesy gibbering about? Man, who would want to put himself in a bummer reality like that?

"You're just on a bummer, Jonesy," he said. "Take it easy.

You're not seeing the universe the way it really is, as if that meant anything. Reality is all in your head. You're just freaking out behind nothing."

"That's it, that's exactly it, I'm freaking out behind nothing. Like zero. Like cipher. Like the void. Nothing is where we're *really* at."

How could he explain it? That reality was really just a lot of empty vacuum that went on to infinity in space and time. The perfect nothingness had minor contaminations of dead matter here and there. A little of this matter had fallen together through a complex series of random accidents to contaminate the universal deadness with trace elements of life, protoplasmic slime, biochemical clockwork. Some of this clockwork was complicated enough to generate thought, consciousness. And that was all there ever was or would ever be anywhere in space and time. Clockwork mechanisms rapidly running down in the cold black void. Everything that wasn't dead matter already would end up that way sooner or later.

"This is the way it really is," Jonesy said. "People used to live in this bummer all the time. It's the way it is, and nothing we can do can change it."

"I can change it," Kip said, taking his pillbox out of a pocket. "Just say the word. Let me know when you've had enough and I'll bring you out of it. Lebemil, peyotadrene, mescamil, you name it."

"You don't understand, man, it's *real*. That's the trip I'm on, I haven't taken anything at all for twelve hours, remember? It's the natural state, it's reality itself, and man, it's awful. It's a horrible bummer. Christ, why did I have to talk myself into this? I don't want to see the universe this way, who needs it?"

Kip was starting to get pissed off—Jonesy was becoming a real bring-down. Why did he have to pick a beautiful day like this to take his stupid nothing trip?

"Then *take* something already," he said, offering Jonesy the pillbox.

Shakily, Jonesy scooped out a cap of peyotedrene and a 15 mg. tab of lebemil and wolfed them down dry. "How did people *live* before psychedelics?" he said. "How could they stand it?"

"Who knows?" Kip said, closing his eyes and staring straight at the sun, diffusing his consciousness into the universe of golden orange light encompassed by his eye lids. "Maybe they had some way of not thinking about it."

VASTER THAN EMPIRES AND MORE SLOW

Ursula K. Le Guin

Since the publication of her novel *The Left Hand of Darkness,* which won both the Hugo and Nebula awards, Ursula Le Guin's star has been on a constantly accelerating rise. Reading any of her stories and novels immediately tells us why: she's a writer of grace, ease, and good clear thinking. Here, in a story of exploration on an alien planet, Ursula Le Guin spins a fascinating and powerful web from strands of logic and mood.

You're looking at a clock. It has hands, and figures arranged in a circle. The hands move. You can't tell if they move at the same rate, or if one moves faster than the other. What does *than* mean? There is a relationship between the hands and the circle of figures, and the name of this relationship is on the tip of your tongue; the hands are . . . something-or-other, at the figures. Or is it the figures that . . . at the hands? What does *at* mean? They are figures —your vocabulary hasn't shrunk at all—and of course you can count, one two three four etc., but the trouble is you can't tell which one is one. Each one is one: itself. Where do you begin? Each one being one, there is no, what's the word, I had it just now, something-ship, between the ones. There is no between. There is only here and here, one and one. There is no there. Maya has fallen. All is here now one.

But if all is now and all here and one all, there is no end. It did not begin so it cannot end. Oh God, here now One get me out of this—

I'm trying to describe the sensations of the average person in NAFAL flight. It can be much worse than this for some, whose time-sense is acute. For others it is restful, like a drug-haze freeing the mind from the tyranny of hours. And for a few the experience is certainly mystical; the collapse of time and relation leading them directly to intuition of the eternal. But the mystic is a rare bird, and the nearest most people get to God in paradoxical time is by inarticulate and anguished prayer for release.

They used to drug people for the long jumps, but stopped the practice when they realized its effects. What happens to a drugged, or ill, or wounded person during near-lightspeed flight is, of course, indeterminable. A jump of ten lightyears should logically make no difference to a victim of measles or gunshot. The body ages only a few minutes; why is the measles patient carried out of the ship a leper, and the wounded man a corpse? Nobody knows, except perhaps the body, which keeps the logic of the flesh, and knows it has lain festering, bleeding, or drugged into mindlessness, for ten years. Many imbeciles having been produced, the Fisher King Effect was established as fact, and they stopped using drugs and transporting the ill, the damaged, and the pregnant. You have to be in common health to go NAFAL, and you have to take it straight.

But you don't have to be sane.

It was only during the earliest decades of the League that Earthmen, perhaps trying to bolster their battered collective ego, sent out ships on enormously long voyages, beyond the pale, over the stars and far away. They were seeking for worlds that had not, like all the known worlds, been settled or seeded by the Founders on Hain, truly alien worlds; and all the crews of these Extreme Surveys were of unsound mind. Who else would go out to collect information that wouldn't be received for four, or five, or six centuries? Received by whom? This was before the invention of the instantaneous communicator; they would be isolated both in space and time. No sane person who has experienced time-slippage of even a few decades between near worlds would volunteer for a round trip of a half millennium. The Surveyors were escapists; misfits; nuts.

Ten of them climbed aboard the ferry at Smeming Port on Pesm, and made varyingly inept attempts to get to know one another during the three days the ferry took getting to their ship, *Gum*. Gum is a Low Cetian nickname, on the order of Baby or Pet. There was one Low Cetian on the team, one Hairy Cetian, two Hainishmen, one Beldene, and five Terrans; the ship was Cetian-built, but chartered by the Government of Earth. Her motley crew came aboard wriggling through the coupling-tube one by one like apprehensive spermatozoa fertilizing the universe. The ferry left, and the navigator put *Gum* underway. She flittered for some hours on the edge of space a few hundred million miles from Pesm, and then abruptly vanished.

When, after ten hours twenty-nine minutes, or 256 years, *Gum* reappeared in normal space, she was supposed to be in the vicinity of Star KG-E-96651. Sure enough, there was the cheerful gold pinhead of the star. Somewhere within a 400-million-kilometer sphere there was also a greenish planet, World 4470, as charted by a Cetian Mapmaker long ago. The ship now had to find the planet. This was not quite so easy as it might sound, given a 400-million-kilometer haystack. And *Gum* couldn't bat about in planetary space at near lightspeed; if she did, she and Star KG-E-96651 and World 4470 might all end up going bang. She had to creep, using rocket propulsion, at a few hundred thousand miles an hour. The Mathematician/Navigator, Asnanifoil, knew pretty well where the planet ought to be, and thought they might raise it within ten E-days. Meanwhile the members of the Survey team got to know one another still better.

"I can't stand him," said Porlock, the Hard Scientist (chemistry, plus physics, astronomy, geology, etc.), and little blobs of spittle appeared on his mustache. "The man is insane. I can't imagine why he was passed as fit to join a Survey team, unless this is a deliberate experiment in non-compatibility, planned by the Authority, with us as guinea pigs."

"We generally use hamsters and Hainish gholes," said Mannon, the Soft Scientist (psychology, plus psychiatry, anthropology, ecology, etc.), politely; he was one of the Hainishmen. "Instead of guinea pigs. Well, you know, Mr. Osden is really a very rare case. In fact, he's the first fully cured case of Render's Syndrome—a variety of infantile autism which was thought to be incurable. The great Terran analyst Hammergeld reasoned that the cause of the autistic condition in this case is a supernormal empathic capacity, and developed an appropriate treatment. Mr. Osden is the first patient to undergo that treatment; in fact he lived with Dr. Hammergeld until he was eighteen. The therapy was completely successful."

"Successful?"

"Why, yes. He certainly is not autistic."

"No, he's intolerable!"

"Well, you see," said Mannon, gazing mildly at the saliva-flecks on Porlock's mustache, "the normal defensive-aggressive reaction between strangers meeting—let's say you and Mr. Osden just for example—is something you're scarcely aware of; habit, manners, inattention get you past it; you've learned to ignore it, to the point where you might even deny it exists. However, Mr. Osden, being an empath, feels it. Feels his feelings, and yours, and is hard put to say which is which. Let's say that there's a normal element of hostility towards any stranger in your emotional reaction to him when you meet him, plus a spontaneous dislike of his looks, or clothes, or handshake—it doesn't matter what. He feels that dislike. As his autistic defense has been unlearned, he resorts to an aggressive-defense mechanism, a response in kind to the aggression which you have unwittingly projected onto him." Mannon went on for quite a long time.

"Nothing gives a man the right to be such a bastard," Porlock said.

"He can't tune us out?" asked Harfex, the Biologist, another Hainishman.

"It's like hearing," said Olleroo, Assistant Hard Scientist, stooping over to paint her toenails with fluorescent lacquer. "No eyelids on your ears. No Off switch on empathy. He hears our feelings whether he wants to or not."

"Does he know what we're *thinking?*" asked Eskwana, the Engineer, looking round at the others in real dread.

"No," Porlock snapped. "Empathy's not telepathy! Nobody's got telepathy."

"Yet," said Mannon, with his little smile. "Just before I

left Hain there was a most interesting report in from one of the recently rediscovered worlds, a hilfer named Rocannon reporting what appears to be a teachable telepathic technique existent among a mutated hominid race; I only saw a synopsis in the HILF *Bulletin,* but—" He went on. The others had learned that they could talk while Hammon went on talking; he did not seem to mind, nor even to miss much of what they said.

"Then why does he hate us?' Eskwana asked.

"Nobody hates you, Ander honey," said Olleroo, daubing Eskwana's left thumbnail with fluorescent pink. The engineer flushed and smiled vaguely.

"He acts as if he hated us," said Haito, the Coordinator. She was a delicate-looking woman of pure Asian descent, with a surprising voice, husky, deep, and soft, like a young bullfrog. "Why, if he suffers from our hostility, does he increase it by constant attacks and insults? I can't say I think much of Dr. Hammergeld's cure, really, Mannon; autism might be preferable . . ."

She stopped. Osden had come into the main cabin.

He looked flayed. His skin was unnaturally white and thin, showing the channels of his blood like a faded roadmap in red and blue. His Adam's apple, the muscles that circled his mouth, the bones and ligaments of his wrists and hands, all stood out distinctly as if displayed for an anatomy lesson. His hair was pale rust, like long-dried blood. He had eyebrows and lashes, but they were visible only in certain lights; what one saw was the bones of the eyesockets, the veining of the lids, and the colorless eyes. They were not red eyes, for he was not really an albino, but they were not blue or gray; colors had canceled out in Osden's eyes, leaving a cold waterlike clarity, infinitely penetrable. He never looked directly at one. His face lacked expression, like an anatomical drawing, or a skinned face.

"I agree," he said in a high, harsh tenor, "that even autistic withdrawal might be preferable to the smog of cheap second-hand emotions with which you people surround me. What are you sweating hate for now, Porlock? Can't stand the sight of me? Go practice some autoeroticism the way you were doing last night, it improves your vibes. —Who the devil moved my tapes, here? Don't touch my things, any of you. I won't have it."

"Osden," said Asnanifoil, the Hairy Cetian, in his large slow voice, "why *are* you such a bastard?"

Ander Eskwana cowered down and put his hands in front of his face. Contention frightened him. Olleroo looked up with a vacant yet eager expression, the eternal spectator.

"Why shouldn't I be?" said Osden. He was not looking at Asnanifoil, and was keeping physically as far away from all of them as he could in the crowded cabin. "None of you constitute, in yourselves, any reason for my changing my behavior."

Asnanifoil shrugged; Cetians are seldom willing to state the obvious. Harfex, a reserved and patient man, said, "The reason is that we shall be spending several years together. Life will be better for all of us if—"

"Can't you understand that I don't give a damn for all of you?" Osden said, took up his microtapes, and went out. Eskwana had suddenly gone to sleep. Asnanifoil was drawing slipstreams in the air with his finger and muttering the Ritual Primes. "You cannot explain his presence on the team except as a plot on the part of the Terran Authority. I saw this almost at once. This mission is meant to fail," Harfex whispered to the Coordinator, glancing over his shoulder. Porlock was fumbling with his fly-button; there were tears in his eyes. I did tell you they were all crazy, but you thought I was exaggerating.

All the same, they were not unjustified. Extreme Surveyors expected to find their fellow team-members intelligent, well-trained, unstable, and personally sympathetic. They had to work together in close quarters and nasty places, and could expect one another's paranoias, depressions, manias, phobias, and compulsions to be mild enough to admit of good personal relationships, at least most of the time. Osden might be intelligent, but his training was sketchy and his personality was disastrous. He had been sent only on account of his singular gift, the power of empathy: properly speaking, of wide-range bioempathic receptivity. His talent wasn't species-specific; he could pick up emotion or sentience from anything that felt. He could share lust with a white rat, pain with a squashed cockroach, and phototropy with a moth. On an alien world, the Authority had decided, it would be useful to know if anything nearby is sentient, and if so, what its feelings towards you are. Osden's title was a new one: He was the team's Sensor.

"What is emotion, Osden?" Haito Tomiko asked him one day in the main cabin, trying to make some rapport with him for once. "What is it, exactly, that you pick up with your empathic sensitivity?"

"Muck," the man answered in his high, exasperated voice. "The psychic excreta of the animal kingdom. I wade through your faeces."

"I was trying," she said, "to learn some facts." She thought her tone was admirably calm.

"You weren't after facts. You were trying to get at me. With some fear, some curiosity, and a great deal of distaste. The way you might poke a dead dog, to see the maggots crawl. Will you understand once and for all that I don't want to be got at, that I want to be left alone?" His skin was mottled with red and violet, his voice had risen. "Go roll in your own dung, you yellow bitch!" he shouted at her silence.

"Calm down," she said, still quietly, but she left him at once and went to her cabin. Of course he had been right about her motives; her question had been largely a pretext, a mere effort to interest him. But what harm in that? Did not that effort imply respect for the other? At the moment of asking the question she had felt at most a slight distrust of him; she had mostly felt sorry for him, the poor arrogant venomous bastard, Mr. No-Skin as Olleroo called him. What did he expect, the way he acted? Love?

"I guess he can't stand anybody feeling sorry for him," said Olleroo, lying on the lower bunk, gilding her nipples.

"Then he can't form any human relationship. All his Dr. Hammergeld did was turn an autism inside out. . . ."

"Poor frot," said Olleroo. "Tomiko, you don't mind if Harfex comes in for a while tonight, do you?"

"Can't you go to his cabin? I'm sick of always having to sit in Main with that damned peeled turnip."

"You do hate him, don't you? I guess he feels that. But I slept with Harfex last night too, and Asnanifoil might get jealous, since they share the cabin. It would be nicer here."

"Service them both," Tomiko said with the coarseness of offended modesty. Her Terran subculture, the East Asian, was a puritanical one; she had been brought up chaste.

"I only like one a night," Olleroo replied with innocent serenity. Beldene, the Garden Planet, had never discovered chastity, or the wheel.

"Try Osden, then," Tomiko said. Her personal instability was seldom so plain as now: a profound self-distrust manifesting itself as destructivism. She had volunteered for this job because there was, in all probability, no use in doing it.

The little Beldene looked up, paintbrush in hand, eyes wide. "Tomiko, that was a dirty thing to say."

"Why?"

"It would be vile! I'm not attracted to Osden!"

"I didn't know it mattered to you," Tomiko said indifferently, though she did know. She got some papers together and left the cabin, remarking, "I hope you and Harfex or whoever it is finish by last bell; I'm tired."

Olleroo was crying, tears dripping on her little gilded nipples. She wept easily. Tomiko had not wept since she was ten years old.

It was not a happy ship; but it took a turn for the better when Asnanifoil and his computer raised World 4470. There it lay, a dark-green jewel, like truth at the bottom of a gravity well. As they watched the jade disc grow, a sense of mutuality grew among them. Osden's selfishness, his accurate cruelty, served now to draw the others together. "Perhaps," Mannon said, "he was sent as a beating-gron. What Terrans call a scapegoat. Perhaps his influence will be good after all." And no one, so careful were they to be kind to one another, disagreed.

They came into orbit. There were no lights on nightside, on the continents none of the lines and clots made by animals who build.

"No men," Harfex murmured.

"Of course not," snapped Osden, who had a viewscreen to himself, and his head inside a polythene bag. He claimed that the plastic cut down on the empathic noise he received from the others. "We're two lightcenturies past the limit of the Hainish Expansion, and outside that there are no men. Anywhere. You don't think Creation would have made the same hideous mistake twice?"

No one was paying him much heed; they were looking with affection at that jade immensity below them, where there was life, but not human life. They were misfits among men, and what they saw there was not desolation, but peace. Even Osden did not look quite so expressionless as usual; he was frowning.

Descent in fire on the sea; air reconnaissance; landing. A plain of something like grass, thick, green, bowing stalks, surrounded the ship, brushed against extended view-cameras, smeared the lenses with a fine pollen.

"It looks like a pure phytosphere," Harfex said. "Osden, do you pick up anything sentient?"

They all turned to the Sensor. He had left the screen and was pouring himself a cup of tea. He did not answer. He seldom answered spoken questions.

The chitinous rigidity of military discipline was quite inapplicable to these teams of Mad Scientists; their chain of command lay somewhere between parliamentary procedure and peck-order, and would have driven a regular service officer out of his mind. By the inscrutable decision of the Authority, however, Dr. Haito Tomiko had been given the title of Coordinator, and she now exercised her prerogative for the first time. "Mr. Sensor Osden," she said, "please answer Mr. Harfex."

"How could I 'pick up' anything from outside," Osden said without turning, "with the emotions of nine neurotic hominids pullulating around me like worms in a can? When I have anything to tell you, I'll tell you. I'm aware of my responsibility as Sensor. If you presume to give me an order again, however, Coordinator Haito, I'll consider my responsibility void."

"Very well, Mr. Sensor. I trust no orders will be needed henceforth." Tomiko's bullfrog voice was calm, but Osden seemed to flinch slightly as he stood with his back to her: as if the surge of her suppressed rancor had struck him with physical force.

The biologist's hunch proved correct. When they began field analyses they found no animals even among the microbiota. Nobody here ate anybody else. All life-forms were photosynthesizing or saprophagous, living off light or death, not off life. Plants: infinite plants, not one species known to the visitors from the house of Man. Infinite shades and intensities of green, violet, purple, brown, red. Infinite silences. Only the wind moved, swaying leaves and fronds, a warm soughing wind laden with spores and pollens, blowing the sweet pale-green dust over prairies of great grasses, heaths that bore no heather, flowerless forests where no foot had ever walked, no eye had ever looked. A warm, sad world, sad and serene. The Surveyors, wandering like picnickers over sunny plains of violet filicaliformes, spoke softly to each other. They knew their voices broke a silence of a thousand million years, the silence of wind and leaves, leaves and wind, blowing and ceasing and blowing again. They talked softly; but being human, they talked.

"Poor old Osden," said Jenny Chong, Bio and Tech, as she piloted a helijet on the North Polar Quadrating run. "All that fancy hi-fi stuff in his brain and nothing to receive. What a bust."

"He told me he hates plants," Olleroo said with a giggle. "You'd think he'd like them, since they don't bother him like we do."

"Can't say I much like these plants myself," said Porlock, looking down at the purple undulations of the North Circumpolar Forest. "All the same. No mind. No change. A man alone in it would go right off his head."

"But it's all alive," Jenny Chong said. "And if it lives, Osden hates it."

"He's not really so bad," Olleroo said, magnanimous. Porlock looked at her sidelong and asked, "You ever slept with him, Olleroo?"

Olleroo burst into tears and cried, "You Terrans are obscene!"

"No she hasn't," Jenny Chong said, prompt to defend. "Have you, Porlock?"

The chemist laughed uneasily: Ha, ha, ha. Flecks of spittle appeared on his mustache.

"Osden can't bear to be touched," Olleroo said shakily. "I just brushed against him once by accident and he knocked me off like I was some sort of dirty . . . thing. We're all just things, to him."

"He's evil," Porlock said in a strained voice, startling the two women. "He'll end up shattering this team, sabotaging it, one way or another. Mark my words. He's not fit to live with other people!"

They landed on the North Pole. A midnight sun smouldered over low hills. Short, dry, greenish-pink bryoform grasses stretched away in every direction, which was all one direction, south. Subdued by the incredible silence, the three Surveyors set up their instruments and collected their samples, three viruses twitching minutely on the hide of an unmoving giant.

Nobody asked Osden along on runs as pilot or photographer or recorder, and he never volunteered, so he seldom left base camp. He ran Harfex's botanical taxonomic data through the on-ship computers, and served as assistant to Eskwana, whose job here was mainly repair and maintenance. Eskwana had begun to sleep a great deal, twenty-five hours or more out of the thirty-two hour day, dropping off in the middle of repairing a radio or checking the guidance circuits of a helijet. The Co-ordinator stayed at base one day to observe. No one else was home except Poswet To, who was subject to epileptic fits; Mannon had plugged her into a therapy-circuit today in a state of preventive catatonia. Tomiko spoke reports into the storage banks, and kept an eye on Osden and Eskwana. Two hours passed.

"You might want to use the 860 microwaldoes in sealing that connection," Eskwana said in his soft, hesitant voice.

"Obviously!"

"Sorry. I just saw you had the 840's there—"

"And will replace them when I take the 860's out. When I don't know how to proceed, Engineer, I'll ask your advice."

After a minute Tomiko looked round. Sure enough, there was Eskwana sound asleep, head on the table, thumb in his mouth.

"Osden."

The white face did not turn; he did not speak, but conveyed impatiently that he was listening.

"You can't be unaware of Eskwana's vulnerability."

"I am not responsible for his psychopathic reactions."

"But you are responsible for your own. Eskwana is essential to our work here, and you're not. If you can't control your hostility, you must avoid him altogether."

Osden put down his tools and stood up. "With pleasure!" he said in his vindictive, scraping voice. "You could not possibly imagine what it's like to *experience* Eskwana's irrational terrors. To have to share his horrible cowardice, to have to cringe with him at everything!"

"Are you trying to justify your cruelty towards him? I thought you had more self-respect." Tomiko found herself shaking with spite. "If your empathic power really makes you share Ander's misery, why does it never induce the least compassion in you?"

"Compassion," Osden said. "Compassion. What do you know about compassion?"

She stared at him, but he would not look at her.

"Would you like me to verbalize your present emotional affect regarding myself?" he said. "I can do so more precisely than you can. I'm trained to analyze such responses as I receive them. And I do receive them."

"But how can you expect me to feel kindly towards you when you behave as you do?"

"What does it matter how I *behave*, you stupid sow, do you think it makes any difference? Do you think the average human is a well of loving kindness? My choice is to be hated or to be despised. Not being a woman or a coward, I prefer to be hated."

"That's rot. Self-pity. Every man has—"

"But I am not a man," Osden said. "There are all of you. And there is myself. I am *one*."

Awed by that glimpse of abysmal solipsism, she kept silent a while; finally she said, with neither spite nor pity, clinically, "You could kill yourself, Osden."

"That's your way, Haito," he jeered. "I'm not depressive and *seppuku* isn't my bit. What do you want me to do here?"

"Leave. Spare yourself and us. Take the aircar and a data-feeder and go do a species count. In the forest; Harfex hasn't even started the forests yet. Take a hundred-square-meter forested area, anywhere inside radio range. But outside empathy range. Report in at eight and twenty-four o'clock daily."

Osden went, and nothing was heard from him for five days but laconic all-well signals twice daily. The mood at base camp changed like a stage set. Eskwana stayed awake up to eighteen hours a day. Poswet To got out her stellar lute and chanted the celestial harmonies (music had driven Osden into a frenzy). Mannon, Harfex, Jenny Chong, and Tomiko all went off tranquilizers. Porlock distilled something in his laboratory and drank it all by himself. He had a hangover. Asnanifoil and Poswet To held an all-night Numerical Epiphany, that mystical orgy of higher mathematics which is the chiefest pleasure of the religious Cetian soul. Olleroo slept with everybody. Work went well.

The Hard Scientist came towards base at a run, laboring through the high, fleshy stalks of the graminiformes. "Something—in the forest—" His eyes bulged, he panted, his mustache and fingers trembled. "Something big. Moving, behind me. I was putting in a benchmark, bending down. It came at me. As if it was swinging down out of the trees. Behind me." He stared at the others with the opaque eyes of terror or exhaustion.

"Sit down, Porlock. Take it easy. Now wait, go through this again. You *saw* something—"

"Not clearly. Just the movement. Purposive. A—an—I don't know what it could have been. Something self-moving. In the trees, the arboriformes, whatever you call 'em. At the edge of the woods."

Harfex looked grim. "There is nothing here that could attack you, Porlock. There are not even microzoa. There *could not* be a large animal."

"Could you possibly have seen an epiphyte drop suddenly, a vine come loose behind you?"

"No," Porlock said. "It was coming down at me, through the branches, fast. When I turned it took off again, away and upward. It made a noise, a sort of crashing. If it wasn't an animal, God knows what it could have been! It was big —as big as a man, at least. Maybe a reddish color. I couldn't see, I'm not sure."

"It was Osden," said Jenny Chong, "doing a Tarzan act." She giggled nervously, and Tomiko repressed a wild feckless laugh. But Harfex was not smiling.

"One gets uneasy under the arboriformes," he said in his polite, repressed voice. "I've noticed that. Indeed, that may be why I've put off working in the forests. There's a hypnotic quality in the colors and spacing of the stems and branches, especially the helically arranged ones; and the spore-throwers grow so regularly spaced that it seems unnatural. I find it quite disagreeable, subjectively speaking. I wonder if a stronger effect of that sort mightn't have produced a hallucination . . . ?"

Porlock shook his head. He wet his lips. "It was there," he said. "Something. Moving with purpose. Trying to attack me from behind."

When Osden called in, punctual as always, at twenty-four o'clock that night, Harfex told him Porlock's report. "Have you come on anything at all, Mr. Osden, that could substantiate Mr. Porlock's impression of a motile, sentient life-form, in the forest?"

Ssss, the radio said sardonically. "No. Bullshit," said Osden's unpleasant voice.

"You've been actually inside the forest longer than any of us," Harfex said with unmitigable politeness. "Do you agree with my impression that the forest ambiance has a rather troubling and possibly hallucinogenic effect on the perceptions?"

Ssss. "I'll agree that Porlock's perceptions are easily troubled. Keep him in his lab, he'll do less harm. Anything else?"

"Not at present," Harfex said, and Osden cut off.

Nobody could credit Porlock's story, and nobody could discredit it. He was positive that something, something big, had tried to attack him by surprise. It was hard to deny this, for they were on an alien world, and everyone who had entered the forest had felt a certain chill and foreboding under the "trees." ("Call them trees, certainly," Harfex had said: "They really are the same thing—only, of course, altogether different.") They agreed that they had felt uneasy, or had had the sense that something was watching them from behind.

"We've got to clear this up," Porlock said, and he asked to be sent as a temporary Biologist's Aide, like Osden, into the forest to explore and observe. Olleroo and Jenny Chong volunteered if they could go as a pair. Harfex sent them all off into the forest near which they were encamped, a vast tract covering four-fifths of Continent D. He forbade side arms. They were not to go outside a fifty-kilo half-circle, which included Osden's current site. They all reported in twice daily, for three days. Porlock reported a glimpse of what seemed to be a large semi-erect shape moving through the trees across the river; Olleroo was sure she had heard something moving near the tent, the second night.

"There are no animals on this planet," Harfex said, dogged.

Then Osden missed his morning call.

Tomiko waited less than an hour, then flew with Harfex to the area where Osden had reported himself the night before. But as the helijet hovered over the sea of purplish leaves, illimitable, impenetrable, she felt a panic despair. "How can we find him in this?"

"He reported landing on the river bank. Find the aircar; he'll be camped near it, and he can't have gone far from his camp. Species-counting is slow work. There's the river."

"There's his car," Tomiko said, catching the bright foreign glint among the vegetable colors and shadows. "Here goes, then."

She put the ship in hover and pitched out the ladder. She and Harfex descended. The sea of life closed over their heads.

As her feet touched the forest floor, she unsnapped the flap of her holster; then glancing at Harfex, who was unarmed, she left the gun untouched. But her hand kept coming back up to it. There was no sound at all as soon as they were a few meters away from the slow, brown river, and the light was dim. Great boles stood well apart, almost regularly, almost alike; they were soft-skinned, some appearing smooth and others spongy, gray or greenish-brown or brown, twined with cablelike creepers and festooned with epiphytes, extending rigid, entangled armfuls of big, saucer-shaped, dark leaves that formed a roof-layer twenty to thirty meters thick. The ground underfoot was springy as a mattress, every inch of it knotted with roots and peppered with small, fleshy-leaved growths.

"Here's his tent," Tomiko said, cowed at the sound of her voice in that huge community of the voiceless. In the tent was Osden's sleeping bag, a couple of books, a box of rations. We should be calling, shouting for him, she thought, but did not even suggest it; nor did Harfex. They circled out from the tent, careful to keep each other in sight through the thick-standing presences, the crowding gloom. She stumbled over Osden's body, not thirty meters from the tent, led to it by the whitish gleam of a dropped notebook. He lay face down between two huge-rooted trees. His head and hands were covered with blood, some dried, some still oozing red.

Harfex appeared beside her, his pale Hainish complexion quite green in the dusk. "Dead?"

"No. He's been struck. Beaten. From behind." Tomiko's fingers felt over the bloody skull and nape and temples. "A weapon or a tool . . . I don't find a fracture."

As she turned Osden's body over so they could lift him, his eyes opened. She was holding him, bending close to his face. His pale lips writhed. A deathly fear came into her. She screamed aloud two or three times and tried to run away, shambling and stumbling into the terrible dusk. Harfex caught her, and at his touch and the sound of his voice, her panic decreased. "What is it? What is it?" he was saying.

"I don't know," she sobbed. Her heartbeat still shook her, and she could not see clearly. "The fear—the . . . I panicked. When I saw his eyes."

"We're both nervous. I don't understand this—"

"I'm all right now; come on, we've got to get him under care."

Both working with senseless haste, they lugged Osden to the riverside and hauled him up on a rope under his armpits; he dangled like a sack, twisting a little, over the glutinous dark sea of leaves. They pulled him into the helijet and took off. Within a minute they were over open prairie. Tomiko locked onto the homing beam. She drew a deep breath, and her eyes met Harfex's.

"I was so terrified I almost fainted. I have never done that."

"I was . . . unreasonably frightened also," said the Hainishman, and indeed he looked aged and shaken. "Not so badly as you. But as unreasonably."

"It was when I was in contact with him, holding him. He seemed to be conscious for a moment."

"Empathy? . . . I hope he can tell us what attacked him."

Osden, like a broken dummy covered with blood and mud, half-lay as they had bundled him into the rear seats in their frantic urgency to get out of the forest.

More panic met their arrival at base. The ineffective brutality of the assault was sinister and bewildering. Since Harfex stubbornly denied any possibility of animal life, they began speculating about sentient plants, vegetable monsters, psychic projections. Jenny Chong's latent phobia reasserted itself, and she could talk about nothing except the Dark Egos which followed people around behind their backs. She and Olleroo and Porlock had been summoned back to base; and nobody was much inclined to go outside.

Osden had lost a good deal of blood during the three or four hours he had lain alone, and concussion and severe contusions had put him in shock and semi-coma. As he came out of this and began running a low fever he called several times for "Doctor," in a plaintive voice: "Doctor Hammergeld . . ." When he regained full consciousness, two of those long days later, Tomiko called Harfex into his cubicle.

"Osden: Can you tell us what attacked you?"

The pale eyes flickered past Harfex's face.

"You were attacked," Tomiko said gently. The shifty gaze was hatefully familiar, but she was a physician, protective of the hurt. "You may not remember it yet. Something attacked you. You were in the forest—"

"Ah!" he cried out, his eyes growing bright and his features contorting. "The forest—in the forest—"

"What's in the forest?"

He gasped for breath. A look of clearer consciousness came into his face. After a while he said, "I don't know."

"Did you see what attacked you?" Harfex asked.

"I don't know."

"You remember it now."

"I don't know."

"All our lives may depend on this. You must tell us what you saw!"

"I don't know," Osden said, sobbing with weakness. He was too weak to hide the fact that he was hiding the answer, yet he would not say it. Porlock, nearby, was chewing his pepper-colored mustache as he tried to hear what was going on in the cubicle. Harfex leaned over Osden and said, "You *will* tell us—" Tomiko had to interfere bodily.

Harfex controlled himself with an effort that was painful to see. He went off silently to his cubicle, where no doubt he took a double or triple dose of tranquilizers. The other men and women, scattered about the big frail building, a long main hall and ten sleeping-cubicles, said nothing, but looked depressed and edgy. Osden, as always, even now, had them all at his mercy. Tomiko looked down at him with a rush of hatred that burned in her throat like bile. This monstrous egotism that fed itself on others' emotions, this absolute selfishness, was worse than any hideous deformity of the flesh. Like a congenital monster, he should not have lived. Should not be alive. Should have died. Why had his head not been split open?

As he lay flat and white, his hands helpless at his sides, his colorless eyes were wide open, and there were tears running from the corners. Tomiko moved towards him suddenly. He tried to flinch away. "Don't," he said in a weak hoarse voice and tried to raise his hands to protect his head. "Don't!"

She sat down on the folding stool beside the cot, and after a while put her hand on his. He tried to pull away, but lacked the strength.

A long silence fell between them.

"Osden," she murmured, "I'm sorry. I'm very sorry. I will you well. Let me will you well, Osden. I don't want to hurt you. Listen, I do see now. It was one of us. That's right, isn't it. No, don't answer, only tell me if I'm wrong; but I'm not. . . . Of course there are animals on this planet: Ten of them. I don't care who it was. It doesn't matter, does it. It could have been me, just now. I realize that. I didn't understand how it is, Osden. You can't see how difficult it is for us to understand. . . . But listen. If it were love, instead of hate and fear. . . . Is it never love?"

"No."

"Why not? Why should it never be? Are human beings all so weak? That is terrible. Never mind, never mind, don't worry. Keep still. At least right now it isn't hate, is it? Sympathy at least, concern, well-wishing. You do feel that, Osden? Is it what you feel?"

"Among . . . other things," he said, almost inaudible.

"Noise from my subconscious, I suppose. And everybody else in the room. . . . Listen, when we found you there in the forest, when I tried to turn you over, you partly wakened, and I felt a horror of you. I was insane with fear for a minute. Was that your fear of me I felt?"

"No."

Her hand was still on his, and he was quite relaxed, sinking towards sleep, like a man in pain who has been given relief from pain. "The forest," he muttered; she could barely understand him. "Afraid."

She pressed him no further, but kept her hand on his and watched him go to sleep. She knew what she felt, and what therefore he must feel. She was confident of it: There is only one emotion, or state of being, that can thus wholly reverse itself, polarize, within one moment. In Great Hainish, indeed, there is one word, ontá for love and for hate. She was not in love with Osden, of course; that is another kettle of fish. What she felt for him was ontá, polarized hate. She held his hand, and the current flowed between them, the tremendous electricity of touch, which he had always dreaded. As he slept, the ring of anatomy-chart muscles around his mouth relaxed, and Tomiko saw on his face what none of them had ever seen—very faint, a smile. It faded. He slept on.

He was tough; next day he was sitting up, and hungry. Harfex wished to interrogate him, but Tomiko put him off. She hung a sheet of polythene over the cubicle door, as Osden himself had often done. "Does it actually cut down your empathic reception?" she asked, and he replied, in the dry, cautious tone they were now using to each other, "No."

"Just a warning, then."

"Partly. More faith-healing. Dr. Hammergeld thought it worked. . . . Maybe it does, a little."

There had been love, once. A terrified child, suffocating in the tidal rush and battering of the huge emotions of adults, a drowning child, saved by one man. Taught to breathe, to live, by one man. Given everything, all protection and love, by one man. Father/mother/God: no other. "Is he still alive?" Tomiko asked, thinking of Osden's incredible loneliness, and the strange cruelty of the great doctors. She was shocked when she heard his forced, tinny laugh. "He died at least two and a half centuries ago," Osden said. "Do you forget where we are, Coordinator? We've all left our little families behind. . . ."

Outside the polythene curtain the eight other human beings on World 4470 moved vaguely. Their voices were low and strained. Eskwana slept; Poswet To was in therapy; Jenny Chong was trying to rig lights in her cubicle so that she wouldn't cast a shadow.

"They're all scared," Tomiko said, scared. "They've all got these ideas about what attacked you. A sort of ape-potato, a giant fanged spinach, I don't know. . . . Even

Harfex. You may be right not to force them to see. That
would be worse, to lose confidence in one another. But why
are we all so shaky, unable to face the fact, going to pieces
so easily? Are we really all insane?"

"We'll soon be more so."

"Why?"

"There *is* something."

He closed his mouth; the muscles of his lips stood out
rigid.

"Something sentient?"

"A sentience."

"In the forest?"

He nodded.

"What is it, then——?"

"The fear." He began to look strained again, and moved
restlessly. "When I fell, there, you know, I didn't lose consciousness at once. Or I kept regaining it. I don't know. It
was more like being paralyzed."

"You were."

"I was on the ground. I couldn't get up. My face was in
the dirt, in that soft leafmold. It was in my nostrils and
eyes. I couldn't move. Couldn't see. As if I was in the
ground. Sunk into it, part of it. I knew I was between two
trees even though I never saw them. I suppose I could feel
the roots. Below me in the ground, down under the ground.
My hands were bloody, I could feel that, and the blood
made the dirt around my face sticky. I felt the fear. It
kept growing. As if they'd finally *known* I was there, lying
on them there, under them, among them, the thing they
feared, and yet part of their fear itself. I couldn't stop sending the fear back, and it kept growing, and I couldn't move,
I couldn't get away. I would pass out, I think, and then the
fear would bring me to again, and I still couldn't move. Any
more than they can."

Tomiko felt the cold stirring of her hair, the readying of
the apparatus of terror. "They: Who are they, Osden?"

"They, it—I don't know. The fear."

"What is he talking about?" Harfex demanded when
Tomiko reported this conversation. She would not let Harfex question Osden yet, feeling that she must protect Osden
from the onslaught of the Hainishman's powerful, over-re-
pressed emotions. Unfortunately, this fueled the slow fire of

paranoid anxiety that burned in poor Harfex, and he thought she and Osden were in league, hiding some fact of great importance or peril from the rest of the team.

"It's like the blind man trying to describe the elephant. Osden hasn't seen or heard the . . . the sentience, any more than we have."

"But he's felt it, my dear Haito," Harfex said with just-suppressed rage. "Not empathically. On his skull. It came and knocked him down and beat him with a blunt instrument. Did he not catch *one* glimpse of it?"

"What would he have seen, Harfex?" Tomiko asked, but he would not hear her meaningful tone; even he had blocked out that comprehension. What one fears is alien. The murderer is an outsider, a foreigner, not one of us. The evil is not in me!

"The first blow knocked him pretty well out," Tomiko said a little wearily, "he didn't see anything. But when he came to again, alone in the forest, he felt a great fear. Not his own fear, an empathic affect. He is certain of that. And certain it was nothing picked up from any of us. So that evidently the native life-forms are not all insentient."

Harfex looked at her a moment, grim. "You're trying to frighten me, Haito. I do not understand your motives." He got up and went off to his laboratory table, walking slowly and stiffly, like a man of eighty, not of forty.

She looked round at the others. She felt some desperation. Her new, fragile, and profound interdependence with Osden gave her, she was well aware, some added strength. But if even Harfex could not keep his head, who of the others would? Porlock and Eskwana were shut in their cubicles; the others were all working or busy with something. There was something queer about their positions. For a while the Coordinator could not tell what it was; then she saw that they were all sitting facing the nearby forest. Playing chess with Asnanifoil, Olleroo had edged her chair around until it was almost beside his.

She went to Mannon, who was dissecting a tangle of spidery brown roots, and told him to look for the pattern-puzzle. He saw it at once, and said with unusual brevity, "Keeping an eye on the enemy."

"What enemy? What do *you* feel, Mannon?" She had a

sudden hope in him as a psychologist, on this obscure ground of hints and empathies where biologists went astray.

"I feel a strong anxiety with a specific spatial orientation. But I am not an empath. Therefore, the anxiety is explicable in terms of the particular stress-situation, that is, the attack on a team member in the forests, and also in terms of the total stress-situation, that is, my presence in a totally alien environment, for which the archetypical connotations of the word 'forest' provide an inevitable metaphor."

Hours later Tomiko woke to hear Osden screaming in nightmare; Mannon was calming him, and she sank back into her own dark-branching pathless dreams. In the morning Eskwana did not wake. He could not be roused with stimulant drugs. He clung to his sleep, slipping further and further back, mumbling softly now and then until, wholly regressed, he lay curled on his side, thumb at his lips, gone.

"Two days: two down. Ten little Indians, nine little Indians. . . ." That was Porlock.

"And you're the next little Indian," Jenny Chong snapped. "Go analyze your urine, Porlock!"

"He is driving us all insane," Porlock said, getting up and waving his left arm. "Can't you feel it? For God's sake, are you all deaf and blind? Can't you feel what he's doing, the emanations? It all comes from him—from his room there—from his mind. He is driving us all insane with fear!"

"Who is?" said Asnanifoil, looming black, precipitous, and hairy over the little Terran.

"Do I have to say his name? Osden, then. Osden! Osden! Why do you think I tried to kill him? In self-defense! To save all of us! Because you won't see what he's doing to us. He's sabotaged the mission by making us quarrel, and now he's going to drive us all insane by projecting fear at us so that we can't sleep or think, like a huge radio that doesn't make any sound, but it broadcasts all the time, and you can't sleep, and you can't think. Haito and Harfex are already under his control, but the rest of you can be saved. I had to do it!"

"You didn't do it very well," Osden said, standing half-naked, all rib and bandage, at the door of his cubicle. "I could have hit myself harder. Hell, it isn't me that's scaring you blind, Porlock, it's out there—there, in the woods!"

Porlock made an ineffectual attempt to assault Osden;

Asnanifoil held him back, and continued to hold him effortlessly while Mannon gave him a sedative shot. He was put away, shouting about giant radios. In a minute the sedative took effect, and he joined a peaceful silence to Eskwana's.

"All right," said Harfex. "Now, by my Gods, you'll tell us what you know and all you know."

Osden said, "I don't know anything."

He looked battered and faint. Tomiko made him sit down before he talked.

"After I'd been three days in the forest, I thought I was occasionally receiving some kind of faint affect."

"Why didn't you report it?"

"Thought I was going spla, like the rest of you."

"That, equally, should have been reported."

"You'd have called me back to base. I couldn't take it. You realize that my inclusion in the mission was a bad mistake. I'm not able to coexist with nine other neurotic personalities at close quarters. I was wrong to volunteer for Extreme Survey, and the Authority was wrong to accept me."

No one spoke; but Tomiko saw, with certainty this time, the flinch in Osden's shoulders and the tightening of his facial muscles as he registered their bitter agreement.

"Anyhow, I didn't want to come back to base because I was curious. Even going psycho, how could I pick up empathic affects when there was no creature to emit them? They weren't bad, then. Very vague. Queer. Like a draft in a closed room, a flicker in the corner of your eye. Nothing, really."

For a moment he had been borne up on their listening: They heard, so he spoke. He was wholly at their mercy. If they disliked him, he had to be hateful; if they mocked him, he became grotesque; if they listened to him, he was the storyteller. He was helplessly obedient to the demands of their emotions, reactions, moods. And there were seven of them, too many to cope with, so that he must be constantly knocked about from one to another's whim. He could not find coherence. Even as he spoke and held them, somebody's attention would wander: Olleroo perhaps was thinking that he wasn't unattractive; Harfex was seeking the ulterior motive of his words; Asnanifoil's mind, which could not be long held by the concrete, was roaming off towards the eternal peace of number; and Tomiko was distracted by pity, by fear. Osden's voice faltered. He lost the thread. "I . . . I thought it must be the trees," he said, and stopped.

"It's not the trees," Harfex said. "They have no more nervous system than do plants of the Hainish Descent on Earth. None."

"You're not seeing the forest for the trees, as they say on Earth," Mannon put in, smiling elfinly; Harfex stared at him. "What about those root-nodes we've been puzzling about for twenty days—eh?"

"What about them?"

"They are, indubitably, connections. Connections among the trees. Right? Now let's just suppose, most improbably, that you knew nothing of animal brain-structure. And you were given one axon, or one detached glial cell, to examine. Would you be likely to discover what it was? Would you see that the cell was capable of sentience?"

"No. Because it isn't. A single cell is capable of mechanical response to stimulus. No more. Are you hypothesizing that individual arboriformes are 'cells' in a kind of brain, Mannon?"

"Not exactly. I'm merely pointing out that they are all interconnected, both by the root-node linkage and by your green epiphytes in the branches. A linkage of incredible complexity and physical extent. Why, even the prairie grass-forms have those root-connectors, don't they? I know that sentience or intelligence isn't a thing; you can't find it in, or analyze it out from, the cells of a brain. It's a function of the connected cells. It is, in a sense, the connection: the connectedness. It doesn't exist. I'm not trying to say it exists. I'm only guessing that Osden might be able to describe it."

And Osden took him up, speaking as if in trance. "Sentience without senses. Blind, deaf, nerveless, moveless. Some irritability, response to touch. Response to sun, to light, to water, and chemicals in the earth around the roots. Nothing comprehensible to an animal mind. Presence without mind. Awareness of being, without object or subject. Nirvana."

"Then why do you receive fear?" Tomiko asked in a low voice.

"I don't know. I can't see how awareness of objects, of others, could arise: an unperceiving response. . . . But there was an uneasiness, for days. And then when I lay between the two trees and my blood was on their roots—" Osden's face glittered with sweat. "It became fear," he said shrilly, "only fear."

"If such a function existed," Harfex said, "it would not be capable of conceiving of a self-moving, material entity, or responding to one. It could no more become aware of us than we can 'become aware' of Infinity."

"The silence of those infinite expanses terrifies me," muttered Tomiko. "Pascal was aware of Infinity. By way of fear."

"To a forest," Mannon said, "we might appear as forest fires. Hurricanes. Dangers. What moves quickly is dangerous, to a plant. The rootless would be alien, terrible. And if it is mind, it seems only too probable that it might become aware of Osden, whose own mind is open to connection with all others so long as he's conscious, and who was lying in pain and afraid within it, actually inside it. No wonder it was afraid—"

"Not 'it,'" Harfex said. "There is no being, no huge creature, no person! There could at most be only a function—"

"There is only a fear," Osden said.

They were all still a while, and heard the stillness outside.

"Is that what I feel all the time coming up behind me?" Jenny Chong asked, subdued.

Osden nodded. "You all feel it, deaf as you are. Eskwana's the worst off, because he actually has some empathic capacity. He could send if he learned how, but he's too weak, never will be anything but a medium."

"Listen, Osden," Tomiko said, "you can send. Then send to it—the forest, the fear out there—tell that we won't hurt it. Since it has, or is, some sort of affect that translates into what we feel as emotion, can't you translate back? Send out a message: We are harmless, we are friendly."

"You must know that nobody can emit a false empathic message, Haito. You can't send something that doesn't exist."

"But we don't intend harm; we are friendly."

"Are we? In the forest, when you picked me up, did you feel friendly?"

"No. Terrified. But that's—it, the forest, the plants, not my own fear, isn't it?"

"What's the difference? It's all you felt. Can't you see," and Osden's voice rose in exasperation, "why I dislike you and you dislike me, all of you? Can't you see that I retransmit every negative or aggressive affect you've felt towards me since we first met? I return your hostility, with thanks. I do it in self-defense. Like Porlock. It is self-defense, though; it's the only technique I developed to replace my original defense of total withdrawal from others. Unfortunately, it creates a closed circuit, self-sustaining and self-reinforcing. Your initial reaction to me was the instinctive antipathy to a cripple; by now, of course, it's hatred. Can you fail to see my point? The forest-mind out there transmits only terror, now, and the only message I can send it is terror, because when exposed to it I can feel nothing except terror!"

"What must we do, then?" said Tomiko, and Mannon replied promptly, "Move camp. To another continent. If there are plant-minds there, they'll be slow to notice us, as this one was; maybe they won't notice us at all."

"It would be a considerable relief," Osden observed stiffly. The others had been watching him with a new curiosity. He had revealed himself, they had seen him as he was, a helpless man in a trap. Perhaps, like Tomiko, they had seen that the trap itself, his crass and cruel egotism, was their own construction, not his. They had built the cage and locked him in it, and like a caged ape he threw filth out through the bars. If, meeting him, they had offered trust, if they had been strong enough to offer him love, how might he have appeared to them?

None of them could have done so, and it was too late now. Given time, given solitude, Tomiko might have built up with him a slow resonance of feeling, a consonance of trust, a harmony; but there was no time, their job must be done. There was not room enough for the cultivation of so great a thing, and they must make do with sympathy, with pity, the small change of love. Even that much had given her strength, but it was nowhere near enough for him. She could see in his flayed face now his savage resentment of their curiosity, even of her pity.

"Go lie down, that gash is bleeding again," she said, and he obeyed her.

Next morning they packed up, melted down the sprayform hangar and living quarters, lifted *Gum* on mechanical drive, and took her halfway round World 4470, over the red and green lands, the many warm-green seas. They had picked out a likely spot on Continent G: a prairie, twenty thousand square kilos of windswept graminiformes. No forest was within a hundred kilos of the site, and there were no lone trees or groves on the plain. The plant-forms occurred only in large species-colonies, never intermingled, except for certain tiny ubiquitous saprophytes and spore-bearers. The team sprayed holomeld over structure forms, and by evening of the thirty-two-hour day they were settled in to the new camp. Eskwana was still asleep and Porlock still sedated, but everyone else was cheerful. "You can breathe here!" they kept saying.

Osden got on his feet and went shakily to the doorway; leaning there he looked through twilight over the dim reaches of the swaying grass that was not grass. There was a faint, sweet odor of pollen on the wind; no sound but the soft, vast sibilance of wind. His bandaged head cocked a little, the empath stood motionless for a long time. Darkness came, and the stars, lights in the windows of the distant house of Man. The wind had ceased; there was no sound. He listened.

In the long night Haito Tomiko listened. She lay still and heard the blood in her arteries, the breathing of sleepers, the wind blowing, the dark veins running, the dreams advancing, the vast static of stars increasing as the universe died slowly, the sound of death walking. She struggled out of her bed, fled the tiny solitude of her cubicle. Eskwana alone slept. Porlock lay straitjacketed, raving softly in his obscure native tongue. Olleroo and Jenny Chong were playing cards, grim-faced. Poswet To was in the therapy niche, plugged in. Asnanifoil was drawing a mandala, the Third Pattern of the Primes. Mannon and Harfex were sitting up with Osden.

She changed the bandages on Osden's head. His lank, reddish hair, where she had not had to shave it, looked strange. It was salted with white, now. Her hands shook as she worked. Nobody had yet said anything.

"How can the fear be here too?" she said, and her voice rang flat and false in the terrific silence of the vegetable night.

"It's not just the trees; the grasses too . . ."

"But we're twelve thousand kilos from where we were this morning; we left it on the other side of the planet."

"It's all one," Osden said. "One big green thought. How long does it take a thought to get from one side of your brain to the other?"

"It doesn't think. It isn't thinking," Harfex said, lifelessly. "It's merely a network of processes. The branches, the epiphytic growths, the roots with those nodal junctures between individuals: They must all be capable of transmitting electrochemical impulses. There are no individual plants, then, properly speaking. Even the pollen is part of the linkage, no doubt, a sort of windborne sentience, connecting overseas. But it is not conceivable. That all the biosphere of a planet should be one network of communications, sensitive, irrational, immortal, isolated . . ."

"Isolated," said Osden. "That's it! That's the fear. It isn't that we're motile, or destructive. It's just that we are. We are other. There has never been any other."

"You're right," Mannon said, almost whispering. "It has no peers. No enemies. No relationship with anything but itself. One alone forever."

"Then what's its function in species-survival?"

"None, maybe," Osden said. "Why are you getting teleological, Harfex? Aren't you a Hainishman? Isn't the measure of complexity the measure of the eternal joy?"

Harfex did not take the bait. He looked ill. "We should leave this world," he said.

"Now you know why I always want to get out, get away from you," Osden said with a kind of morbid geniality. "It isn't pleasant, is it—the other's fear? . . . If only it were an animal intelligence. I can get through to animals. I get along with cobras and tigers; superior intelligence gives one the advantage. I should have been used in a zoo, not on a human team. . . . If I could get through to the damned stupid potato! If it wasn't so overwhelming. . . . I still pick up more than the fear, you know. And before it panicked it had a—there was a serenity. I couldn't take it in, then, I didn't realize how big it was. To know the whole daylight, after all, and the whole night. All the winds and the lulls together. The winter stars and the summer stars at the same time. To have roots, and no enemies. To be entire. Do you see? No invasion. No others. To be whole. . . ."

He had never spoken before, Tomiko thought.

"You are defenseless against it, Osden," she said. "Your

personality has changed already. You're vulnerable to it. We may not all go mad, but you will, if we don't leave."

He hesitated, then he looked up at Tomiko, the first time he had ever met her eyes—a long, still look, clear as water.

"What's sanity ever done for me?" he said, mocking. "But you have a point, Haito. You have something there."

"We should get away," Harfex muttered.

"If I gave in to it," Osden mused, "could I communicate?"

"By 'give in,'" Mannon said in a rapid, nervous voice, "I assume that you mean, stop sending back the empathic information which you receive from the plant-entity: stop rejecting the fear, and absorb it. That will either kill you at once, or drive you back into total psychological withdrawal, autism."

"Why?" said Osden. "Its message is *rejection*. But my salvation is rejection. It's not intelligent. But I am."

"The scale is wrong. What can a single human brain achieve against something so vast?"

"A single human brain can perceive pattern on the scale of stars and galaxies," Tomiko said, "and interpret it as Love."

Mannon looked from one to the other of them; Harfex was silent.

"It'd be easier in the forest," Osden said. "Which of you will fly me over?"

"When?"

"Now. Before you all crack up or go violent."

"I will," Tomiko said.

"None of us will," Harfex said.

"I can't," Mannon said. "I . . . I am too frightened. I'd crash the jet."

"Bring Eskwana along. If I can pull this off, he might serve as a medium."

"Are you accepting the Sensor's plan, Coordinator?" Harfex asked formally.

"Yes."

"I disapprove. I will come with you, however."

"I think we're compelled, Harfex," Tomiko said, looking at Osden's face, the ugly white mask transfigured, eager as a lover's face.

Olleroo and Jenny Chong, playing cards to keep their thoughts from their haunted beds, their mounting dread, chattered like scared children. "This thing, it's in the forest, it'll get you—"

"Scared of the dark?" Osden jeered.

"But look at Eskwana, and Porlock, and even Asnanifoil—"

"It can't hurt you. It's an impulse passing through synapses, a wind passing through branches. It is only a nightmare."

They took off in a helijet, Eskwana curled up still sound asleep in the rear compartment, Tomiko piloting, Harfex and Osden silent, watching ahead for the dark line of forest across the vague gray miles of starlit plain.

They neared the black line, crossed it; now under them was darkness.

She sought a landing place, flying low, though she had to fight her frantic wish to fly high, to get out, get away. The huge vitality of the plant-world was far stronger here in the forest, and its panic beat in immense dark waves. There was a pale patch ahead, a bare knoll-top a little higher than the tallest of the black shapes around it—the not-trees; the rooted; the parts of the whole. She set the helijet down in the glade, a bad landing. Her hands on the stick were slippery, as if she had rubbed them with cold soap.

About them now stood the forest, black in darkness.

Tomiko cowered down and shut her eyes. Eskwana moaned in his sleep. Harfex's breath came short and loud, and he sat rigid, even when Osden reached across him and slid the door open.

Osden stood up; his back and bandaged head were just visible in the dim glow of the control-panel as he paused stooping in the doorway.

Tomiko was shaking. She could not raise her head. "No, no, no, no, no no, no," she said in a whisper. "No. No. No."

Osden moved suddenly and quietly, swinging out of the doorway, down into the dark. He was gone.

I am coming! said a great voice that made no sound.

Tomiko screamed. Harfex coughed; he seemed to be trying to stand up, but did not do so.

Tomiko drew in upon herself, all centered in the blind eye in her belly, in the center of her being; and outside that there was nothing but the fear.

It ceased.

She raised her head, slowly unclenched her hands. She sat up straight. The night was dark, and stars shone over the forest. There was nothing else.

"Osden," she said, but her voice would not come. She spoke again, louder, a lone bullfrog croak. There was no reply.

She began to realize that something had gone wrong with Harfex. She was trying to find his head in the darkness, for he had slipped down from the seat, when all at once, in the dead quiet, in the dark rear compartment of the craft, a voice spoke. "Good," it said.

It was Eskwana's voice. She snapped on the interior lights and saw the engineer lying curled up, asleep, his hand half over his mouth.

The mouth opened and spoke. "All well," it said.

"Osden—"

"All well," said the soft voice from Eskwana's mouth.

"Where are you?"

Silence.

"Come back."

Wind was rising. "I'll stay here," the soft voice said.

"You can't stay—"

Silence.

"You'd be alone, Osden!"

"Listen." The voice was fainter, slurred, as if lost in the sound of wind. "Listen. I will you well."

She called his name after that, but there was no answer. Eskwana lay still. Harfex lay stiller.

"Osden!" she cried, leaning out the doorway into the dark, wind-shaken silence of the forest of being. "I will come back. I must get Harfex to the base. I will come back, Osden!"

Silence and wind in leaves.

They finished the prescribed survey of World 4470, the eight of them; it took them forty-one days more. Asnanifoil and one or another of the women went into the forest daily at first, searching for Osden in the region around the bare knoll; though Tomiko was not in her heart sure which bare knoll they had landed on that night in the very heart and vortex of terror. They left piles of supplies for Osden, food enough for fifty years—clothing, tents, tools. They did not go on searching; there was no way to find a man alone, hiding, if he wanted to hide, in those unending labyrinths and dim corridors vine-entangled, root-floored. They might have passed within arm's reach of him and never seen him.

But he was there; for there was no fear any more.

Rational, and valuing reason more highly after an intolerable experience of the immortal mindless, Tomiko tried to understand rationally what Osden had done. But the words escaped her control. He had taken the fear into himself, and accepting, had transcended it. He had given up his self to the alien, an unreserved surrender that left no place for evil. He had learned the love of the Other, and thereby had been given his whole self. But this is not the vocabulary of reason.

The people of the Survey team walked under the trees, through the vast colonies of life, surrounded by a dreaming silence, a brooding calm that was half-aware of them and wholly indifferent to them. There were no hours. Distance was no matter. Had we but world enough and time . . . The planet turned between the sunlight and the great dark; winds of winter and summer blew fine, pale pollen across the quiet seas.

Gum returned after many surveys, years, and light-years, to what had several centuries ago been Smeming Port on Pesm. There were still men there to receive (incredulously) the team's reports and to record its losses: Biologist Harfex, dead of fear, and Sensor Osden, left as a colonist.

ALL THE LAST WARS
AT ONCE

George Alec Effinger

More and more of the people I know tell
me they've stopped reading newspapers:
"It's just a big bringdown every morning;
who needs it?" Considering the amount of
social and racial bitterness, religious obtuse-
ness, and general bad will there is in the
world, it's not surprising that our daily news
is considerably less than inspiring. (Yesterday
in New York a bank robber had to abandon
the premises in mid-heist because someone
else had phoned in a bomb threat.) George
Alec Effinger, meditating on such matters,
wrote this wry tale of how we might get all
the nonsense out of our systems for good, and
maybe it would serve us right at that.

We interrupt this p—
—upt this program to—
—terrupt our regularly scheduled programming to bring
you this bulletin pieced together from the archives of the
General Motors Corporation.

"Good afternoon. This is Bob Dunne, NBC News in New
Haven, Connecticut. We're standing here in the lobby of the
Hotel Taft in New Haven, where the first international racial
war has just been declared. In just a few seconds, the two

277

men responsible will be coming out of that elevator. (Can you hear me?)

"—elevator. Those of you in the western time zones are probably already—"

The elevator doors opened. Two men emerged, smiling and holding their hands above their heads in victorious, self-congratulatory boxers' handshakes. They were immediately mobbed by newsmen. One of the two men was exceptionally tall, and black as midnight in Nairobi. The other was short, fat, white, and very nervous. The black man was smiling broadly, the white man was smiling and wiping perspiration from his face with a large red handkerchief.

"—C News. The Negro has been identified as the representative of the people of color of all nations. He is, according to the mimeographed flyer distributed scant minutes ago, Mary McLeod Bethune Washington, of Washington, Georgia. The other man with him is identified as Robert Randall La Cygne, of La Cygne, Kansas, evidently the delegate of the Caucasian peoples. When, and by whom, this series of negotiations was called is not yet clear.

"At any rate, the two men, only yesterday sunk in the sticky obscurity of American life, have concluded some sort of bargaining that threatens to engulf the entire world in violent reaction. The actual content of that agreement is still open to specu—"

"—or at any later date."

A close-up on Washington, who was reading from a small black notebook.

"We have thus reached, and passed, that critical moment. This fact has been known and ignored by all men, on both sides of the color line, for nearly a generation. Henceforth, this situation is to be, at least, honest, if bloodier. Bob and I join in wishing you all the best of luck, and may God bless."

"Mr. Washington?"

"Does this necessarily mean—"

"—iated Press here, Mr. Washing—"

"Yes? You, with the hat."

"Yes, sir. Vincent Reynolds, UPI. Mr. Washington, are we to understand that this agreement has some validity? You are aware that we haven't seen any sort of credentials—"

Washington grinned. "Thank you. I'm glad you brought

that up. Credentials? Just you wait a few minutes, and listen outside. Ain't no stoppin' when them rifles start poppin'!"

"Mr. Washington?"

"Yes?"

"Is this to be an all-out, permanent division of peoples?"

"All-out, yes. Permanent, no. Bob and I have decided on a sort of statute of limitations. You go out and get what you can for thirty days. At the end of the month, we'll see what and who's left."

"You can guarantee that there will be no continuation of hostilities at the end of the thirty days?"

"Why, sure! We're all growed up, now, ain't we? Sure, why, you can trust *us!*"

"Then this is a war of racial eradication?"

"Not at all," said Bob La Cygne, who had remained silent, behind Washington's broad seersucker back. "Not at all what I would call a war of eradication. 'Eradicate' is an ugly term. 'Expunge' is the word we arrived at, isn't it, Mary Beth?"

"I do believe it is, Bob."

Washington studied his notebook for a few seconds, ignoring the shouting newsmen around him. No attempt was made by the uniformed guards to stop the pushing and shoving, which had grown somewhat aggravated. Then he smiled brightly, turning to La Cygne. They clasped hands and waved to the flashing bulbs of the photographers.

"No more questions, boys. You'll figure it all out soon enough; that's enough for now." The two men turned and went back into the waiting elevator.

(Tock tockatock tocka tock tock) "And now, the Six O'Clock Report (tocka tock tocka tocka), with (tockatock) Gil Monahan."

(Tocka tocka tock tock tocka)

"Good evening. The only story in the news tonight is the recently declared official hostilities between members of all non-Caucasian races and the white people of the world. Within minutes of the original announcement, open warfare broke out in nearly every multi-racially populated area in the U.S. and abroad. At this moment the entire globe is in turmoil; the scene everywhere flickers between bloody combat in the streets and peaceful lulls marked by looting and destruction of private property.

"What has happened, in effect, is a thirty-day suspension of all rational codes of conduct. The army and National Guard are themselves paralyzed due to their own internal conflicts. A state of martial law has been declared by almost all governments, but, to our knowledge, nowhere has it been effectively enforced.

"There seems to be absolutely no cooperation between members of the opposite sides, on any level. Even those who most sympathized with the problems of the other are engaged in, using Mary McLeod Bethune Washington's terms, 'getting their own.' Interracial organizations, social groups, and even marriages are splintering against the color barrier.

"We have some reports now from neighboring states that may be of importance to our viewers, concerning the conditions in these areas at the present time. A state of emergency has been declared for the following municipalities in New Jersey: Absecon, Adelphia, Allendale, Allenhurst, Allentown, Allenwood, Alloway, Alpha . . . Well, as my eye travels over this list of some eight or nine hundred towns, I notice that only a few *aren't* listed, notably Convent Station and Peapack. You can pretty well assume that things are bad *all* over. That goes for the New York, Pennsylvania, and Connecticut regions as well.

"We have some footage that was shot in Newark about ten minutes after the New Haven declaration. It's pretty tense out there now. The expert analysts in the news media are astounded that the intense polarization and outbreaks of rioting occurred so quickly. Let's take a look at those films now.

"Apparently there's some diffi—

"I don't know, what can . . . experiencing ourselves some of this interference with . . . refusal to even . . .

"—rifying. They're running around out there like maniacs, shooting and—

"—flames and the smoke is—you can see the clouds against the sky, between the buildings like waves of—"

It was a pink mimeographed factsheet. Frowning, he stuffed it into his pocket. "Factsheet," eh? It had been several days since Stevie had heard a fact that he could trust.

Nobody was saying *anything* worth listening. The factsheets had begun the second day with the expected clutter of charges and accusations, but soon everyone realized that this wasn't going to be that kind of war. Nobody gave a good goddamn *what* happened to anyone else. On the third day, the few angry allegations that were made were answered with "our own sources do not indicate that, in fact, any such incident actually occurred" or with a curt "T.S., baby!" or, finally, no reply at all. Now the factsheets just bragged, or warned, or threatened.

Stevie was hitchhiking, which was a dangerous thing to do, but no more dangerous than sitting in an apartment waiting for the blazing torches. He felt that if he were going to be a target, a moving target offered the better odds.

He carried a pistol and a rifle that he had liberated from Abercrombie & Fitch. The hot morning sun gleamed on the zippers and studs of his black leathers. He stood by the side of the parkway, smiling grimly to himself as he waited for a ride. Every car that came around the curve was a challenge, one that he was more than willing to accept. There wasn't much traffic lately, and for that Stevie was sorry. He was really getting to dig this.

A car approached, a late model black Imperial with its headlights burning. He set himself, ready to dodge into the ditch on the side of the road. Stevie stared through the windshield as the car came nearer. He let out his breath suddenly: It was a white chick. It looked like she had liberated the car; maybe she was looking for someone to team up with. Even if she was a dog, it would beat hitching.

The Imperial passed him, slowed, and stopped on the road's shoulder. The chick slid over on the seat, rolling down the window on the passenger's side and shouting to him.

"Hurry up, you idiot. I don't want to sit here much longer."

He ran to the car, pulling open the door to get in. She slammed it shut again, and Stevie stood there confused.

"What the hell—"

"Shut up," she snapped, handing him another pink factsheet. "Read this. And hurry it up."

He read the factsheet. His throat went dry and he began to feel a buzz in his head. At the top of the page was the familiar, fisted Women's Lib symbol. In regulation incendiary rhetoric below it, a few paragraphs explained that it had been decided by the uppermost echelon to strike now for freedom. During the period of severe disorientation, women the world over were taking the opportunity to beat down the revisionist male supremist pigs. Not just the oppressed racial minorities can express their militancy, it said. The female popular liberation front knew no color boundaries. Who did they think they were kidding? Stevie thought.

"You're gonna get plugged by some black bitch, you know that?" he said. He looked up at her. She had a gun pointed at him, aimed at his chest. The buzz in his head grew louder.

"You wanna put that sheet back on the pile? We don't have enough to go around," she said.

"Look," said Stevie, starting to move toward the car. The girl raised the pistol in a warning. He dove to the ground, parallel to the car, and rolled up against the right front wheel. The girl panicked, opening the door to shoot him before he could get away. Stevie fired twice before she sighted him, and she fell to the grassy shoulder. He didn't check to see if she were dead or merely wounded; he took her pistol and got in the car.

"My fellow Americans." The voice of the President was strained and tired, but he still managed his famous promiseless smile. The picture of the Chief Executive was the first to disturb the televisions' colored confetti snow for nearly two weeks.

"We are met tonight to discuss the intolerable situation in which our nation finds itself. With me this evening"—the President indicated an elderly, well-dressed Negro gentleman seated at a desk to the left of the President's—"I have invited the Rev. Dr. Roosevelt Wilson, who will speak to you from his own conscience. Rev. Wilson is known to many of you as an honest man, a community leader, and a voice of collaboration in these times of mistrust and fiscal insecurity."

Across the nation, men in dark turtlenecks ran down searing channels of flame, liberated television sets in their gentle grasp, running so that they might see this special telecast. Across the nation men and women of all persuasions looked at Wilson and muttered, "Well, isn't he the clean old nigger!"

Rev. Wilson spoke, his voice urgent and slow with emotion. "We must do everything that our leaders tell us. We cannot take the law into our own hands. We must listen to the promptings of reason and calm, and find that equitable solution that I'm sure we all desire."

The TV broadcast had been a major accomplishment. Its organization had been a tribute to the cooperation of many dissatisfied men who would rather have been out liberating lawn furniture. But the message of these two paternal figures of authority was more important.

"Thank you, Dr. Wilson," said the President. He stood, smiling into the camera, and walked to a large map that had been set up to his right. He took a pointer in one hand.

"This," he said, "is our beleaguered nation. Each green dot represents a community where the violence that plagues us has gone beyond containable limits." The map was nearly solid green, the first time the USA had been in that condition since the early seventeenth century. "I have asked for assistance from the armed forces of Canada, Mexico and Great Britain, but although I mailed the requests nearly two weeks ago, I have yet to receive a reply. I can only assume that we are on our own.

"Therefore, I will make one statement concerning official government policy. As you know, this state of affairs will technically come to an end in about fifteen days. At that time, the government will prosecute *severely* anyone connected with any further disruptions of Federal activities. This is not merely an empty threat; it con—"

A young black man ran before the camera, turning to shout an incoherent slogan. Rev. Wilson saw the pistol in the boy's hand and stood, his face contorted with fear and envy. "The business of America *is* business!" he screamed, and then dropped back into his seat as the black militant shot. The President clutched his chest and cried, "We *must* not . . . lose . . ." and fell to the floor.

The cameras seemed to swing at random, as men rushed about confusedly. From somewhere a white man appeared, perhaps one of the technicians, with his own pistol. He hurried to the desk shouting, "For anarchy!" and shot Dr. Wilson point-blank. The white assassin turned, and the black assassin fired at him. The two killers began a cautious but noisy gun battle in the studio. Here most viewers turned off their sets. "In very poor taste," they thought.

The sign outside: SECOND NATIONAL BANK OF OUR LORD, THE ENGINEER. UNIVERSAL CHURCH OF GOD OR SOME SORT OF COSMIC EMBODIMENT OF GOD.

Above the entrance to the church fluttered a hastily made banner. The masculine symbol had been crudely painted on a white sheet; the white flag indicated that the worshippers were white males and that blacks and women were "welcome" at their own risk. The population was now split into four mutually antagonistic segments. The separate groups began to realize that there was some point in keeping their members together in little cadres. The streets and apartment buildings were death traps.

Inside the church the men were silent in prayer. They were led by an elderly deacon, whose inexperience and confusion were no greater or less than any in the congregation.

"Merciful God," he prayed, "in whatever Form the various members of our flock picture You, corporal Entity or insubstantial Spirit, we ask that You guide us in this time of direst peril.

"Brother lifts sword against brother, and brother against sister. Husband and wife are torn asunder against Your holiest ordainments. Protect us, and show us our proper response. Perhaps it is true that vengeance is solely Yours; but speak to us, then, concerning Limited Cautionary Retaliation, and other alternatives. We would see a sign, for truly we are lost in the mires of day-to-day living."

The deacon continued his prayer, but soon there began a series of poundings on the door. The deacon stopped for just a second, looking up nervously, his hand straying to his sidearm. When nothing further happened he finished the prayer and the members of the congregation added, if they chose, their amens.

At the end of the service the men rose to leave. They stood at the door, in no hurry to abandon the sanctuary of the church. At last the deacon led them out. It was immediately noticed that a yellow factsheet had been nailed to the outside of the door. The Roman Catholics of the neighborhood had decided to end the centuries-long schism. Why not now, when everybody else was settling their differences? A Final Solution.

A bullet split wood from the door frame. The men standing on the stoop jumped back inside. A voice called from the street, "You damn commie atheist Protestants! We're gonna wipe you out and send your lousy heretic souls straight to Hell!" More gunfire. The stained glass windows of the church shattered, and there were cries from inside.

"They got one of the elders!"

"It's those crummy Catholics. We should have got them when we had the chance. Damn it, now they got us holed up in here."

The next day a blue factsheet was circulated by the Jewish community explaining that they had finally gotten tired of having their gabardine spat on, and that everybody'd just have to watch out. Around the world the remaining clusters of people fractured again, on the basis of creed.

It was getting so you didn't know *who* you could trust.

Stevie was heading back toward the city when the car went. It made a few preliminary noises, shaking and rattling slower, and then it stopped. For all he knew it might simply have been out of gas. There were eight days left in the prescribed thirty, and he needed a ride.

He took the rifle and the two pistols from the Imperial and stood by the side of the road. It was a lot more dangerous to hitch now than it had been before, for the simple reason that the odds were that anyone who happened by would probably be on the other side of *one* of the many ideological fences. He was still confident, though, that he would be safely picked up, or be able to wrest a car away from its owner.

There was very little traffic. Several times Stevie had to jump for cover as a hostile driver sped by him, shooting wildly from behind the wheel. At last an old Chevy stopped for him, driven by a heavy white man whom Stevie judged to be in his late fifties.

"Come on, get in," said the man.

Stevie climbed into the car, grunting his thanks and settling warily back against the seat.

"Where you going?" asked the man.

"New York."

"Um. You, uh, you a Christian?"

"Hey," said Stevie, "right now we ain't got any troubles at all. We can just drive until we get where we're going. We only have eight days, right? So if we leave off the questions, eight days from now *both* of us'll be happy."

"All right. That's a good point, I guess, but it defeats the whole purpose. I mean, it doesn't seem to enter into the spirit of things."

"Yeah, well, the spirit's getting a little tired."

They rode in silence, taking turns with the driving. Stevie noticed that the old man kept staring at the rifle and two pistols. Stevie searched the car as best he could with his eyes, and it looked to him as though the old man was unarmed himself. Stevie didn't say anything.

"You seen a factsheet lately?" asked the man.

"No," said Stevie. "Haven't seen one in days. I got tired of the whole thing. *Now* who's at it?"

The old man looked at him quickly, then turned back to the road. "Nobody. Nothing new." Stevie glanced at the man now, studying his face curiously. Nothing new.

After a while the man asked him for some bullets.

"I didn't think that you had a gun," said Stevie.

"Yeah. I got a .38 in the glove compartment. I keep it there, where I'm less likely to use it."

"A .38? Well, these shells wouldn't do you any good, anyhow. Besides, I don't really want to give them up yet."

The man looked at him again. He licked his lips, appearing to make some decision. He took his eyes off the road for a moment and lunged across the seat in a dive for one of the loaded pistols. Stevie slammed the edge of his hand into the older man's throat. The man choked and collapsed on the seat. Stevie switched off the engine and steered the car to the side of the road, where he opened the door and dumped the still body.

Before he started the car again, Stevie opened the glove compartment. There was an unloaded revolver and a crumpled factsheet. Stevie tossed the gun to the ground by the old man. He smoothed out the wrinkled paper. The youth of the world, it proclaimed, had declared war on everyone over the age of thirty years.

"How you coming with that factsheet?"

The thin man in the green workshirt stopped typing and looked up. "I don't know. It's hard making out your crummy handwriting. Maybe another fifteen minutes. Are they getting restless out there?"

The man in the jacket gulped down some of his lukewarm coffee. "Yeah. I was going to make an announcement, but what the hell. Let 'em wait. They had their vote, they know what's coming. Just finish that factsheet. I want to get it run off and put up before them goddamn Artists beat us to it."

"Look, Larry, them queers'll never think of it in the first place. Calm down."

The man in the workshirt typed in silence for a while. Larry walked around the cold meeting hall, pushing chairs back in place and chewing his cigar nervously. When the stencil was finished, the man in the workshirt pulled it out of the typewriter and handed it to Larry. "All right," he said, "there it is. Maybe you better go read it to them first. They been waiting out there for a couple of hours now."

"Yeah, I guess so," said Larry. He zipped up his green jacket and waited for the man in the workshirt to get his coat. He turned off the lights and locked the door to the hall. Outside was a huge crowd of men, all white and all well into middle age. They cheered when Larry and the other man came out. Larry held up his hands for quiet.

"All right, listen up," he said. "We got our factsheet here. Before we go and have it run off, I'm going to let you hear it. It says just like what we voted for, so you all should be pretty satisfied."

He read the factsheet, stopping every now and then to wait through the applause and cheers of the men. He looked out at the crowd. They're all brawny veteran-types, he thought. That's what we are: We're Veterans. We been through it all. We're the ones who know what's going on. We're the Producers.

The factsheet explained, in simple language unlike the bitter diatribes of other groups, that the laborers—the Producers—of the world had gotten fed up with doing all the work while a large portion of the population—the goddamn queer Artists—did nothing but eat up all the fruits of honest nine-to-five work. Artists contributed nothing, and wasted large amounts of our precious resources. It was simple logic to see that the food, clothing, shelter, money and recreational facilities that were diverted from the Producers' use was as good as thrown into the garbage. The Producers worked harder and harder, and got back less and less. Well then, what could you expect to happen? Everything was bound to get worse for everybody.

The men cheered. It was about time that they got rid of the parasites. No one complained when you burned off a leech. And no one could complain when you snuffed out the leechlike elements of normal, organized, Productive society.

Larry finished reading the sheet and asked for questions and comments. Several men started talking, but Larry ignored them and went on speaking himself.

"Now, this doesn't mean," he said, "that we gotta get everybody that doesn't work regular hours like we do. You see that some of the peoole are hard to tell whether they're Producers like us, or just lousy addict Artists. Like the people that make TV. We can use them. But we have to be careful, because there's a lot of Artists around who are trying to make us think that they're really Producers. Just remember: If you can use it, it's not Art."

The crowd cheered again, and then it began to break up. Some of the men stood around arguing. One of the small groups of Producers that was slowly walking to the parking lot was deeply involved in debating the boundaries separating Artists and Producers.

"I mean, where are we going to stop?" said one. "I don't like the way this divisioning is going. Pretty soon there won't be any groups left to belong to. We'll all be locked up in our homes, afraid to see anybody at all."

"It's not doing us any good," agreed another. "If you go out and get what you want, I mean, take something from a store or something, why, everybody knows you got it when you bring it home. Then *you're* the target. I got less now than when this all started."

A third man watched the first two grimly. He pulled out a factsheet of his own from the pocket of his jacket. "That's commie talk," he said. "You're missing the point of the whole thing. Let me ask you a question. Are you right- or left-handed?"

The first man looked up from the factsheet, puzzled. "I don't see that it makes any difference. I mean, I'm basically left-handed, but I write with my right hand."

The third man stared angrily, in disbelief.

Bang.

YANG and YIN: Male and female. Hot and cold. Mass and energy. Smooth and crunchy. Odd and even. Sun and moon. Silence and noise. Space and time. Slave and master. Fast and slow. Large and small. Land and sea. Good and evil. On and off. Black and white. Strong and weak. Regular and filter king. Young and old. Light and shade. Fire and ice. Sickness and health. Hard and soft. Life and death.

If there *is* a plot, shouldn't you know about it?

One more hour.

Millions of people hid in their holes, waiting out the last minutes of the wars. Hardly anyone was out on the streets yet. No one shouted their drunken celebrations that little bit ahead of schedule. In the night darkness Stevie could still hear the ragged crackings of guns in the distance. Some suckers getting it only an hour from homefree.

The time passed. Warily, people came out into the fresher air, still hiding themselves in shadows, not used yet to walking in the open. Guns of the enthusiasts popped; they would never get a chance like this again, and there were only fifteen minutes left. Forty-second Street chromium knives found their lodgings in unprotected Gotham throats and shoulders.

Times Square was still empty when Stevie arrived. Decomposing corpses sprawled in front of the record and porno shops. A few shadowy forms moved across the streets, far away down the sidewalk.

The big ball was poised. Stevie watched it, bored, with murderers cringing around him. The huge lighted New Year's globe was ready to drop, waiting only for midnight and for the kissing New Year's VJ-Day crowds. There was Stevie, who didn't care, and the looters, disappointed in the smoked-out, gunfire black, looted stores.

It said it right up there: 11:55. Five more minutes. Stevie pushed himself back into a doorway, knowing that it would be humiliating to get it with only five minutes left. From the vague screams around him he knew that some were still finding it.

People were running by now. The square was filling up. 11:58 and the ball was *just* hanging there: The sudden well of people drew rapid rifle-fire, but the crowd still grew. There was the beginning of a murmur, just the hint of the war-is-over madness. Stevie sent himself into the stream, giving himself up to the release and relief.

11:59. . . . The ball seemed . . . to tip . . . and *fell!* 12:00! The chant grew stronger, the New York chant, the smugness returned in all its sordid might. "We're Number One! We're Number One!" The cold breezes drove the shouting through the unlit streets, carrying it on top of the burnt and fecal smells. It would be a long time before what was left would be made livable, but We're Number One! There were still sporadic shots, but these were the usual New York Town killers, doing the undeclared and time-honored violence that goes unnoticed.

We're Number One!

Stevie found himself screaming in spite of himself. He was standing next to a tall, sweating black. Stevie grinned; the black grinned. Stevie stuck out his hand. "Shake!" he said. "We're Number One!"

"We're Number One!" said the black. "I mean, it's *us!* We gotta settle all this down, but, I mean, what's left is *ours!* No more fighting!"

Stevie looked at him, realizing for the first time the meaning of their situation. "Right you are," he said with a catch in his voice. "Right you are, Brother."

"Excuse me."

Stevie and the black turned to see a strangely dressed woman. The costume completely hid any clue to the person's identity, but the voice was very definitely feminine. The woman wore a long, loose robe decorated fancifully with flowers and butterflies. Artificial gems had been stuck on, and the whole thing trimmed with cheap, dimestore "gold-and-silver" piping. The woman's head was entirely hidden by a large, bowl-shaped woven helmet, and from within it her voice echoed excitedly.

"Excuse me," she said. "Now that the preliminary skirmishes are over, don't you think we should get on with it?"

"With what?" asked the black.

"The Last War, the final one. The war against ourselves. It's senseless to keep avoiding it, now."

"What do you mean?" asked Stevie.

The woman touched Stevie's chest. "There. Your guilt.

Your frustration. You don't really feel any better, do you? I mean, women don't really hate men; they hate their own weaknesses. People don't really hate other people for their religion or race. It's just that seeing someone different than you makes you feel a little insecure in your own belief. What you hate is your own doubt, and you project the hatred onto the other man."

"She's right!" said the black. "You know, I wouldn't mind it half so much if they'd hate me because of *me;* but nobody ever took the trouble."

"That's what's so frustrating," she said. "If anyone's ever going to hate the *real* you, you know who it'll have to be."

"You're from that Kindness Cult, aren't you?" the black said softly.

"*Shinsetsu,*" she said. "Yes."

"You want us to meditate or something?" asked Stevie. The woman dug into a large basket that she carried on her arm. She handed each of them a plump cellophane package filled with a colorless fluid.

"No." said the black as he took his package. "Kerosene."

Stevie held his bag of kerosene uncertainly, and looked around the square. There were others dressed in the *Shinsetsu* manner, and they were all talking to groups that had formed around them.

"Declare war on myself?" Stevie said doubtfully. "Do I have to publish a factsheet first?" No one answered him. People nearby were moving closer so they could hear the *Shinsetsu* woman. She continued to hand out the packages as she spoke.

Stevie slipped away, trying to get crosstown, out of the congested square. When he reached a side street he looked back: Already the crowd was dotted with scores of little fires, like scattered piles of burning leaves in the backyards of his childhood.

THE FOURTH PROFESSION

Larry Niven

Though I referred earlier to Larry Niven's reputation as a science-oriented writer, the reputation isn't completely congruent with Niven's work. To be sure, there's always an awareness of the workings of scientific reality even in his fantasy stories, but at the same time Niven realizes that good stories need believable characters to bring ideas to life. Here is an excellent example of Niven's evolving and strengthening abilities: a tale of a super race of aliens, and an ordinary human being. (Ordinary?)

The doorbell rang around noon on Wednesday.

I sat up in bed and—it was the oddest of hangovers. My head *didn't* spin. My sense of balance was quiveringly alert. At the same time my mind was clogged with the things I knew: facts that wouldn't relate, churning in my head.

It was like walking the high wire while simultaneously trying to solve an Agatha Christie mystery. Yet I was doing neither. I was just sitting up in bed, blinking.

I remembered the Monk, and the pills. How many pills?

The bell rang again.

Walking to the door was an eerie sensation. Most people pay no attention to their somesthetic senses. Mine were clamoring for attention, begging to be tested—by a backflip, for instance. I resisted. I don't have the muscles for doing backflips.

293

I couldn't remember taking any acrobatics pills.

The man outside my door was big and blond and blocky. He was holding an unfamiliar badge up to the lens of my spy-eye, in a wide hand with short, thick fingers. He had candid blue eyes, a square, honest face—a face I recognized. He'd been in the Long Spoon last night, at a single table in a corner.

Last night he had looked morose, introspective, like a man whose girl has left him for Mr. Wrong. A face guaranteed to get him left alone. I'd noticed him only because he wasn't drinking enough to match the face.

Today he looked patient, endlessly patient, with the patience of a dead man.

And he had a badge. I let him in.

"William Morris," he said, identifying himself. "Secret Service. Are you Edward Harley Frazer, owner of the Long Spoon Bar?"

"Part-owner."

"Yes, that's right. Sorry to bother you, Mr. Frazer. I see you keep bartender's hours." He was looking at the wrinkled pair of underpants I had on.

"Sit down," I said, waving at the chair. I badly needed to sit down myself. Standing, I couldn't think about anything but standing. My balance was all conscious. My heels would not rest solidly on the floor. They barely touched. My weight was all on my toes; my body insisted on standing that way.

So I dropped onto the edge of the bed, but it felt like I was giving a trampoline performance. The poise, the grace, the polished ease! Hell. "What do you want from me, Mr. Morris? Doesn't the Secret Service guard the President?"

His answer sounded like rote-memory. "Among other concerns, such as counterfeiting, we do guard the President and his immediate family and the President-elect, and the Vice President if he asks us to." He paused. "We used to guard foreign dignitaries too."

That connected. "You're here about the Monk."

"Right." Morris looked down at his hands. He should have had an air of professional self-assurance to go with the badge. It wasn't there. "This is an odd case, Frazer. We took it because it used to be our job to protect foreign visitors, and because nobody else would touch it."

"So last night you were in the Long Spoon guarding a visitor from outer space."

"Just so."

"Where were you night before last?"

"Was that when he first appeared?"

"Yah," I said, remembering. "Monday night . . ."

He came in an hour after opening time. He seemed to glide, with the hem of his robe just brushing the floor. By his gait he might have been moving on wheels. His shape was wrong, in a way that made your eyes want to twist around to straighten it out.

There is something queer about the garment that gives a Monk his name. The hood is open in front, as if eyes might hide within its shadow, and the front of the robe is open too. But the loose cloth hides more than it ought to. There is too much shadow.

Once I thought the robe parted as he walked toward me. But there seemed to be nothing inside.

In the Long Spoon was utter silence. Every eye was on the Monk as he took a stool at one end of the bar, and ordered.

He looked alien, and was. But he *seemed* supernatural.

He used the oddest of drinking systems. I keep my house brands on three long shelves, more or less in order of type. The Monk moved down the top row of bottles, right to left, ordering a shot from each bottle. He took his liquor straight, at room temperature. He drank quietly, steadily, and with what seemed to be total concentration.

He spoke only to order.

He showed nothing of himself but one hand. That hand looked like a chicken's foot, but bigger, with lumpy-looking, very flexible joints, and with five toes instead of four.

At closing time the Monk was four bottles from the end of the row. He paid me in one-dollar bills, and left, moving steadily, the hem of his robe just brushing the floor. I testify as an expert: He was sober. The alcohol had not affected him at all.

"Monday night," I said. "He shocked the hell out of us. Morris, what was a Monk doing in a bar in Hollywood? I thought all the Monks were in New York."

"So did we."

"Oh?"

"We didn't know he was on the West Coast until it hit the newspapers yesterday morning. That's why you didn't see more reporters yesterday. We kept them off your back. I came in last night to question you, Frazer. I changed my mind when I saw that the Monk was already here."

"Question *me*. Why? All I did was serve him drinks."

"Okay, let's start there. Weren't you afraid the alcohol might kill a Monk?"

"It occurred to me."

"Well?"

"I served him what he asked for. It's the Monks' own doing that nobody knows anything about Monks. We don't even know what shape they are, let alone how they're put together. If liquor does things to a Monk, it's his own lookout. Let *him* check the chemistry."

"Sounds reasonable."

"Thanks."

"It's also the reason I'm here," said Morris. "We know too little about the Monks. We didn't even know they existed until something over two years ago."

"Oh?" I'd only started reading about them a month ago.

"It wouldn't be that long, except that all the astronomers were looking in that direction already, studying a recent nova in Saggittarius. So they caught the Monk starship a little sooner; but it was already inside Pluto's orbit.

"They've been communicating with us for over a year. Two weeks ago they took up orbit around the Moon. There's only one Monk starship, and only one ground-to-orbit craft, as far as we know. The ground-to-orbit craft has been sitting in the ocean off Manhattan Island, convenient to the United Nations Building, for those same two weeks. Its crew are supposed to be all the Monks there are in the world.

"Mr. Frazer, we don't even know how your Monk got out here to the West Coast! Almost anything you could tell us would help. Did you notice anything odd about him, these last two nights?"

"Odd?" I grinned. "About a Monk?"

It took him a moment to get it, and then his answering smile was wan. "Odd for a Monk."

"Yah," I said, and tried to concentrate. It was the wrong

move. Bits of fact buzzed about my skull, trying to fit themselves together.

Morris was saying, "Just talk, if you will. The Monk came back Tuesday night. About what time?"

"About four thirty. He had a case of—pills—RNA . . ."

It was no use. I knew too many things, all at once, all unrelated. I knew the name of the Garment to Wear Among Strangers, its principle and its purpose. I knew about Monks and alcohol. I knew the names of the five primary colors, so that for a moment I was blind with the memory of the colors themselves, colors no man would ever see.

Morris was standing over me, looking worried. "What is it? What's wrong?"

"Ask me anything." My voice was high and strange and breathless with giddy laughter. "Monks have four limbs, all hands, each with a callus heel behind the fingers. I know their names, Morris. Each hand, each finger. I know how many eyes a Monk has. One. And the whole skull is an ear. There's no word for *ear*, but medical terms for each of the —resonating cavities—between the lobes of the brain . . ."

"You look dizzy. You don't sample your own wares, do you, Frazer?"

"I'm the opposite of dizzy. There's a compass in my head. I've got absolute direction. Morris, it must have been the pills."

"Pills?" Morris had small, squarish ears that couldn't possibly have come to a point. But I got that impression.

"He had a sample case full of—education pills . . ."

"Easy now." He put a steadying hand on my shoulder. "Take it easy. Just start at the beginning, and talk. I'll make some coffee."

"Good." Coffee sounded wonderful, suddenly. "Pot's ready. Just plug it in. I fix it before I go to sleep."

Morris disappeared around the partition that marks off the kitchen alcove from the bedroom/living room in my small apartment. His voice floated back. "Start at the beginning. He came back Tuesday night."

"He came back Tuesday night," I repeated.

"Hey, your coffee's already perked. You must have plugged it in in your sleep. Keep talking."

"He started his drinking where he'd left off, four bottles from the end of the top row. I'd have sworn he was cold sober. His voice didn't give him away . . ."

His voice didn't give him away because it was only a whisper, too low to make out. His translator spoke like a computer, putting single words together from a man's recorded voice. It spoke slowly and with care. Why not? It was speaking an alien tongue.

The Monk had had five tonight. That put him through the ryes and the bourbons and the Irish whiskeys, and several of the liqueurs. Now he was tasting the vodkas.

At that point I worked up the courage to ask him what he was doing.

He explained at length. The Monk starship was a commercial venture, a trading mission following a daisy chain of stars. He was a sampler for the group. He was mightily pleased with some of the wares he had sampled here. Probably he would order great quantities of them, to be freeze-dried for easy storage. Add alcohol and water to reconstitute.

"Then you won't be wanting to test all the vodkas," I told him. "Vodka isn't much more than water and alcohol."

He thanked me.

"The same goes for most gins, except for flavorings." I lined up four gins in front of him. One was Tanqueray. One was a Dutch gin you have to keep chilled like some liqueurs. The others were fairly ordinary products. I left him with these while I served customers.

I had expected a mob tonight. Word should have spread. *Have a drink in the Long Spoon, you'll see a Thing from Outer Space.* But the place was half empty. Louise was handling them nicely.

I was proud of Louise. As with last night, tonight she behaved as if nothing out of the ordinary was happening. The mood was contagious. I could almost hear the customers thinking: *We like our privacy when we drink. A Thing from Outer Space is entitled to the same consideration.*

It was strange to compare her present insouciance with the way her eyes had bugged at her first sight of a Monk.

The Monk finished tasting the gins. "I am concerned for the volatile fractions," he said. "Some of your liquors will lose taste from condensation."

I told him he was probably right. And I asked, "How do you pay for your cargos?"

"With knowledge."

"That's fair. What kind of knowledge?"

The Monk reached under his robe and produced a flat sample case. He opened it. It was full of pills. There was a large glass bottle full of a couple hundred identical pills; and these were small and pink and triangular. But most of the sample case was given over to big, round pills of all colors, individually wrapped and individually labelled in the wandering Monk script.

No two labels were alike. Some of the notations looked hellishly complex.

"These are knowledge," said the Monk.

"Ah," I said, and wondered if I was being put on. An alien can have a sense of humor, can't he? And there's no way to tell if he's lying.

"A certain complex organic molecule has much to do with memory," said the Monk. "Ribonucleic acid. It is present and active in the nervous systems of most organic beings. Wish you to learn my language?"

I nodded.

He pulled a pill loose and stripped it of its wrapping, which fluttered to the bar like a shred of cellophane. The Monk put the pill in my hand and said, "You must swallow it now, before the air ruins it, now that it is out of its wrapping."

The pill was marked like a target in red and green circles. It was big and bulky going down.

"You must be crazy," Bill Morris said wonderingly.

"It looks that way to me, too, now. But think about it. This was a Monk, an alien, an ambassador to the whole human race. He wouldn't have fed me anything dangerous, not without carefully considering all the possible consequences.

"He wouldn't, would he?"

"That's the way it seemed." I remembered about Monks and alcohol. It was a pill memory, surfacing as if I had known it all my life. It came too late . . .

"A language says things about the person who speaks it, about the way he thinks and the way he lives. Morris, the Monk language says a lot about Monks."

"Call me Bill," he said irritably.

"Okay. Take Monks and alcohol. Alcohol works on a

Monk the way it works on a man, by starving his brain cells a little. But in a Monk it gets absorbed more slowly. A Monk can stay high for a week on a night's dedicated drinking.

"I knew he was sober when he left Monday night. By Tuesday night he must have been pretty high."

I sipped my coffee. Today it tasted different, and better, as if memories of some Monk staple foods had worked their way as overtones into my taste buds.

Morris said, "And you didn't know it."

"Know it? I was counting on his sense of responsibility!"

Morris shook his head in pity, except that he seemed to be grinning inside.

"We talked some more after that—and I took some more pills."

"Why?"

"I was high on the first one."

"It made you drunk?"

"Not drunk, but I couldn't think straight. My head was full of Monk words all trying to fit themselves to meanings. I was dizzy with nonhuman images and words I couldn't pronounce."

"Just how many pills did you take?"

"I don't remember."

"Swell."

An image surfaced. "I do remember saying, 'But how about something unusual? *Really* unusual.' "

Morris was no longer amused. "You're lucky you can still talk. The chances you took, you should be a drooling idiot this morning!"

"It seemed reasonable at the time."

"You don't remember how many pills you took?"

I shook my head. Maybe the motion jarred something loose. "That bottle of little triangular pills. I know what they were. Memory erasers."

"Good God! You didn't . . ."

"No, no, Morris. They don't erase your whole memory. They erase pill memories. The RNA in a Monk memory pill is tagged somehow, so that the eraser pill can pick it out and break it down."

Morris gaped. Presently he said, "That's incredible. The education pills are wild enough, but *that* . . . You see what they must do, don't you? They hang a radical on each and every RNA molecule in each and every education pill. The active principle in the eraser pill is an enzyme for just that radical."

He saw my expression and said, "Never mind, just take my word for it. They must have had the education pills for a hundred years before they worked out the eraser principle."

"Probably. The pills must be very old."

He pounced. "How do you know that?"

"The name for the pill has only one syllable, like *fork*. There are dozens of words for kinds of pill reflexes, for swallowing the wrong pill, for side effects depending on what species is taking the pill. There's a special word for an animal-training pill, and another one for a slave-training pill. Morris, I think my memory is beginning to settle down."

"Good!"

"Anyway, the Monks must have been peddling pills to aliens for thousands of years. I'd guess tens of thousands."

"Just how many kinds of pill were in that case?"

I tried to remember. My head felt congested . . .

"I don't know if there was more than one of each kind of pill. There were four stiff flaps like the leaves of a book, and each flap had rows of little pouches with a pill in each one. The flaps were maybe sixteen pouches long by eight across. Maybe. Morris, we ought to call Louise. She probably remembers better than I do, even if she noticed less at the time."

"You mean Louise Schu the barmaid? She might at that. Or she might jar something loose in your memory."

"Right."

"Call her. Tell her we'll meet her. Where's she live, Santa Monica?"

He'd done his homework, all right.

Her phone was still ringing when Morris said, "Wait a minute. Tell her we'll meet her at the Long Spoon. And tell her we'll pay her amply for her trouble."

Then Louise answered and told me I'd jarred her out of a sound sleep, and I told her she'd be paid amply for her trouble, and she said what the hell kind of a crack was *that?*

After I hung up I asked, "Why the Long Spoon?"

"I've thought of something. I was one of the last customers out last night. I don't think you cleaned up."

"I was feeling peculiar. We cleaned up a little, I think."

"Did you empty the wastebaskets?"

"We don't usually. There's a guy who comes in in the morning and mops the floors and empties the wastebaskets and so forth. The trouble is, he's been home with the flu the last couple of days. Louise and I have been going early."

"Good. Get dressed, Frazer. We'll go down to the Long Spoon and count the pieces of Monk cellophane in the wastebaskets. They shouldn't be too hard to identify. They'll tell us how many pills you took."

I noticed it while I was dressing. Morris's attitude had changed subtly. He had become proprietary. He tended to stand closer to me, as if someone might try to steal me, or as if I might try to steal away.

Imagination, maybe. But I began to wish I didn't know so much about Monks.

I stopped to empty the percolator before leaving. Habit. Every afternoon I put the percolator in the dishwasher before I leave. When I come home at three A.M. it's ready to load.

I poured out the dead coffee, took the machine apart, and stared.

The grounds in the top were fresh coffee, barely damp from steam. They hadn't been used yet.

There was another Secret Service man outside my door, a tall Midwesterner with a toothy grin. His name was George Littleton. He spoke not a word after Bill Morris introduced us, probably because I looked like I'd bite him.

I would have. My balance nagged me like a sore tooth. I couldn't forget it for an instant.

Going down in the elevator, I could feel the universe shifting around me. There seemed to be a four-dimensional map in my head, with me in the center and the rest of the universe traveling around me at various changing velocities.

The car we used was a Lincoln Continental. George drove. My map became three times as active, recording every touch of brake and accelerator.

"We're putting you on salary," said Morris, "if that's agreeable. You know more about Monks than any living man. We'll class you as a consultant and pay you a thousand dollars a day to put down all you remember about Monks."

"I'd want the right to quit whenever I think I'm mined out."

"That seems all right," said Morris. He was lying. They would keep me just as long as they felt like it. But there wasn't a thing I could do about it at the moment.

I didn't even know what made me so sure.

So I asked, "What about Louise?"

"She spent most of her time waiting on tables, as I remember. She won't know much. We'll pay her a thousand a day for a couple of days. Anyway, for today, whether she knows anything or not."

"Okay," I said, and tried to settle back.

"You're the valuable one, Frazer. You've been fantastically lucky. That Monk language pill is going to give us a terrific advantage whenever we deal with Monks. They'll have to learn about us. We'll know about them already. Frazer, what does a Monk look like under the cowl and robe?"

"Not human," I said. "They only stand upright to make us feel at ease. And there's a swelling along one side that looks like equipment under the robe, but it isn't. It's part of the digestive system. And the head is as big as a basketball, but it's half hollow."

"They're natural quadrupeds?"

"Yah. Four-footed, but climbers. The animal they evolved from lives in forests of like giant dandelions. They can throw rocks with any foot. They're still around on Center; that's the home planet. You're not writing this down."

"There's a tape recorder going."

"Really?" I'd been kidding.

"You'd better believe it. We can use anything you happen to remember. We still don't even know how your Monk got out here to California."

My Monk, forsooth.

"They briefed me pretty quickly yesterday. Did I tell you? I was visiting my parents in Carmel when my supervisor called me yesterday morning. Ten hours later I knew just about everything anyone knows about Monks. Except you, Frazer.

"Up until yesterday we thought that every Monk on

Earth was either in the United Nations Building or aboard the Monk ground-to-orbit ship.

"We've been in that ship, Frazer. Several men have been through it, all trained astronauts wearing lunar exploration suits. Six Monks landed on Earth—unless more were hiding somewhere aboard the ground-to-orbit ship. Can you think of any reason why they should do that?"

"No."

"Neither can anyone else. And there are six Monks accounted for this morning. All in New York. Your Monk went home last night."

That jarred me. "How?"

"We don't know. We're checking plane flights, silly as that sounds. Wouldn't you think a stewardess would notice a Monk on her flight? Wouldn't you think she'd go to the newspapers?"

"Sure."

"We're also checking flying saucer sightings."

I laughed. But by now that sounded logical.

"If that doesn't pan out, we'll be seriously considering teleportation. Would you . . ."

"That's it," I said without surprise. It had come the way a memory comes, from the back of my mind, as if it had always been there. "He gave me a teleportation pill. That's why I've got absolute direction. To teleport I've got to know where in the universe I am."

Morris got bug-eyed. "You can teleport?"

"Not from a speeding car," I said with reflexive fear. "That's death. I'd keep the velocity."

"Oh." He was edging away as if I had sprouted horns. More memory floated up, and I said, "Humans can't teleport anyway. That pill was for another market."

Morris relaxed. "You might have said that right away."

"I only just remembered."

"Why did you take it, if it's for aliens?"

"Probably for the location talent. I don't remember. I used to get lost pretty easily. I never will again. Morris, I'd be safer on a high wire than you'd be crossing a street with the Walk sign."

"Could that have been your 'something unusual'?"

"Maybe," I said. At the same time I was somehow sure that it wasn't.

Louise was in the dirt parking lot next to the Long Spoon. She was getting out of her Mustang when we pulled up. She waved an arm like a semaphore and walked briskly toward us, already talking. "Alien creatures in the Long Spoon, forsooth!" I'd taught her that word. "Ed, I keep telling you the customers aren't human. Hello, are you Mr. Morris? I remember you. You were in last night. You had four drinks. All night."

Morris smiled. "Yes, but I tipped big. Call me Bill, okay?"

Louise Schu was a cheerful blonde, by choice, not birth. She'd been working in the Long Spoon for five years now. A few of my regulars knew my name; but they all knew hers.

Louise's deadliest enemy was the extra twenty pounds she carried as padding. She had been dieting for some decades. Two years back she had gotten serious about it and stopped cheating. She was *mean* for the next several months. But, clawing and scratching and half starved every second, she had worked her way down to one hundred and twenty-five pounds. She threw a terrific celebration that night and—to hear her tell it afterward—ate her way back to one-forty-five in a single night.

Padding or not, she'd have made someone a wonderful wife. I'd thought of marrying her myself. But my marriage had been too little fun, and was too recent, and the divorce had hurt too much. And the alimony. The alimony was why I was living in a cracker box, and also the reason I couldn't afford to get married again.

While Louise was opening up, Morris bought a paper from the coin rack.

The Long Spoon was a mess. Louise and I had cleaned off the tables and collected the dirty glasses and emptied the ash trays into waste bins. But the collected glasses were still dirty and the waste bins were still full.

Morris began spreading newspaper over an area of floor. And I stopped with my hand in my pocket.

Littleton came out from behind the bar, hefting both of the waste bins. He spilled one out onto the newspaper, then the other. He and Morris began spreading the trash apart.

My fingertips were brushing a scrap of Monk cellophane. I'd worn these pants last night, under the apron.

Some impulse kept me from yelling out. I brought my hand out of my pocket, empty. Louise had gone to help the others sift the trash with their fingers. I joined them.

Presently Morris said, "Four. I hope that's all. We'll search the bar too."

And I thought: Five.

And I thought: I learned five new professions last night. What were the odds that I'll want to hide at least one of them?

If my judgment was bad enough to make me take a teleport pill intended for something with too many eyes, what else might I have swallowed last night?

I might be an advertising man, or a superbly trained thief, or a Palace Executioner skilled in the ways of torture. Of I might have asked for something really unpleasant, like the profession followed by Hitler or Alexander the Great.

"Nothing here," Morris said from behind the bar. Louise shrugged agreement. Morris handed the four scraps to Littleton and said, "Run these out to Douglass. Call us from there.

"We'll put them through chemical analysis," he said to Louise and me. "One of them may be real cellophane off a piece of candy. Or we might have missed one or two. For the moment, let's assume there were four."

"All right," I said.

"Does it sound right, Frazer? Should it be three, or five?"

"I don't know." As far as memory went, I really didn't.

"Four, then. We've identified two. One was a course in teleportation for aliens. The other was a language course. Right?"

"It looks that way."

"What else did he give you?"

I could feel the memories floating back there, but all scrambled together. I shook my head.

Morris looked frustrated.

"Excuse me," said Louise. "Do you drink on duty?"

"Yes," Morris said without hesitation.

And Louise and I weren't on duty. Louise mixed us three gin-and-tonics and brought them to us at one of the padded booths.

Morris had opened a flattish briefcase that turned out to be part tape recorder. He said, "We won't lose anything now. Louise, let's talk about last night."

"I hope I can help."

"Just what happened in here after Ed took his first pill?"

"Mmm." Louise looked at me askance. "I don't know when he took that first pill. About one I noticed that he was acting strange. He was slow on orders. He got drinks wrong.

"I remembered that he had done that for a while last fall, when he got his divorce . . ."

I felt my face go stiff. That was unexpected pain, that memory. I am far from being my own best customer; but there had been a long lost weekend about a year ago. Louise had talked me out of trying to drink and bartend too. So I had gone drinking. When it was out of my system I had gone back to tending bar.

She was saying, "Last night I thought it might be the same problem. I covered for him, said the orders twice when I had to, watched him make the drinks so he'd get them right.

"He was spending most of his time talking to the Monk. But Ed was talking English, and the Monk was making whispery noises in his throat. Remember last week, when they put the Monk speech on television? It sounded like that.

"I saw Ed take a pill from the Monk and swallow it with a glass of water."

She turned to me, touched my arm. "I thought you were crazy. I tried to stop you."

"I don't remember."

"The place was practically empty by then. Well, you laughed at me and said that the pill would teach you not to get lost! I didn't believe it. But the Monk turned on his translator gadget and said the same thing."

"I wish you'd stopped me," I said.

She looked disturbed. "I wish you hadn't said that. I took a pill myself."

I started choking. She'd caught me with a mouthful of gin and tonic.

Louise pounded my back and saved my life, maybe. She said, "You don't remember that?"

"I don't remember much of anything coherent after I took the first pill."

"Really? You didn't seem loaded. Not after I'd watched you awhile."

Morris cut in. "Louise, the pill you took. What did the Monk say it would do?"

"He never did. We were talking about me." She stopped to think. Then, baffled and amused at herself, she said, "I don't know how it happened. All of a sudden I was telling the story of my young life. To a Monk. I had the idea he was sympathetic."

"The *Monk?*"

"Yes, the Monk. And at some point he picked out a pill and gave it to me. He said it would help me. I believed him. I don't know why, but I believed him, and I took it."

"Any symptoms? Have you learned anything new this morning?"

She shook her head, baffled and a little truculent now. Taking that pill must have seemed sheer insanity in the cold grey light of afternoon.

"All right," said Morris. "Frazer, you took three pills. We know what two of them were. Louise, you took one, and we have no idea what it taught you." He closed his eyes a moment, then looked at me. "Frazer, if you can't remember what you took, can you remember rejecting anything? Did the Monk offer you anything . . ." He saw my face and cut it off.

Because that had jarred something . . .

The Monk had been speaking his own language, in that alien whisper that doesn't need to be more than a whisper because the basic sounds of the Monk language are so unambiguous, so easily distinguished, even to a human ear. *This teaches proper swimming technique. A ——— can reach speeds of sixteen to twenty-four ——— per ——— using these strokes. The course also teaches proper exercises . . .*

I said, "I turned down a swimming course for intelligent fish."

Louise giggled. Morris said, "You're kidding."

"I'm not. And there was something else." That swamped-in-data effect wasn't as bad as it had been at noon. Bits of data must be reaching cubbyholes in my head, linking up, finding their places.

"I was asking about the shapes of aliens. Not about Monks, because that's bad manners, especially from a race that hasn't yet proven its sentience. I wanted to know about other aliens. So the Monk offered me three courses in unarmed combat techniques. Each one involved extensive knowledge of basic anatomy."

"You didn't take them?"

"No. What for? Like, one was a pill to tell me how to kill an armed intelligent worm, but only if I was an unarmed intelligent worm. I wasn't *that* confused."

"Frazer, there are men who would give an arm and a leg for any of those pills you turned down."

"Sure. A couple of hours ago you were telling me I was crazy to swallow an alien's education pill."

"Sorry," said Morris.

"You were the one who said they should have driven me out of my mind. Maybe they did," I said, because my hypersensitive sense of balance was still bothering the hell out of me.

But Morris's reaction bothered me worse. *Frazer could start gibbering any minute. Better pump him for all he's worth while I've got the chance.*

No, his face showed none of that. Was I going paranoid?

"Tell me more about the pills," Morris said. "It sounds like there's a lot of delayed reaction involved. How long do we have to wait before we know we've got it all?"

"He did say something . . ." I groped for it, and presently it came.

It works like a memory, the Monk had said. He'd turned off his translator and was speaking his own language, now that I could understand him. The sound of his translator had been bothering him. That was why he'd given me the pill.

But the whisper of his voice was low, and the language was new, and I'd had to listen carefully to get it all. I remembered it clearly.

The information in the pills will become part of your memory. You will not know all that you have learned until you need it. Then it will surface. Memory works by association, he'd said.

And: *There are things that cannot be taught by teachers. Always there is the difference between knowledge from school and knowledge from doing the work itself.*

"Theory and practice," I told Morris. "I know just what he meant. There's not a bartending course in the country that will teach you to leave the sugar out of an Old Fashioned during rush hour."

"*What* did you say?"

"It depends on the bar, of course. No posh bar would let itself get that crowded. But in an ordinary bar, anyone who orders a complicated drink during rush hour deserves what he gets. He's slowing the bartender down when it's crucial, when every second is money. So you leave the sugar out of an Old Fashioned. It's too much money."

"The guy won't come back."

"So what? He's not one of your regulars. He'd have better sense if he were."

I had to grin. Morris was shocked and horrified. I'd shown him a brand new sin. I said, "It's something every bartender ought to know about. Mind you, a bartending school is a trade school. They're teaching you to survive as a bartender. But the recipe calls for sugar, so at school you put in the sugar or you get ticked off."

Morris shook his head, tight-lipped. He said, "Then the Monk was warning you that you were getting theory, not practice."

"Just the opposite. Look at it this way, Morris . . ."

"Bill."

"Listen, Bill. The teleport pill can't make a human nervous system capable of teleportation. Even my incredible balance, and it *is* incredible, won't give me the muscles to do ten quick backflips. But I do know what it *feels* like to teleport. That's what the Monk was warning me about. The pills give field training. What you have to watch out for are the reflexes. Because the pills don't change you physically."

"I hope you haven't become a trained assassin."

One must be wary of newly learned reflexes, the Monk had said.

Morris said, "Louise, we still don't know what kind of an education you got last night. Any ideas?"

"Maybe I repair time machines." She sipped her drink, eyed Morris demurely over the rim of the glass.

Morris smiled back. "I wouldn't be surprised."

The idiot. He meant it.

"If you really want to know what was in the pill," said Louise, "why not ask the Monk?" She gave Morris time to look startled, but no time to interrupt. "All we have to do is open up and wait. He didn't even get through the second shelf last night, did he, Ed?"

"No, by God, he didn't."

Louise swept an arm about her. "The place is a mess, of course. We'd never get it clean in time. Not without help. How about it, Bill? You're a government man. Could you get a team to work here in time to get this place cleaned up by five o'clock?"

"You know not what you ask. It's three-fifteen now!"

Truly, the Long Spoon was a disaster area. Bars are not meant to be seen by daylight anyway. Just because our worlds had been turned upside down, and just because the Long Spoon was clearly unfit for human habitation, we had been thinking in terms of staying closed tonight. Now it was too late . . .

"Tip Top Cleaners," I remembered. "They send out a four-man team with its own mops. Fifteen bucks an hour. But we'd never get them here in time."

Morris stood up abruptly. "Are they in the phone book?"

"Sure."

Morris moved.

I waited until he was in the phone booth before I asked, "Any new thoughts on what you ate last night?"

Louise looked at me closely. "You mean the pill? Why so solemn?"

"We've got to find out before Morris does."

"Why?"

"If Morris has his way," I said, "they'll classify my head Top Secret. I know too much. I'm likely to be a political prisoner the rest of my life; and so are you, if you learned the wrong things last night."

What Louise did then, I found both flattering and comforting. She turned upon the phone booth where Morris was making his call a look of such poisonous hatred that it should have withered the man where he stood.

She believed me. She needed no kind of proof, and she was utterly on my side.

Why was I so sure? I had spent too much of today guessing at other people's thoughts. Maybe it had something to do with my third and fourth professions . . .

I said, "We've got to find out what kind of pill you took. Otherwise Morris and the Secret Service will spend the rest of their lives following you around, just on the off chance that you know something useful. Like me. Only they *know* I know something useful. They'll be picking my brain until Hell freezes over."

Morris yelled from the phone booth. "They're coming! Forty bucks an hour, paid in advance when they get here!"

"Great!" I yelled.

"I want to call in. New York." He closed the folding door.

Louise leaned across the table. "Ed, what are we going to do?"

It was the way she said it. We were in it together, and there was a way out, and she was sure I'd find it—and she said it all in the sound of her voice, the way she leaned toward me, the pressure of her hand around my wrist. *We.* I felt power and confidence rising in me; and at the same time I thought: *She couldn't do that yesterday.*

I said, "We clean this place up so we can open for business. Meanwhile you try to remember what you learned last night. Maybe it was something harmless, like how to catch trilchies with a magnetic web."

"Tril . . . ?"

"Space butterflies, kind of."

"Oh. But suppose he taught me how to build a faster-than-light motor?"

"We'd bloody have to keep Morris from finding out. But you didn't. The English words for going faster than light —hyperdrive, space warp—they don't have Monk translations except in math. You can't even say 'faster than light' in Monk."

"Oh."

Morris came back grinning like an idiot. "You'll never guess what the Monks want from us now."

He looked from me to Louise to me, grinning, letting the suspense grow intolerable. He said, "A giant laser cannon."

Louise gasped, "What?" and I asked, "You mean a launching laser?"

"Yes, a launching laser. They want us to build it on the Moon. They'd feed our engineers pills to give them the specs and to teach them how to build it. They'd pay off in more pills."

I needed to remember something about launching lasers. And how had I known what to call it?

"They put the proposition to the United Nations," Morris was saying. "In fact, they'll be doing all of their business through the UN, to avoid charges of favoritism, they say, and to spread the knowledge as far as possible."

"But there are countries that don't belong to the UN," Louise objected.

"The Monks know that. They asked if any of those nations had space travel. None of them do, of course. And the Monks lost interest in them."

"Of course," I said, remembering. "A species that can't develop spaceflight is no better than animals."

"Huh?"

"According to a Monk."

Louise said, "But what *for?* Why would the Monks want a laser cannon? And on our Moon!"

"That's a little complicated," said Morris. "Do you both remember when the Monk ship first appeared, two years ago?"

"No," we answered more or less together.

Morris was shaken. "You didn't notice? It was in all the papers. Noted Astronomer Says Alien Spacecraft Approaching Earth. No?"

"No."

"For Christ's sake! I was jumping up and down. It was like when the radio astronomers discovered pulsars, remember? I was just getting out of high schoool."

"Pulsars?"

"Excuse me," Morris said overpolitely. "My mistake. I tend to think that everybody I meet is a science fiction fan. Pulsars are stars that give off rhythmic pulses of radio energy. The radio astronomers thought at first that they were getting signals from outer space."

Louise said, "You're a science fiction fan?"

"Absolutely. My first gun was a Gyro-Jet rocket pistol. I bought it because I read Buck Rogers."

I said, "Buck who?" But then I couldn't keep a straight face. Morris raised his eyes to Heaven. No doubt it was there that he found the strength to go on.

"The noted astronomer was Jerome Finney. Of course he hadn't said anything about Earth. Newspapers always get that kind of thing garbled. He'd said that an object of artificial, extraterrestrial origin had entered the solar system.

"What had happened was that several months earlier, Jodrell Bank had found a new star in Saggittarius. That's the direction of the galactic core. Yes, Frazer?"

We were back to last names because I wasn't a science fiction fan. I said, "That's right. The Monks came from the galactic hub." I remembered the blazing night sky of Center. My Monk customer couldn't possibly have seen it in his lifetime. He must have been shown the vision through an education pill, for patriotic reasons, like kids are taught what the Star Spangled Banner looks like.

"All right. The astronomers were studying a nearby nova, so they caught the intruder a little sooner. It showed a strange spectrum, radically different from a nova and much more constant. It even got stranger. The light was growing brighter at the same time the spectral lines were shifting toward the red.

"It was months before anyone identified the spectrum.

"Then one Jerome Finney finally caught wise. He showed that the spectrum was the light of our own sun, drastically blue-shifted. Some kind of mirror was coming at us, moving at a hell of a clip, but slowing as it came."

"Oh!" I got it then. "That would mean a light-sail!"

"Why the big deal, Frazer? I thought you already knew."

"No. This is the first I've heard of it. I don't read the Sunday supplements."

Morris was exasperated. "But you knew enough to call the laser cannon a launching laser!"

"I just now realized why it's called that."

Morris stared at me for several seconds. Then he said, "I forgot. You got it out of the Monk language course."

"I guess so."

He got back to business. "The newspapers gave poor Finney a terrible time. You didn't see the political cartoons either? Too bad. But when the Monk ship got closer it started sending signals. It *was* an interstellar sailing ship, riding the sunlight on a reflecting sail, and it was coming here."

"Signals. With dots and dashes? You could do that just by tacking the sail."

"You *must* have read about it."

"Why? It's so obvious."

Morris looked unaccountably ruffled. Whatever his reasons, he let it pass. "The sail is a few molecules thick and nearly five hundred miles across when it's extended. On light pressure alone they can build up to interstellar velocities—but it takes them a long time. The acceleration isn't high.

"It took them two years to slow down to solar system velocities. They must have done a lot of braking before our telescopes found them, but even so they were going far too fast when they passed Earth's orbit. They had to go inside Mercury's orbit and come up the other side of the sun's gravity well, backing all the way, before they could get near Earth."

I said, "Sure. Interstellar speeds have to be above half the speed of light, or you can't trade competitively."

"What?"

"There are ways to get the extra edge. You don't have to depend on sunlight, not if you're launching from a civilized system. Every civilized system has a moon-based launching laser. By the time the sun is too far away to give the ship a decent push, the beam from the laser cannon is spreading just enough to give the sail a hefty acceleration without vaporizing anything."

"Naturally," said Morris, but he seemed confused.

"So that if you're heading for a strange system, you'd naturally spend most of the trip decelerating. You can't count on a strange system having a launching laser. If you know your destination is civilized, that's a different matter."

Morris nodded.

"The lovely thing about the laser cannon is that if anything goes wrong with it, there's a civilized world right there to fix it. You go sailing out to the stars with trade goods, but you leave your launching motor safely at home. Why is everybody looking at me funny?"

"Don't take it wrong," said Morris. "But how does a paunchy bartender come to know so much about flying an interstellar trading ship?"

"What?" I didn't understand him.

"Why did the Monk ship have to dive so deep into the solar system?"

"Oh, that. That's the solar wind. You get the same problem around any yellow sun. With a light-sail you can get push from the solar wind as well as from light pressure. The trouble is, the solar wind is just stripped hydrogen atoms. Light bounces from a light-sail, but the solar wind just hits the sail and sticks."

Morris nodded thoughtfully. Louise was blinking as if she had double vision.

"You can't tack against it. Tilting the sail does from nothing. To use the solar wind for braking you have to bore straight in, straight toward the sun," I explained.

Morris nodded. I saw that his eyes were as glassy as Louise's eyes.

"Oh," I said. "Damn, I must be stupid today. Morris, that was the third pill."

"Right," said Morris, still nodding, still glassy-eyed. "That must have been the unusual, *really* unusual profession you wanted. Crewman on an interstellar liner. Jesus."

And he should have sounded disgusted, but he sounded envious.

His elbows were on the table, his chin rested on his fists. It is a position that distorts the mouth, making one's expression unreadable. But I didn't like what I could read in Morris's eyes.

There was nothing left of the square and honest man I had let into my apartment at noon. Morris was a patriot now, and an altruist, and a fanatic. He must have the stars for his nation and for all mankind. Nothing must stand in his way. Least of all, me.

Reading minds again, Frazer? Maybe being captain of an interstellar liner involves having to read the minds of the crew, to be able to put down a mutiny before some idiot can take a heat point to the *mpff glip habbabub,* or however a Monk would say it; it has something to do with straining ketones out of the breathing-air.

My urge to acrobatics had probably come out of the same pill. Free fall training. There was a lot in that pill.

This was the profession I should have hidden. Not the Palace Torturer, who was useless to a government grown too subtle to need such techniques; but the captain of an interstellar liner, a prize too valuable to men who have not yet reached beyond the Moon.

And I had been the last to know it. Too late, Frazer.

"Captain," I said. "Not crew."

"Pity. A crewman would know more about how to put a ship together. Frazer, how big a crew are you equipped to rule?"

"Eight and five."

"Thirteen?"

"Yes."

"Then why did you say eight and five?"

The question caught me off balance. Hadn't I . . . ? Oh. "That's the Monk numbering system. Base eight. Actually, base two, but they group the digits in threes to get base eight."

"Base two. Computer numbers."

"Are they?"

"Yes. Frazer, they must have been using computers for a long time. Aeons."

"All right." I noticed for the first time that Louise had collected our glasses and gone to make fresh drinks. Good, I could use one. She'd left her own, which was half full. Knowing she wouldn't mind, I took a swallow.

It was soda water.

With a lime in it. It had looked just like our gin and tonics. She must be back on the diet. Except that when Louise resumed a diet, she generally announced it to all and sundry . . .

Morris was still on the subject. "You use a crew of thirteen. Are they Monk or human or something else?"

"Monk," I said without having to think.

"Too bad. Are there humans in space?"

"No. A lot of two-feet, but none of them are like any of the others, and none of them are quite like us."

Louise came back with our drinks, gave them to us, and sat down without a word.

"You said earlier that a species that can't develop spaceflight is no better than animals."

"According to the Monks," I reminded him.

"Right. It seems a little extreme even to me, but let it pass. What about a race that develops spaceflight and then loses it?"

"It happens. There are lots of ways a space-going species can revert to animal. Atomic war. Or they just can't live with the complexity. Or they breed themselves out of food, and the world famine wrecks everything. Or waste products from the new machinery ruins the ecology."

" 'Revert to animal.' All right. What about nations? Suppose you have two nations next door, same species, but one has space flight . . ."

"Right. Good point, too. Morris, there are just two countries on Earth that can deal with the Monks without dealing through the United Nations. Us, and Russia. If Rhodesia or Brazil or France tried it, they'd be publicly humiliated."

"That could cause an international incident." Morris's jaw tightened heroically. "We've got ways of passing the warning along so that it won't happen."

Louise said, "There are some countries I wouldn't mind seeing it happen to."

Morris got a thoughtful look—and I wondered if everybody would get the warning.

The cleaning team arrived then. We'd used Tip Top Cleaners before, but these four dark women were not our usual team. We had to explain in detail just what we wanted done. Not their fault. They usually clean private homes, not bars.

Morris spent some time calling New York. He must have been using a credit card; he couldn't have that much change.

"That may have stopped a minor war," he said when he got back. And we returned to the padded booth. But Louise stayed to direct the cleaning team.

The four dark women moved about us with pails and spray bottles and dry rags, chattering in Spanish, leaving shiny surfaces wherever they went. And Morris resumed his inquisition.

"What powers the ground-to-orbit ship?"

"A slow H-bomb going off in a magnetic bottle."

"Fusion?"

"Yah. The attitude jets on the main starship use fusion power too. They all link to one magnetic bottle. I don't know just how it works. You get fuel from water or ice."

"Fusion. But don't you have to separate out the deuterium and tritium?"

"What for? You melt the ice, run a current through the water, and you've got hydrogen."

"Wow," Morris said softly. "Wow."

"The launching laser works the same way," I remembered. What else did I need to remember about launching lasers? Something dreadfully important.

"Wow. Frazer, if we could build the Monks their launching laser, we could use the same techniques to build other fusion plants. Couldn't we?"

"Sure." I was in dread. My mouth was dry, my heart was pounding. I almost knew why. "What do you mean, *if?*"

"And they'd pay us to do it! It's a damn shame. We just don't have the hardware."

"What do you mean? We've *got* to build the launching laser!"

Morris gaped. "Frazer, what's wrong with you?"

The terror had a name now. "My God! What have you told the Monks? Morris, listen to me. You've got to see to it that the Security Council promises to build the Monks' launching laser."

"Who do you think I am, the Secretary-General? We can't build it anyway, not with just Saturn launching configurations." Morris thought I'd gone mad at last. He wanted to back away through the wall of the booth.

"They'll do it when you tell them what's at stake. And we can build a launching laser, if the whole world goes in on it. Morris, look at the good it can do! Free power from seawater! And light-sails work *fine* within a system."

"Sure, it's a lovely picture. We could sail out to the moons of Jupiter and Saturn. We could smelt the asteroids for their metal ores, using laser power . . ." His eyes had momentarily taken on a vague, dreamy look. Now they snapped back to what Morris thought of as reality. "It's the kind of thing I daydreamed about when I was a kid. Someday we'll do it. Today—we just aren't ready."

"There are two sides to a coin," I said. "Now, I know how this is going to sound. Just remember there are reasons. Good reasons."

"Reasons? Reasons for what?"

"When a trading ship travels," I said, "it travels only from one civilized system to another. There are ways to tell whether a system has a civilization that can build a launching laser. Radio is one. The Earth puts out as much radio flux as a small star.

"When the Monks find that much radio energy coming from a nearby star, they send a trade ship. By the time the ship gets there, the planet that's putting out all the energy is generally civilized. But not so civilized that it can't use the knowledge a Monk trades for.

"Do you see that they *need* the launching laser? That ship out there came from a Monk colony. This far from the axis of the galaxy, the stars are too far apart. Ships launch by starlight and laser, but they brake by starlight alone, because they can't count on the target star having a launching laser. If they had to launch by starlight too, they probably wouldn't make it. A plant-and-animal cycle as small as the life-support system on a Monk starship can last only so long."

"You said yourself that the Monks can't always count on the target star staying civilized."

"No, of course not. Sometimes a civilization hits the level at which it can build a launching laser, stays there just long enough to send out a mass of radio waves, then reverts to animal. That's the point. If we tell them we can't build the laser, we'll be animals to the Monks."

"Suppose we just refuse? Not *can't* but *won't*."

"That would be stupid. There are too many advantages. Controlled fusion . . ."

"Frazer, think about the cost." Morris looked grim. He wanted the laser. He didn't think he could get it. "Think about politicians thinking about the cost," he said. "Think about politicians thinking about explaining the cost to the taxpayers."

"Stupid," I repeated, "and inhospitable. Hospitality counts high with the Monks. You see, we're cooked either way. Either we're dumb animals, or we're guilty of a criminal breach of hospitality. And the Monk ship *still* needs more light for its light-sail than the sun can put out."

"So?"

"So the captain uses a gadget that makes the sun explode."

"The," said Morris, and "He," and "Explode?" He didn't know what to do. Then suddenly he burst out in great loud cheery guffaws, so that the women cleaning the Long Spoon turned with answering smiles. He'd decided not to believe me.

I reached across and gently pushed his drink into his lap.

It was two-thirds empty, but it cut his laughter off in an instant. Before he could start swearing, I said, "I am not playing games. The Monks will make our sun explode if we don't build them a launching laser. Now go call your boss and tell him so."

The women were staring at us in horror. Louise started toward us, then stopped, uncertain.

Morris sounded almost calm. "Why the drink in my lap?"

"Shock treatment. And I wanted your full attention. Are you going to call New York?"

"Not yet." Morris swallowed. He looked down once at the spreading stain on his pants, then somehow put it out of his mind. "Remember, I'd have to convince him. I don't believe it myself. Nobody and nothing would blow up a sun for a breach of hospitality!"

"No, no, Morris. They have to blow up the sun to get to the next system. It's a serious thing, refusing to build the launching laser! It could wreck the *ship!*"

"Screw the ship! What about a whole planet?"

"You're just not looking at it right . . ."

"Hold it. Your ship is a trading ship, isn't it? What kind of idiots would the Monks be, to exterminate one market just to get on to the next?"

"If we can't build a launching laser, we aren't a market."

"But we might be a market on the next circuit!"

"What next circuit? You don't seem to grasp the *size* of the Monks' marketplace. The communications gap between Center and the nearest Monk colony is about . . ." I stopped to transpose. ". . . sixty-four thousand years! By the time a ship finishes one circuit, most of the worlds she's visited have already forgotten her. And then what? The colony world that built her may have failed, or refitted the spaceport to service a different style of ship, or reverted to animal; even Monks do that. She'd have to go on to the next system for refitting.

"When you trade among the stars, *there is no repeat business.*"

"Oh," said Morris.

Louise had gotten the women back to work. With a corner of my mind I heard their giggling discussion as to whether Morris would fight, whether he could whip me, etc.

Morris asked, "How does it work? How do you make a sun go nova?"

"There's a gadget the size of a locomotive fixed to the —main supporting strut, I guess you'd call it. It points straight astern, and it can swing sixteen degrees or so in any direction. You turn it on when you make departure orbit. The math man works out the intensity. You beam the sun for the first year or so, and when it blows, you're just far enough away to use the push without getting burned."

"But how does it work?"

"You just turn it on. The power comes from the fusion

tube that feeds the attitude jet system . . . Oh, you want to know why does it make a sun explode. I don't know that. Why should I?"

"Big as a locomotive. And it makes suns explode." Morris sounded slightly hysterical. Poor bastard, he was beginning to believe me. The shock had hardly touched me, because truly I had known it since last night.

He said, "When we first saw the Monk light-sail, it was just to one side of a recent nova in Saggittarius. By any wild chance, was that star a market that didn't work out?"

"I haven't the vaguest idea."

That convinced him. If I'd been making it up, I'd have said yes. Morris stood up and walked away without a word. He stopped to pick up a bar towel on his way to the phone booth.

I went behind the bar to make a fresh drink. Cutty over ice, splash of soda; I wanted to taste the burning power of it.

Through the glass door I saw Louise getting out of her car with her arms full of packages. I poured soda over ice, squeezed a lime in it, and had it ready when she walked in.

She dumped the load on the bar top. "Irish coffee makings," she said. I held the glass out to her and she said, "No thanks, Ed. One's enough."

"Taste it."

She gave me a funny look, but she tasted what I handed her. "Soda water. Well, you caught me."

"Back on the diet?"

"Yes."

"You never said *yes* to that question in your life. Don't you want to tell me all the details?"

She sipped at her drink. "Details of someone else's diet are boring. I should have known that a long time ago. To work! You'll notice we've only got twenty minutes."

I opened one of her paper bags and fed the refrigerator with cartons of whipping cream. Another bag held perking coffee. The flat, square package had to be a pizza.

"Pizza. Some diet," I said.

She was setting out the percolators. "That's for you and Bill."

I tore open the paper and bit into a pie-shaped slice. It was a deluxe, covered with everything from anchovies to salami. It was crisp and hot, and I was starving.

I snatched bites as I worked.

There aren't many bars that will keep the makings for Irish coffee handy. It's too much trouble. You need massive quantities of whipping cream and ground coffee, a refrigerator, a blender, a supply of those glass figure-eight-shaped coffee perkers, a line of hot plates, and—most expensive of all—room behind the bar for all of that. You learn to keep a line of glasses ready, which means putting the sugar in them at spare moments to save time later. Those spare moments are your smoking time, so you give that up. You learn not to wave your arms around because there are hot things that can burn you. You learn to half-whip the cream, a mere spin of the blender, because you have to do it over and over again, and if you overdo it the cream turns to butter.

There aren't many bars that will go to all that trouble. That's why it pays off. Your average Irish coffee addict will drive an extra twenty minutes to reach the Long Spoon. He'll also down the drink in about five minutes, because otherwise it gets cold. He'd have spent half an hour over a Scotch and soda.

While we were getting the coffee ready, I found time to ask, "Have you remembered anything?"

"Yes," she said.

"Tell me."

"I don't mean I know what was in the pill. Just—I can do things I couldn't do before. I think my way of thinking has changed. Ed, I'm worried."

"Worried?"

She got the words out in a rush. "It feels like I've been falling in love with you for a very long time. But I haven't. Why should I feel that way so suddenly?"

The bottom dropped out of my stomach. I'd had thoughts like this—and put them out of my mind, and when they came back I did it again. I couldn't afford to fall in love. It would cost too much. It would hurt too much.

"It's been like this all day. It scares me, Ed. Suppose I feel like this about every man? What if the Monk thought I'd make a good call girl?"

I laughed much harder than I should have. Louise was getting really angry before I was able to stop.

"Wait a minute," I said. "Are you in love with Bill Morris too?"

"No, of course not!"

"Then forget the call girl bit. He's got more money than I do. A call girl would love him more, if she loved anyone, which she wouldn't, because call girls are generally frigid."

"How do you know?" she demanded.

"I read it in a magazine."

Louise began to relax. I began to see how tense she really had been. "All right," she said, "but that means I really am in love with you."

I pushed the crisis away from us. "Why didn't you ever get married?"

"Oh . . ." She was going to pass it off, but she changed her mind. "Every man I dated wanted to sleep with me. I thought that was wrong, so . . ."

She looked puzzled. "Why did I think that was wrong?"

"Way you were brought up."

"Yes, but . . ." She trailed off.

"How do you feel about it now?"

"Well, I wouldn't sleep with *any*one, but if a man was worth dating he might be worth marrying, and if he was worth marrying he'd certainly be worth sleeping with, wouldn't he? And I'd be crazy to marry someone I hadn't slept with, wouldn't I?"

"I did."

"And look how that turned out! Oh, Ed, I'm sorry. But you did bring it up."

"Yah," I said, breathing shallow.

"But I used to feel that way too. Something's changed."

We hadn't been talking fast. There had been pauses, gaps, and we had worked through them. I had had time to eat three slices of pizza. Louise had had time to wrestle with her conscience, lose, and eat one.

Only she hadn't done it. There was the pizza, staring at her, and she hadn't given it a look or a smell. For Louise, that was unusual.

Half-joking, I said, "Try this as a theory. Years ago you must have sublimated your sex urge into an urge for food. Either that or the rest of us sublimated our appetites into a sex urge, and you didn't."

"Then the pill un-sublimated me, hmm?" She looked thoughtfully at the pizza. Clearly its lure was gone. "That's what I mean. I didn't used to be able to outstare a pizza."

"Those olive eyes."

"Hypnotic, they were."

"A good call girl should be able to keep herself in shape." Immediately I regretted saying it. It wasn't funny. "Sorry," I said.

"It's all right." She picked up a tray of candles in red glass vases and moved away, depositing the candles on the small square tables. She moved with grace and beauty through the twilight of the Long Spoon, her hips swaying just enough to avoid the sharp corners of tables.

I'd hurt her. But she'd known me long enough; she must know I had foot-in-mouth disease . . .

I had seen Louise before and known that she was beautiful. But it seemed to me that she had never been beautiful with so little excuse.

She moved back by the same route, lighting the candles as she went. Finally she put the tray down, leaned across the bar and said, "I'm sorry. I can't joke about it when I don't *know*."

"Stop worrying, will you? Whatever the Monk fed you, he was trying to help you."

"I love you."

"What?"

"I love you."

"Okay. I love you too." I use those words so seldom that they clog in my throat, as if I'm lying, even when it's the truth. "Listen, I want to marry you. Don't shake your head. I want to marry you."

Our voices had dropped to whispers. In a tormented whisper, then, she said, "Not until I find out what I *do*, what was in the *pill*. Ed, I can't trust myself until then!"

"Me too," I said with great reluctance. "But we can't wait. We don't have time."

"What?"

"That's right, you weren't in earshot. Sometime between three and ten years from now, the Monks may blow up our sun."

Louise said nothing. Her forehead wrinkled.

"It depends on how much time they spend trading. If we can't build them the launching laser, we can still con them into waiting for a while. Monk expeditions have waited as long as . . ."

"Good Lord. You mean it. Is that what you and Bill were fighting over?"

"Yah."

Louise shuddered. Even in the dimness I saw how pale she had become. And she said a strange thing.

She said, "All right, I'll marry you."

"Good," I said. But I was suddenly shaking. Married. Again. Me. Louise stepped up and put her hands on my shoulders, and I kissed her.

I'd been wanting to do that for—five years? She fitted wonderfully into my arms. Her hands closed hard on the muscles of my shoulders, massaging. The tension went out of me, drained away somewhere. Married. Us. At least we could have three to ten years.

"Morris," I said.

She drew back a little. "He can't hold you. You haven't done anything. Oh, I *wish* I knew what was in that pill I took! Suppose I'm the trained assassin?"

"Suppose I am? We'll have to be careful of each other."

"Oh, we know all about you. You're a starship commander, an alien teleport, and a translator for Monks."

"And one thing more. There was a fourth profession. I took four pills last night, not three."

"Oh? Why didn't you tell Bill?"

"Are you kidding? Dizzy as I was last night, I probably took a course in how to lead a successful revolution. God help me if Morris found *that* out."

She smiled. "Do you really think that was what it was?"

"No, of course not."

"Why did we do it? Why did we swallow those pills? We should have known better."

"Maybe the Monk took a pill himself. Maybe there's a pill that teaches a Monk how to look trustworthy to a generalized alien."

"I did trust him," said Louise. "I remember. He seemed so sympathetic. Would he really blow up our sun?"

"He really would."

"That fourth pill. Maybe it taught you a way to stop him."

"Let's see. We know I took a linguistics course, a course in teleportation for Martians, and a course in how to fly a light-sail ship. On that basis . . . I probably changed my mind and took a karate course for worms."

"It wouldn't hurt you, at least. Relax. . . . Ed, if you remember taking the pills, why don't you remember what was in them?"

"But I don't. I don't remember anything."

"How do you know you took four, then?"

"Here." I reached in my pocket and pulled out the scrap of Monk cellophane. And knew immediately that there was something in it. Something hard and round.

We were staring at it when Morris came back.

"I must have cleverly put it in my pocket," I told them. "Sometime last night, when I was feeling sneaky enough to steal from a Monk."

Morris turned the pill like a precious jewel in his fingers. Pale blue it was, marked on one side with a burnt orange triangle. "I don't know whether to get it analyzed or take it myself, now. We need a miracle. Maybe this will tell us—"

"Forget it. I wasn't clever enough to remember how fast a Monk pill deteriorates. The wrapping's torn. That pill has been bad for at least twelve hours."

Morris said a dirty thing.

"Analyze it," I said. "You'll find RNA, and you may even be able to tell what the Monks use as a matrix. Most of the memories are probably intact. But don't swallow the damn thing. It'll scramble your brains. All it takes is a few random changes in a tiny percentage of the RNA."

"We don't have time to send it to Douglass tonight. Can we put it in the freezer?"

"Good. Give it here."

I dropped the pill in a sandwich-size plastic Baggy, sucked the air out the top, tied the end, and dropped it in the freezer. Vacuum and cold would help preserve the thing. It was something I should have done last night.

"So much for miracles," Morris said bitterly. "Let's get down to business. We'll have several men outside the place tonight, and a few more in here. You won't know who they are, but go ahead and guess if you like. A lot of your customers will be turned away tonight. They'll be told to watch the newspapers if they want to know why. I hope it won't cost you too much business."

"It may make our fortune. We'll be famous. Were you maybe doing the same thing last night?"

"Yes. We didn't want the place too crowded. The Monks might not like autograph hounds."

"So that's why the place was half empty."

Morris looked at his watch. "Opening time. Are we ready?"

"Take a seat at the bar. And look nonchalant, dammit."

Louise went to turn on the lights.

Morris took a seat to one side of the middle. One big square hand was closed very tightly on the bar edge. "Another gin and tonic. Weak. After that one, leave out the gin."

"Right."

"Nonchalant. Why should I be nonchalant? Frazer, I had to tell the President of the United States of America that the end of the world is coming unless he does something. I had to talk to him myself!"

"Did he buy it?"

"I hope so. He was so goddam calm and reassuring, I wanted to scream at him. God, Frazer, what if we can't build the laser? What if we try and fail?"

I gave him a very old and classic answer. "Stupidity is always a capital crime."

He screamed in my face. "Damn you and your supercilious attitude and your murdering monsters too!" The next second he was ice-water calm. "Never mind, Frazer. You're thinking like a starship captain."

"I'm what?"

"A starship captain has to be able to make a sun go nova to save the ship. You can't help it. It was in the pill."

Damn, he was right. I could *feel* that he was right. The pill had warped my way of thinking. Blowing up the sun that warms another race *had* to be immoral. Didn't it?

I couldn't trust my own sense of right and wrong!

Four men came in and took one of the bigger tables. Morris's men? No. Real estate men, here to do business.

"Something's been bothering me," said Morris. He grimaced. "Among all the things that have been ruining my composure, such as the impending end of the world, there was one thing that kept nagging at me."

I set his gin-and-tonic in front of him. He tasted it and said, "Fine. And I finally realized what it was, waiting there in the phone booth for a chain of human snails to put the President on. Frazer, are you a college man?"

"No. Webster High."

"See, you don't really talk like a bartender. You use big words."

"I do?"

"Sometimes. And you talked about 'suns exploding', but

you knew what I meant when I said 'nova.' You talked about 'H-bomb power,' but you knew what fusion was."

"Sure."

"I got the possibly silly impression that you were learning the words the instant I said them. Parlez-vous français?"

"No. I don't speak any foreign languages."

"None at all?"

"Nope. What do you think they teach at Webster High?"

"Je parle la langue un peu, Frazer. Et tu?"

"Merde de cochon! Morris, je vous dit—oops."

He didn't give me a chance to think it over. He said, "What's fanac?"

My head had that *clogged* feeling again. I said, "Might be anything. Putting out a zine, writing to the lettercol, helping put on a Con—Morris, what *is* this?"

"That language course was more extensive than we thought."

"Sure as hell, it was. I just remembered. Those women on the cleaning team were speaking Spanish, but I understood them."

"Spanish, French, Monkish, technical languages, even fannish. What you got was a generalized course in how to understand languages the instant you hear them. I don't see how it could work without telepathy."

"Reading minds? Maybe." Several times today, it had felt like I was guessing with too much certainty at somebody's private thoughts.

"Can you read *my* mind?"

"That's not quite it. I get the feel of *how* you think, not *what* you're thinking. Morris, I don't like the idea of being a political prisoner."

"Well, we can talk that over later." *When my bargaining position is better,* Morris meant. *When I don't need the bartender's good will to con the Monk.* "What's important is that you might be able to read a Monk's mind. That could be crucial."

"And maybe he can read mine. And yours."

I let Morris sweat over that one while I set drinks on Louise's tray. Already there were customers at four tables. The Long Spoon was filling rapidly; and only two of them were Secret Service.

Morris said, "Any ideas on what Louise Schu ate last

night? We've got *your* professions pretty well pegged down. Finally."

"I've got an idea. It's kind of vague." I looked around. Louise was taking more orders. "Sheer guesswork, in fact. Will you keep it to yourself for a while?"

"Don't tell Louise? Sure—for a while."

I made four drinks and Louise took them away. I told Morris, "I have a profession in mind. It doesn't have a simple one or two word name, like teleport or starship captain or translator. There's no reason why it should, is there? We're dealing with aliens."

Morris sipped at his drink. Waiting.

"Being a woman," I said, "can be a profession, in a way that being a man can never be. The word is *housewife*, but it doesn't cover all of it. Not nearly."

"Housewife. You're putting me on."

"No. You wouldn't notice the change. You never saw her before last night."

"Just what kind of change have you got in mind? Aside from the fact that she's beautiful, which I did notice."

"Yes, she is, Morris. But last night she was twenty pounds overweight. Do you think she lost it all this morning?"

"She *was* too heavy. Pretty, but also pretty well padded." Morris turned to look over his shoulder, casually turned back. "Damn. She's still well padded. Why didn't I notice before?"

"There's another thing. By the way, have some pizza."

"Thanks." He bit into a slice. "Good, it's still hot. Well?"

"She's been staring at that pizza for half an hour. She bought it. But she hasn't tasted it. She couldn't possibly have done that yesterday."

"She may have had a big breakfast."

"Yah." I knew she hadn't. She'd eaten diet food. For years she'd kept a growing collection of diet food, but she'd never actively tried to survive on it before. But how could I make such a claim to Morris? I'd never even been in Louise's apartment.

"Anything else?"

"She's gotten good at nonverbal communication. It's a very womanly skill. She can say things just by the tone of her voice or the way she leans on an elbow or . . ."

"But if mind reading is one of *your* new skills . . ."

"Damn. Well—it used to make Louise nervous if someone touched her. And she never touched anyone else." I felt myself flushing. I don't talk easily of personal things.

Morris radiated skepticism. "It all sounds very subjective. In fact, it sounds like you're making yourself believe it. Frazer, why would Louise Schu want such a capsule course? Because you haven't described a housewife at all. You've described a woman looking to persuade a man to marry her." He saw my face change. "What's wrong?"

"Ten minutes ago we decided to get married."

"Congratulations," Morris said, and waited.

"All right, you win. Until ten minutes ago we'd never even kissed. I'd never made a pass, or vice versa. No, damn it, I don't believe it! I *know* she loves me; I ought to!"

"I don't deny it," Morris said quietly. "That would be why she took the pill. It must have been strong stuff, too, Frazer. We looked up some of your history. You're marriage shy."

It was true enough. I said, "If she loved me before, I never knew it. I wonder how a Monk could know."

"How would he know about such a skill at all? Why would he have the pill on him? Come on, Frazer, you're the Monk expert!"

"He'd have to learn from human beings. Maybe by interviews, maybe by—well, the Monks can map an alien memory into a computer space, then interview that. They may have done that with some of your diplomats."

"Oh, *great*."

Louise appeared with an order. I made the drinks and set them on her tray. She winked and walked away, swaying deliciously, followed by many eyes.

"Morris. Most of your diplomats, the ones who deal with the Monks, they're men, aren't they?"

"Most of them. Why?"

"Just a thought."

It was a difficult thought, hard to grasp. It was only that the changes in Louise had been all to the good from a man's point of view. The Monks must have interviewed many men. Well, why not? It would make her more valuable to the man she caught—or to the lucky man who caught her . . .

"Got it."

Morris looked up quickly. "Well?"

"Falling in love with me was part of her pill learning. A *set*. They made a guinea pig of her."

"I wondered what she saw in you." Morris's grin faded. "You're serious. Frazer, that still doesn't answer . . ."

"It's a slave indoctrination course. it makes a woman love the first man she sees, permanently, and it trains her to be valuable to him. The Monks were going to make them in quantity and sell them to men."

Morris thought it over. Presently he said, "That's awful. What'll we do?"

"Well, we can't tell her she's been made into a domestic slave! Morris, I'll try to get a memory eraser pill. If I can't—I'll marry her, I guess. Don't look at me that way," I said, low and fierce. "I didn't do it. And I can't desert her now!"

"I know. It's just—oh, put gin in the next one."

"Don't look now," I said.

In the glass of the door there was darkness and motion. A hooded shape, shadow-on-shadow, supernatural, a human silhouette twisted out of true . . .

He came gliding in with the hem of his robe just brushing the floor. Nothing was to be seen of him but his flowing grey robe, the darkness in the hood and the shadow where his robe parted. The real estate men broke off their talk of land and stared, popeyed, and one of them reached for his heart-attack pills.

The Monk drifted toward me like a vengeful ghost. He took the stool we had saved him at one end of the bar.

It wasn't the same Monk.

In all respects he matched the Monk who had been here the last two nights. Louise and Morris must have been fooled completely. But it wasn't the same Monk.

"Good evening," I said.

He gave an equivalent greeting in the whispered Monk language. His translator was half on, translating my words into a Monk whisper, but letting his own speech alone. He said, "I believe we should begin with the Rock and Rye."

I turned to pour. The small of my back itched with danger.

When I turned back with the shot glass in my hand, he was holding a fist-sized tool that must have come out of his robe. It looked like a flattened softball, grooved deeply for five Monk claws, with two parallel tubes poking out in my direction. Lenses glinted in the ends of the tubes.

"Do you know this tool? It is a . . ." and he named it.

I knew the name. It was a beaming tool, a multi-frequency laser. One tube locked on the target; thereafter the aim was maintained by tiny flywheels in the body of the device.

Morris had seen it. He didn't recognize it, and he didn't know what to do about it, and I had no way to signal him.

"I know that tool," I confirmed.

"You must take two of these pills." The Monk had them ready in another hand. They were small and pink and triangular. He said, "I must be convinced that you have taken them. Otherwise you must take more than two. An overdose may affect your natural memory. Come closer."

I came closer. Every man and woman in the Long Spoon was staring at us, and each was afraid to move. Any kind of signal would have trained four guns on the Monk. And I'd be fried dead by a narrow beam of X-rays.

The Monk reached out with a third hand/foot/claw. He closed the fingers/toes around my throat, not hard enough to strangle me, but hard enough.

Morris was cursing silently, helplessly. I could feel the agony in his soul.

The Monk whispered, "You know of the trigger mechanism. If my hand should relax now, the device will fire. Its target is yourself. If you can prevent four government agents from attacking me, you should do so."

I made a palm-up gesture toward Morris. *Don't do anything.* He caught it and nodded very slightly without looking at me.

"You can read minds," I said.

"Yes," said the Monk—and I knew instantly what he was hiding. He could read everybody's mind, except mine.

So much for Morris's little games of deceit. But the Monk could not read my mind, and I could see into his own soul.

And, reading his alien soul, I saw that I would die if I did not swallow the pills.

I placed the pink pills on my tongue, one at a time, and swallowed them dry. They went down hard. Morris watched it happen and could do nothing. The Monk felt them going down my throat, little lumps moving past his finger.

And when the pills had passed across the Monk's finger, I worked a miracle.

"Your pill-induced memories and skills will be gone within two hours," said the Monk. He picked up the shot glass of Rock and Rye and moved it into his hood. When it reappeared it was half empty.

I asked, "Why have you robbed me of my knowledge?"

"You never paid for it."

"But it was freely given."

"It was given by one who had no right," said the Monk. He was thinking about leaving. I had to do something. I knew now, because I had reasoned it out with great care, that the Monk was involved in an evil enterprise. But he must stay to hear me or I could not convince him.

Even then, it wouldn't be easy. He was a Monk crewman. His ethical attitudes had entered his brain through an RNA pill, along with his professional skills.

"You have spoken of rights," I said. In Monk. "Let us discuss rights." The whispery words buzzed oddly in my throat; they tickled; but my ears told me they were coming out right.

The Monk was startled. "I was told that you had been taught our speech, but not that you could speak it."

"Were you told what pill I was given?"

"A language pill. I had not known that he carried one in his case."

"He did not finish his tasting of the alcohols of Earth. Will you have another drink?"

I felt him guess at my motives, and guess wrong. He thought I was taking advantage of his curiosity to sell him my wares for cash. And what had he to fear from me? Whatever mental powers I had learned from Monk pills, they would be gone in two hours.

I set a shot glass before him. I asked him, "How do you feel about launching lasers?"

The discussion became highly technical. "Let us take a special case," I remember saying. "Suppose a culture had been capable of starflight for some sixty-fours of years— or even for eights of times that long. Then an asteroid slams into a major ocean, precipitates an ice age . . ." It had happened once, and well he knew it. "A natural disaster can't spell the difference between sentience and nonsentience, can it? Not unless it affects brain tissue directly."

At first it was his curiosity that held him. Later it was me. He couldn't tear himself loose. He never thought of it. He was a sailship crewman, and he was cold sober, and he argued with the frenzy of an evangelist.

"Then take the general case," I remember saying. "A world that cannot build a launching laser is a world of animals, yes? And Monks themselves can revert to animal."

Yes, he knew that.

"Then build your own launching laser. If you cannot, then your ship is captained and crewed by animals."

At the end I was doing all the talking. All in the whispery Monk tongue, whose sounds are so easily distinguished that even I, warping a human throat to my will, need only whisper. It was a good thing. I seemed to have been eating used razor blades.

Morris guessed right. He did not interfere. I could tell him nothing, not if I had had the power, not by word or gesture or mental contact. The Monk would read Morris's mind. But Morris sat quietly drinking his tonic-and-tonics, waiting for something to happen. While I argued in whispers with the Monk.

"But the ship!" he whispered. "What of the ship?" His agony was mine; for the ship must be protected . . .

At one-fifteen the Monk had progressed halfway across the bottom row of bottles. He slid from the stool, paid for his drinks in one-dollar bills, and drifted to the door and out.

All he needed was a scythe and hour glass, I thought, watching him go. And what I needed was a long morning's sleep. And I wasn't going to get it.

"Be sure nobody stops him," I told Morris.

"Nobody will. But he'll be followed."

"No point. The Garment to Wear Among Strangers is a lot of things. It's bracing; it helps the Monk hold human shape. It's a shield and an air filter. And it's a cloak of invisibility."

"Oh?"

"I'll tell you about it if I have time. That's how he got out here, probably. One of the crewmen divided, and then one stayed and one walked. He had two weeks."

Morris stood up and tore off his sport jacket. His shirt

was wet through. He said, "What about a stomach pump
for you?"

"No good. Most of the RNA-enzyme must be in my
blood by now. You'll be better off if you spend your time
getting down everything I can remember about Monks,
while I can remember anything at all. It'll be nine or ten
hours before everything goes." Which was a flat-out lie, of
course.

"Okay. Let me get the dictaphone going again."

"It'll cost you money."

Morris suddenly had a hard look. "Oh? How much?"

I'd thought about that most carefully. "One hundred thousand dollars. And if you're thinking of arguing me down,
remember whose time we're wasting."

"I wasn't." He was, but he'd changed his mind.

"Good. We'll transfer the money now, while I can still
read your mind."

"All right."

He offered to make room for me in the booth, but I
declined. The glass wouldn't stop me from reading Morris's soul.

He came out silent; for there was something he was
afraid to know. Then: "What about the Monks? What about
our sun?"

"I talked that one around. That's why I don't want him
molested. He'll convince others."

"Talked him around? How?"

"It wasn't easy." And suddenly I would have given my
soul to sleep. "The profession pill put it in his genes; he
must protect the ship. It's in me too. I know how strong
it is."

"Then . . ."

"Don't be an ass, Morris. The ship's perfectly safe where
it is, in orbit around the Moon. A sailship's only in danger
when it's between stars, far from help."

"Oh."

"Not that that convinced him. It only let him consider
the ethics of the situation rationally."

"Suppose someone else unconvinces him?"

"It could happen. That's why we'd better build the launching laser."

Morris nodded unhappily.

The next twelve hours were rough.

In the first four hours I gave them everything I could remember about the Monk teleport system, Monk technology, Monk family life, Monk ethics, relations between Monks and aliens, details on aliens, directions of various inhabited and uninhabited worlds—everything. Morris and the Secret Service men who had been posing as customers sat around me like boys around a campfire, listening to stories. But Louise made us fresh coffee, then went to sleep in one of the booths.

Then I let myself slack off.

By nine in the morning I was flat on my back, staring at the ceiling, dictating a random useless bit of information every thirty seconds or so. By eleven there was a great black pool of lukewarm coffee inside me, my eyes ached marginally more than the rest of me, and I was producing nothing.

I was convincing, and I knew it.

But Morris wouldn't let it go at that. He believed me. I felt him believing me. But he was going through the routine anyway, because it couldn't hurt. If I was useless to him, if I knew nothing, there was no point in playing soft. What could he lose?

He accused me of making everything up. He accused me of faking the pills. He made me sit up, and damn near caught me that way. He used obscure words and phrases from mathematics and Latin and fan vocabulary. He got nowhere. There wasn't any way to trick me.

At two in the afternoon he had someone drive me home.

Every muscle in me ached; but I had to fight to maintain my exhausted slump. Else my hindbrain would have lifted me onto my toes and poised me against a possible shift in artificial gravity. The strain was double, and it hurt. It had hurt for hours, sitting with my shoulders hunched and my head hanging. But now—if Morris saw me walking like a trampoline performer . . .

Morris's man got me to my room and left me.

I woke in darkness and sensed someone in my room. Someone who meant me no harm. In fact, Louise. I went back to sleep.

I woke again at dawn. Louise was in my easy chair, her

feet propped on a corner of the bed. Her eyes were open. She said, "Breakfast?"

I said, "Yah. There isn't much in the fridge."

"I brought things."

"All right." I closed my eyes.

Five minutes later I decided I was all slept out. I got up and went to see how she was doing.

There was bacon frying, there was bread already buttered for toasting in the Toast-R-Oven, there was a pan hot for eggs, and the eggs scrambled in a bowl. Louise was filling the percolator.

"Give that here a minute," I said. It only had water in it. I held the pot in my hands, closed my eyes and tried to remember . . .

Ah.

I knew I'd done it right even before the heat touched my hands. The pot held hot, fragrant coffee.

"We were wrong about the first pill," I told Louise. She was looking at me very curiously. "What happened that second night was this. The Monk had a translator gadget, but he wasn't too happy with it. It kept screaming in his ear. Screaming English, too loud, for my benefit.

"He could turn off the part that was shouting English at me, and it would still whisper a Monk translation of what *I* was saying. But first he had to teach me the Monk language. He didn't have a pill to do that. He didn't have a generalized language-learning course either, if there is one, which I doubt.

"He was pretty drunk, but he found something that would serve. The profession it taught me was an old one, and it doesn't have a one-or-two-word name. But if it did, the word would be *prophet!*"

"Prophet," said Louise. "Prophet?" She was doing a remarkable thing. She was listening with all her concentration, and scrambling eggs at the same time.

"Or disciple. Maybe *apostle* comes closer. Anyway, it included the Gift of Tongues, which was what the Monk was after. But it included other talents too."

"Like turning cold water into hot coffee?"

"Miracles, right. I used the same talent to make the little pink amnesia pills disappear before they hit my stomach. But an apostle's major talent is persuasion.

"Last night I convinced a Monk crewman that blowing up suns is an evil thing.

"Morris is afraid that someone might convert him back. I don't think that's possible. The mind-reading talent that goes with the prophet pill goes deeper than just reading minds. I read souls. The Monk is my apostle. Maybe he'll convince the whole crew that I'm right.

"Or he may just curse the *hachiroph shisp,* the little old nova maker. Which is what I intend to do."

"Curse it?"

"Do you think I'm kidding or something?"

"Oh, no." She poured our coffee. "Will that stop it working?"

"Yes."

"Good," said Louise. And I felt the power of her own faith, her faith in me. It gave her the serenity of an idealized nun.

When she turned back to serve the eggs, I dropped a pink triangular pill in her coffee.

She finished setting breakfast and we sat down. Louise said, "Then that's it. It's all over."

"All over." I swallowed some orange juice. Wonderful, what fourteen hours' sleep will do for a man's appetite. "All over. I can go back to my fourth profession, the only one that counts."

She looked up quickly.

"Bartender. First, last, and foremost, I'm a bartender. You're going to marry a bartender."

"Good," she said, relaxing.

In two hours or so the slave sets would be gone from her mind. She would be herself again: free, independent, unable to diet, and somewhat shy.

But the pink pill would not destroy real memories. Two hours from now, Louise would still know that I loved her; and perhaps she would marry me after all.

I said, "We'll have to hire an assistant. And raise our prices. They'll be fighting their way in when the story gets out."

Louise had pursued her own thoughts. "Bill Morris looked awful when I left. You ought to tell him he can stop worrying."

"Oh, no. I *want* him scared. Morris has got to talk the rest of the world into building a launching laser, instead of just throwing bombs at the Monk ship. And we *need* the launching laser."

"Mmm! That's good coffee. Why do we need a launching laser?"

"To get to the stars."

"That's Morris's bag. You're a bartender, remember? The fourth profession."

I shook my head. "You and Morris. You don't see how *big* the Monk marketplace is, or how thin the Monks are scattered. How many novas have you seen in your lifetime?

"Damn few," I said. "There are damn few trading ships in a godawful lot of sky. There are things out there besides Monks. Things the Monks are afraid of, and probably others they don't know about.

"Things so dangerous that the only protection is to be somewhere else, circling some other star, when it happens here! The Monk drive is our lifeline and our immortality. It would be cheap at any price . . ."

"Your eyes are glowing," she breathed. She looked half hypnotized, and utterly convinced. And I knew that for the rest of my life, I would have to keep a tight rein on my tendency to preach.

RECENT SELECTIONS FROM THE PUBLISHER OF THE BEST SCIENCE FICTION IN THE WORLD

Current Adult Fantasy from Ballantine Books